crossing borders

STORIES AND ESSAYS ABOUT TRANSLATION

ALSO BY LYNNE SHARON SCHWARTZ

FICTION

Two-Part Inventions
The Writing on the Wall
Referred Pain
In the Family Way
The Fatigue Artist
Leaving Brooklyn
Disturbances in the Field
The Melting Pot and Other Subversive Stories
Acquainted with the Night
Balancing Acts
Rough Strife

NONFICTION

Not Now, Voyager
The Emergence of Memory: Conversations with W. G. Sebald (editor)
Ruined by Reading
Face to Face
We Are Talking About Homes
A Lynne Sharon Schwartz Reader

POEMS

No Way Out But Through
In Solitary
See You in the Dark

CHILDREN'S BOOKS

The Four Questions

TRANSLATIONS

Smoke over Birkenau, by Liana Millù
A Place to Live: Selected Essays of Natalia Ginzburg
Aldabra, by Silvana Gandolfi

To Naomi and Eva,
Hope you enjoy this,
Love,
Lynne

crossing borders

STORIES AND ESSAYS ABOUT TRANSLATION

EDITED BY

LYNNE SHARON SCHWARTZ

SEVEN STORIES PRESS

new york · oakland · london

Seven Stories Press
140 Watts Street
New York, NY 10013
sevenstories.com

Library of Congress Cataloging-in-Publication Data

Names: Schwartz, Lynne Sharon, editor author.
Title: Crossing borders : stories and essays about translation / edited by
   Lynne Sharon Schwartz.
Description: New York : Seven Stories Press, 2017.
Identifiers: LCCN 2017003722 | ISBN: 9781609807917 (hardback) | ISBN:
9781609809744 (paperback)
Subjects: LCSH: Short stories, American. | American fiction--20th century. |
   Translating and interpreting--Fiction. | Translators--Fiction. |
   Translating and interpreting. | BISAC: LANGUAGE ARTS & DISCIPLINES /
   Translating & Interpreting. | FICTION / Anthologies (multiple authors). |
   LITERARY COLLECTIONS / Essays.
Classification: LCC PS648.T725 C76 2017 | DDC 418/.02--dc23
LC record available at https://lccn.loc.gov/2017003722

Printed in the United States of America

9 8 7 6 5 4 3 2 1

contents

Introduction. 7

Michelle Herman, "Auslander" 15

Joyce Carol Oates, "The Translation" 51

Chana Bloch, "Crossing the Border"* 77

Sharon May, "The Wizard of Khao-I-Dang". 105

Lucy Ferriss, "The Difficulty of Translation" 125

Primo Levi, "On Translating and Being Translated,"*
    translated by Zaia Alexander 141

Svetlana Velmar-Jancovic, "Sima Street,"
    translated by Bogdan Rakic. 147

Lydia Davis, "French Lesson I: *Le Meurtre*" 157

Michael Scammell, "The Servile Path"* 165

Todd Hasak-Lowy, "The Task of This Translator" 187

Susan Daitch, "Asylum" 215

Harry Mathews, "Translation and the Oulipo"* 233

Norman Lavers, "The Translator" 245

Robin Hemley, "The Perfect Word" 255

Laura Esther Wolfson, "In Love with Russian"* 271

Courtney Angela Brkic, "The Translator" 281

David Huddle, "The Interrogation of the Prisoner Bung
    by Mister Hawkins and Sergeant Tree". 295

Lynne Sharon Schwartz, "Her Native Tongue". 307

Author Biographies 311

Acknowledgments. 317

* Essay

Introduction

I first got the notion of translating when I was learning Italian by reading Natalia Ginzburg, one of Italy's greatest writers of the twentieth century: novelist, essayist, biographer, chronicler of the war years and the stunned, chaotic melancholy of the postwar period. Her essays were marvels of emotional and psychological penetration, written in deceptively simple language, simple enough for a beginner. Although Ginzburg wrote of a kind of suffering I could only imagine—her internal exile during the war, the Fascists' murder of her husband—I felt an immediate affinity with her idiom. The shape and structure of the sentences felt familiar, almost as if I could have written them myself—they followed so closely the patterns and syntax my own mind generated. Except I hadn't lived the life and I didn't know the language. Still, I wanted to get close to those sentences, get inside them.

The best way to do this was to translate them, which I did. A labor of love, narcissistic, like communing with myself in a new tongue.

From there I became interested in the process itself. Transferring words, thoughts, sounds from one language to another. A kind of alchemy, and as usual with alchemical experiments, it takes a near miracle to make it yield anything precious. But this near miracle occurs more often than one might expect. Translation has been going on for millennia. There have always been intrepid and willing translators like those who brought Homer and the Trojan War to Western Europe, or the Italian novellas of the Renaissance to Britain, for which Shakespeare was clearly grateful. Not to mention the translators of the King James version of the Bible. The examples are countless, and in recent times have come from every continent and every era. They are the cultural foundation that has shaped us, that we take for granted. The ways we conduct private and public affairs would be quite different without them.

All the while there have been ready detractors. Their disparagements are well known: Chana Bloch refers to several in her essay, "Crossing the Border" (which suggested the title for this collection). My favorite is by Cervantes, that translation is "the other side of the tapestry." Not a bad definition, come to think of it; it's provocative and yields a striking visual image, curious in itself, if not something we'd want to hang on the wall. And of course there's the often-cited Italian equation: "traduttore = traditore," translator means traitor, which has endured not because it's true but because it's clever.

What I strove to be while translating Ginzburg was the opposite of a traitor. An accomplice. I wanted to work alongside her toward the same end—bringing her vision to readers, resounding in my native tongue rather than hers. To manage this I needed to find the places where her sensibility and my own connected, like wires that produce sparks. These points of connection would have nothing to do with biographical similarities; they were not anything that could be named. I imagined her inside my head and gave her my excellent facility with English. At the same time I tried to inhabit her, to feel what it was she felt compelled to find words for, her Italian words. An odd form of intimacy. A neat, if impossible, acrobatic feat. Later I realized I was following along the lines of the seventeenth-century British poet John Dryden's definition of translation. When he was translating Virgil, he said, he wanted Virgil to speak as if he were living in the seventeenth century and writing in English.

Translation theorists have taken issue with this definition—indeed with every rival definition—on a number of grounds. As the number of translated works has grown, so the theoretical baggage has grown along with them, dragged behind on wheels, as it were. Translation theory is rife with novelty, argument, enthusiasm, and controversy—all of which shows that translation itself is alive and well. Some of the controversies are oppositional and unsolvable, like nature versus nurture. Should translations be faithful (to the letter?) or free (to the point of paraphrase?). Even broader is the question of whether translation is possible at all. Can one language ever render all the verbal, intellectual, aural subtleties and connotations of another? The great German critic Walter Benjamin, in his famous, inspiring, and occasionally impenetrable essay, "The Task of the Translator," comes down on the side of the possibles. Translation, he writes, "expresses the central reciprocal relationship between languages." Since all languages are interrelated in what they hope to express, Benjamin posits a "pure language," an abstraction of all of the world's languages, from which each translation draws and in which each partakes. "It is the task of the translator to release in his own language that pure language which is under the spell of another, to liberate the language imprisoned in a work in his re-creation of that work." I especially like the notion of our English being imprisoned in, say, Sophocles's Greek, and needing the translator's strong hands to release it.

The contemporary critic George Steiner takes a similarly positive view of translation's efficacy: the central theme of his great book *After Babel* is, "Inside or between languages, human communication equals translation." In the simplest terms, finding words for an inchoate idea or feeling is a form of translation; giving it shape and voice is another stage of the process; and having it heard and comprehended completes the translation cycle. And that is only the beginning of communication. (Speaking of communication, it is a pity that the United States lags far behind other developed countries in translating major works from all over the world. Visit a bookstore in other urban centers and you'll find dozens of translated books, many that of them important American works. Publishers and bookstores here don't reciprocate.)

In any event, I suspect most translators are not influenced by theory as they work; I know from experience that writers don't write with critics' voices in their heads—unless they want to provoke a migraine.

I became far more absorbed in practice than in theory. The more I translated, the more I was enchanted by the inner process, the peculiar cohabitation that takes place within the translator. This enchantment persisted even when I translated authors for whom I didn't start out feeling any spectacular affinity. Even so, the task required a kind of moving into the thought processes of another. When I was done I felt I knew those authors, the same way you might a know a stranger you share an intimate dance with, a perfect dancing partner, who teaches you new steps, and the feel of whose body in motion you never forget.

On a more selfish level, I loved the process because it felt like writing; it had all the piquant delights of seeking and finding words, arranging and rearranging them, molding the sentences like Play-Doh, taking them apart and molding them again, and again. And all this without having to make anything up! It was all done for you, waiting on the page. It offered the most pleasurable parts of writing, without the burden—or nuisance—of invention.

Translating may feel like writing, it is a form of writing, but in fact the art it resembles most is acting. The actor starts with words on a page—the given, the text—that present and define a character. His or her job is to recreate that character, to give it tangible life by using his own body's movements and gestures, his own voice and inflections. Like the translator, the actor must find her way into the writer's vision, and then find an analogue of that vision within herself. So we can speak of Olivier's Hamlet in contrast to Kevin Kline's Hamlet, say, as we do of Pope's translation of Homer in contrast to Robert Fagles's. Or the many versions of Dante, a work that great poets in English cannot resist; there are so many translations, and so many fine ones.

Since I'm primarily a fiction writer, I began wondering what other fiction writers would make of the task of the translator—to use Walter Benjamin's famous phrase (appropriated with high irony in Todd Hasak-Lowy's story). I searched out examples of stories in which translation or translators were the major theme. I was surprised by what I found: how many there were, and how many wonderful writers had been provoked by the subject. It was no surprise, though, that two of the situations that occurred most frequently—as the pages that follow will show—are love and war. They are situations that afford the greatest opportunities for misunderstanding, impulsive action, disappointment, illusion, and disillusion. In Joyce Carol Oates's story, "The Translation," the American "cultural emissary" to an Eastern European country falls in love with the colleague he gets to know through a translator; but when he's assigned a new, less personally appealing translator, the love vanishes like unspoken words. Does he love the woman, or the translator, or some phantasmal merging of both? In "The Translator," Lucy Ferriss shows the unease and incomprehension a young American living abroad feels toward her lover—again in an unnamed Eastern European country—who speaks so many languages that she cannot place him, except in an opaque silence. And Susan Daitch's "Asylum" illustrates translation of a different kind—movie subtitles; the full impact of her many-layered story is not realized until the end.

I was curious, too, about what other translators made of the enigmatic alchemy simmering in their heads as they worked. Luckily a number have told their stories. Chana Bloch recalls her engagement with the Song of Songs, which required audacity in addition to skill and love; after reading her essay, our comprehension of the Song of Songs is changed forever. Michael Scammell's essay on translating two early works of Nabokov—by accident, as it were—while he was still a graduate student is an amusing and revealing account of the lengthy correspondence he carried on not with the author himself, but with Nabokov's wife and spokesperson, Vera. And if undertaking to translate takes nerve, offering oneself up for translation does as well. Primo Levi's take on translation—he himself did a great deal of it—seems less kindly toward the process. Instead he is wary of the many pitfalls that await both the translator and the translated. Like Levi, I remember looking at some translated works of mine with a kind of dread; sometimes I felt relief, and sometimes I recoiled in shock and horror. And Laura Esther Wolfson, in a wry personal essay, describes conducting her marriage in Russian, her husband's native tongue: could this have been a factor in the demise of the relationship? She thinks not, but cunningly suggests evidence to the contrary.

I was also surprised by how much of the fiction employs a similar framework: the United States at war, or after a war, sending its military to deal with the locals, some of whom may be secret rebels or refugees hoping to emigrate. The stories by David Huddle (set in Korea), Courtney Angela Brkic (in an unnamed Middle Eastern country), and Sharon May (set in Cambodia) share an implicit outrage at the ignorance of the occupiers. These characters make misguided use of interpreters, who in turn make use of them. Deceptions proliferate. Much is said; little is understood.

Besides the misunderstandings of language, magnified by interpreters whose allegiance is ambiguous, there are insurmountable cultural differences that no amount of translation can erase. Because of custom and usage, a Cambodian hoping to emigrate, in "The Wizard of Khao-I-Dang," cannot say his brother's name or the year of his birth in a way that will satisfy the American interrogator. Finally, there is the matter of individual will: in fiction as in life, not everyone wants to be understood. To some characters, misunderstanding in love or war brings a distinct advantage.

Svetlana Velmar-Janovic's "Sima Street" is based on a historical event in Belgrade, but given the events of the '90s in Bosnia and Serbia, it refers pointedly to modern times. And Norman Lavers's story "The Translator" presents a translator with unpopular liberal views in an unnamed country, grown old, half starved, who's spent her life shunted in and out of prison. In the midst of doing a most unusual translation of *Hamlet*, she is interrupted yet again by the police banging at her door.

The sober, ascetic translator of Michelle Herman's "Auslander" lives up to her name: an outsider. She keeps her life orderly and keeps her distance from emotional entanglement, but she cannot resist the work of a brilliant Rumanian poet—a task that embroils her in the disorderly lives of others.

A number of the stories take a half-playful attitude toward translation: both Todd Hasak-Lowy's and Robin Hemley's protagonists feel justly inadequate to the translation tasks demanded of them. Hemley's character is faced with the absurdity of adding gay sex to translations of classic Chinese poetry; while the reader chuckles, the hero is forced into an uneasy self-awareness. Hasak-Lowy's story spirals by leaps and bounds into farce, at the same time that it raises old-world ghosts of past wars, persecutions, and sacrifices. And in "French Lesson I: *Le Meurtre*," Lydia Davis plays slyly with words and their dissemblings: she lays the guilty words out like pieces of a puzzle, leaving it to the reader to reconstruct the plot, as in a true murder mystery.

Like translation itself, the situations are rarely simple. I find the variations in tone and style and mood a constant refreshment. The task of the reader, like that of the translator, is examination, interpretation, and above all, pleasure in the marvels that language can accomplish.

Auslander

BY MICHELLE HERMAN

The translator, Auslander, was at first flattered. She listened, astonished, for a full minute before the caller—Rumanian, she had guessed after his initial words of praise—paused for a breath, allowing her the opportunity to thank him.

"No, no," he said. "It is I who should thank you, and furthermore apologize for disturbing you at your home. Naturally I am aware that this was most presumptuous. I admit I hesitated a long while before I placed the call. Still, it was difficult to resist. When I read the contributors' notes and discovered that you 'lived and worked in New York City,' I felt it was a great stroke of luck. I must tell you I was surprised that your telephone number was so easily obtained from Directory Assistance."

Auslander laughed. "I've never found it necessary to keep the number a secret. I'm not exactly in the position of getting besieged with calls from admiring readers."

"You are far too modest," the Rumanian said. He spoke hoarsely but with a certain delicacy, as if he were whispering. "Your essay was truly quite something. Such insight! Your understanding of the process of translating poetry is complete, total."

"It's kind of you to say so," Auslander said. She had begun to shiver. The telephone call had caught her just as she was preparing to lower herself into the bathtub, and she wished she had thought to grab a towel when she'd rushed to answer the phone.

"I assure you I am not being kind," he said. "Your work impressed me greatly. It is so difficult to write of such matters with cleverness and charm as well as intelligence. I imagine you are a poet yourself?"

"No, not actually," Auslander said. Her teeth were chattering now. "Could you possibly hold on for just a second?" She set the receiver down and clambered over the bed to shut the window. Across the small courtyard a man sat at his kitchen table laying out a hand of solitaire. He looked up at Auslander and she stared back for an instant before she remembered that she was naked. As she yanked down the bamboo shade, the man raised his hand in slow expressionless salute.

"Oh, I fear I *have* interrupted you," the Rumanian said when she returned to the phone.

"Not at all." Auslander cradled the receiver on her shoulder as she dug through a heap of clothes on the floor. She extracted a flannel shirt and shrugged her arms into it. "Really, it was very good of you to call."

"Good of me? No, no, not in the least." He was nearly breathless. "Your essay was *outstanding*. Brilliant, I should say."

"My goodness," Auslander said. She sat down on the bed and buried her feet in the tangle of shirts and jeans and sweaters.

"Marvelous work. Profound. I do not exaggerate."

She was beginning to feel embarrassed. "You're much too kind," she murmured, and quickly, before he could protest again, she said, "Tell me, how did you happen to come across the essay?"

"Oh"—he laughed, a taut, high-pitched sound—"I read everything, everything. I haunt the periodical room of the library. Nothing is obscure to me. The quarterlies, the academic journals, they all fascinate me, utterly. And I admit also that I have a particular interest in translation."

"A university library, it must be?"

"Ah, my God! How rude of me!" There was a soft thump, and Auslander imagined him smacking his fist to his forehead. "I am so sorry. I have not properly introduced myself. My name is Petru Viorescu. I am a student—a graduate student—at Columbia University."

Auslander smiled into the phone. A Rumanian: she had been right. "Well, Mr. Viorescu, I'm grateful for your compliments. It was very thoughtful of you to call." This was greeted with silence. Auslander waited; he remained mute. She was just starting to become uneasy when he cleared his throat, and lowering his hushed voice still further said, "Miss Auslander, I do not want to appear in any way aggressive. Yet I wondered if it might be possible for us to meet."

"To meet?"

"Yes. You see, what I want to propose is a working meeting. Or, rather, a meeting to discuss the possibility . . . the possibility of working." He spoke quickly, with a nervous edge to his voice. "In your essay you write of the problems of translating some of the more diffuse, associative poetry in the Romance languages—of the light, respectful touch necessary for such work."

"Yes," she said. Cautious now.

"You have this touch, of course."

"I hope so," Auslander said.

"You even mentioned, specifically mentioned, a number of modern Rumanian poets. This was a great surprise and pleasure to me. I should add that I myself am Rumanian."

"Yes."

"Your biographical note included the information that you are fluent in nine languages. I assume, on the basis of your remarks in the second section of the essay, that my own is one."

"Your assumption is correct."

"And you are familiar with a great deal of Rumanian poetry."

"'A great deal,' I don't know about, Mr. Viorescu."

"You are feeling a little bit impatient with me now, yes?" He coughed out his odd laugh again. "Bear with me, please, for another moment. Have you in fact done any translation from the Rumanian as yet?"

Of course, Auslander thought. She struck her own forehead lightly with her palm. *A poet.* "Some," she said. A *student* poet yet. More than likely a very bad one. Unpublished, it went without saying. She sighed. Vanity! Only this had prevented her from assessing the matter sooner.

"I thought so. I would be most grateful if you would consider meeting with me to discuss a project I have in mind."

"I'm afraid I'm quite busy," Auslander said.

"I assure you I would not take up very much of your time. A half hour perhaps, no more."

"Yes, well, I'm afraid I can't spare even that."

"Please," he said. "It might be that ten or fifteen minutes would be sufficient."

Irritated, she said, "You realize, of course, that you haven't described the nature of this project."

"Oh, that is not possible at the moment." It occurred to her then that he actually was whispering. Always such drama with poets! "I do not mean to be secretive, believe me," he said. "It is only that I am unable to speak freely. But if you could spare a few minutes to see me . . ."

"I'm sorry," she said.

"Please."

It was not desperation—not exactly that—that she heard in this invocation. But surely, she thought, it was something akin to it. Urgency. Despair? Oh, nonsense, she told herself. She was being fanciful; she had proofread too many romance novels lately. With this thought she felt a pang of self-pity. She had lied when she'd said she was busy. She had not had any real work since early fall; she had been getting by with freelance proofreading—drudgery, fools' work: romances and science fiction, houseplant care and rock star biographies. But that was beside the point, of course. Busy or not, she had every right to say no. She had refused such requests before, plenty of times. Those letters, so pathetic, forwarded to her by the journal or publisher to which they had been sent, asking her to translate a manuscript "on speculation"—they wrote letters that were like listings in *Writers' Market*, these young poets!—she had never had the slightest difficulty answering. But naturally it was easier to write a brief apologetic note than to disengage oneself politely on the phone. Still, it was only a matter of saying no, and saying it firmly so it would be clear the discussion was at an end.

Viorescu had fallen silent again. A manipulation, Auslander thought grimly. He was attempting to stir up guilt. And for what should she feel guilty? As if her sympathy were in the public domain! What did he think, did he imagine that publishing a scholarly essay in *Metaphrasis* meant she was a celebrity, someone with charity to spare?

"I'm assuming that your intent is to try to convince me to undertake the translation of a manuscript," she said. "First I must tell you that my services are quite expensive. Furthermore, you have read only a single essay which concerns approaches to translation and which tells you nothing whatsoever about my abilities as a translator."

"On the contrary," he said. "I have read two volumes of your translations, one from the Italian, one from the Portuguese, and a most remarkable group of poems in a quarterly, translated from the German. I apologize for not mentioning this earlier; I excuse myself by telling you I feared you would question my motives, the sincerity of my praise. So much flattery, you see. But I assure you I am entirely sincere. I have not been as thorough as I might have been in my research—my time is limited, you understand, by my own studies—but I am certain I have seen enough of your work to know that it is of the highest caliber. I am well aware that the finest poem can lose all of its beauty in the hands of a clumsy translator. The work I read was without exception excellent."

Speechless, Auslander picked angrily at the frayed cuff of her shirt.

"And, naturally, I would expect to pay you whatever fee you are accustomed to receiving. I am hardly a wealthy man—as I say, I am a student. 'Independently poor' is how I might describe my financial status"—that curious little laugh again—"but this of course is important, it is not a luxury."

Auslander could not think of a word to say. She looked around at the disorder in her bedroom, a tiny perfect square littered with clothes and papers and precarious towers of books, and through the doorway, into the kitchen, where the tub stood full on its stubby clawed legs. The water was probably cold as a stone by now.

"All right," she said finally. "I'll meet with you. But only for half an hour, no more. Is that understood?" Even as she spoke these cautionary words she felt foolish, ashamed of herself.

But he was not offended. "That's fine," he said. "That's fine." She had been prepared for a crow of triumph. Yet he sounded neither triumphant nor relieved. Instead he had turned distracted; his tone was distant. Auslander had a sudden clear vision of him thinking: *All right, now this is settled. On to the other.*

They set a time and place, and Auslander—herself relieved that the conversation was over—hung up the phone and went into the kitchen. The bathwater had indeed turned quite cold. As she drained some of it and watched the tap stream out a rush of fresh hot water, she resolved to put the Rumanian out of her mind.

The tenor of the conversation had left her feeling vaguely anxious, but there was nothing to be done for it. She would know soon enough what she had gotten herself into. She would undoubtedly be sorry, that much was already clear. It seemed to her that she was always getting herself into something about which she would be certain to be sorry later.

IN TRUTH, Auslander at thirty-four had no serious regrets about her life. For all her small miscalculations, all the momentary lapses in judgment that only proved to her that she'd do better to attend to her instincts, in the end there was nothing that really upset the steady balance she had attained. She had lived in the same small Greenwich Village apartment for a dozen years; she had a few friends she trusted and who did not make especially great demands on her time or spirit; her work was work she liked and excelled in. The work in particular was a real source of pleasure to her; and yet it was not the work she had set out to do. She had begun as a poet, and she had not, she thought, been a very bad one. Still, she had known by her freshman year at college that she would never be a very good one. She had been able to tell the difference even then between true poets and those who were only playing at it for their own amusement. Poetry as self-examination or catharsis was not for her—not enough for her—and knowing she would never be one of the few real poets, she gave it up without too much sorrow.

The decision to make her way as a translator of other, better, poets' work was one that hardly needed to be made: she found she had been moving toward it steadily for years, as if by intent. As early as the fifth grade she had discovered that languages came easily to her: the Hebrew lessons her father had insisted on were a snap, a pleasure; Yiddish, which was spoken at home, she taught herself to read and write. In junior high school she learned French, swallowing up long lists of words as if she'd been hungering for them all her young life. At that age she took this as a matter of course; it was only later that she came to understand that facility with languages was considered a talent, a special gift. By her sixteenth birthday she was fully fluent in French, Hebrew, Yiddish, and Spanish. By eighteen she had added German and Italian, and by the time she had completed her undergraduate education she had mastered Portuguese, Rumanian, and Russian as well. Her choice to become a translator, she knew, was a kind of compromise between aspirations and ability; but it was a compromise that satisfied her.

She knew her limits. This, Auslander believed, was her best trait. She did not deceive herself and thus could not disappoint herself. She always knew where she stood. She was aware, for example, that she was not a beauty. She was content with her looks, however, for they were certainly good enough ("for my purposes," she had told a former lover, a painter who had wondered aloud if she were ever sad about not being "a more conventionally pretty type"). When she troubled to make even a half-hearted effort she was quite attractive—neatly if eccentrically dressed, solid looking, "an indomitable gypsy," in the words of the painter. Her unruly black hair and eyebrows, her wide forehead and prominent nose, her fine posture—about which her father had been insistent along with the Hebrew classes—all of this made an impression. Her figure, another ex-lover had told her, was that of a Russian peasant—he meant her strong legs and broad shoulders and hips. The notion amused her (though the man, finally, did not; he was a biochemist with little in the way of real imagination— his stolidness, which she had at first interpreted as a charming imperturbability, depressed her after several months). She knew she was the kind of woman of whom other women said, "She's really very striking, don't you think?" to men who shrugged and agreed, without actually looking at her, in order to keep the peace. And yet there was a particular sort of man who appreciated her brand of attractiveness—men by and large a decade or so older than herself, intelligent and good-natured men who had a tendency to brood, even to be sullen, and whose wit was mocked by self-criticism. In any case, she was not "on the market." She had no call to compete with the slim, lively blondes or the dramatic dark young beauties who weaved like lovely ribbons through the city, brilliantly pretty and perpetually bored and lonely. Auslander watched them at publication parties and post-reading parties, in Village cafes and restaurants and bars, and she eavesdropped on their talk with mild interest: there was a hunt on in the city; there was always talk—she heard it everywhere—about the lack of available, desirable men. Auslander herself was not lonely, never bored. She liked having a man in her life, and frequently she did, but she was most at ease alone, and she grew uncomfortable when a man tried to force himself too far into her affairs. It made her nervous to have a man   no matter how much she cared for him—poking about in her things, clattering through cabinets and riffling through her books, cooking pasta in her kitchen, sitting casually in her desk chair.

Auslander's boyfriends—a ridiculous word, she thought, when the men she knew were over forty (though the men themselves seemed to like it)—always started off admiring her "independence" and "self-sufficiency." Later, they would accuse her of "fear of commitment," "obsessive self-reliance." Her most recent affair, with a poet named Farrell—a very good poet, whose work she admired greatly, and the first, and only, poet with whom she had ever been involved in this way—had dissolved after nearly a year into a series of nasty arguments: he called her inflexible and cold; she pronounced him infantile, morbidly dependent. In the end she slept with a young novelist she met at the Ninety-Second

Street Y, and carelessly let Farrell discover it. He drank himself into a rage and howled at her, pounding the refrigerator and the bathtub with his fists, and hurled a bottle of shampoo across the room; the plastic split and pale orange globs spattered the walls. She watched in mute amazement, breathless with fear, as he flung himself around her kitchen in a fury, bellowing like an animal. Finally she slammed out of the apartment without a word, and when she returned an hour and a half later he was asleep on her bedroom floor, curled like a shell among her clothes. She spent the night sitting wide awake and shivering at her desk, and in the morning when he rose he only nodded at her and said, "Well, all right, then," and left.

She had not seen him since—it had been five weeks now—and she had found that she missed him. This itself was disturbing. If he was gone, she wanted him gone, done with. She yearned for clarity; ambivalence unnerved her. They had been a bad match, she told herself. Farrell was so demanding, and what did he want from her after all? To be a different sort of person than she was? He needed constant attention and she couldn't give it to him. But there was no getting around the fact that she liked him. More than liked him. She was fonder of him than she had been of anyone in years—perhaps ever in her life. She wasn't even entirely sure why she had slept with the young writer except that she had felt suffocated. She'd needed to poke her way out, shake things up. But still she had taken a good deal of pleasure in Farrell's company before their battling had begun.

This had happened again and again, this cycle of pleasure and discontent. Auslander could not help but wonder sometimes if she was simply picking the wrong men. To hear other women talk, most men were afraid of involvement. Her friend Delia, a playwright, had confessed to her that the man she'd been seeing for the last two years complained constantly about feeling trapped.

"He says he wants to be close," she told Auslander, "but then he admits that the whole notion of togetherness terrifies him." Why then was it that the men Auslander knew seemed only too eager to cast in their lots with her? Delia laughed. She said, "Oh, sure. You ought to try taking one of them up on it sometime. He'd be out the door so fast you wouldn't know what hit you. Take Farrell, for instance. Do you think he'd know what to do with you if he had you? He'd be scared to death."

Auslander wasn't so sure. Not that it mattered anymore. Farrell, she felt certain, was out of the picture for good. They had spoken on the phone a couple of times, but he was still angry with her, and the last time they'd talked—he had telephoned her, drunk, in the dead middle of the night—he had called her a "cold ungiving bitch."

It was of Farrell that Auslander was thinking as she readied herself for her appointment with Petru Viorescu. It wasn't that she was imagining a romance with the Rumanian. She expected that she would read a few of his poems, gently tell him she could not translate them, and they would never meet again. No, it was only that this was the first time in more than a month that she had dressed and tidied herself knowing that she was going to meet with a man. She had been keeping to herself since the explosion with Farrell, seeing only the occasional woman friend—Delia or Margot or Kathleen, all of whom lived nearby—for lunch or coffee. She had not even attended a reading or seen a play or a movie since that night. It struck her now that it was as if she had been in hiding. *Hiding from what?* she wondered, surprised at herself. Afraid that Farrell would sneak up behind her on the street or in a theater? And if he did? What did it matter?

Displeased, she shook off the thought and took a few steps back from the full-length mirror behind her bedroom door, considering herself. She grimaced. What a specter! Brushing and tugging and straightening, turning this way and that. There was something demeaning, Auslander thought, about thinking of one's appearance. Still, it was unavoidable. She tipped her head, squinting at herself. She looked all right. She had decided it would be wise to appear a trifle stern, and in gray corduroy slacks and a black sweater, boots, no jewelry, no scarves, her hair in a single long braid, she was satisfied that she had achieved the appropriate effect. Nodding to herself, she swept out of the room, snatched up her long coat and her gloves, and was off, even looking forward to the meeting now as a kind of mild diversion.

In the Peacock Cafe she had no trouble spotting him. He had the hollow, unhealthy look of a youngish poet—mid-thirties, she guessed, somewhat older than she had expected—and wore the uniform of a graduate student: shirt and tie, corduroy jacket and blue jeans. He was very slight. As she took him in with a glance from the doorway, she calculated that he was about her own height, certainly no taller than five-six at most. He sat smoking a cigarette and tapping a teaspoon against a coffee mug at one of the small round tables in the front of the cafe.

Auslander went in flourishing her coat and smacking her gloves together, her braid flapping behind her, and moved straight to his table and extended her hand. "Mr. Viorescu?"

He started, and half-stood so abruptly the mug clattered against the sugar bowl. "Ah, Miss Auslander?"

Auslander nodded and sat down across from him. There was an alert, tensely intelligent look about him, she thought—almost an animal-like keenness.

"You are younger than I had imagined," he said. His presence of mind seemed to have returned to him. He was assessing her quite coolly.

She thought of saying: *You are older and shorter.* But she only nodded.

"I don't know why I should have expected that you would be older—perhaps fifty." He grinned and tilted back his chair, folding his arms across his chest. His smile made her uncomfortable and reminded her that the meeting was not likely to be a pleasant one for her. "Would you like a cappuccino? Or an espresso perhaps?"

"American coffee, thank you." She decided not to remove her coat; she would make it clear that she meant to stick by her half-hour time limit. Viorescu continued to grin at her, and she was relieved when the waitress finally idled by to take her order. They sat in silence until she returned with the coffee. Then the Rumanian leaned forward and placed his hands flat on the table. "I know you are busy, so I shall come to the point immediately. Would you be interested in undertaking the translation of the work of a poet who is, I assure you, quite brilliant, a magnificent talent, and who has never been published in English?"

Auslander raised her eyebrows. "I see you are not of the opinion that modesty is a virtue."

"Modesty?" Momentarily he was confused. Then, at once, he began to laugh. "Oh, yes, that is very good, very good."

Auslander, herself confused, did not know what to say.

"I am so sorry—I should have realized. You of course imagined that I was the poet. Yes, I would have drawn the same conclusion." He chuckled softly. "Ah, but my God, imagine me a poet! A fond wish, as it happens, but without even the smallest glimmer of hope." He shook his head. "No, no, look here. It is my wife of whom I am speaking. The poet Teodora Viorescu."

"You're not a poet?"

"Not in the slightest." He lifted his hands from the table and turned them palms up. "As it happens, I have no ability in this area at all. In fact, I have thought to try to translate a number of my wife's poems. I believed I might manage it. But I find it takes a poet to do such work, or—you said you were not yourself a poet—a rather exceptional talent which I do not possess. It was a hopeless task, hopeless. The results were . . . earthbound. Do you know what I mean by this? The poetry was lost."

Auslander sipped her coffee as she mulled this over. Finally she said, "Your wife . . . I take it she is unable to translate her own work?"

"Ah, well, you see, this is the problem. She has not the command of English I have. She has had some . . . some reluctance to learn the language as fully as she might. Oh, she is able to express herself perfectly well in spoken English. As for writing . . . that is another matter altogether."

"Yes." Auslander nodded. "This is often the case."

"I had hoped you might recognize her name, though it is understandable if you do not. Her reputation was only beginning to become established in our country when we left. She was thought of then as one of the most promising young poets in Rumania. She was very young, you understand—nineteen—but still she had published a small book and her work was included in two quite prestigious anthologies."

"Viorescu," Auslander murmured. "She has always published under this name?"

"Yes. We married when she was seventeen."

"Seventeen!"

He shrugged. "We have known each other since we were children. I was the best friend of her eldest brother."

"I see," Auslander said politely.

"And in any case, over the last eight years you most certainly would not have heard of her. Since we came to the United States there has been nothing to hear."

"Is she writing at all?"

"Oh, she is writing, she is writing all the time. But she writes only in Rumanian. None of the work has been published."

"How is it that she has never before had any interest in having her poems translated?"

"Well, it is somewhat more complicated than that." He shifted in his seat. "You see, even now she insists she has no interest."

"But then . . ." Auslander narrowed her eyes. "You're discussing this with me without her permission?"

He poked at his pack of cigarettes with his index finger, pushing it around in a small circle. His eyes followed its path.

"You must realize that I could not possibly consider the translation of a writer's work against her wishes."

He did not raise his eyes. "Well, here is the problem," he said. "I am very . . . I am very concerned about her. I fear . . . She is not—how can I say this correctly? She is not adjusting. She is languishing here. A poet needs a certain amount of attention to thrive. Teo is not thriving. I fear for her."

"Still it doesn't seem—"

"We are not thriving," he said. Now he looked at Auslander. "She sits awake at night and writes; the poems she puts in a drawer in the bedroom. She will not discuss them. She refuses to consider the possibility of their translation. She is angry—all the time she seems angry. Often she will not even speak to me."

"Well, this is a personal matter," Auslander said, "between the two of you only."

He continued as if she had not spoken. "Teo is rather frail, you see. She has headaches, she does not sleep well. Frequently she is depressed. I feel strongly that she cannot continue this way. She has no life outside her part-time job at the university. She has no friends, no one to talk with. She says I am her only friend. And it was I who took her away from her family and a promising career."

"She is sorry she left Rumania?"

"Not quite sorry, no. The situation there was untenable, impossible. Worse for her than for me. She is a Jew—only nominally, of course; it is virtually impossible to practice Judaism in our country. But this in itself made life difficult for her. No, we were completely in agreement about leaving. But here . . . she is always unhappy. Her poetry, her most recent work—it makes me weep to read it, it is so full of sorrow. The poems are spectacular: violent and beautiful. But it is as if she is speaking only to herself."

"Perhaps this is the way she wants it."

Again he ignored her. "I have thought for a long time about finding a translator for her. I believe that if she were able to hold in her hand a translation of one of her poems, if it were precisely the right translation—she would change her mind. But how to find the person capable of this! It was daunting to me; it seemed beyond my abilities. When I read your essay in *Metaphrasis*, however, I was certain I had found Teo's translator. I have no doubt of this, still. I feel it, I feel it in my heart. As I read that essay, it was like a sign: I knew you were the one. With absolute clarity I knew also that you would be sympathetic to the problem . . . the unusual situation."

"Naturally, I'm sympathetic. But what can I do? Without her approval I could not translate a word of her writing. Surely you understand that. What you're asking of me is not only unethical, it's unfeasible. Without the participation of your wife . . ." She shook her head. "I'm sorry. It's impossible."

Viorescu's expression was impassive as he tapped a cigarette from his pack and placed it between his lips. As he lit it, he breathed out, in rapid succession, two dark streams of smoke.

"But I would still like to see some of her poems," Auslander said. She did not know herself if she were being merely polite or if he had indeed called upon her curiosity. In any case it seemed to her absolutely necessary to make this offer; she could not refuse to read his wife's work after all he had said.

Viorescu took the cigarette from his mouth and looked at it.

Then he waved it at Auslander. "Ah, yes, but are you quite sure that itself would not be 'unethical'?"

His petulance, she decided, was excusable under the circumstances. He was disappointed; this was understandable. Calmly, she said, "I see no reason why it should be." She kept her eyes on his cigarette as she spoke. "Unless, of course, you would simply prefer that I not read them."

He smiled, though faintly. "No, no. I had hoped that in any event you would want to read them." From a satchel hung on the back of his chair he produced a manila envelope. He laid it on the table between them. It was quite thick. The sight of it moved her, and this came as a surprise. Viorescu folded his hands and set them atop the envelope. "I have chosen mostly those poems written in the last year or so, but also there is a quantity of her earlier work, some of it dating from our first few years in this country. I have also included a copy of her book, which I thought you would be interested in seeing."

"Yes," Auslander said. "I would, thank you."

"It is, I believe, a fair sample of Teo's work. It should give you a true sense of what she is about. See for yourself that I have not been overly generous in my praise."

"You're very proud of her."

"Yes, naturally." He spoke brusquely enough so that Auslander wondered if she had offended him. "Perhaps this is hard for you to understand. Teo is . . . she is not only my wife, she is like my sister. I have known her since she was six years old and I was twelve. We were family to each other long before our marriage."

A dim alarm went off in Auslander's mind—a warning that confidences were ahead. This was her cue to change the subject, no question about it. But she remained silent. Altogether despite herself she was touched.

"Ah, you find this poignant," Viorescu said, startling her.

Embarrassed, she nodded.

"Yes, well, perhaps it is. That we have been so close for so much of our lives is itself touching, I suppose. But we are not . . . She is . . . Ah, well." He shrugged and smiled, vaguely.

Auslander cautioned herself: *This is none of your business; you want no part of this.* But she felt drawn in; she couldn't help asking, "What were you about to say?" And yet as she spoke she groaned inwardly.

"Oh—only that something has been lost. This is maybe not so unusual after so many years, I think." He closed his eyes for an instant. "Something lost," he murmured. "Yes, it may be that she is lost to me already. Well, it is my own fault. I have not been a help to her. I have done a great deal of damage."

At once Auslander realized she did not want to hear any of this. *Not another word,* she thought, and she imagined herself rising immediately, bidding him good-bye and taking off—she did not even have to take the package of poems. What was the point of it? Did she honestly think there was a chance she might discover a hidden genius? Who was she kidding?

"It is very bad, very bad," he muttered.

A mistake, Auslander thought. Sitting here listening, offering to read the poetry of his wife—all a mistake. She could feel her chest tightening against what she suddenly felt was certain to be a perilous intrusion into her life. For it would get worse with every moment: confessions led to further confessions. No more. She wanted no more of Viorescu and his poet wife.

He pushed the envelope toward her. "Here, I can see you are impatient. I did not mean to keep you so long."

She picked up the envelope. "It's true, I should be going." She half-rose, awkwardly, and drew the envelope to her chest. "Ah— shall I phone you after I've read these?"

"I will phone you." He smiled at her, broadly this time. "I

should like to thank you in advance for your time. I am very grateful."

Auslander felt uneasy. "I hope I've made it completely clear that I'm not going to be able to take Teodora on."

"After you have read the poems," he said, "perhaps you will change your mind."

"I'm afraid not."

"You have agreed to read them, after all."

"I am always interested in good poetry," Auslander said stiffly. "If your wife's work is as you say, I would be doing myself a disservice by not reading it."

"Indeed," he said, and now he laughed—his telephone laugh, that short curious bark. "I will phone you next week."

She could feel his eyes on her back as she retreated, the envelope of poems under her arm. For his sake—and for the sake of the unknown, unhappy Teodora—she hoped the poems were not dreadful. She did not have much confidence in this hope, however; the excitement that had begun to stir in her only moments ago had already left her entirely.

By the time she had passed through the café's door and emerged onto the street, she was convinced the work would turn out to be inept. As she crossed Greenwich Avenue, her coat whipping about her legs, her head bowed against the wind, she was imagining her next conversation with Viorescu. She would be gentle; there would be no need to tell him the truth about his wife's work. If he deceived himself, he deceived himself. It was not her responsibility.

AS IT turned out, Viorescu had neither lied to her nor deceived himself. Teodora Viorescu's poems were extraordinary. Auslander, after reading the first of them, which she had idly extracted from the envelope and glanced at as she sat down to her dinner, had in her astonishment risen from the table, dropping her fork to her plate with a clatter, and reached for the envelope to shake out the remainder of its contents. A batch of poems in hand, she ate her broiled chicken and rice without the slightest awareness of so doing. She could hardly believe her eyes. The poems jumped on the pages, full of terror, queer dangerous images of tiny pointed animal faces, blood raining through the knotted black branches of trees, fierce woods that concealed small ferocious creatures. And the language! The language was luminous, electrifying. What a haunted creature the poet herself must be! Auslander thought as she at last collapsed against her pillows at half-past twelve. She had been reading for five hours, had moved from table to desk to bed, and she had not yet read all the poems Viorescu had given her, but she intended to, tonight. She needed however to rest for a moment. She was exhausted; her eyes burned.

For ten minutes she lay listening to the dim apartment sounds of night: refrigerator, plumbing, upstairs creaks and groans, downstairs murmurs. Then she sat up again, stacked her pillows neatly behind her, and set again to reading. When she had read all of the poems once, she began to reread; after a while she got up and fetched a legal pad. For some time she reread and made notes on the pad, resisting with difficulty the urge to go to her desk for a batch of the five-by-seven cards she used to make notes on work she was translating. Finally she gave in, telling herself it was simply easier to use the index cards, their feel was more familiar, and with a supply of the cards beside her she worked until dawn in something of a feverish state, feeling like one of the poet's own strange night creatures as she sat wild-haired and naked in her bed, chewing on her fingers and the end of her pen, furiously scratching out notes as the gray-bluish light rose around her.

For days, anxiously, she awaited Viorescu's call. On the fifth day she checked the telephone directory and was half-relieved to find no listing; she knew she should not phone him. But she felt foolish, waiting. Dimly she was reminded of her adolescence—a hateful time—as she stared at the phone, willing it to ring. After each of her ventures out of the apartment—her few forays to the supermarket and the library, her one trip uptown to return the galleys of a gothic romance—she hastened to her answering machine. The playback yielded up several invitations to functions that didn't interest her, a number of calls from friends, one from her mother, one from Farrell.

"Do you miss me, Harriet, my love? Are you lonely?"

Auslander breathed impatiently, fists against her thighs. Farrell's message was intended of course to make her angry. He never called her "Harriet" except to taunt her. *Well, let him,* she thought. She would not allow him to upset her. She had been less preoccupied lately with missing him; she had other things on her mind (and she'd like the chance to tell him that, she thought)—though the sound of his voice on the tape, it was true, sent a shiver of sorrow and loneliness through her. "Has it hit you yet that you're all alone? Are you enjoying it, as anticipated? Or are you sorry? Or are you not alone—have you already found someone else to resist loving?" There was a pause, then, harsher: "Don't call me back. I've changed my mind; I don't want to talk to you after all."

Eight days passed; then nine. On the tenth day—once again as she was about to take a bath, one leg over the side of the tub—the phone rang and she knew instantly it was the poet's husband.

He was cheerful. "So? What do you make of my Teodora?"

Auslander felt it would be wise to be guarded. "Well, she's something, all right. An original, no question."

"You enjoyed her work, then?"

She could not remain cautious; she was too relieved to hear from him.

"'Enjoyed?' Ha! She's a terror, your wife. The real thing, astonishing stuff."

Viorescu was cackling. "Yes, yes, it's true, absolutely true. She is one of a kind, a wonder, a gem!"

Auslander stood beside the bed coiling and uncoiling the telephone cord about her wrist as they went on to talk about the poems. She excused herself to get her notes, and then she was able to quote directly from them; Viorescu was delighted. She had just launched into some observations about one of the most recent poems when she happened to glance up and saw that the man across the way was standing at his window staring blankly at her. Good lord, she thought, he would begin to imagine she strolled around naked for his benefit. She sat down on the bed, her back to the window, and pulled the blanket up around her.

"Listen, Petru," she said, "I've been thinking. I really ought to meet Teodora."

He clicked his tongue. "Well, as you know, this is not such a simple matter. I am not sure it is possible at all right now."

"It may be difficult," she said, "but surely we can manage it."

"Tell me, have you given any further thought to the question of translating her work?"

"I've already told you I would not consider it without her full cooperation."

"But you are interested! Well, this is good news indeed. Of course you must meet her. Let me think . . . Why don't you come to dinner? Let us say, next Friday night?"

"Are you sure?"

"Yes, of course. But it would be best not to let her know immediately that you are a translator."

Auslander was discomfited. "Are you sure this is necessary?" she said. "If I'm not to be a translator, who am I? How did we meet?"

"Oh, I shall say I met you at an academic function. Teo never attends department functions with me."

"An academic function," Auslander echoed. She recalled then

that she had never asked him what his area of study was. "What department is it that I am to be associated with?"

"Philosophy," he said with a short laugh. "That is my department. My specialization is Nietzsche."

"Wonderful," Auslander said. "You can tell Teo I'm a renowned Nietzsche scholar and I'll remain silent all evening."

"I can tell her that you are Hannah Arendt and she would not know the difference," Viorescu said dryly.

"Are you sure all this intrigue is necessary? Maybe you ought to simply tell her the truth."

"No. She would suspect a plot."

"Has she such a suspicious nature?"

"It does not take much," he said, "to arouse suspicious thoughts. Why take such a chance? We can tell her the truth after an hour, two hours perhaps, once she is comfortable in your presence."

For the second time, Auslander hung up the phone after talking to the Rumanian and found herself wondering what she was letting herself in for. Gloomily she paced around her bedroom—the man across the way, she noted as she went to the window to pull down the shade, was no longer looking out—and tried to convince herself that she was in no danger of becoming personally involved with the Viorescus. They needed a translator, she told herself; it was not necessary to be their friend. Still, she didn't like the circumstances; they did not lend themselves to a smooth working relationship. Even assuming that all went well—that Teodora was willing, that she could be reasoned with—the project was likely to be full of difficulties and strains, starting out the way it was. Already she had agreed to this preposterous masquerade! It was clear enough that between Viorescu and his wife there were problems, serious problems. Auslander hated the thought of these complications.

But the poetry! Auslander shook her head, tugged at her hair as she circled the room. *Oh, the poetry!*

SHE WOULD have recognized Teodora Viorescu at once, Auslander felt. Had she passed her on Sixth Avenue a day or two ago, she was certain she would have thought: *Might this not be the poet?* Small and pale, with hair like a slick black cap cut so short her ears stuck out pointedly from beneath it, she felt her way through the room toward Auslander like a swimmer.

"I'm very pleased to meet you," Auslander said. "Petru has told me a great deal about you." She took the poet's small hand in hers. It was very cold.

"So you are Miss Auslander."

"Just Auslander is fine."

"Ah, yes, so my husband told me." She smiled. Her face was perfectly round, her eyes also—oddly—round. How white her skin was! As if she truly never saw daylight. And how grave she looked, even as she smiled. It was in the eyes, Auslander thought. Her eyes were the eyes of one of her own imaginary creatures: liquid-black with floating pinpoints of light, emitting a steady watchful beam.

During dinner there was small talk. The food was Rumanian, traditional, Viorescu explained. He seemed very nervous and spoke at length about ingredients and methods of cooking. Auslander avoided meeting his eyes; she was sure it was plain to Teodora that something was up. Teodora herself kept her eyes downcast and picked at her food; between the Viorescus barely a word passed.

Auslander helped Viorescu move the table back into the kitchen and pile the dishes in the sink; he tried to whisper to her but she waved him away impatiently. Enough of this, she thought. She returned to the living room to find the poet sitting on the windowseat, gazing out upon Riverside Drive. Auslander seated herself on the end of the couch nearest the window and said, "Please, Teodora, won't you tell me about your work? Your husband informs me that you are a fine poet."

"There is nothing to tell." She turned slowly toward Auslander. Her tone and facial expression were remote. Auslander recalled what Farrell had told her when she'd described a famous poet she'd met as "terribly cool and remote." "Wrong again, Auslander," he had said. "Not remote. Only massively depressed and riddled with anxiety—like me."

Auslander tried again. "Petru tells me you published a book in Rumania."

"Yes."

"And have you any interest in publishing your work in the United States?"

Teodora glanced over at her husband, who had entered the room silently and positioned himself by the bookshelves opposite the couch where Auslander sat, and spoke quietly to him in Rumanian. Auslander heard only snatches of what she said. "Unfair"—she heard this word several times—and "You should have told me." Once, clearly, she heard the poet say "unforgivable," and then—her heart sank—she heard unmistakably the Rumanian for "translator." Viorescu did not speak. Finally Teodora turned again to Auslander. "I am sorry if we have put you to any trouble. I do not wish for my work to be translated into English." Abruptly she stood and left the room.

Auslander started to rise, but Viorescu said, "Please, Auslander. There is nothing we can do."

"What do you mean 'nothing we can do'?" She was astounded. "I thought you were so eager to convince her."

"I believed she might be convinced. Apparently I was wrong."

"But you didn't even *try*."

"It would be pointless. She is very angry at having been deceived."

"Why didn't you just tell her what I was here for in the first place?"

"You must realize that it would not have mattered either way. She is obviously beyond—"

"You're giving up. I can't believe it. You do this whole . . ." She sank back into the couch and looked up at him in amazement. "And giving up so easily!"

"Easily!" He laughed hoarsely. "I have been trying for years to talk her into having her work translated. I am giving up now finally." He shook his head. "There is a story—do you know it?—about a famous philosopher who decided, after long consideration, to become a vegetarian. For many years he lived as a vegetarian. He spoke and wrote of it, of course, since under the circumstances such a decision could not be a private matter only. He spoke brilliantly, in fact, and movingly, on the moral logic of his choice. Then one day he sat down to his table and began to eat a steak. His students, as you would imagine, were quite agitated when they saw this. Why the change? they cried. What had happened? And the famous philosopher said, 'Ah, well, it was time to give it a rest.'"

"There is no relevance to this story, Petru," Auslander said wearily.

"Oh, I quite disagree, Auslander, my friend. But in any event don't you find it a charming story?"

"I have other things on my mind," she said. "Tell me. Why doesn't Teo want her work translated? What does she say when you ask her?"

"She says, 'Because I say so.'"

"But that's a child's logic."

"No. It's a parent's logic, rather. The child asks, 'Why not?' The parent says, 'Only because I say not.'"

"Well, then." Auslander shrugged and stood up. She was angrier and more disappointed than she could have predicted. "I guess that's it. Shall I mail the poems back to you?"

"Are you in a rush to be rid of them?" He smiled at her. "No, my friend. Let us not altogether give up. May I telephone you tomorrow?"

"What's the point?"

"Oh, I shall talk to her tonight. Perhaps it would be wise to tell her you've already read her work, extend your compliments. It will depend on her spirits."

"But I thought . . ." Auslander stopped herself. There was no sense trying to follow him. "All right, fine. Call me."

"Tell me something," he said as he walked with her to the door and helped her into her coat. "Are you absolutely certain that if her work were translated it would be publishable here?"

"Oh, without question," Auslander said. Then a thought came to her. "Why? Do you think it will help if Teo knows this? Because if you like, I can make a few calls tomorrow, ask around, get a feel for it." Instantly she regretted this offer. Who on earth could she call to discuss the work of an untranslated Rumanian poet? Without work to show, what could she expect an editor to say? It was nonsense, absurd.

"That would be very kind."

"I should go now," Auslander said, her hand on the doorknob. As she went down the hall to the elevator, she reflected that it was a miracle that she had escaped without having made any further promises.

On the subway heading back to the Village, she removed from her Danish schoolbag the envelope containing Teodora's poems. She was not sure why she hadn't told Viorescu she had the poems with her—evidently she wasn't ready yet to part with them. She flipped through the pages until she found the one she wanted. From the front pocket of her bag she took out a pen and the packet of index cards she had begun to keep on Teodora's work, and she sifted through the cards, stopping at the one headed "In the Cold Field, In the Troubled Light." She ran her eyes quickly down the card; besides the title, she had already, automatically, cast a number of lines into English as she made her notes. She sighed and turned to the poem itself. Then, pen in hand, using the canvas bag as a lap-desk, she began the translation.

HE DID not even bother to say hello. "She wants no part of it," Viorescu announced. "She will not discuss it."

"What did you tell her? Did you explain—"

"I pleaded, I made promises, I was a madman." He laughed miserably. "She made me sleep on the couch."

"That's none of my affair," Auslander said sharply.

"I want to apologize for all the trouble you have taken."

"Yes, well, here's a surprise for you," she said. She took a deep breath and then told him about the poems she had translated last night, working until four o'clock, until she couldn't see clearly anymore.

"My God, that's . . . Is this really true? How marvelous! Please, will you read them to me?"

For half an hour she read Viorescu his wife's poems. She had rough versions—very rough in some cases—of eight poems already; one or two were quite polished, almost perfect.

"But this is wonderful! Incredible! Oh, we must convince her. Do you think . . . what if we did as I had thought to begin with . . ."

"I don't know. If you were to simply show her these translations she might get very angry. She might—quite justifiably—feel invaded."

"She might feel complimented."

"She might. You would know better than I."

Auslander was not altogether sure of this, however. His track record did not seem to be the best.

SEVERAL DAYS passed. Auslander continued to translate the poems. There was no logic in it, she knew; she had almost no hope by now that Teodora would agree to have this done. She was translating the poems because she wanted to; there was no other reason. She was working at it late on Saturday afternoon when there was a knock on her door. Surprised, her first thought was of Farrell. Nobody ever dropped by without calling. Farrell himself had done so only once, and he would surely only do it now if he were drunk. Cautiously she went to the door and stood listening.

"Auslander, are you there?"

It was Petru Viorescu. She snapped away the police lock and swung the door open. He looked terrible.

"Petru! What on earth's the matter?"

"May I come in?" He brushed past her and heaved himself into her desk chair. He looked around. "What is this room? Bathroom, study, kitchen?"

Auslander closed and locked the door. "What's going on? You look like hell."

"I want to tell you something. I need to discuss this with someone. I am going to lose my mind."

"Is it about Teodora?" she asked anxiously. "Has something happened?"

"Oh, something has happened, yes, but not what you imagine. You think she is so fragile! You are afraid that she has tried to commit suicide, that she has had a 'nervous breakdown.' No," he said. "She is made of iron, my wife." He laughed, but then after a second he placed his head in his hands and began to weep. Auslander stood back, uncertain what was expected of her. Finally he stopped crying; he looked up at her and very calmly told his story: He had met a young woman, someone in his department. He was in love; there was nothing to be done for it.

"I don't understand," Auslander said. "When did this happen? Just this week?"

"Months ago," he said. "Months."

"But I don't understand," she repeated. "Have you . . . ?"

"I have not slept with her, if that is your question."

"But then . . . Have you told Teo about this?"

"Of course." He seemed offended at the implication that he might not have.

"But why? You haven't done anything. What is there to tell? You are . . . you have a crush, Petru, only that."

"No, no. It is not a crush. I am in love."

Auslander was at a loss. "Well, what do you want to do?" Then immediately she said, "Never mind. I don't want to know."

He began to weep again. Auslander wanted to scream. Suddenly a suspicion came to her. "Tell me something," she said. "How much does this business with the other woman—"

"Ana," Viorescu said.

"I don't want to know her name! How much does it have to do with Teo's refusal to have the poems translated?"

"How much does anything have to do with anything?"

"Don't speak to me that way, I won't stand for it," she snapped at him. "Answer me truthfully." She began to pace around the kitchen. "What's going on here? What is this all about? When did you tell Teo about this woman?"

"Months ago," he said. "As soon as I knew. I could not keep my feelings secret from her. We tell each other everything, we always have; we are brother and sister, inseparable."

"But you fancy yourself in love with someone else," she said sarcastically.

"One has nothing to do with the other. You must yourself know that."

"You're not planning to leave Teo?"

"No, I am not going to leave her. The question is whether she will leave me."

"But why has it come to this now, if she's known all these months? What's changed?" At once Auslander had the answer. "Petru," she said, "did the idea of having her poems translated somehow backfire on you?"

He shrugged.

"Did you come up with the notion of getting me to do this in the first place as a way of . . . of placating her? Giving her something of her own? Did you think that having me translate her poems might make things all right between the two of you?"

"This is partly true, yes."

"You could have just bought her flowers," Auslander said bitterly. "It would have saved a lot of trouble."

"I have bought her flowers," he said. "And in any case the trouble, it seems to me, was worth it. No? You don't agree? You understand that this was not the only reason I wanted to have the work translated, do you not? I have been discussing the matter with her for years, years. Long before I knew Ana, long before I met you. Years!" he said angrily. "She will not listen to reason. And what is a poet without readers? I have been her only reader for too long."

Auslander continued to stalk the kitchen, twisting her hands together as she paced. For a long time she did not speak. Finally she sighed and said, "Well, now there are two of us."

"Yes," Viorescu said. "Yes, exactly. Now there are two of us."

THE CALL from Teodora the following night woke her.

"I am sorry to be disturbing you at so late an hour," the poet said. "But I will not be long. I wanted only to say one thing. I understand that Petru has been troubling you with problems of a personal nature."

Auslander was too startled to respond.

"I apologize for this," Teodora said. "I want you to know that I have asked him not to trouble you any further."

"Oh, really, it hasn't been all that much trouble," Auslander said.

"In all events he will not be calling you again."

"Oh, that isn't—" Auslander began. But it was too late; the poet had already hung up.

AUSLANDER DID not for a moment seriously consider the possibility that she would not hear from Viorescu. Thus she was not in the least surprised when three days later he called. There was a note of hysteria in his voice, however, which alarmed her.

"What is it, Petru? What's wrong now?"

"She wants to leave me! She says she has had enough, she is fed up. Auslander, please, I need your help. Will you call her? Explain to her? Please?"

"Explain what?" Auslander said. "I don't understand it myself."

"Please. She is at home now. I am in the library. You could call her right now and she could talk to you freely, she is alone."

"I'm sorry, I can't."

"But she wants to leave me!"

"Petru, I can't help you with this. It should be plain by now that I can't. There's nothing I can do."

"Yes, there is. But you refuse! You refuse to help!"

Auslander could not think of what else to do, so she hung up the phone. She stood staring at it. It began to ring again instantly.

She lifted the receiver. "Please don't do this," she said.

"Jesus, Auslander, you're right on top of it tonight, aren't you. I haven't even started doing anything yet."

"Oh, Farrell. I thought you were someone else."

"I wish I were."

"Please," she said, "not tonight. Look, I don't mean to be rude, but are you calling to give me the business? Because if you are, I don't think I'm up to it."

"No, actually I thought I'd take my business elsewhere." He sighed. "You're not laughing, love. What's the matter? Is something really wrong?"

"No, Farrell," she said flatly, "nothing's really wrong."

"Well, shall I tell you why I called? See, I've got this idea. What if I gave up drinking? How would that be?"

"How would it be how?"

"Come on, Auslander. You've always complained about my drinking. What if I stopped?"

"I don't know." Suddenly she felt like crying.

"Hey, what's going on with you? Are you really all right? You sound awful."

"I'm all right," she said. Then, after a second, "No, I'm not. I guess I'm not. I don't know."

"Is there anything I can do?"

She shook her head before she remembered that he couldn't see her. "No," she said. "Not a thing."

"Well, what do you think? Do you think it would make a difference? In our relationship, I mean. Do you think it would help?"

"Look, Farrell," she said, "if you want to quit drinking, then quit drinking. You know perfectly well that I think you ought to. I've said it enough times. But if you're going to do it, do it for yourself, not for me. I don't want to be responsible for the decision."

"Oh, sure, that's right. How could I have forgotten? You don't want to be responsible for anything or anyone, do you?"

"Farrell, please."

"Please what? I am making a perfectly reasonable gesture toward straightening things out between us, and you're just tossing it right back in my face."

"That's not what I mean to do."

"No? What do you mean to do, then? Tell me."

"I don't know."

"You don't, do you."

"No." She realized she was gripping the phone so hard her fingers ached. "I don't."

"Tell me something, will you? *Do* you miss me? Ever? Do you even think about me?"

"Of course I think about you. I think about you a lot. I wonder about how your work is going. I wonder how life's treating you."

He laughed softly. "Oh, Auslander, my love, you should know. Life's not treating me at all—I'm paying my own way."

INTO BED with her that night she took the envelope of Teodora's poems and all of Farrell's poetry that she had in the apartment—all the poems of his that she had in typescript, all the magazines that had his poems in them, his four chapbooks, even some stray handwritten lines on pages torn from legal pads, which he'd left scattered about the apartment on nights he couldn't sleep. She read all of it, every line, Teodora's and Farrell's both, read until she felt stunned and overburdened, and fell into a sleep that was a kind of stupor. Under the blanket of poems, dreaming, she turned and tossed in her sleep; poems crackled and fluttered, flew off the bed, alighted on the floor.

It was months before she heard from Viorescu again. He called to tell her that Teodora had killed herself. He had returned from the library late at night and found her. There was no note. "She left nothing," he said. He spoke of the funeral and of Teodora's family. Several times he wept, but very quietly. Auslander listened without saying anything. When he had said all he had to say, she waited, expecting to hear herself tell him that she was sorry, but she remained silent.

For a moment they were both silent. Finally Viorescu said, "There is something else I must tell you. Teodora destroyed all of her work—all the poems she wrote from the time we left Rumania. I have searched the apartment; she was very thorough. Every copy of every poem is gone."

Now Auslander was able to make herself speak. "I'm sorry," she said.

"You are not surprised, I imagine."

"That she destroyed her poems. No, I suppose I'm not."

He hesitated. "You understand that you now have the only copy of her work."

"Yes."

Again they were silent.

"You want the poems translated," Auslander said.

"This is not the time to discuss this, of course," he said. "But after a reasonable amount of time has passed, yes."

"Yes, I see," she said.

"And in the meantime you will be careful, will you not?"

"With the poems? Of course."

"Well, then . . . We will speak."

As she went to her desk and removed the envelope from the center drawer, where it had remained undisturbed for months, Auslander thought briefly of Farrell's poems, which that same morning months ago she had set on the top shelf of her bedroom closet. She saw them in her mind—the bundle of poems secured by a rubber band, surrounded by the accumulated clutter of years: stacks of letters; shoeboxes full of photographs, postcards, cancelled checks; spiral-bound notebooks dating back to graduate school. Then the image vanished and she sat down at her desk; she flipped open the oak box in which her index cards were filed and removed the cards on Teodora—the notes and the dozen translations she had done. One at a time she laid the cards on her desk, as slowly and precisely as a storefront fortune teller, spreading them out carefully in a fan, one corner of each card touching the next. When she had come to the end of the cards, she shook the poems themselves out of the envelope. Now the desktop was littered with poetry. For a time she sat looking at all that she had spilled out there. Then she scooped up everything and stood, hugging the papers and cards tightly to her chest. She crossed the kitchen and with some difficulty unhooked the police lock. In the hallway she hesitated for an instant only; then she moved quickly. With one arm she held the poet's work; with her free hand she pulled open the door to the incinerator chute. It was a matter of seconds; then it was done.

The Translation

BY JOYCE CAROL OATES

What were the words for *woman, man, love, freedom, fate?*—in this strange land where the architecture and the country-side and the sea with its dark choppy waters and the very air itself seemed to Oliver totally foreign, unearthly? He must have fallen in love with the woman at once, after fifteen minutes' conversation. Such perversity was unlike him. He had loved a woman twenty years before; had perhaps loved two or even three women in his lifetime; but had never fallen in love, had never been in love; such melodramatic passion was not his style. He had spoken with her only for fifteen minutes at the most, and not directly: through the translator assigned to him. He did not know her at all. Yet that night he dreamed of rescuing her.

"I am struck and impressed," he said politely, addressing the young woman introduced to him as a music teacher at the high school and a musician—a violist—herself, "with the marvelous old buildings here . . . the church that is on the same street as my hotel . . . yes? . . . You know it? . . . And with the beauty of the parks, the trees and flowers, everything so well-tended, and the manner of the people I have encountered . . . they are friendly but not effusive, they appear so very . . . so very healthy," he said, hearing his voice falter, realizing that he was being condescending—as if it surprised him, the fact that people in this legendary, long-suffering nation were not very different from people anywhere. But his translator translated the speech and the young woman appeared to agree, nodding, smiling as if to encourage him. Thank God he had not offended her. "I am very grateful to have been allowed a visa," he said. "I have never visited a country that has struck me in such a way . . . an immediate sense of, of . . . how shall I put it? . . . of something like nostalgia . . . do you know the expression, the meaning? . . . nostalgia . . . emotion for something once possessed but now lost, perhaps not now even accessible through memory . . ."

If he was making a fool of himself with this speech, and by so urgently staring at the woman, Alisa, the others did not appear to notice; they listened intently, even greedily, as Oliver's young translator repeated his words, hardly pausing for breath. He was a remarkable young man, probably in his early twenties, and Oliver had the idea that the translator's presence and evident goodwill toward him were freeing his tongue, giving him a measure of happiness for the first time since he had left the United States. For the first time, really, in many years. It was marvelous, magical, to utter his thoughts aloud and to hear, then, their instantaneous translation into a foreign language—to sit with his translator at his left hand, watching the effect of his words upon his listeners' faces as they were translated. An eerie, uncanny experience . . . unsettling and yet exciting, in a way Oliver could not have explained. He had not liked the idea of relying upon a translator; one of his failings, one of the disappointments of his life, had always been a certain shyness or coolness in his character, which it was evidently his fate not to alter, and he had supposed that travel in a country as foreign as this one, and as formally antagonistic to the United States, would be especially difficult since he knew nothing of the language. But in fact the translator was like a younger brother to him, like a son. There was an intimacy between them and a pleasurable freedom, even an unembarrassed lyricism in Oliver's remarks, that he could not possibly have anticipated.

Of course his mood was partly attributable to the cognac, and to the close, crowded, overheated room in which the reception was being held, and to his immediate attraction for the dusky-haired, solemn young woman with the name he could not pronounce— *Alisa* was as close as he could come to it; he would have to ask the translator to write it out for him when they returned to the hotel. It would not last, his mood of gaiety. But for the present moment he was very happy merely to hear these people speak their language, a melodic play of explosive consonants and throaty vowels; it hardly mattered that his translator could manage to translate only a fraction of what was being said. He was happy, almost euphoric. He was intoxicated. He had to restrain himself from taking one of Alisa's delicate hands in his own and squeezing it, to show how taken he was by her. *I know you are suffering in this prison state of yours,* he wanted to whisper to her, *and I want, I want to do something for you . . . want to rescue you, save you, change your life . . .*

The director of the Lexicographic Institute was asking him a courteous, convoluted question about the current state of culture in his own nation, and everyone listened, frowning, as if with anxiety, while, with one part of his mind, Oliver made several statements. His translator took them up at once, transformed them into those eerie, exquisite sounds; the director nodded gravely, emphatically; the others nodded; it seemed to be about what they had anticipated. One of the men, white-haired, diminutive, asked something in a quavering voice, and Oliver's translator hesitated before repeating it. "Dr. Crlejevec is curious to know— is it true that your visual artists have become artists merely of the void—that is, of death—that they are exclusively morbid, that they have turned their backs on life?" The translator blushed, not quite meeting Oliver's gaze, as if he were embarrassed by the question. But the question did not annoy Oliver. Not in the least.

He disliked much of contemporary art anyway and welcomed the opportunity to express his feelings, warmly, knowing that what he said would endear him to these people. It pleased him most of all that Alisa listened so closely. Her long, nervous fingers toyed with a cameo brooch she wore at her throat; her gray eyes were fixed upon his face. "Art moves in a certain tendril-like manner . . . in many directions, though at a single point in history one direction is usually stressed and acclaimed . . . like the evolutionary gropings of nature to my way of thinking. Do you see? The contemporary pathway is but a tendril, a feeler, an experimental gesture . . . Because it is obsessed with death and the void and the annihilation of self, it will necessarily die . . . It pronounces its own death sentence."

The words were translated; the effect was instantaneous; Oliver's pronouncement seemed to meet with approval. The director, however, posed another question. He was a huge man in his fifties, with a ruddy, beefy face and rather coarse features, though his voice seemed to Oliver quite cultured. ". . . But in the meantime, does it not do damage? . . . to the unformed, that is, to the young, the susceptible . . . does it not do irreparable damage, such deathly art?"

Oliver's high spirits could not be diminished. He only pretended to be thinking seriously before he answered, "Not at all! In my part of the world, serious art is ignored by the masses; the unformed, the young, the susceptible are not aware of its existence."

He had expected his listeners to laugh. But they did not laugh. The young woman murmured something, shaking her head. Oliver's translator said to him, "She says she is shocked . . . unless, of course, you are joking."

The conversation shifted. Oliver was taken to other groups of people, was introduced by his translator, was made to feel important, honored. From time to time he glanced back at the young woman—when he saw her preparing to leave, he was stricken; he wanted to tell his translator to stop her, but of course that would have been indecorous. *I want to do something for you. Anything. I want . . .* But it would have been indecorous.

"SHE IS a fine person, very hard-working, very trustworthy," Liebert was saying slowly. "Not my friend or even acquaintance, but my sister's . . . my older sister, who was her classmate. She is a very accomplished violist, participated in a festival last spring in Moscow, but also a very fine teacher here, very hardworking, very serious."

"Is she married?" Oliver asked.

They were being driven in a shiny black taxicab along an avenue of trees in blossom—acacia, lime—past buildings of all sizes, some very old, some disconcertingly new, of glass and poured concrete and steel, and from time to time the buildings fell back and a monument appeared, sudden, grandiose, rather pompous—not very old either, Oliver noted. Postwar.

"There is some difficulty, yes," the translator said, "with the husband . . . and with the father as well. But I do not know, really. I am not an acquaintance of hers, as I said. She lives her life, I live mine. We meet a few times a year, at gatherings like the one last night . . . She too does translations, though not into English. Into Italian and German exclusively."

"Then she is married? You mentioned a husband? . . ."

Liebert looked out the window, as if embarrassed by Oliver's interest. He was not unwilling to talk about the young woman, but not willing either. For the first time in their three days' acquaintance, Oliver felt the young man's stubborn nature. "They have not been together in one place for many years, as I understand it," he said. "The husband, not an acquaintance of my own, is some years older than she . . . a doctor, I believe . . . a research specialist in an area I know nothing of. He is in another city. He has been in another city, and Alisa in this city, for many years."

"I'm sorry to hear that," Oliver said sincerely. "She struck me as sweet, vulnerable . . . possibly a little lonely? I don't like to think that she may be unhappy."

Liebert shrugged his shoulders.

"Unhappy, so?" he murmured.

They drove through a square and Oliver's attention was drawn to an immense portrait of a man's face, a poster three stories high.

"Amazing!" he said without irony.

"It is not amazing, it is ordinary life," Liebert said. "We live here."

". . . She isn't unhappy, then? No more than most?"

"There is not the—what is the word?—the compulsion to analyze such things, such states of mind," Liebert said with a vague air of reproach. "It is enough to complete the day—working hard, doing one's obligations. You understand? Leisure would only result in morbid self-scrutiny and the void, the infatuation with the void, which is your fate."

"My fate?" Oliver said. "Not mine. Don't confuse me with anyone else."

Liebert mumbled an apology.

They drove on in silence for a few minutes. They were approaching a hilly area north of the city; in the near distance were mountains of a peculiar magenta color, partly obscured by mist. Oliver felt, still, that uncharacteristic euphoria, as if he were in a dream, a kind of paradise, and on all sides miracles ringed him in. He had not been prepared for the physical beauty of this place, or for the liveliness of its people. And his translator, Liebert, was quite a surprise. He spoke English with very little accent, clear voiced, boyish, attentive to Oliver's every hesitation or expression of curiosity, exactly as if he could read Oliver's thoughts. He took it as his by Joyce Carol Oates

solemn duty, evidently, to make Oliver comfortable in every way. His manner was both shy and composed, childlike and remarkably mature. He had a sweet, melancholy, shadowed face with a head of thick, dark, curly hair and a widow's peak above a narrow forehead; his cheekbones were Slavic; his complexion was pale but with a faint rosy cast to it, as if the blood hummed warmly close beneath the skin. Large brown eyes, a long nose, ears too large for his slender face . . . something about him put Oliver in mind of a nocturnal animal, quick, furtive, naturally given to silence. In general he had an ascetic appearance. No doubt he was very poor, in his ill-fitting tweed suit and scuffed brown shoes, his hair crudely cut, so short that it emphasized the thinness of his neck and the prominence of his Adam's apple. Not handsome, perhaps, but attractive in his own way. Oliver liked him very much.

"If you would like, perhaps another meeting could be arranged," he said softly. "That is, it would not be impossible."

"Another meeting? With her?"

"If you would like," Liebert said.

LOVE: loss of equilibrium. Imbalance. Something fundamental to one's being, an almost physical certainty of self, is violated. Oliver had loved women in the past and he had felt, even, this distressing physical urgency, this anxiety before; but it had never blossomed so quickly, based on so little evidence. The night of the reception at the Institute he had slept poorly, rehearsing in his sleep certain phrases he would say to Alisa, pleading with her, begging her. For what? And why? She was a striking woman, perhaps not beautiful; it was natural that he might be attracted to her, though his experiences with women in recent years had been disappointing. But the intensity of his feeling worried him. It was exactly as if something foreign to his nature had infiltrated his system, had found him vulnerable, had shot his temperature up by several degrees. And he rejoiced in it, despite his worry and an obscure sense of shame. He really rejoiced in it. He woke, poured himself some of the sweet-tasting brandy he had left on his night table, lay back upon the goose-feather pillows, and thought of her. Was it possible he could see her again? Under what pretext? He was leaving in four days. Possibly he could extend his visit. Possibly not.

He recalled her bony, broad cheekbones, the severity of her gaze, her rather startled smile. A stranger. One of many strangers. In this phase of his life, Oliver thought, he met only strangers; he had no wish to see people he knew.

I love you. I want—what do I want? . . . I want to know more about you.

A mistake, but he could not resist pouring more brandy into the glass. It tasted like sweet, heavy syrup at first and then, after a few seconds, like pure alcohol, blistering, acidic. One wished to obliterate the strong taste with the sweet—the impulse was to sip a little more.

According to his clock in its small leather traveling case, it was three-fifteen.

"I want . . . what do I want?" he murmured aloud.

LIEBERT TRANSLATED for Oliver: "She says that the 'extravagance' you speak of in Androv's chronicles . . . and in our literature generally . . . is understood here as exaggeration . . . Metaphors? . . . metaphors, yes, for interior states. But we ourselves, we are not extravagant in our living."

"Of course I only know Androv's work in translation," Oliver said quickly. "It reads awkwardly, rather like Dreiser . . . do you know the name, the novelist? . . . One of our distinguished American novelists, no longer so popular as he once was . . . I was enormously impressed with the stubbornness, the resiliency, the audacity of Androv's characters, and despite his technique of exaggeration they seemed to me very lifelike." He paused, in order to give Liebert the opportunity to translate. He was breathing quickly, watching Alisa's face. They were having a drink in the hotel lounge, a dim, quiet place where morose potted plants of a type Oliver did not recognize grew more than six feet high, drooping over the half-dozen marble tables. Oliver was able to see his own reflection in a mirror across the room; the mirror looked smoky, webbed as if with a spider's web; his own face hovered there indistinct and pale. His constant, rather nervous smile was not visible.

In the subdued light of the hotel lounge, Alisa seemed to him more beautiful than before. Her dark hair was drawn back and fastened in an attractive French twist. It was not done carelessly into a bun or a knot, the way many local women wore their hair; it shone with good health. She wore a white blouse and, again, the old-fashioned cameo brooch, and a hip-length sweater of some coarse dark wool, and a nondescript skirt that fell well below her knees. Her eyes were slightly slanted, almond shaped, dark, glistening; her cheekbones, like Liebert's, were prominent. Oliver guessed her to be about thirty-five, a little older than he had thought. But striking—very striking. Every movement of hers charmed him. Her mixture of shyness and composure, her quick contralto voice, her habit of glancing from Oliver to Liebert to Oliver again, almost flirtatiously—he knew he was staring rudely at her but he could not look away.

"She says: Of course we have a reputation for audacity; how else could we have survived? The blend of humor and morbidity . . . the bizarre tall tales . . . 'deaths and weddings,' if you are familiar with the allusion? . . . no? . . . she is referring to the third volume of *The Peasants*," Liebert murmured. Oliver nodded as if he were following all this. In fact, he had lost track of the conversation; the woman fascinated him; he was vexed with the thought that he had seen her somewhere before, had in some way known her before . . . And he had read only the first two volumes of Androv's massive work. "From the early fifteenth century, as you know, most of the country has been under foreign dominion . . . The most harsh, the Turks . . . centuries of oppression . . . Between 1941 and 1945 alone there were two million of us murdered . . . Without the 'extravagance' and even the mania of high spirits, how could we have survived?"

"I know, I understand, I am deeply sympathetic," Oliver said at once.

He could not relax, though he had had two drinks that afternoon. Something was urgent, crucial—he must not fail—but he could not quite comprehend what he must do. An American traveler, not really a tourist, prominent enough in his own country to merit the designation of "cultural emissary"—the State Department's term, not his own—he heard his own accent and his own predictable words with a kind of revulsion, as if here, in this strange, charming country, the personality he had created for himself over a forty-three-year period were simply inadequate: shallow, superficial, hypocritical. He had not suffered. He could pretend knowledge and sympathy, but of course he was an impostor; he had not suffered except in the most ordinary of ways—an early, failed marriage, a satisfactory but not very exciting profession, the stray, undefined disappointments of early middle age. He listened to the woman's low, beautifully modulated voice and to his translator's voice; he observed their perfect manners, their rather shabby clothing, and judged himself inferior. He hoped they would not notice. Liebert, who had spent so many patient hours with him, must sense by now his own natural superiority; must have some awareness of the irony of their relative positions. Oliver hoped the young man would not resent him, would not turn bitterly against him before the visit came to a conclusion. It seemed to him an ugly fact of life that he, Oliver, had money, had a certain measure of prestige, however lightly he valued it, and had, most of all, complete freedom to travel anywhere he wished. The vast earth was his—as much of it as he cared to explore. Other cultures, other ways of life were open to his investigation. Even the past was his, for he could visit places of antiquity, could assemble countless books and valuable objects, could pursue any interest to its culmination. As the editor and publisher of a distinguished magazine, which featured essays on international culture with as little emphasis as possible upon politics, Oliver was welcome nearly anywhere; he knew several languages—French, German, Italian, Spanish—and if he did not know a country's language a skillful interpreter was assigned to him and there was rarely any difficulty. Though he was accustomed to think of himself as colorless, as a failure—he had wanted to be a poet and a playwright, as a young man—it was nevertheless true that he was a success and that he had a certain amount of power. Alisa and Liebert, however, were powerless; in a sense they were prisoners.

Of course they proclaimed their great satisfaction with postwar events. The Nazis had been driven back, another world power had come to their aid, the government under which they now lived was as close to perfection as one might wish. Compared to their tumultuous, miserable past, how sunny their present seemed!—of course they were happy. But they were prisoners just the same. They could not leave their country. It might even be the case that they could not leave this particular city without good cause. Oliver happened to know that nearly one third of the population was involved, on one level or another, in espionage—neighbors reporting on neighbors, relatives on relatives, students on teachers, teachers on supervisors, friends on friends. It was a way of life. As Liebert had said one day, it was nothing other than ordinary life for them.

Oliver knew. He knew. The two of them were fortunate just to have jobs that weren't manual labor; they were fortunate to be as free as they were, talking with an American. He believed he could gauge their fate in the abstract, in the collective, no matter that the two of them were really strangers to him. He knew and he did sympathize and, in spite of his better judgment, he wished that he could help them.

At dusk they walked three abreast along the sparsely lit boulevard, the main street of the city. Oliver was to be taken to a workingman's cafe; he was tired of the hotel food, the expensive dinners. They spoke now of the new buildings that were being erected south of the city, along the sea cliff; they told Oliver that he must take time to visit one of the excavations farther to the south—he would see Roman ornaments, coins, grave toys, statuary. "Alisa says the evidence of other centuries and other civilizations is so close to us," Liebert murmured. "We are unable to place too much emphasis upon the individual, the ephemeral. Do you see? I have often thought along those lines myself."

"Yes, I suppose so—I suppose that's right," Oliver said slowly.

Alisa said something to him, looking up at him. Liebert, on his right side, translated at once: "Future generations are as certain as the past—there is a continuity—there is a progress, an evolution. It is clear, it is scientifically demonstrable."

"Is it?" Oliver said, for a moment wondering if it might be so. "Yes—that's possible—I'm sure that's possible."

Liebert translated his words and Alisa laughed.

"Why is she laughing? What did you say?" Oliver asked, smiling.

"I said—only what you said. I translated your words faithfully," Liebert said rather primly.

"She has such a ready, sweet laugh," Oliver said. "She's so charming, so unconscious of herself . . . Ask her, Liebert, where she's from . . . where she went to school . . . where she lives . . . what her life is like."

"All that?" Liebert asked. "So much!"

"But we have all evening, don't we?" Oliver said plaintively. ". . . All night?"

THAT DAY he had been a guest at the district commissioner's home for a two-hour luncheon. He had been driven to the village where the poet Hisjak had been born. Along with another guest of honor, an Italian novelist, he had been shown precious documents—the totally illegible manuscripts of an unknown writer, unknown at least to Oliver—kept in a safe in a museum. The first two evenings of his visit had been spent at endless dinners. He had witnessed a troupe of youthful dancers in rehearsal; he had admired the many statues of heroes placed about the city; he had marveled over the Byzantine domes, the towers and vaulting roofs and fountains. But his hours with Alisa and Liebert were by far the most enjoyable; he knew he would never forget them.

They ate a thick, greasy stew of coarse beef and vegetables, and many slices of whole-grain bread and butter, and drank two bottles of wine of a dry, tart nature, quite unfamiliar to Oliver. The three of them sat at a corner table in an utterly unimpressive restaurant; like a diner, it was, crude and brightly lit and noisy as an American diner. At first the other patrons took notice of them, but as time passed and the restaurant grew noisier, they were able to speak without being overheard. Oliver was very happy. He felt strangely free, like a child. The food was delicious; he kept complimenting them and asking Liebert to tell the waitress, and even to tell the cook; the bread, especially, seemed extraordinary—he insisted that he had never tasted bread so good. "How can I leave? Where can I go from here?" he said jokingly. They were served small, flaky tarts for dessert, and Oliver ate his in two or three bites, though he was no longer hungry and the oversweet taste, apricots and brandy and raw dark sugar, was not really to his liking.

"You are all so wonderful . . ." he said.

Alisa sat across from him, Liebert sat to his left. The table was too small for their many dishes and glasses and silverware. They laughed together like old friends, easily, intimately. Alisa showed her gums as she laughed—no self-consciousness about her— utterly natural, direct. Her eyes narrowed to slits and opened wide again, sparkling. The wine had brought a flush to her cheeks. Liebert too was expansive, robust. He no longer played the role of the impoverished, obsequious student. Sometimes he spoke to Oliver without feeling the necessity to translate his English for Alisa; sometimes he and Alisa exchanged remarks, and though Oliver did not know what they were saying, or why they laughed so merrily, he joined them in their laughter. Most of the time, however, Liebert translated back and forth from Oliver to Alisa, from Alisa to Oliver, rapidly, easily, always with genuine interest. Oliver liked the rhythm that was established: like a game, like a piece of music, like the bantering of love. Oliver's words in English translated into Alisa's language, Alisa's words translated into Oliver's language, magically. Surely it was magic. Oliver asked Alisa about her background, about the village she had grown up in; he asked her about her parents, about her work. It turned out that her father had been a teacher also, a music teacher at one of the colleges—"very distinguished and well loved"—but he had become ill, there was no treatment available, he had wanted to return to his home district to die. Oliver listened sympathetically. There was more to it, he supposed, there was something further about it . . . but he could not inquire. And what about the husband? But he could not inquire, he did not dare.

"You are all so remarkably free of bitterness," he said.

Liebert translated. Alisa replied. Liebert hesitated before

saying: "Why should we be bitter? We live with complexity. You wish simplicity in your life . . . good divided sharply from evil, love divided from hate . . . beauty from ugliness. We have always been different. We live with complexity; we would not recognize the world otherwise."

Oliver was staring at Alisa. "Did you really say that?" he asked.

"Of course she said that. Those words exactly," Liebert murmured.

"She's so . . . she's so very . . . I find her so very charming," Oliver said weakly. "Please don't translate! Please. Do you see? It's just that I find her so . . . I admire her without reservation," he said, squeezing Liebert's arm. "I find it difficult to reply to her. Central Europe is baffling to me; I expected to be meeting quite different kinds of people; your closed border, your wartime consciousness that seems never to lift, your reputation for . . . for certain inexplicable . . ." Both Liebert and Alisa were watching him, expressionless. He fell silent. Absurdly, he had been about to speak of the innumerable arrests and imprisonments, even of the tortures reported in the West, but it seemed to him now that perhaps these reports were lies. He did not know what to believe.

"Freedom and constraint cannot be sharply divided, the one from the other," Liebert said coldly. "Freedom is a relative thing. It is relative to the context, to the humanity it . . . serves? . . . shelters. For instance, your great American cities, they are so famed, they are 'free,' you would boast, citizens can come and go as they wish . . . each in his automobile, isn't that so? But, in fact, we know that your people are terrified of being hurt by one another. They are terrified of being killed by their fellow citizens. In this way," Liebert said, smiling, "in this way it must be judged that the nature of freedom is not so simple. But it is always political."

"There's a difference between self-imposed restrictions and . . . and the restrictions of a state like yours," Oliver said, obscurely hurt, blinking. He had no interest in defending his nation. He did not care about it at all, not at the moment. "But perhaps you are correct; the issue is always political, even when it is baffling and obscure . . . In America we have too much freedom and the individual is free to hurt others, this is an excess of . . . am I speaking too quickly? . . . this is an excess rather than . . . But I don't wish to talk of such things," he said softly. "Not tonight. It is more important, our being together. Do you agree? Yes? Ask Alisa—does she agree?"

They agreed. They laughed together like old friends.

"Alisa says we must live our lives in the interstices of the political state," Liebert said slyly, "like sparrows who make their nests on window ledges or street lamps. They are happy there until the happiness stops. We are happy until it stops. But perhaps it will not stop for many years—who can predict? Political oppression is no more a disaster than an accident on the highway or a fatal disease or being born crippled . . ."

"Disaster is disaster," Oliver said thickly. "What do we care? There isn't time. I must leave in a few days . . . I admire you both so very, very much. You're noble, you're brave, you're attractive . . . she is beautiful, isn't she? . . . beautiful! I've never met anyone so intelligent and beautiful at the same time, so vivacious, good-natured . . . Will you tell her that? Please?"

Liebert turned to her and spoke. She lowered her head, fussed with her hair, reddened slightly, frowned. A long moment passed. She glanced shyly at Oliver. Seeing the desperation in his eyes, she managed to smile.

"Thank you," Oliver whispered. "Thank you both so very much."

SOMETHING WAS stinging him.

Bedbugs?

His arms were curiously leaden; he could not move; he could not rake his nails against his sides, his abdomen, his buttocks, his back. He groaned but did not wake. The stinging became a single sweeping flame that covered his body, burned fiercely into his eyes.

"Alisa?" he said. "Are you here? Are you hiding?"

He was in the Old City, the City of Stone. Much of it had been leveled during the war, but there were ancient buildings—fortresses, inns, cathedrals. The weight of time. The weight of the spirit. On all sides, voices were chattering in that exquisite, teasing language he could not decipher. They were mocking him, jeering at him. They knew him very well. He was to be led to their shrine, where a miracle would be performed. The holy saint of Toskinjevec, patron saint of lepers, epileptics, the crippled and the insane and the fanatic . . . He was being hurried along the cobblestone streets. There were heavy oak doors with iron hinges; there were rusted latches and locks; walls slime-green with mold, beginning to crumble. Footsteps rang and echoed. Liebert held his hand, murmured words of comfort, stroked his head. He wanted only to obey. "Where is she? Is she already there?" he whispered. Liebert told him to be still—he must not speak! Someone was following them. Someone wished to hurt them. Oliver saw, in a panic, the greenish copper steeple of an old church; he could take refuge in its ruins; no one would find them there. The main part of the building had been reduced to rubble. A wall remained, and on this wall were posters of the great president—charmingly candid shots that showed the man with one of his children, and in a peasant's costume, with a rifle raised to his shoulder and one eye squinted shut, and on the ledge above a waterfall, his arm raised in a salute to the crowd gathered below. Oliver hurried. Someone would stand guard for them—one of the men he had seen in the restaurant, had seen without really considering; a young black haired man who had been playing chess with a friend, and who had not glanced up a single time at Oliver and his friends. But now he would stand guard. Now he was to be trusted.

They descended into a cellar. Everywhere there were slabs of stone, broken plasterboard, broken glass. Weeds grew abundantly in the cracks. "Hurry," Liebert urged, dragging him forward. Then Oliver was with her, clutching at her. By a miracle they were together. He kissed her desperately, recklessly. She pretended to resist.

"No, there isn't time, there isn't enough time," he begged. "No, don't stop me . . ." She went limp; she put her arms around his neck; they struggled together, panting, while the young translator urged them on, anxious, a little annoyed. Oliver's entire body stung. Waves of heat swept over him and broke into tiny bits so that he groaned aloud. He wanted her so violently, he was so hungry for her, for her or for something . . . "How can I bring you with me?" he said. "I love you, I won't surrender you."

She spoke in short, melodic phrases. He could not understand. Now she too was anxious, clutching at him, pressing herself against him. Oliver could not bear it. He was going mad. Then, out of the corner of his eye, he happened to see someone watching them. The police! But no, it was a poorly dressed old man, a cripple, peering at them from behind a broken wall. He was deformed; his legs were mere stumps. Oliver stared in a panic. He could not believe what he saw. Behind the old man were two or three others, half crawling, pushing themselves along through the debris by the exertions of their arms, their legs cut off at the thigh. They were bearded, wide-eyed, gaping, moronic. He understood that they were moronic.

Oliver tried to lead Alisa away, but she resisted. Evidently the men were from a nearby hospital and were harmless. They had been arrested in an abortive uprising of some sort years before, and punished in ways fitting their audacity; but now they were harmless, harmless . . .

His sexual desire died at once. The dream died at once.

HE COULD not sleep. The dream had left him terrified and nauseated.

During the past few years, life had thinned out for Oliver. It had become insubstantial, unreal, too spontaneous to have much value. Mere details, pieces, ugly tiny bits. Nothing was connected and nothing made sense. Was this life? This idle, pointless flow? He had watched it, knowing that one must be attentive, one must be responsible. But he had not really believed in it. There was no internal necessity, no order, only that jarring spontaneity, a world of slivers and teasing fragments. Ugly and illusory.

Here, however, things seemed different. He could breathe here. There were travelers who could not accept the reality of the countries they visited and who yearned, homesick, for their own country, for their own language; but Oliver was not one of them. He would not have cared—not for a moment!—if the past were eradicated, his home country destroyed and erased from history.

He poured brandy into a glass, his fingers steady.

"Would I mourn? . . . Never."

The dream had frightened him but it was fading now. It was not important. He had had too much to eat, too much to drink. His emotional state was unnatural. Love was an imbalance: he was temporarily out of control. But he would be all right. He had faith in himself.

The woman lived in a one-room apartment, Liebert had informed him. She shared it with another teacher at the high school, a woman. Should Oliver wish to visit her there—how could it be arranged? She could not come to the hotel. That was out of the question. Liebert had muttered something about the possibility of the other woman's going to visit her family . . . though this would involve some expenses . . . She would need money. It would be awkward but it could be arranged. If so, then Alisa would be alone and Oliver would be welcome to visit her. There might be danger, still. Or was there no danger? Oliver really did not know.

"And what of her husband?" Oliver had asked hesitantly.

"Ah—there is no risk. The man is in a hospital at Kanleža, in the mountains . . . he is receiving treatment for emotional maladjustment . . . a very sad case. Very sad. It is tragic, but he is no risk; do not worry about him," Liebert said softly.

They looked at each other for a moment. Oliver warmed, reddened. He did not know if he was terribly ashamed or simply excited.

"I love her," he whispered. "I can't help it."

Liebert might not have heard, he had spoken so softly. But he did not ask Oliver to repeat his words.

"How much money would the woman need?" Oliver asked helplessly.

They had been here, in this room. The money had changed hands and Liebert had gone and Oliver had undressed at once, exhausted from the evening, from all the eating and drinking and talking. He had wanted only to sleep. His fate was decided: he would meet Alisa the following day, he would extend his visit for another week, perhaps, in order to see her every day. But now he must sleep, he was sick with exhaustion. And so he had slept. But dreams disturbed him; in them he was trying to speak, trying to make himself understood, while strangers mocked and jeered. The last dream, of Alisa and the deformed old men, was the most violent of all, a nightmare of the sort he had not had for years. When he woke he felt debased, poisoned. It was as if a poison of some sort had spread throughout his body.

He sat up, leafing through a guidebook in English, until dawn.

"BUT I don't understand. Where is Mr. Liebert?"

His new translator was a stout, perspiring man in his fifties, no more than five feet four inches tall. He wore a shiny black suit with a vest and oversized buttons of black plastic. Baldness had enlarged his round face. His eyebrows were snarled and craggy, his lips pale, rubbery. With a shrug of shoulders he dismissed Liebert. "Who knows? There was important business. Back home, called away. Not your concern."

He smiled. Oliver stared, thinking, *He's a nightmare, he's from a nightmare.* But the man was real, the bright chilly morning was real. Oliver's dismay and alarm were real. He tried to protest, saying that he had liked Liebert very much, the two of them had understood each other very well; but the new translator merely smiled stupidly, as before. "I am your escort now and your translator," he repeated.

Oliver made several telephone calls, but there was nothing to be done.

"I do not have the acquaintance of Mr. Liebert," he said as they walked out together. One eyelid descended in a wink. "But there is no lack of sympathy. It is all the same. A nice day, isn't it? That is acacia tree in blossom, is lovely, eh? Every spring."

The man's accent was guttural. Oliver could not believe his bad luck. He walked in a trance, thinking of Alisa, of Liebert— Liebert, who had been so charming, so quick. It did not seem possible that this had happened.

That day he saw the posters of his dream. He saw a tarnished coppery green steeple rising above a ruined church. He saw, in the distance, long, low, curiously narrow strips of cloud or mist rising from the sea, reaching into the lower part of the city. Beside him the squat, perspiring man chattered in babyish English, translated signs and menus, kept asking Oliver in his mechanical chirping voice, "It is nice, eh? Spring day. Good luck." From time to time he winked at Oliver as if there were a joke between them.

Oliver shuddered.

The city looked different. There was too much traffic—buses, motorbikes, vans of one kind or another—and from the newer section of the city, where a number of one-story factories had been built, there came invisible clouds of poison. The sky was mottled; though it was May 15, it was really quite cold.

"Where is Liebert?" Oliver asked, more than once. "He and I were friends . . . we understood each other . . ."

They went to a folk museum where they joined another small group. Oliver tried to concentrate. He smiled, he was courteous as always, he made every effort to be civil. But the banalities—the idiotic lies! His translator repeated what was said in a thick, dull voice, not passing judgment as Liebert would have done, slyly—and Oliver was forced to reply, to say something. He stammered, he heard his voice proclaiming the most asinine things—bald, blunt compliments, flattery. Seven or eight men in a group for an endless luncheon, exchanging banalities, hypocritical praise, chatter about the weather and the blossoming trees and the National Ballet. The food was too rich, and when Oliver's came to him it was already lukewarm. The butter was unsalted and taste-less. One of the men, a fat, pompous official, exactly like an official in a political cartoon, smoked a cigar and the smoke drifted into Oliver's face. He tried to bring up the subject of his first translator but was met with uncomprehending stares.

Afterward he was taken, for some reason, to the offices of the Ministry of Agriculture; he was introduced to the editor of a series of agricultural pamphlets; it was difficult for him to make sense of what was being said. Some of these people spoke English as well as his translator did, and he had the idea that others merely pretended not to know English. There was a great deal of chatter. He thought of Alisa and felt suddenly exhausted. He would never get to her now—it was impossible. Beside him, the fat sweating man kept close watch. What was being said?—words. He leaned against a gritty windowsill, staring absently out at the innumerable rooftops, the ugly chimneys and water tanks, the banal towers. He remembered the poison of his dream and could taste it in the air now; the air of this city was remarkably polluted.

"You are tired now? Too much visit? You rest, eh?"

"Yes."

"You leave soon, it was said? Day after tomorrow?"

"Yes. I think so."

There were streetcars, and factory whistles. Automobile horns. In the street someone stared rudely at him. Oliver wondered what these people saw—a tall, sandy-haired man in his early forties, distracted, haggard, rather vain in his expensive clothes? They looked at his clothes, not at him. At his shoes. They did not see him at all; they had no use for him.

"You are maybe sick?"

"A little. I think. Yes."

"Ah!" he said, in a parody of sympathy. "You go to room, rest. Afterward, perk up. Afterward there is plan for evening—yes? All set?"

"Evening? I thought this evening was free."

The man winked. "She is friend—old friend. Sympathizes you."

"I don't understand," Oliver stammered.

"All understand. All sympathize one another," the man said cheerfully.

"IS WEALTHY? Own several automobiles? What about house—houses? Parents are living? How many brothers and sisters? Is married has children? How many? Names?"

The three of them sat together, not in Alisa's room but in another cafe. Oliver was paying for their drinks. He was paying for everything. The woman's curt, rude questions were being put to him in clusters and he managed to answer, as succinctly as possible, trying not to show his despair. When his translator repeated Oliver's answers, Alisa nodded emphatically, always the same way, her eyes bright, deliberately widened. Wisps of hair had come loose about her forehead; it annoyed Oliver that she did not brush them away. She was a little drunk, her laughter was jarring, she showed her gums when she laughed—he could hardly bear to watch her.

"Say like our country very much? Good. New place going up— there is new company, Volkswagen—many new jobs. When you come back, another year, lots new things. You are friendly, always welcome. Very nice. Good to know . . ."

The conversation seemed to rattle on without Oliver's intervention. He heard his voice, heard certain simpleminded replies. Alisa and the fat man laughed merrily. They were having a fine time. Oliver drank because he had nothing else to do; whenever he glanced at his watch, the other looked at it also, with childish, open avarice. Time did not pass. He dreaded any mention of the room, of the alleged roommate who had left town, but he had the idea that if he refused to mention it, the others would not mention it either. They were having too good a time, drinking . . . They murmured to each other in their own language and broke into peals of laughter, and other patrons, taking notice, grinned as if sharing their good spirits.

"Is nice place? All along here, this street. Yes? Close to hotel. All close. She says: Is wife of yours pretty? Young? Is not jealous, you on long trip, take airplane? Any picture of wife? Babies?"

"No wife," Oliver said wearily. "No babies."

"No—? Is not married?"

"Is not," Oliver said.

"Not *love?* Not once?"

"Not," he said.

The two of them exchanged incredulous looks. Then they laughed again and Oliver sat silent, while their laughter washed about him.

BEING DRIVEN to the airport he saw, on the street, a dark-haired cyclist pedaling energetically—a young long-nosed handsome boy in a pullover sweater—Liebert—his heart sang: *Liebert.* But of course it was not Liebert. It was a stranger, a boy of about seventeen, no one Oliver knew. Then again at the airport he saw him. Again it was Liebert. A mechanic in coveralls, glimpsed in a doorway, solemn, dark-eyed, with a pronounced widow's peak and prominent cheekbones: Liebert. He wanted to push his way through the crowd to him. To his translator. He wanted to touch him again, wanted to squeeze his hands, his arm. But of course the young man was a stranger—his gaze was dull, his mouth slack. Oliver stared at him just the same. The plane was loading, it was time for him to leave, yet he stood there, paralyzed.

"What will I do for the rest of my life?" he called to the boy.

Crossing the Border

BY CHANA BLOCH

We've all heard the nasty quips about translation. "Poetry is what gets lost in translation," said Robert Frost; "translators are traitors," say the Italians; the French expression, "*les belles infidèles*," implies that a translation (feminine in French) can be either beautiful or faithful, not both. All too often, publishers, editors, and reviewers treat translators with disrespect. A translation is seen as the handmaiden of the male original, a creature of a lesser order, fashioned from the primal rib. Why would any sensible person choose to engage in this much-maligned art? I must confess: for more than fifty years I have translated from Yiddish and Hebrew, and have found that work to be one of the joys of my life.

First of all, there is the pleasure of reading. Translating a poem is a particularly intimate form of reading, close and slow. Once you and that poem start living together, you get to know its pulse and body heat, a sensual pleasure. Then there's the intellectual charge that comes from problem-solving. The most resistant passages often yield the greatest satisfaction. That kind of work keeps the blood circulating in the brain. As a remedy for aging, it's even better than drinking red wine. And there's food for the spirit, too, when you live in the presence of something larger than yourself. George Steiner has written, "Without [translation], we would live in arrogant parishes bordered by silence." Translation enables us to cross the parish border and discover what's out there in the world.

I was drawn to translation because I am a poet. As a young writer, in a workshop with Robert Lowell, I submitted, along with my own poems, some translations of Abraham Sutzkever, the great Yiddish poet who died in 2010. Lowell told me, "You can learn to write from your own translations." His suggestion proved to be the most helpful advice I ever received about writing. Later I discovered that W. S. Merwin had heard the same thing from Pound. If he wanted to be a writer he should write every day, Pound told him, but since he was too young to have anything worth writing about, he ought to translate. Pound spoke of the value of translation "as a means of continually sharpening a writer's awareness of the possibilities of his own language."

A translator needs to know at least one language very well: her own. You might say that translation is a form of apprenticeship—not to a master craftsman, but to the genius of the language itself. When you translate you are constantly choosing among alternatives in order to convey meaning, register, image, mood, music; each time you choose, you are exercising muscles that you need in shaping your own work. It's a strenuous but efficient way of teaching yourself to write. For that reason, when I taught poetry workshops or courses about poetry, I always made a point of including translations. In class we compared different versions of poems by Wang Wei, Akhmatova, Baudelaire, Rilke, Lorca, and Celan as a way of learning how a poem is put together, what makes it tick, how much of it can be gotten into English.

Yiddish and Hebrew figure in my personal history and they are intertwined—at times fiercely—in Jewish literary history. Though I had studied other languages, I had a specific reason for choosing to translate from Yiddish and Hebrew. I grew up as a first-generation American, living between two cultures. My parents came to this country from tiny villages, *shtetlekh*, in the Ukraine. At home they spoke English, not Yiddish, but they sent me to a Yiddish *folkshul* every day after school. (Not to Hebrew school; Hebrew belonged to the men and the boys.) I began to study Hebrew as an undergraduate at Cornell and as a graduate student of Judaic Studies at Brandeis, and continued during two extended stays in Jerusalem. In my twenties, I discovered that translation offered me a way of honoring the creativity in these two languages, more meaningful by far than the "nostalgia *yiddishkayt*" that often passes for Jewish identity. Once I was engaged in this work, I felt a responsibility to help save what might otherwise be lost, and to contribute something of substance to American-Jewish culture.

Yiddish began its life about a thousand years ago in Northern Italy, and then evolved in the Rhineland as a Germanic language with Romance and Hebrew-Aramaic components, written in Hebrew characters. As the Jews migrated eastward from the thirteenth century to the sixteenth, Yiddish absorbed elements of Slavic as well. In Eastern Europe, Hebrew-Aramaic was *loshn koydesh*, "the holy tongue," reserved for the man's world of study and worship; Yiddish was *mame-loshn*, "the mother tongue" of home and marketplace, of everyday life. Yiddish was originally called *Yiddish-taytsh* or simply *Taytsh*, from the word for "German," Deutsch. *Fartaytshn* meant to gloss a Hebrew text by giving a word-by-word equivalent in the Jewish vernacular—at first Aramaic, later Yiddish, Ladino, and other languages. In modern Yiddish, *fartaytshn* is still one of the verbs for "translate," revealing the Jewish nexus between translation and interpretation.

Isaac Bashevis Singer recognized the uniqueness of Yiddish in his Nobel Prize speech in 1978:

The high honor bestowed upon me by the Swedish Academy is also a recognition of the Yiddish language—a language of exile, without a land, without frontiers, not supported by any government, a language which possesses no words for weapons, ammunition, military exercises, war tactics; a language that was despised by both Gentiles and emancipated Jews . . . There are some who call Yiddish a dead language, but so was Hebrew called for two thousand years . . . Yiddish has not yet said its last word.

A STIRRING prophecy, worthy of a master of fantasy! In sober fact, Hitler and Stalin murdered the writers and readers and speakers of Yiddish, dealing a catastrophic blow as well to the language itself. In America, Yiddish survives mostly in a debased form, in jokes and wisecracks and the handful of words that have made it into Webster's: *schlep, schmooze, schmear, schmatte, shtick, schlock.* (This is proclaimed in some quarters as a cultural achievement.) Today Yiddish is spoken in the ultra-Orthodox community, and one might say it is enjoying an afterlife in the academy, taught in many colleges here and abroad, but that's not the same as being a living language. Modern Yiddish literature flourished only from the end of the nineteenth century until the middle of the twentieth. As Benjamin Harshav put it: "a brilliant performance and . . . a tragic exit from an empty hall."

The Yiddish writers I translated shared an urgency to be heard that was different from anything I'd encountered among writers of English. For the former, translation was a necessary condition of survival. Who, after all, was reading them in Yiddish? Or who would be, in the future? Two of the major figures of post-war Yiddish literature in the U.S. were Isaac Bashevis Singer (1904–1991), who had an international reputation, and Jacob Glatstein (1896–

by Chana Bloch

1971), hardly known outside the Yiddish world. Cynthia Ozick has written a painful and hilarious novella, *Envy; or, Yiddish in America*, about Ostrover, the fiction writer (a thinly-veiled portrait of Singer), and Edelshtein, the poet (a harsh caricature of Glatstein)—Ostrover reaching a large audience through his translators, Edelshtein desperate because he has none. As Ozick frames the issue:

> Ostrover's glory was exactly in this: that he required translators! Though he wrote only in Yiddish, his fame was American, national, international. They considered him a "modern." Ostrover was free of the prison of Yiddish!

The unhappy Edelshtein bemoans his outcast state:

> And why Ostrover? Why not somebody else? . . . Ostrover should be the only one? Everyone else sentenced to darkness, Ostrover alone saved?

I read Ozick's novella with some interest because I had translated both Singer and Glatstein, and because the young girl whom the Yiddish poet begs to translate his work ("twenty-three years old . . . an American girl . . . crazy for literature") is called Hannah. But the pathetic Yiddish poet in Ozick's story bears no resemblance to the real-life Glatstein, nor am I Ozick's Hannah. Jacob Glatstein was a poet of great distinction whose work I admired.

It was not by chance that the first poem I translated was Glatstein's "Smoke":

> From the crematory flue
> A Jew aspires to the Holy One.
> And when the smoke of him is gone,

His wife and children filter through.

Above us, in the height of sky,
Saintly billows weep and wait.
God, wherever you may be,
There all of us are also not.

THE BITTER irony in that voice gripped me, haunted me, would not let go until I had turned it into English.

Glatstein's form was a given: the clipped rhythms and tightly-rhymed quatrains are a way of containing grief and despair. What stopped me were the neologisms in stanza 1, nouns that Glatstein turned into verbs (*kroyzt, knoyln*) to suggest the motion of the smoke, winding upwards like a *kroyz*, "a curl" (of smoke or hair), unwinding like a *knoyl*, "a ball" (of thread or string). Literal equivalents seemed to me clumsy and pedantic, and they lacked the bite of the Yiddish. I chose "aspires" and "filter through" for their ironic edge, "aspires" to evoke the ideal of the aspiring mind, and "filter through" to suggest the harrowing domesticity of Glatstein's metaphor.

In the Introduction to his *Imitations* (1958)—not really translations but rather adaptations of European poetry—Robert Lowell writes that "the usual reliable translator gets the literal meaning but misses the tone, and . . . in poetry, tone is, of course, everything. I have been reckless with literal meaning," he goes on to say, "and labored hard to get the tone." I wondered: had I let go of the literal meaning in order to get the tone? I sent my version to Glatstein with a letter half-apologizing for the freedoms I had taken. He wrote back at once, inviting me to translate more of his work. And so I learned at the start two of the cardinal rules of translation: first, it's not just a matter of finding word-for-word equivalents, and second, it's the tone that makes the music. (This may be better in French: *c'est le ton qui fait la musique.* It's a familiar enough saying, and "tone" in English is inexact.) Translation, as the Jewish textual tradition teaches us, is a form of interpretation, and to a greater or lesser degree, it necessarily involves transformation.

Despite his considerable achievements, Isaac Bashevis Singer was viewed with disdain in Yiddishist literary circles, and not simply because of writers' envy, as Ozick's story suggests. Naomi Seidman discusses the response to Singer in her wide-ranging and illuminating book about translation, *Faithful Renderings: Jewish-Christian Difference and the Politics of Translation.* In the words of Irving Saposnik, a critic she quotes, Singer was "an entrepreneur, a skillful marketer of both his image and his imagination," who gave the American audience just what it wanted: "sharp edges were smoothed, ethnic quirks turned into old world charm . . . and Bashevis crossed over from the mundane obscurity of a Yiddish writer to being the darling of the literary world." Seidman has an apt phrase for this kind of crossover: she calls it "translation-as-assimilation."

Saul Bellow brought Singer to national attention with his pungent, idiomatic translation of "Gimpel the Fool," published in 1953 in the *Partisan Review.* Bellow conveys the feel of Singer's Yiddish, but, as Naomi Seidman and Janet Hadda have noted, he quietly omits what might be offensive to a Gentile reader: the derogatory epithets *shiksa* and *goy*, along with a line that implies the virgin birth is foolishness no Jew would ever believe. Bellow's partner-in-crime, Eliezer Greenberg, gets the blame for those omissions, but I can't help wondering if Singer himself had anything to do with it.

Seidman's chapter on Singer got me thinking about my own

experience. Thanks to the detective efforts of Paul Hamburg, the Judaica librarian at the University of California at Berkeley, who tracked my versions of Singer to the University of Texas at Austin, I now have copies of a few drafts of the stories I translated. Even in that limited sample I found some evidence for what the critics were saying. Singer worked closely with me, as he did with all his translators. We would meet over prune Danish at the Automat on the Upper West Side to go over my drafts. Having checked those against the originals, I can now see that where I missed nuances of the Yiddish, he did not bother to correct me. His changes were mostly directed at making the stories more accessible to an American audience. I had deliberately retained a few Yiddish words, assuming that the reader would be able to infer their meaning from the context. Singer changed rebbetsin ("rabbi's wife") to "saint," and *Mogen Dovid* to "Star of David." He crossed out *le-chayim* and wrote "to your health," but then thought better of it. Where one of his characters says, "She married a Litvak," he crossed out "Litvak" and wrote "Lithuanian." But a *Litvak* is not just a person from Lithuania, or Latvia or Russia; it's a Jewish character type scorned by the *Galitzyaner* Jews as a cold rationalist, lacking in emotional depth. (Czeslaw Milosz was a Lithuanian, but he was *not* a *Litvak*!)

My translations of Singer are billed as a collaboration between me and Elizabeth Pollet, but that wasn't exactly the case. Singer turned over my versions to Pollett, an American-Jewish novelist, for further editing; her task was apparently to make the stories read like current American fiction, so she upgraded the sentence structure in places where I had left a trace of Yiddish syntax. Singer's readiness to have his originals retouched reveals how eager he was to reach an American audience. When we worked together, I was too much a beginner to question his approach. Today it's clear to me that what gets lost in translation-by-assimilation is the distinctive savor of the culture, just as it does in the bland versions of ethnic foods prepared for the American palate.

Lost in Translation is the title of a memoir by Eva Hoffman; the subtitle is *A Life in a New Language* (1989). Hoffman writes about emigrating with her family in 1959, when she was a girl of thirteen, from Kracow to Vancouver, where she was to acquire, along with a new language, "a whole new geography of emotions." Her memoir demonstrates again and again the inseparability of language from culture. In one of the most telling anecdotes, Hoffman ponders her relationship with her American boy-friend: "Should you marry him? the question comes in English. Yes. Should you marry him? the question echoes in Polish. No." Asking the question in a different language prompts an entirely different set of cultural assumptions and elicits an antithetical response. Recent research on psycholinguistics confirms as much: when bilingual people switch from one language to another, they start thinking differently, too. A Polish-speaking Jew, Hoffman had to reinvent herself in English: as she put it, "I have to translate myself without becoming assimilated"—a good plan of action for anyone engaged in translation.

It is more difficult to translate poetry than prose, and considerably more difficult to translate an ancient text than a contemporary one, which is to say that translating the Song of Songs proved to be an unusually rewarding project. If you have a question when you are translating a living author, you can often get the answer straight from (pardon me) the source's mouth. When you are translating an ancient text, there's no author to consult, and there are many more questions than answers. Who wrote the Song? Certainly not King Solomon. Could it have been a woman? When was it written? Was it a collection of lyrics or a unified whole? I was fortunate to have as my collaborator Ariel Bloch, who was a professor of Semitic linguistics at the University of California at Berkeley. We dealt with those questions, and others as perplexing, in our introduction, presenting the evidence for our conclusions while admitting that finally there is no certainty.

The Song of Songs celebrates the sexual awakening of a young, unmarried woman and her lover; it is the only love poem that has survived from ancient Israel. While it was most likely composed as a poem about erotic love, the rabbis read it as an allegory about the love of God and the people of Israel; this interpretation, along with the attribution to King Solomon, helped it to survive the final cut of the canon-makers. The Church Fathers in turn read the Song as a dialogue between Christ and his Bride, the Church. Once it became part of the Holy Scriptures, the Song demanded exegesis befitting its holiness, and religious interpretations of one kind or another prevailed for two millennia. Some of the more extravagant "findings" of the exegetes now seem very curious: the Shulamite's two breasts, for example, were said to signify Moses and Aaron, or the Old and the New Testaments. The passion in the Song rises at times to 120 degrees in the shade, but in the long history of exegesis and translation, the temperature drops precipitously.

Exegetes and translators commonly presented the young lovers as yearning for one another from a respectable distance, though in doing so they were ignoring the plain sense of the Hebrew. In 4:16, the Shulamite invites her beloved: "Let my lover come into his garden / and taste its delicious fruit," and he replies:

> I have come into my garden,
> my sister, my bride,
> I have gathered my myrrh and my spices,
> I have eaten from the honeycomb,

by Chana Bloch

I have drunk the milk and the wine. (Song 5:1)

THE VERB "to come into" or "to enter" often has a sexual meaning in biblical Hebrew. And the metaphors of feasting suggest fulfillment, especially since the verbs are in the perfect tense (*bati, ariti, akhalti, shatiti*: "I have come, I have gathered, I have eaten, I have drunk"), which signifies a completed action, i.e., consummation. Translators who resort to a noncommittal present tense (I come, I gather, I eat, I drink) or an infinitive construction (I have come to gather) are toning down the lover's exultant song of gratified desire. And the Shulamite, a young woman as spirited and assertive as Juliet, gets subdued as well. In almost every translation up to our own day (the King James Version is a notable exception), we find her wearing a veil, a reading not supported by the Hebrew. That incongruous veil, like the fig leaf of Renaissance painting and sculpture, is a sign of the discomfort of the exegetes. Even contemporary translations may blunt the full intensity of the text because, as so often in the history of translation, misreadings get passed down uncritically from one generation to the next.

The best known English translation is, of course, the King James Version (1611). The King James is a monumental achievement, with an immense impact on our literature, and its rendering of the Song has been justly beloved by generations of readers for its rich textures and resounding cadences—not the usual product of committee work. However, advances in biblical scholarship during the past four centuries have shown many of its readings to be in error, including some of the best-known verses, such as "Stay me with flagons, comfort me with apples" (2:5), or "terrible as an army with banners" (6:10). And its language is often dated, for example, "I am sick of love" (2:5), or the unfortunate "My beloved put in his hand by the hole of the door, and my bowels were moved for him" (5:4). The language of the KJV was conceived for liturgical purposes and was somewhat archaic even in the seventeenth century; its formal, stately music doesn't convey the heat, the speed, the erotic intensity of the original. One would hardly know that this is a poem about *young* lovers.

Deciphering the Hebrew text proved to be more difficult than Ariel and I had anticipated. The Song is one of the most enigmatic books in the Bible, far more obscure and problematic than a reader of English might suppose, in part because it has an unusually high proportion of rare words and constructions. Resolving the puzzles in the Hebrew was Ariel's assignment. Once the two of us had a reasonably clear sense of what the Hebrew was saying, it was my task to embody that reading—unexpurgated—in English that sounded like poetry.

A poem about erotic love no longer seems shocking, and the Shulamite, with her veil off, is a figure we recognize. In our day it is the innocence of the Song that has the power to surprise—a freshness of spirit now all but lost to us. The language of the Song is at once voluptuous and reticent, an effect achieved through the medium of metaphor. The Shulamite's invitation—"Let my lover come into his garden / and taste its delicious fruit" (4:16)—is characteristic both in what it asserts and what it leaves unexpressed. Ariel and I felt that none of the English translations conveyed the rare combination of sensuousness and delicacy that makes the Hebrew so captivating.

Seamus Heaney writes in the introduction to his translation of *Beowulf:* "It is one thing to find lexical meanings for the words . . . but it is quite another thing to find the tuning fork that will give you the note and pitch for the overall music of the work." Searching for the proper register in English took us through a cartonful of drafts. A change in any one verse often demanded a change in several others. But then translation is labor-intensive work. It requires not just imagination, but also patience and perseverance (some would call it obsessiveness). By trial and error we found our way to the stylistic register we sought, steering a course between what Robert Alter calls "the extremes of clunky sexual explicitness and the pastels of greeting-card poetry, which are equal if opposite violations of the original."

Language that is too explicit cheapens the Song. Here is how a distinguished scholar cranked up the heat in his translation in the Anchor Bible Series: "Your vulva [is] a rounded crater; / May it never lack punch!" (7:3). This translation, with its three howlers, illustrates why a translator needs to be sensitive to questions of style. By "crater" this scholar meant a mixing bowl, and by "punch" he meant spiced wine, though it seems he did not stop to think about the associations of those words in English. But "vulva" takes the prize. The sexual organs are never named in the Song, though they are of course suggested many times over. The word *shorerekh* means "your navel," not "your vulva"; in any case, the anatomical term "vulva" is barbaric given the elegantly evocative language of the Song. Our translation reads:

> Your navel is the moon's
> bright drinking cup.
> May it brim with wine!

"THE PASTELS of greeting-card poetry" might well describe a recent verse translation that attempts to universalize the Song: the Shulamite becomes a "princess," the daughters of Jerusalem "city women," Ein Gedi an "oasis," the rose of Sharon "a wildflower thriving" in "sandy earth," Mount Gilead "the slopes," Mount Carmel a "majestic mountain," and "the tower of Lebanon / that looks toward Damascus" a "tower that overlooks the hills." All the distinctive markers have been deleted—the place names that situate the action, along with their music, as sonorous in English as it is in Hebrew. What is the point of domesticating the ancient and the foreign? It's like tourist travel made easy: the travel agent smooths the way so you are as comfortable as if you had never left home.

The concision of biblical Hebrew, most pronounced in the poetic books and a special delight in the Song, is often the first casualty in translation. Biblical Hebrew is an inflected language, which means that it does much of its semantic work with prefixes and suffixes, the conjugation of verbs and declension of nouns. The compact phrase *bati le-gani* requires six words in English: "I-have-come into-my-garden" (5:1). The last thing one should do is pad the lines to fill out some rhyme scheme or metrical scheme, foreign to biblical Hebrew, which would constrict or contort their natural rhythmical flow. The text itself offers some clues to the translator. The Shulamite invites her lover, "Take me by the hand, let us run together" (1:4, *moshkheni acharekha narutza*), and she describes him as "a gazelle, a wild stag . . . bounding over the mountains" (2:9, 8). The young lovers of the Song are full of the animal energy of youth, and the Hebrew lines are accordingly sinewy, graceful, lithe. How to convey that energy in English? "Think like a deer," a friend advised.

The opening verses of the Song set the tone, so each word counts:

> Kiss me, make me drunk with your kisses!
> Your *dodim*
> are better than wine. (Song 1:2)

The plural noun *dodim* is almost always translated as "love," which is imprecise and evasive, given that it refers specifically to lovemaking. *Dodim* occurs only three other times in the Bible—in the Book of Proverbs, where a seductive woman tempts a clueless young man, "Come, let us drink our fill of *dodim*, let us make love all night long, for my husband is not at home" (Prov. 7:18–19), as well as in Ezekiel's denunciations of Jerusalem as an unfaithful wife or a harlot (Ezek. 16:8 and 23:17). Since *dodim* in the Song clearly refers to an *activity*, not just a state of mind, we translated it with the verbal noun "loving": "Your sweet loving / is better than wine."

I'd like to look briefly at a lyric spoken by each of the lovers. Here is the Shulamite in her passionate and dramatic mode:

> Now he has brought me to the house of wine,
> and his flag over me is love.
>
> Let me lie among vine blossoms,
> in a bed of apricots!
> I am in the fever of love.
>
> His left hand beneath my head,
> his right arm
> holding me close.
>
> Daughters of Jerusalem, swear to me
> by the gazelles, by the deer in the field,
> that you will never awaken love until it is ripe.
> (Song 2:4–7)

Nearly every word in 2:5 gave us pause. "Stay me with flagons, comfort me with apples" is the well-known King James translation of *samkhuni ba-ashishot, rapduni ba-tapuchim*. However, *samkhuni* and *rapduni* are not verbs of feeding, as is commonly assumed, but rather of upholstery, as the roots *smk* and *rpd* reveal. The image here is of plumping up a bed in preparation for an erotic encounter, as in Proverbs 7:16–17: "I have spread my couch with fine Egyptian

linen; I have perfumed my bed with myrrh, aloes, and cinnamon."
(The Shulamite sounds a bit like the seductive woman in Proverbs,
whose come-hither, of course, is presented as a cautionary tale.)

Some readers have objected, "Put the apples back in the Song
of Songs" demanding "an apple for an apple"—reparations for
the loss of Paradise, though in the Garden of Eden, of course,
there is no "apple," simply the generic "fruit." *Tappuach* means
"apple" in modern Hebrew, and it has usually been translated as
"apple" in the Song, but botanists believe that it more likely refers
to the apricot, a fruit that is abundant in Israel and has been since
biblical times. The apple tree is not native to the area, and was
introduced comparatively recently. Wild apples are small, hard
and acidic, while apricots are soft, golden, fleshy and fragrant.
Since the fruit of the apricot tree is an image for the lover himself
(2:3), "apricot" is more suitable on all counts.

"I am sick of love," is the King James translation of *cholat ahava
ani*. In the King's English of the seventeenth century, that would
have meant "stricken by passion"; in colloquial English today, "I
am sick of love" means "leave me alone, I've had enough." Many
translations try to salvage this phrase by putting a patch on it, but
"I am sick with love" sounds to me like bad English; another possibility, "I am faint with love," is much too Victorian. I can still
remember the day when, after months of wrestling with this verse,
the word "fever" occurred to me: "I am in the fever of love." I was
so high that I went out the door and ran four miles.

And now the young lover, who speaks these lines in praise of
the Shulamite:

> You have ravished my heart,
> my sister, my bride,
> ravished me with one glance of your eyes,
> one link of your necklace.

And oh, your sweet loving,
my sister, my bride.
The wine of your kisses, the spice
of your fragrant oils.

Your lips are honey, honey and milk
are under your tongue,
your clothes hold the scent of Lebanon.
    (Song 4:9-4:11)

Specificity is always preferred where the Hebrew is specific, as
in *dodim* ("loving"), but it may be misleading where the Hebrew
is indeterminate. When the lover speaks of the Shulamite's *salmah*
(4:11), which we translated as "clothes," we couldn't be sure precisely
what she was wearing, but the real question was how to convey
whatever it was in English. "Cloak" and "mantle" seemed too
old-fashioned, "gown" and "garment" too formal, "robes" too regal,
"tunic" too Greek, "dress" too contemporary. Such terms are time-
bound, culture-bound; they convey nuances that are alien to the
Hebrew, and are constricting, in the way that illustrations in a book
often limit rather than stir the imagination. A prominent New York
artist was commissioned by Random House to prepare artwork
which, thankfully, was not used in our book; in one illustration he
had the Shulamite wearing a red sundress with spaghetti straps.

In a poetic (as opposed to a scholarly) translation, sound and
rhythm are essential elements, part of the sensual experience of the
reader. The Hebrew of the Song is rich in assonance and alliteration.
Sometimes we were able to suggest the play of sound in the Hebrew:

Nofet tittofnah siftotayikh kallah
devash ve-chalav tachat leshonekh
ve-reach salmotayikh ke-reach levanon.

Your lips are honey, honey and milk
are under your tongue,
your clothes hold the scent of Lebanon. (Song 4:11)

But it wasn't always possible to replicate the music of a given verse, so we used alliteration and assonance wherever we could; for example:

They beat me, they bruised me,
they tore the shawl from my shoulders,
those watchmen of the walls. (Song 5:8)

Translating an ancient text is in some ways analogous to the process of restoring a work of art that has been dulled by time. In the 1980s a team of conservators examined the frescoes on the ceiling of the Sistine Chapel, using infrared light to penetrate the surface, and then, with meticulous care, set about removing five centuries of grime, soot, smoke, and varnish. Their work revealed unexpectedly brilliant colors, hues of turquoise and orange that seemed quite unlike Michelangelo—that is, unlike the Michelangelo of tradition, who was thought to favor a much more subdued palette. The colors of the Song in our translation are brighter, its music more sensuous, than in other versions. Those charms of the Song are not our invention; they belong to the pleasures of the original Hebrew. Our aim was to restore in English the passion and intensity, the magical freshness, of this great ancient poem.

In modern Hebrew poetry, the Song of Songs became the model for a boldly secular eroticism, explicitly challenging the allegorical interpretations, notably in the work of Yehuda Amichai

(1924–2000), one of the great love poets—indeed, one of the great poets—of our time. His poetry is enormously popular in Israel—recited at weddings and funerals, taught in the schools, set to music—and it has been translated into over forty languages, including Catalan, Estonian, Korean, Serbo-Croatian, and Vietnamese. When I first met Amichai in Berkeley in the late 1960s, I had already found my way to his poems, attracted by their emotional vitality, their salty wit and skeptical intelligence.

Translating from modern Hebrew presents an unusual challenge. Hebrew was revived as a vernacular only about a hundred years ago, and modern Hebrew preserves, even in everyday speech, the resonance of all its historical layers. Even the simplest words remain charged with ancient, often sacred meanings. A common term like *davar*, which means "word" or "thing," can also refer to a prophetic vision; *makom*, "place," and *shem*, "name," are familiar ways of referring to God. The theological connotations of biblical and rabbinic language are present everywhere in Amichai's poetry, often as the object of his irony. Hebrew verbs and nouns are typically based on tri-consonantal roots that embody some general idea. Since the root system of Hebrew creates a kind of "component awareness," the archaic layers of the language, as well as new-minted expressions, are generally transparent to readers. Amichai is able to draw upon the whole history of the language—biblical, rabbinic, medieval, and modern—alluding irreverently to texts from earlier periods without any sense of strain, and relying on his audience to recognize the allusions.

Biblical expressions that sound perfectly natural in colloquial Hebrew may seem stilted or bookish in an English poem. One can suggest some of the semantic effects possible in Hebrew, for example, by juxtaposing words of Germanic or Latinate origin, though it would be jarring to introduce a word from *Beowulf* or *The Canterbury Tales* into a poem in colloquial English. What's more, Amichai's dialogue with the Bible, the Midrash and the liturgy is only part of the story. He draws equally on vernacular Israeli culture—popular songs, Jewish jokes, nursery rhymes, doggerel, children's games, legal language, military slang. He was influenced by English poetry as well; in fact, it was his chance discovery of the *Faber Book of Modern Verse* that first got him started as a writer. As he told Chana Kronfeld in an interview, it "opened [his] eyes to things [he] didn't know were possible in poetry." Amichai's poetry is noted for its playfulness and wit, and it moves easily from one stylistic register to another. The norms of English tend to resist rapid shifts in register, so a translation that attempts to reproduce every nuance of his Hebrew would very likely seem muddled.

Amichai himself would acknowledge this readily. What's more, his view of the relation between poet and translator calls into question the usual hierarchy. He doesn't regard the poet as inspired creator, acclaimed for his originality, as in the Romantic tradition, but quite the contrary: as a *translator* of sorts, a simple link in the chain of transmission. The poet-as-translator appears in an early poem, "And Let Us Not Get Excited" (1962), as a middleman who passes on "words from one person to another, one tongue to other lips / . . . the way a father passes down / the facial features of his dead father to his son." And in a later poem, "Conferences, Conferences: Malignant Words, Benign Speech" (1998), the poet-as-translator figures prominently, confronting the institutional abuse of language in politics or academia, and toiling to "make honey, like bees, from all the buzz and babble." Notice how Amichai's linking of poetry and translation dismisses the common clichés about translation as betrayal and loss.

Those issues bedevil discussions about translation. But what does "free" mean? And what exactly gets "lost"? My examples come from two of Amichai's love poems.

"A Precise Woman" appears in *The Selected Poetry* (1986), which

by Chana Bloch

I translated with Stephen Mitchell. At that time I was living in
Jerusalem. Stephen worked with Professor Chana Kronfeld
in Berkeley and mailed me his drafts. I spent many afternoons
reading our translations aloud to Yehuda and getting his response.
In "A Precise Woman," his feedback was especially helpful. Here
the poet writes in praise of his beloved:

> A precise woman with a short haircut brings order
> to my thoughts and my dresser drawers,
> moves feelings around like furniture
> into a new arrangement.
> A woman whose body is cinched at the waist and
>   firmly divided
> into upper and lower,
> with weather-forecast eyes
> of shatterproof glass.
> Even her cries of passion follow a certain order,
> one after the other:
> tame dove, then wild dove,
> then peacock, wounded peacock, peacock, peacock,
> then wild dove, tame dove, dove dove
> thrush, thrush, thrush.
>
> A precise woman: on the bedroom carpet
> her shoes always point away from the bed.
> (My own shoes point toward it.)

This is how the six lines at the end of stanza 1, "Even her
cries . . . thrush, thrush, thrush" sound in Hebrew:

> *Afilu tsa'akot ha-ta'avah lefi seder,*
> *achat acharey ha-shniya ve-lo me'urbavot:*

yonat bayit, achar kakh yonat bar,
achar kakh tavas, tavas patsua, tavas, tavas.
Achar kakh yonat bar, yonat bayit, yona yona
tinshemet, tinshemet, tinshemet.

The word I've translated as "thrush" is *tinshémet* in Hebrew, and its modern dictionary definition is "barn owl," which would give us "barn owl, barn owl, barn owl." What is one to do? I lifted mine eyes unto the Bible, whence help often comes. But *tinshemet* appears only three times in the Bible, and no one seems to know what it means. In Leviticus 11:18 (and Deuteronomy 14:16), the *tinshemet*, along with the vulture and the bat, is listed among the unclean birds that Jews are prohibited from eating; in the Bibles I consulted, it is translated variously as "swan" (King James), "water hen" (Revised Standard Version), and "little owl" (New English Bible). To add to the confusion, in the same chapter of Leviticus (11:30), the *tinshemet* appears in a list of unclean creeping things; here I found it translated as "mole" (King James) and "chameleon" (Revised Standard, New English Bible).

When I turned back to the Hebrew, it struck me that Amichai was not thinking of any of these "abominations." I asked him whether he chose *tinshemet* for its sound as well as its meaning, and he confirmed my guess. *Tinshemet* is based on the root *nasham*, "to breathe," and in this context, the sibilant *sh* suggests breathing, or, I should say, heavy breathing. So I found "thrush," perched between albatross and zebra finch, in my trusty thesaurus. But since I'm a little shaky on the names of birds—I know a hawk from a handsaw and an owl from a pussycat, that's about it—I was relieved to see that *Webster's* identifies the thrush as a European bird, which brings it within Amichai's purview. Then I discovered, in his "Seven Laments for the War Dead," that Amichai once read about the thrush in an old German zoology text. And so it came to pass that the lady recovers from her passion—in English—like a thrush. This example shows that what's called a "free" translation is usually not, as you might suppose, the result of an unfettered flight of the imagination. When you're translating a poem of Amichai's, you open the Bible (or rather, the Bibles), the concordance, the dictionary, the thesaurus, the complete works of the poet—and let your fingers do the walking. Only then can you fly.

Chana Kronfeld and I were honored when Amichai asked us to translate *Open Closed Open* (2000), his magnum opus, and sadly, his last book. I'd like to say a word about our process of collaboration on *Open Closed Open*, and more recently on *Hovering at a Low Altitude: The Collected Poetry of Dahlia Ravikovitch* (2009). Even if my Hebrew weren't rusty—which it is—it would never be as good as that of a native speaker. Chana is a native speaker of Hebrew and I of English, so our debates on language and its context gave real meaning to current theories about translation as a negotiation between cultures. To translate is literally to "carry across," from the Latin *trans + ferre*—that is, to carry something across the borders of language and culture that separate us from an unknown country on the other side. Those borders or barriers are generally invisible to the reader, though they are all too clear to the translator who must work her way across or around them. In our intense and absorbing conversations, Chana and I often had the feeling that Hebrew and English language and culture were talking to each other over the divide, and that together we were enacting a border crossing. Our method was dialogue: in the way that Talmudic scholars study a text together by raising alternative possibilities, we debated every word and every turn of phrase.

Some of the time I would prepare rough drafts as a starting point. Then Chana would explain what I missed: "This line comes from the Talmud, and this is a pop song, and this is army slang, and this is children's talk, and this line comes from a skit in the 1980s that everyone knew." Readers outside Israel have tended to oversimplify the meaning of Amichai's work, to blunt his irony, the critical edge of his Hebrew, and even to present him as a religious poet. We were determined to render the full range of his voices, from the colloquial to the densely allusive, while retaining in English the natural ease of his poetic idiom.

Chana would talk about the nuances of words and their cultural context, and I would struggle with what English can and cannot convey. Often she would urge me to push against the boundaries of English, to give the foreignness a tangible presence in the poem, resisting the common tendency to bleach out the cultural particularity. This is a rhetorical strategy that Walter Benjamin famously advocates in his essay, "The Task of the Translator": to "expand and deepen [one's] language by means of the foreign language." Through my work with Chana, I've come to appreciate more deeply the value of this approach, which is gaining recognition in current theories of translation. If you travel to another place, you should come back with something you couldn't find at home. This assumes that the reader is willing to make a bit of an effort, but why assume otherwise?

Amichai's "I Studied Love" is part of a sequence "Gods Change, Prayers Are Here to Stay," where he boldly takes the measure of the Orthodox Jewish practices he grew up with. Here he writes that he learned about love in the Orthodox synagogue of his childhood, with its strict separation of the sexes and subordination of women, by studying the women "on the other side" of the partition:

> I studied love in my childhood in my childhood
> synagogue

in the women's section with the help of the women
    behind the partition
that locked up my mother with all the other
    women and girls.
But the partition that locked them up locked me
    up
on the other side. They were free in their love while
    I remained
locked up with all the men and boys in my love,
    my longing.
I wanted to be there with them and to know their
    secrets
and say with them, "Blessed be He who has made
    me
according to his will." And the partition—
a lace curtain white and soft as summer dresses,
    swaying
on its rings and loops of wish and would,
lu-lu loops, lullings of love in the locked room.
And the faces of women like the face of the moon
    behind the clouds
or the full moon when the curtain parts: an
    enchanted
cosmic order. At night we said the blessing
over the moon outside, and I
thought about the women.

Why is the poet so busily studying the women's faces in the synagogue? Isn't the purpose of the partition to keep him from doing
just that, to keep him focused on his prayers? The Hebrew for partition is *mechitza*. That rabbinic term comes from the root *chatza*,
"to cut, divide, or cross a dividing line." In Modern Hebrew *chutz*

la-aretz means "abroad," *la-chatsot et ha-gvul* means "to cross the border," and the plural form, *mechitzot* "barriers," may occur in the phrase "linguistic and cultural barriers."

The poet describes himself as longing to cross a cultural barrier—a barrier that stopped the translators short. As Naomi Seidman writes, translation is "a border zone," and "what does not succeed in crossing the border is at least as interesting as what makes it across." To most English readers, "Blessed be He who has made me according to His will"—*Baruch she-asani kirtsono*—is unambiguously pious. If they cannot identify this verse as part of the morning prayers recited by women, they will not recognize just how iconoclastic it is—first, because Amichai wishes to say the woman's blessing instead of the man's, and second, because the man's blessing happens to be *Baruch she-lo asani isha*, "Blessed be He who has not made me a woman." In our notes to the poem we quote the man's blessing, though we know that a footnote cannot begin to express how that bit of knowledge radically alters the way the poem reads. More often than not, a note points to a problem rather than resolving it. It signals to the reader: "The following bit of culture stuff, which we will now define in a few words, is something that cannot be defined in a few words."

In the Song of Songs and Amichai's "I Studied Love," women are the bearers of a special wisdom about love. Written more than two millennia apart, these works are nothing short of astonishing when read in the context of traditional Jewish culture, where women have been and still are accorded a subordinate role. In the Song, the brothers who rebuke and threaten the Shulamite about her sexual behavior, and the "watchmen of the walls" who assault her, exemplify the social strictures that mark the woman as "Other." The partition in the Orthodox synagogue serves much the same function.

It is Amichai's openness to the Other that enables him to write the poetry of a whole human being—one of the reasons for his immense appeal. "What's it like to be a woman?" he asks in an early poem. In a poem published after the 1967 war, we find him on Yom Kippur, in the Old City of Jerusalem, standing before the shop of an Arab—a notions shop, much like his father's, which was burned down in Germany—trying to make sense of the parallels between the two men and the tragic history that divides them.

The *mechitza* is one of the many partitions and checkpoints and walls that we humans erect. In Amichai's poem the *mechitza* separates man and woman, and as I have been suggesting, self and Other. Making a translation, or reading one, is about crossing the boundary between self and Other. Amichai's "I Studied Love" tells us that some essential knowledge about "the other side" is "locked up" behind the *mechitza*, and yet, with effort and empathy, it can be retrieved. The same is true of the knowledge of other ages, other cultures, locked away behind the barriers of language—knowledge that we need in order to be fully human and we may retrieve in the act of imaginative understanding that we call translation.

The Wizard of Khao-I-Dang

BY SHARON MAY

Tom treats me like a servant in the day, but he invites me to drink with the Australian embassy staff in the evening. He's new on the Thai border and my least favorite of the immigration officers, arrogant and short-tempered. But I accept his offer because I consider this, too, part of my job, not only to work as a Cambodian interpreter but also to try to educate the staff, as I've been here longer than any of them. Besides, I know he'll buy the beer, and without the alcohol, I cannot sleep.

Tonight all three of them are there—Tom, Richard, Sandra—sitting at a table outside the Bamboo Garden, which caters mostly to foreigners, under a hand-lettered sign that says BAMBU GARDIN. I am the only Cambodian man—the only Cambodian here. The other two translators—Thais who speak Khmer with an accent, and who have their own families to return to in the evening—are absent. Only I have nowhere better to go.

My favorite of the three Australian officers, Sandra, looks about forty years old, pale and fleshy. She wears a red felt hat with a floppy brim, as if she must shield herself from the soft glow of the streetlights. Dark freckles dot her body, like bugs in a sack of rice, speckling her face, her neck, her arms. Of the three embassy officers, she is the kindest, and the most emotional, especially when she's drunk.

Tonight, after her fourth beer, she leans her face close to mine and says, "These poor people. How can you stand it?"

Her tears embarrass me.

I don't want pity. What I want is for them to understand. Of course this is a foolish desire. I know what the Buddha teaches: desire is the cause of suffering. And so I have tried to eradicate desire from my heart. I have tried to weaken its pull on my mind. But still it remains. A wanting. A deep lake of yearning, wide as the Tonle Sap, which expands more than ten times its size during the monsoon, only to shrink again in the dry season.

Even after we have lost everything, we still want something. Having escaped from Cambodia to Thailand, the people stuck in Khao-I-Dang camp want to get to America or Australia or England—or any country that will have them. They want this not for themselves, but for their children. I, who made it to Australia and then came back to the camps to help my people, want to go home to Cambodia. And the immigration officers, what do they want?

THE NEXT morning, Tom doesn't look at me or the Cambodian applicant, who has been bused here from Khao-I-Dang for this interview, along with the other hundred refugees waiting outside the building for their turn. I suspect Tom is tired or hungover. He stares at the file lying on the table and absently twirls an orange Fanta bottle clockwise with his thumb and forefinger. Water drops cover the glass like beads of sweat, except near the lip, which he wipes with a handkerchief now before taking a sip. He drinks a dozen bottles of orange Fanta a day, because—as he confided to me when he first arrived a month ago, nervous and sweating—he is afraid of the water, afraid of the ice, and isn't taking any bloody chances. So every morning in the Aranyaprathet market I fill an ice chest to keep the bottles cold.

"When were you born?" Tom finally asks the applicant, who stares intently at the floor while I translate the question into

Khmer. He wears the cheap, off-white plastic sandals distributed in the camp last week. One of the side straps has broken.

"I'm a Rat," the man answers, glancing up at me, not Tom.

Of course I don't translate this directly. The man, Seng Veasna according to the application, nervously holds his hands sandwiched between his knees. Seng Veasna means "good destiny." He looks about fifty, the father of the small family sitting in a half circle before the officer's wooden desk. I calculate quickly, counting back the previous Years of the Rat until I reach the one that best suits his age.

"Nineteen thirty-six," I say to Tom. He checks the answer against the birth date on the application, submitted by Seng Veasna's relatives in Australia. The numbers must match, as well as the names, or the officer will think the man is lying and reject the application. Each question is a problem with a single correct answer, except that a family's future—not an exam grade—is at stake.

It is my job to solve these problems. To calculate. To resolve inconsistencies.

I did not wish to become a translator or to perform these tricks. I had wanted to become a mathematician and had almost finished my baccalaureate when the Khmer Rouge took over in 1975. I'd planned to teach high school, but it was not my fate. Instead, I now work in this schoolhouse made of timber and tin, at the site of an abandoned refugee camp. This building alone still stands, used for immigration interviews. Inside, three tables for three teams are set in a wide triangle, far enough apart that we can see but not hear each other.

The arrangement reminds me of the triangle I have traveled from Cambodia to Thailand to Australia—and now back again, to Thailand, retracing my journey. After the fall of the Khmer Rouge in 1979, I left Cambodia, crossing the minefields to a camp like this one on the Thai border. Australia accepted me. In Melbourne,

I washed dishes in a refugee hostel and took English classes. Language has always come easily to me, as have numbers. Before the war I'd studied French and some English, and like a fool I'd kept an English dictionary with me after the Khmer Rouge evacuated us from the city. For this stupidity I almost lost my life; when a soldier discovered the book, I survived by claiming I used the pages for toilet paper—very soft, I told him, ripping out a few to demonstrate.

After the Khmer Rouge, I learned some Vietnamese from the occupying soldiers. In the refugee camp, I learned a little Thai. When I first arrived in Australia, English sounded like snake language, with so many S's, hissing and dangerous. But then the words began to clarify, not individually but in patterns, like the sequence of an equation. A door opened, and I no longer felt trapped. I still felt like a stranger, though, useless, alone. I had no wife, no children to keep me there. After three years, I got my Australian passport and returned to Thailand.

First I worked in a transit camp in Bangkok, where the refugees who had been accepted must pass medical tests before they can be sent abroad. The foreign aid workers didn't trust me, because I was Cambodian. And I didn't want to be in Bangkok. After six months I heard the Australian embassy needed translators on the border. That's where I wanted to be, where I could be useful. I jumped at the chance. One step closer to Cambodia, to home.

I had to come back. I think it is my fate to work in a schoolhouse after all.

"Why did you leave Cambodia?" Tom asks the applicant now.

Of all the questions, I dread this one the most. When I translate it into Khmer, Seng Veasna laughs, lifting his hands and opening them in the air in a wide gesture of surrender. For the first time during the interview, he looks relaxed, as if all the tension has drained from his body.

"Doesn't he know what happened in our country?" he asks me. His tone is intimate, personal. For the moment, he has forgotten his fear. He seems to have forgotten even the presence of the embassy officer, although I have not.

"You must tell him," I say in Khmer. I understand the purpose of this question is to distinguish between economic and political refugees, but I also know that this man cannot answer, any more than the last applicant, who just looked at me in disbelief. He cannot answer any more than I can. Still, I urge him, "Just tell the truth."

The man shakes his head no. He cannot speak. He can only laugh. I want to tell him I know this is a nonsense question, a question they do not need to ask.

Why did you leave Cambodia?

I've told the embassy staff many times that if they ask this question, they can never get the right answer. I've explained to the other two officers—although not yet to this new one, Tom— that nearly two million people died. One quarter of the people in Cambodia died in less than four years. Then the Vietnamese invaded. There was no food, no medicine, no jobs. Everyone has lost family. Myself, I lost my mother and father, two brothers, one sister, six aunts and uncles, seventeen cousins. The numbers I can say; the rest I cannot.

Even now, the fighting continues in Cambodia and on the border. Sometimes in this schoolhouse the muffled boom of heavy artillery interrupts the interviews.

"Why is he laughing?" Tom asks.

"He does not understand the question."

"Ask him again. How can he not know why he bloody left the country?"

I see Tom's bottle of Fanta is almost empty. I take another from the ice chest, pop off the cap, wipe the lip with a clean handkerchief, and set it on his desk before turning back to Seng Veasna to explain in Khmer. "I know you don't want to remember. But you must tell him what you've gone through." When the man still does not speak, I add, "Uncle, if you don't answer he will reject your application."

At that, Seng Veasna glances quickly at Tom then back to the floor and begins to talk, without raising his eyes. I repeat his story in English, the story I have heard so many times in infinite variations, the same story that is my own. And when Seng Veasna is finally through and the interview finished, to my relief the officer Tom stamps the application ACCEPTED. One done. Ten families still wait outside. The morning is not yet half over.

HERE'S WHAT I don't say to the immigration officers:

Try to imagine. The camp is like prison, nothing to do but wait and go crazy. Forget your iced bottles of Fanta and beer. Forget your salary that lets you live like a king while you make the decisions of a god.

Imagine. It is like magic. You wake up one morning and everything is gone. The people you love, your parents, your friends. Your house. Like in the film I saw twice in Australia, *The Wizard of Oz*. I watched it first with my second brother's son, who was six, who had been born on the border but raised in Melbourne and cannot even speak Khmer properly. The flying monkeys scared him so much I had to turn off the video. But those monkeys reminded me of home, of when I worked in the forest surrounding Lake Tonle Sap. They reminded me of the monkey god Hanuman and his army, who helped Rama rescue Sita. So, later, after my nephew went to sleep, I watched the rest of the movie. The next week I rented the video and watched it again alone. I didn't like the singing and dancing, so I fast-forwarded through those parts. But the girl's wanting to go home—that I understood. And I understood, too, the wizard who has no power, who cannot even help himself, although he also secretly wishes to return home.

I want to tell the immigration officers—imagine you are in that movie. Then maybe you will understand. You are the girl. Only there is no home to return to. And instead of Oz, you have woken up in a refugee camp.

Each day you have nothing to do but worry and, if you are lucky enough to have a ration card, to wait like a beggar for handouts of rice and canned, half-rancid fish. At night after the foreign aid workers leave, the soldiers who are supposed to protect you steal what few possessions you still have, and they rape your wives and your daughters. You want only to get out. To find a new home.

Every day you hope for an announcement on the loudspeaker that an embassy is conducting interviews. You hope for America but any country will do: France, England, Australia. You check the list on the wall, search for your name, squeezing your body in between the others. The people clustered around the wall have a certain rank smell, almost sweet. You wish you could wash this stink from your own body and purify yourself of this place, of this longing. On one side of you stands a husband who has waited for years, checking this same wall; on the other, a mother who's been rejected twice and so has little hope, yet she still comes to look. Behind you a father squats in the sun: he can't read, so his son checks for him while he waits. If you're lucky enough to be listed, you must be prepared to go to the interview the following day.

Imagine. The bus picks you up early in the morning, exiting the gate past the Thai guards with their machine guns, taking you out of the camp for the first time in the years since you arrived. As the bus rattles over the rutted road, your mind clenches in fear. The child in front of you presses her face to the window, enraptured. She points at the rice fields, the water buffalo, the cows, which she has never seen before because she was born in the camp. "What's that?" she asks, curious. "And that?" Her father names these things for her. You know he is thinking of the interview ahead, as you are, and how much depends on it, how her future depends on it; perhaps he is thinking, too, of how the shirt he has cleaned and pressed is already stained with sweat.

ALL THE questions are difficult. Especially the ones that seem the simplest to the immigration officer. What is your name? Where were you born? How old are you?

Take, for example, this morning, when officer Richard asks a young man, "What is your brother's name?"

"Older brother Phal," the boy answers. He is skinny, frightened.

"What is his *full* name?" Richard, over six feet tall, has wide shoulders and a large belly like a Chinese Buddha. Although he smiles often, his height and massive torso scare the applicants, especially when he leans toward them as he does now, both elbows planted on the table, intently studying the boy. The young man stares at the floor. He looks like a real Khmer—wide cheekbones, full lips, chocolate skin. "Don't be scared," Richard says. "Take it easy. We're not going to do anything to you. Just try to answer correctly, honestly."

Still the boy hesitates. I worry Richard may take this as a sign he is lying about his relationship to the sponsor, although I've tried to explain to him that Cambodians don't call their relatives by their given names; it's not polite. You call them brother or sister, aunt or uncle, or you use nicknames, so you may not know the full given name. Then there are the names you may have used under the Khmer Rouge, to hide your background to save your family's lives, or your own. I have explained this all before, but it does no good.

In the end, Richard says, "I'm sorry," and stamps the front page REJECTED.

I can do nothing. Although siblings have lower priority, I believe the familial relationship is not the problem. Rather, the boy is dark-skinned and speaks no English. Richard, like the others, prefers the light-skinned Cambodians, who have more Chinese blood, softer features, who can speak at least some English. If they are young and pretty, and female, even better.

Just as important is the officer's mood, yet another variable I must consider. Tom is more likely to accept an applicant when he has been to a brothel the night before. Sandra is more likely to approve after she has received a letter from her children in Brisbane. Richard, usually in good spirits, is most dangerous when he has a hangover or digestive problems. Today, he seems to have neither trouble. He has not been running to the toilet or popping paracetamol pills for a headache, so I don't know why the day doesn't seem to get easier.

The next couple is neither young nor pretty. The wife's lips and teeth are stained red from chewing betel nut.

"When was your seventh son born?" Richard asks.

The husband and wife look at each other, confused.

"Was it eight or nine years ago?" the man asks his wife.

"Nine," she says. "No, eight."

"No, tell him eight." The wife gives her husband a scolding look, then smiles weakly at the officer, showing her stained teeth. By now Richard is laughing and shaking his head.

"Eight," I translate.

"Do they know his birth *date*?"

The husband looks again at his wife. "Dry season," she says. "I remember it had stopped raining already."

"Around December or January," I translate. Then I add, "It's not that they're lying. It's that these things aren't important. Birth dates are not registered until a child enters school, if then."

"How can you not know when your own child was born?"

Richard asks me. His generous belly shakes as he laughs. He does not really want an answer, so I say nothing.

"What's wrong?" the wife asks me.

"Never mind," I say. "Don't worry."

I am forever in between.

To the people in the camp, I explain again and again. "Look, you must remember your full names and birth dates. In Cambodia it's not important, but in the West, it's very important. If you don't know, make them up. One person in the family must write all the answers down, and everyone must remember. You must practice."

They look at me funny at first, not quite believing me, like Richard watches me now, still chuckling. Because he is amused, I calculate he will accept the couple. I decide to say nothing and just smile back.

THAT NIGHT at the Bamboo Garden, Richard calls the owner to our table. "Your food is spot-on, very *aroy*," Richard says, emphasizing and mispronouncing the Thai word for delicious, using the wrong tone. "But, mate, that sign is spelled wrong."

The owner, a slight man in his sixties, nods his head. "Yes. Thank you. Yes."

"I mean, you gotta fix that spelling." Richard points to the sign above him. "Darith, can you explain to him?"

Shit, I think, even here I have to translate. In polite language, I tell the owner in Thai that the big foreigner loves the food very much.

The owner smiles. Richard nods, happy to be understood. I think that's the end of it. But then Richard pulls a long strip of toilet paper—which is used in place of napkins—from the pink plastic container in the center of the table. In large block letters, using the pen he keeps in his shirt pocket, he writes: BAMBOO

GARDEN. He underlines the double O and the E, then points again at the misspelled sign.

The owner's face darkens, without me having to explain. "Thank you. Yes, I fix," he says, as he takes the piece of toilet paper from Richard's outstretched hand.

THE YOUNG woman sitting in front of the desk this morning is both pretty and light-skinned. Her hair, recently washed, is combed neatly into a shiny ponytail that falls below her narrow waist. As she passed me to take her seat, I could smell the faint sweet scent of shampoo. She wears a carefully ironed white blouse, and a trace of pink lipstick which she must have borrowed from a friend or relative to make herself up for this occasion. Officer Tom, to whom I have been assigned today, watches the girl with interest, charmed. Her sponsor is only a cousin, so normally she would have little chance of being accepted.

"What do you do in the camp?" he asks. "Do you work?"

The young lady speaks softly. Out of politeness, she doesn't meet his eyes. "Yes, I work, but . . ." Her voice trails off and then she turns to me, blushing. "I don't want to say, it's a very low job."

"What is it?"

"I work in the CARE bakery, making bread."

Tom eyes me suspiciously. "Why are you talking to her?"

I could answer him straight, but I'm annoyed with him today. I did not sleep well last night. I am getting sick of this job, this place. For all I do, it seems I have done nothing. "She was talking to me," I snap back. "That's why I talked to her."

"What did she say?"

"She says she doesn't want to tell you, because she feels embarrassed." As if on cue, she turns her head away. Her ponytail ripples down her back.

"What exactly does she *do* in the camp?" Tom says this in an insinuating way, as if he suspects she's a prostitute. I don't like the way he looks at her. Maybe he is undressing her in his mind right now. For her part, the girl waits quietly in the chair, knees drawn together, looking at her hands lying still on her knees. Her fingernails are clean, cut short. This, too, she remembered to do for the interview.

"She has a wonderful job," I say to Tom. "You know the bread from the CARE bakery in Khao-I-Dang, the French bread you eat every morning? She is the baker."

"That's very good. Why didn't you say so in the first place?" He relaxes back in his chair and takes a drink from the Fanta bottle. I don't know how he can drink this stuff, or how I can watch him drink it all day. I submerge the thought and clear my head to concentrate on the task at hand. He continues, "Ask her what she is going to do if she gets accepted to Australia."

"What are you going to do in Australia—tell him you're going to open a bakery," I say, all in one sentence.

Raising her head to face him now, she answers in a sweet, composed voice, "I want to open a bakery shop in Australia."

I translate. "She wants to work in a bakery in Australia, and when she can save enough money, to open her own bread shop."

"Good, good," he says, and stamps the application ACCEPTED.

THAT NIGHT at dinner with Sandra and Richard, Tom asks me out of the blue, "Why did you come back here?"

The restaurant sign is gone, creating an empty space over our heads. In response to Tom's question, I shrug my shoulders and look away, hoping he'll get distracted, perhaps by the attractive waitress waiting to refill our glasses. I glance at her and she comes forward to pour more beer for everyone.

"You came back, didn't you?" Tom persists after the waitress has stepped back into the shadows. "Your mother's Australian, isn't she? And your father is Cambodian?"

I've heard this rumor, too, mostly from foreigners. I think it is their way of explaining why I can speak English.

"No, I am all Cambodian," I say. "But I have Australian citizenship."

"So you went through the Khmer Rouge and all that?" asks Richard.

"Yes. All that."

Sandra, who knows this, watches me. Her jaw tenses under the shadow of her hat.

"I don't get it," Tom says. "Why would you come back? Seems to me everyone else is trying to get out of here." He laughs, lifting his glass. "Myself included. Cheers, mate."

I lift my glass. "Cheers," I say. I should leave it at that.

Sandra is still watching me with concern, her eyebrows drawn together. "How about that storm this afternoon?" she asks, to change the subject. "I couldn't hear a thing."

Maybe it is the beer. I don't know. I look straight at Tom. "You don't know how much the people feel," I say. He doesn't respond.

"I couldn't hear a thing," Sandra repeats, more forcefully this time. "I can't believe how loud rain is on a tin roof."

"Yeah," says Richard. "I had to stop an interview."

"The way you treat people, you don't know anything," I say, still looking directly at Tom. He shifts in his chair and dips a spring roll into sweet red sauce. With his other hand he ticks the Formica table-top. His eyes study the waitress. As if he hasn't even heard me. I often feel this way around the immigration officers, invisible. Sometimes they talk about the Cambodians, calling them lazy or stupid, as if I am not there, or as if they have forgotten that I, too, am Khmer.

"If you ask me, these people don't really want to come to your country," I continue. "If you open the gate, they will go back to Cambodia. They won't even say good-bye." I want to stop, but I can't. "And don't ask them why they leave the country. You think they want to leave their home? They laugh when you ask them that. You should know. The real situation is that they want to survive."

Sandra has stopped talking. Richard looks into the half-empty beer glass, then takes a sip. Tom loudly crunches on another spring roll. I don't know why they are the way they are. It's not that none of them cares. There is Sandra, and others like her. And they are sent from country to country, without time to learn the difference between Cambodia and Vietnam. It's not easy for them. I tell myself that they are just worn down, but the new arrivals have the same assumed superiority, the unquestioned belief that they know everything: what is wrong, what is right—that they are somehow more *human*. I signal to the waitress for another round.

THE NEXT night, instead of beer, Tom orders me a Fanta orange soda, grinning as he slides the bottle across the table toward me. The restaurant sign is still gone.

"No, thanks," I say.

"Go ahead, mate."

"No, thank you," I say again.

"Why not?" asks Tom.

"Oh, leave him alone," says Sandra.

I stare at the orange bottle.

"It won't kill you," says Tom.

"No, not me." I try to make light of it. "I gave that stuff up a long time ago, in 1976."

Tom laughs. So does Richard in his booming voice. For all of their attention to dates from the applicants, for all their insistence that the numbers must match exactly, they ignore what those dates mean. But I am telling the truth. It was 1976, the second year under the Khmer Rouge regime. It was the rainy season, cold and miserable. I lived in a single men's labor camp on a hill in the rice fields. One night I heard the guards calling, "We got the enemy! We got the enemy!" What *enemy*, I thought. We were in the middle of nowhere. The real purpose of the guards was to keep the workers from trying to escape or steal food at night. When I opened my eyes, I couldn't see the man sleeping next to me. Clouds blocked the stars. Then I noticed the feeble flames from lit pieces of rubber tire, burned for lamplight, and got up to see what had happened.

Near the compound's kitchen, three Khmer Rouge leaders gathered around a skinny man kneeling in the mud, his elbows tied tightly behind his back. His shoulders were pulled back like a chicken's wings, tensing the tendons in his neck. He had dark skin and long hair that fell below his bound wrists. I'd heard rumors of resistance fighters, "long hairs" who lived in the forest around Lake Tonle Sap, but I had never seen one and did not believe until then that they really existed. I had thought them the product of our collective imagining, our wishing someone had the courage to fight back.

Comrade Sok kicked the man in his side, and he fell over into the mud. Sok was a big man, twice the size of the prisoner. When Sok kicked him again, the man's head hit a water buffalo yoke lying at the edge of the kitchen. One of the other leaders pulled his head up. The prisoner's eyes were closed. Comrade Sok said, "Why do you resist? What do you struggle for?"

The man seemed only half-conscious. He opened his eyes briefly, then closed them again and spoke very clearly, slowly enunciating each word. "I struggle for all of you, brothers, not for myself."

"You struggle for me? We have already liberated the country." Sok kicked him again. "We have no need of your help."

The man said once more, "I struggle for you."

Then they threw him like a sack of rice into an oxcart. Everyone was watching. We couldn't help him. We couldn't do anything.

The next day, while I was cleaning the abscesses on my feet using water boiled with sour leaves, the oxcart returned—without the man, loaded instead with bottles of soft drinks and cigarette cartons. Comrade Sok explained this was our reward for capturing the enemy: one bottle for three people, one pack of cigarettes for ten people. The next time we captured the enemy, we would receive an even greater reward.

The cigarette packets were Fortunes, with a lion insignia. The soda bottles were Miranda orange. I teased the two younger boys with whom I shared the soft drink, dividing the bottle into thirds, the top being the largest, the bottom the smallest. "What part do you want?" I asked. Of course they chose the top two portions. "Okay, I'll take the bottom," I said. "You don't mind if I drink my portion first . . ."

"No, that's not right," they protested together. I was only making fun. I poured the drink into three tin bowls we usually used to eat the rice ration, giving the boys most of it. They were excited about the soda, which they hadn't tasted in a long time, if ever. But all the while I was trying to make them laugh, I felt sad. A man was killed for this.

The drink was flat, not even enough liquid to fill my mouth.

THE APPLICATION lying on the table today in front of Sandra is a difficult case. This morning, when I dropped the files on each of the three officers' tables, I made sure this one came to her. The sponsor in Australia, a daughter, got citizenship by claiming a woman was her mother. Now that the daughter is in Australia, she claims the woman is not actually her mother, but rather her aunt, and that the woman sitting before us now is her real mother.

The mother hands me the letter from her daughter, which I translate. In it, the daughter explains that this woman is her real mother and confesses she lied before. She did not know her mother was alive then. She was alone in the camp, with no one to take care of her. That's why she lied.

Sandra asks me, "Do you think they are really mother and daughter?"

"Yes," I say, and hand her the letter, which she adds to the file lying open before her, with the previous and current applications and small black-and-white photos. "You can even see the daughter looks like her."

"Well, they cannot do that," Sandra says. "She lied. The law is the law."

"I can tell you, this is a story many people face, not just these two. They do not intend to lie, but because of the circumstances they must do it, believe me. Think of your own daughter, if you were separated." And then I add, "Of course it's up to you, not me."

"She lied," Sandra says. "It's finished. I have to reject them."

"I can't tell them straight like that," I say. "Would you let me explain nicely to them the reason they are getting rejected?"

"All right, go ahead."

So I take a chance, a calculated risk. There is nothing to lose now. I know Sandra loves her own children, and also that she has a good heart. I say to the mother in a soft, even voice, "Look, your daughter lied to the embassy even though she knew what she was doing was wrong. A country like Australia is not like Cambodia. The law is the law. When you say someone is your mother, she's got to be your mother. Now she cannot change her story. So from now on, I don't think you will be able to meet your daughter anymore for the rest of your life."

Tears began to well in the mother's eyes. I feel bad for what I am doing, but I know there is no other way. I keep my voice firm, steady, and continue, "So now, after all you've been through in Cambodia, after how hard you struggled to keep your family together, to survive, now you are separated forever."

The mother begins to wail, a long piercing sound that fills the entire room, so that the teams at the other two tables turn around to look at us. "Oh, my daughter, I will never see you again!" she cries. I translate what she says for Sandra. "After all we survived in the Pol Pot time—when you were starving, I risked my life to steal food for you. When you got sick, I looked after you. When you could not walk, I carried you in my arms. And now you lie. You lie and you are separated from me. I cannot see you for the rest of my life. *Ouey . . .*"

I translate it all, word for word. The father is crying now, too, but silently. He sits in a wooden chair, with his back straight. Their young son watches his mother's face and sobs as well, echoing her wails.

"Please, tell them to go now," Sandra says. She looks away and wipes her eyes with the back of her hand.

In Khmer, I dismiss the family. "Go, go. Don't cry anymore. Even if you die, nobody cares. You will never see your child anymore."

As the mother walks away, the applicants at the other tables watch her leave. The building is silent except for her voice. She cries all the way out of the building, gripping her husband's arm. Her son whimpers too, clinging to her legs through the sarong, almost tripping her.

I start to laugh. "Well, Sandra, that's it," I say. "Send them back to the Killing Fields. Don't worry. There are more coming."

Sandra looks at me, stunned. She opens her mouth and closes it again, without saying anything, like a fish gulping seawater. The freckled skin around her eyes is red and puffy. I can see the beating of her blood beneath the translucent skin of her left temple, a small pulsing disk, like the flutter of a bird's heart. She looks away, down to the table, and starts idly shifting through the papers. She isn't really looking at them.

"I'll get the next family," I say.

She nods, her face still turned away from me. I grab the list and go call the next family from the dozens of others waiting outside the building. Some stand in the sun. Others squat in the shade of three small coconut trees, fanning away flies.

"Keo Narith," I say. No one steps forward. The crowd looks agitated, nervous. The mother is still crying. "My daughter, I can never see you again!" A group has gathered around her, asking, "What happened? What happened?"

"Keo Narith!" I call again.

Still, no one answers. I remember the name because it rhymes with my own, and I saw the family members board the bus when they were called in the morning. They must be hiding somewhere now in the crowd or behind the coconut trees or around the corner of the building. I hear a man to the left of me say, "The embassy is not happy today. They reject easily." It's true, when too many people are rejected, the next applicants don't dare answer. They'd rather wait for months or years until they get back on the list again.

AFTER WE drive back to Aranyaprather, the embassy staff meets again for dinner at the Bamboo Garden. The owner has fixed the sign: two small, oblong O's are now squeezed into the space that held the U, and the I has been changed to an E, but the shades of paint don't quite match. Tom and Richard are talking the usual bullshit. Richard expands on his most recent stomach problems. Tom no longer talks about leaving. He has a Thai girlfriend now, a prostitute he claims is a waitress at the bar who has never slept with a man before him. "She's been saving herself," he says.

Sandra looks at him, disgusted, and interjects, "Yeah, right. You really believe that?"

As the men continue talking, Sandra turns to me and whispers, "Darith, I changed it. I changed the file, when I got back. I'm letting them go."

I say quietly, "You made the right decision."

"I know," she says, her eyes shining, urgent. "I understand."

I think, there is more than any of us can understand. I feel something I cannot express: an opening, an exit. It is like the feeling I had when I first crossed the border after the end of the Khmer Rouge regime: gratitude, mixed with weariness and hunger. The day I arrived I could still taste the foul pond water I'd drunk in darkness the night before, so thirsty, not seeing until morning the body of a woman in the pond, close to where I slept on the embankment. I didn't know then what would come, how many years I would work before returning to the border I'd fled. I wonder, does Sandra—who, out of the corner of my eye, I can see is still watching me as I glance down at my beer glass—really understand? How many families will remain stuck in the camp if I can no longer do this job? I weigh all of this: duty, desire, two halves of an equation, as I turn the glass in my hand.

All the while in my heart I am thinking, hoping, I can quit now. I can leave this place. It's time to go home.

The Difficulty of Translation

BY LUCY FERRISS

Kate worked in one of those gray European cities whose monstrous eighteenth-century buildings abide within cages of scaffolding. Over its cupolas and steeples hovered the maws of bright yellow cranes. Everything was being restored: halls of justice, fountains, Doric columns, statues of long-forgotten soldiers and poets. In the few vacant lots where history had gnawed out the root of the old civilization, towers of glass and onyx loomed like spears hurled down from another planet, warning the natives.

Winter was passing for her, had passed almost, in a damp miasma of dog droppings and soiled newspapers backed against the deserted circular fountains. All the unrestored cast-metal statues sported a chartreuse green. Kate wondered frequently, repetitiously, whether their casters had been aware of the corrosive tendency of brass, whether they had planned for centuries of empire-supported polishers to keep the brass shiny. Perhaps they hadn't minded the onset of this druggy green sign of seniority.

Seagulls circled above the leathery surface of the pond she passed daily. Truck vendors sold sausage sandwiches and fried potatoes with spicy mayonnaise dressings, which Kate bought for a shiny coin and ate with a thin red plastic fork. The first bite burned the roof of her mouth, and the last tasted of the animal grease in which everything was cooked. She noticed these things. She was falling in love, and it scared her.

THE SMALL, pleasant office where Kate worked sat at the bottom of steep granite steps that led from the massive city hall to the theater district. Kate's job was to appraise antiques for export to the United States. She had arrived here, three years ago, because she was having an affair with the export manager. When he died in a car accident shortly after her arrival, she had stayed on. The firm liked her work—she had a careful eye, and a kind manner with the old ladies whose crystal she rejected—and Personnel managed somehow (she didn't ask) to renew her papers each year. And each year she stayed, though summer passed hesitantly and winter made her think always of the wars this city and others like it had barely survived. Lines for bread, she thought; dung burned for fuel.

She spoke the language passably. Once a week or more she was invited to a dinner party at which others her age—bureaucrats, young lawyers, antique dealers—chatted excitedly around her and she soaked up their energy like a sponge going red with the excellent wine. Her thoughts felt simple to her on these occasions. The vocabulary at hand contained none of the shadings she was used to. In the empty, half-sober moments after she'd returned to her flat, she wondered sometimes if her party companions thought simple thoughts—but that was her American prejudice at work, filtering out whatever subtleties it couldn't immediately process. She went to bed with the vapor of mystery. What did anyone think, really, and was language just a bowl to contain it? On rare occasions she missed the manager who had brought her here, the one who had died on a hairpin turn in the neighboring mountains. But she had scarcely known him, when you got down to it, and the years had smudged him into the gray of the city, until when she dreamed of him, he was speaking in this other language, the one that made thoughts simple.

She fell in love not at a party but at a sidewalk stand, the one nearest her office, where she waited in spring mist for a grated lamb sandwich and a can of beer to make her lunch. The man in front of her spent his waiting time fooling with a fancy pocket calculator. He seemed nervous, and she thought maybe she would help him, when his turn came, with the strange names of the sandwiches. The day was windy, she would remember later; it had been windy for more than a week and her hair was going tangled and coarse at the ends. She had learned to tie a scarf around her neck like the local people, but she would not wear their loose-knitted hats.

He ordered a large sausage sandwich with Andalusian sauce, a beer, and a package of pork rinds. He placed the order fluently, in the slack dialect of men who depend on such food, and he adjusted what she noticed were large hands to carry it all to one of two splintery green benches in the small park by the food stand. By the time she made her way to the other bench, he had spread his lunch on either side and was eating calmly in the wind with a thick text spread over his knees. He wouldn't spill a drop of grease on his neat pants and sweater, she thought, and she practiced the phrase in the local language a few times before she realized, suddenly that she had said it, aloud and in English: "I bet you won't spill a drop of grease on those pants."

"I've spilled plenty in the past," he said. He didn't look up. He spoke like someone from the Midwest. "One learns."

"Your book won't flop closed, either. Mine always flops closed, if I don't have a hand free."

"You have to choose heavy pages." With a long pinky, he turned the page, then looked over. His lips were full and almost feminine, shining a bit with oil from the sandwich. "There are restaurants," he said.

"I'm inside all morning."

"You work here, then?"

She nodded in the vague direction of her office. He didn't even glance, but smiled cunningly, as if he'd already mapped the route. "This isn't a city, you know," he said, crunching pork rind. "It's a work zone."

"Will they ever finish, do you think?"

He shrugged. "They restored the Coliseum. And those were Italians."

"They have better weather."

He said something she didn't understand.

"What?"

"Polish saying. 'Plant in the rain and the roots grab hold.'" He pushed the last of the sandwich into his mouth and washed it down. Closing the book, he stood and wiped his hands on his paper napkin. (Where had he gotten that napkin? They never gave her one, at the stand.) Then he reached into his inside jacket pocket and pulled out a card. *J. Roscher*, it read. *Simultaneous translation & interpretation. French, German, Dutch, Italian, Polish, English.*

HE TOOK her first to an Indian place several blocks into a questionable district of the city, where they ate papadums and a lightly saffroned, greaseless lamb. (She initiated the phone call, though not the rendezvous. She invented the pretext of needing to translate a Dutch inscription on a silver bowl.) Next they tried a very expensive, tiny Japanese pocket where he selected varieties of raw fish that she never knew swam in the sea. At the third restaurant, his neighborhood favorite, a round fussy woman prepared them both chicken waterzoi and plied them with a bright green aperitif while they waited. Kate got up her courage to ask about his scar, a neat slice in the shape of an acute accent running from his left earlobe toward his prominent Adam's apple. She had not noticed it the first day, at the lunch stand, but as he swallowed and spoke, she found her eyes straying there.

"A memory," he said, tasting the excellent though slightly sweet wine he'd ordered, "of my roustabout days."

She loved the way he used slang, not inappropriately, but with the imagination of someone who has discovered rather than inherited. The picture of Joaquim—that was his given name, not quite compatible with the "J." of the card—with his pursed lips and fair forehead, as a roustabout, made her laugh.

"I almost died," he said.

"I'm sorry."

"That's quite all right," he said. "Anyhow, I lived."

Smiling at him over the narrow rim of the aperitif glass, Kate realized she had begun dreaming about Joaquim's face and body, the slouch in his posture, the sleepy weight of his eyelids, the hair he combed straight back from his high forehead like a symphony conductor. That night he came back with her to the ground-floor apartment she had been renting since the export manager's death, and they made love with a competence that, at least on Kate's part, just managed to hint at her wild rush of feeling. While they were at it, Joaquim murmured to her in German, French, Italian, Polish, and one other language that could have been Danish or Norwegian. Later he lay with a hand cupping her breast and told her a funny story in English about the first American girl he had known, who had exclaimed over the shape and behavior of his uncircumcised penis.

"How," Kate asked sleepily, suffused with love, "do you hold all those languages in your head?"

"How does a mother hold all her babies in her arms?" he asked her back. "How does a criminal hold all his crimes in his conscious? How does a composer hear all the instruments in the symphony?"

Kate did not answer; she was not supposed to answer. She was supposed to lie with her head on Joaquim's bony chest and smell the wine-sweetened exhalations of his pores. Only as she drifted off to sleep did she catch his error. *Conscience*, he had meant, not *conscious*. The kind of mistake that even a native might make.

WHAT SCARED her were the silences. What she knew about Joaquim might have explained them. He had been born, he told her, in Holland, but had moved to Paris with his mother, who took up with a Polish diplomat. They lived five years in Chicago. "And the rest, as they say, is history," he said, swirling a lock of Kate's trimmed hair.

Silence was the space between one language and another, the place of memory. But that explanation, for Kate, didn't suffice. She wanted to know what he was really. She watched him sleep and wondered what language he dreamed in. When he spent the evening at her flat, he brought classical CDs and sat listening to Palestrina or Messaien. She could cook or watch the news or sit with him, holding his hand, but he would not hold up his end of a conversation. He wasn't angry, he told her, or bored. He was just emptying his reservoir of words, drifting back to the original *da*.

Out in the world, he was full of words. The international courts kept him on retainer; he also translated sometimes for visiting theater troupes and TV crews. In his spare time, he was translating World War I accounts from Italian into German. Thus the heavy tome, which he had been reading in the wind, and the calculator, which was a translation device.

As the days warmed they went biking together, through the beech forest just outside the city that had once been the king's domain. The paths criss-crossed, dead-ended, climbed around hills and dove into gullies. The sun, out at last, glinted through the tall beeches, their leaves lime green. Once they took lunch at a former cloister in the midst of the woods, where people much taller and more beautiful than Kate's co-workers sat with their large sleek

dogs at outdoor wooden tables drinking Abbey beer and rosé wine
and eating open-faced peasant sandwiches of white cheese sprin-
kled with radishes and onions. Ten feet from them, new families
of ducks and coots, hoping for tosses of bread, cruised the edge
of the pond once used by the monks as a fishery. The baby coots
had bright red beaks and pushed their heads along, pigeon-like
imitating their stern bourgeois parents.

"*Comme tu es belle dans cette lumière*," said Joaquim. "*Wie sch*
bist du in diesem Licht. É bella alla luce—"

"I get it," Kate interrupted. He looked hurt. "I'm sorry,"
said.

"No problem. It is hard to switch gears. You look lovely
light."

"Thank you, darling," she said.

He turned his attention to the pond and took a long
of his beer. "Watch the egret," he said. He gestured wit
glass toward a thin gray bird stepping daintily around
wall edging the pond. Leaning his long neck over th
bird came up with a small fish, which he wriggled dow
there was a movement high in a willow tree. "Ah," sai

"What? What's in the tree?"

"The fellow who got there first."

A larger egret swooped out of the thick branche
pass at the fishing bird, then landed on the far side

"Maybe they're male and female," Kate said, wa
egret jump away to take refuge in the overhang of
"This could be a mating ritual."

"Dream on, Pollyanna," said Joaquim, and she
Pollyanna, away to ask him about later. The larger egret sta
the pond. The other patrons were watching now. One woman had
pulled a video recorder out of her satchel. Soon, as the newcomer
wandered out of his haven, the big egret launched a stealth attack,

flying low and straight over the surface of the pond. At the last moment, while Kate held her breath, the newcomer took to the air. The birds climbed, glided, flapped, turned. Faster on account of his wider wing span, the pond's defender kept coming up on the intruder from below, his beak out, ready to peck belly or wing. They flew through the fountain in the middle of the pond, over the willows; they pivoted as sharply as they could. The woman with the video camera kept squeaking, but Kate could not make a sound.

Finally, the bigger egret chased away the newcomer—first to a willow tree that shook with its weight, and finally away from the pond, out over the vast beech woods. Then the winner sloped down to a rock, gave a little shiver, and posed, immobile, on one leg.

"Now," said Kate, "he'll be all alone."

"That's how he likes it," said Joaquim.

"I was rooting for the littler guy," she said. She took a bite of her white-cheese sandwich. She could taste the rye field in the bread, the milked cow in the cheese.

"It is all about territory," he said. And then in an undertone, not meant for her to hear, "*Es gibt immer am Heimat. Tu chodzi nie o ziemie.*"

That night they ate oysters at his apartment, a tidy, elegant top story of a family house. His Italian war volumes lay scattered about the sitting room. CDs of chamber and orchestral music—no voices—lined the shelves. From the open window to the balcony came the throaty lyric of the local nightingale. Down below lay the tiny, carefully partitioned gardens that ran behind the tall houses, the length of the block. Kate pictured lifting the brick walls that separated them, the way one might lift the cardboard honeycomb of a wine case, and letting the gardens run together in a lush city forest.

by Lucy Ferriss

Later she lay awake, watching his face move through sleep. She herself had dreams in which she spoke her second language perfectly, without accent, and her thoughts in these dreams were as thick and beveled as crystal, though they vanished when she woke.

SHE WENT to watch him work. He had promised her it would be dull. He sat in a glassed booth at one of the courts, where one fishing industry took another's dumping practices before the bar, or one country's pharmaceuticals objected to another's patenting practices. This litigation had to do with exporting antiques from the European Union, he had told her, an issue in which she might take a passing interest. "Passing!" exclaimed Kate.

On the first truly hot day of summer, she took an afternoon off work. Dressed in an uncharacteristic sleeveless dress of bleeding blue madras, she rode the subway to the end of the line and then stood by the city's outer wasteland of industry to catch a rumbling bus to the glassed-in complex that held the courts. On the bus, which was crowded, several men glanced approvingly at her. Kate had grown prettier since falling in love. Her export manager had liked her for her youth and competence and possibly for her hair, which in good weather hung in thick chestnut curls just over her shoulders. But she had been shy back then, and since his death she had taken to hunching her shoulders in what seemed the constant chill of the city. She no longer looked American—she never walked from the hip as the American tourists did, nor did she raise her voice above the other commuters on the subway. But on this ride out to the halls of European justice, she stood tall in her foreignness. She was like the new buildings, designed by architects from the Orient or California, and not like the crabbed and crutched representatives of a vanished empire.

Joaquim had left her name at the desk. The stern woman who sat there took her passport and gave her a nametag. Huge modern paintings hung on the high blond walls of the corridors; it felt more like an auction house than a courthouse. She made her way up to the fourth floor and down a long gallery to a set of heavy wooden doors, where a coterie of dark-suited men stood conferring. A pair of them glanced at her. She smiled apologetically and slipped inside the chamber.

There was a fair crowd of spectators. A few sat straight and listened to the proceedings—three judges at the front and lawyers with documents and arguments in what Joaquim had told Kate would be Polish. The others sat hunched on the long benches with headphones plastered to their ears. The nationality bringing the case, Joaquim had explained, was allowed to argue in its own language—and sure enough, two of the three judges had their own earphones, like old wigs. The respondents could argue in that same language or in either French or English. All arguments and opinions would be translated into nine languages, fourteen if the matter involved the constitution of the European Union.

All these things Kate understood. But as she slipped into one of the benches toward the back of the room, the silence and strangeness felt more alien to her than anything she had encountered in her three years of living abroad. The lawyer arguing gestured mightily with his hands but spoke in a hurried, muted Polish directed at the one judge without earphones. That judge would nod, or lift an eyebrow, and perhaps five seconds later, as the translation came through the other judges' earphones, they would mimic her gesture.

Before she reached for the black headpiece dangling from a hook at her knees, Kate scanned the elevated glass booths at the front of the courtroom. There, in the third one, sat Joaquim. He, too, was gesturing, with even more alacrity and purpose than the lawyer. He kept putting the tips of his fingers to his forehead and then letting them spring away, as if he had yanked a difficult thought from his brain. *Deutsch*, a white label on his booth read. Kate clapped the earphones on her head and turned the dial to German. There was Joaquim's voice, no mistaking it: the rising vowels, the almost undetectable lisp, the emphatic *schwas*. But the intensity of his voice was something altogether different. She was used to light irony, to coy allusions and elliptical phrasing. Even without understanding the German, she knew from the voice coming through the headpiece and the body movements of the man in the glass booth that he meant every word he said.

Kate turned the dial to the next language, Italian, and scanned the booths. She matched a woman to the voice, a plump olive-skinned matron with her hair in a bun. Like Joaquim, she gestured, but her words were less fluid, more full of stops and rushed starts. Kate turned again, to English. *Following Section Three of the 1973 accords,* the male voice said, *these transactions are in keeping with the—with the fundamental principle of estate sales and free distribution. Museum purchasing is entailed by Section Five, Part Three. There we have granted the plaintiff his remedy. Here in specific we are talking about Louis Quinze jaundiced intaglio.*

Not *jaundiced,* Kate thought. He must have meant *varnished.* The translator—a balding fellow in the booth nearest her, who kept adjusting his round glasses—sounded British, but then Joaquim could sound American. Perhaps the two words, *jaundiced* and *varnished,* sounded the same in the original; or perhaps the lawyer had used another word that meant yellowing, and the translator had come up with *jaundiced* before he understood the meaning of the whole sentence, and now it was too late. The words tumbled on. "The worst," Joaquim had told her, "is German into French or English. You have to hold the entire sentence in your head until the speaker finally lands on that darn verb at the end, and then you recite it all in order while the speaker goes right on to the next subject."

"That darn verb," Kate had repeated, and looped her arms around him.

The arguments dragged on. Spectators came and went. It seemed the Poles bringing the case believed that lost Jewish treasures, just now uncovered, were being plundered without regard for the butchered culture they represented. But the arguments waxed more technical. In the glass booths, after a half-hour, new translators entered from the back, clapped headphones over their ears, adjusted their microphones, and between one breath and the next relieved the one who had been at the task. When Joaquim left his post, Kate rose and exited to the wide, hushed corridor.

Joining her, Joaquim pressed a hand into the small of Kate's back and steered her to the elevator and down into a small courtyard ringed by the building. He looked ravaged; as soon as they were outside he pulled out his pack and lit a cigarette. They sat at a small iron table. The sun had gone behind a scrim of clouds and Kate shivered in her blue dress. Joaquim leaned over, smoke in his breath, and kissed her.

"So what do you think?" she said.

"About what?"

"This case. It seems to me they've got a point. No one's brought found estates to us yet, but I'd think we'd pause before shipping anything abroad. There ought to be laws."

Joaquim looked at her intently. "Katerina," he said, "I don't know anything about the case."

"Well, neither do I, really, but just from what you were saying—"

"I don't even know what I was saying." He drew on the cigarette and stared at a corner of the courtyard. "It's just words," he said. "As soon as I hear them I must remold them. I get them to make sense in German—"

"Or French. Or English."

"Yes, or Italian, and then they leave me while the other words are pouring in. My dear, I know less about 'the case' than the mouse who nibbles in the corner."

"Oh," said Kate. Then there seemed nothing more to say. Joaquim smoked. Just when she thought he was annoyed with her, he took her hand. His warm fingers stroked her palm. Tentatively, she reached out and touched his scar, which was no more than a rough indentation on his neck.

After ten minutes, he glanced at his watch. "Time for me to go back in," he said.

"And make with the words again," said Kate.

"Yah. And make the words."

SHE BEGAN bringing Joaquim with her to the little soirees her friends had. He conversed readily, if not at length. Her friends, for their part, accepted Joaquim as one of their own. It was only as they were walking home through the long, late twilight that Kate felt her lover shedding the conviviality of the evening like a coat that had grown too heavy for the warm air.

"If you don't like them," she said at last, "we don't have to go, next time."

But they did go. And Kate would introduce herself to a new arrival. "Yes, I'm American. And Joaquim is—well, I guess Joaquim is everything. Or nothing." The new person would laugh indulgently, and Joaquim would smile patiently, and Kate would glow.

"You should see where he works," she found herself explaining one night. "It's this complete Tower of Babel, only disassembled. I mean, there they are discussing stolen Jewish property from the Holocaust, for God's sake, and Joaquim here is politely translating from Polish into German."

"What would you rather?" asked the person she was speaking to. "That he go to war over the past?"

"No! Only there should be substance, don't you think? Not just strings of legal terms."

They turned to Joaquim, who smiled thinly. "Much," he said, "gets lost in translation."

To her own surprise, Kate was becoming at once comfortable and cruel. She pushed for a raise at work and began to dress like the people they had seen in the Abbey garden. She corrected Joaquim when he used *lay* for *lie* or claimed to be hungered. She walked taller and laughed louder.

In short—Kate told herself frequently—she had changed.

WHEN SHE broke off with him, she told her friends at one of the soirees that she could be with someone who thought in another language, but not with someone who thought in no language at all. She was speaking more fluently by then. The words she had adopted had become plastic. She could say one thing and mean another, or mean two things at once. She cracked jokes, told stories about her childhood. For a short time she dated the retail manager at a rival export house, a square-jawed soccer player who had grown up in the city.

Through the cool, damp summer, she looked occasionally for Joaquim at the sidewalk lunch stand. He had not seemed hurt by the breakup. He had regarded her thoughtfully and kissed tenderly and said almost nothing. She dreamed several times of his scar, of how he had gotten it—a bar fight in Chicago, a near escape as a spy in Poland. And then she thought of him little, until the scaffolding came down on the little theater near her office.

All through one lunch she watched the workers bringing down the tiers of planks and ropes and metal tubing, their teamwork a delicate dance of climbings and lowerings. The day was windy, like the day she had met Joaquim, only it was autumn blowing in now. The workers had to step carefully, once the guard rails came down.

Underneath the scaffolding, the theater had been scraped and whitewashed, its cornices replaced, its windows refitted. Over the door, a polished brass Cupid aimed its bow at passersby, who turned to point. Kate wanted to tell someone in her office how the theater looked like a newborn baby, fragile and robust at once. But she knew them, the locals and the Americans. Like most antique dealers, they preferred the new. The theater with the scaffolding and the theater restored looked more or less the same to them.

The next day, leaving work early, Kate took the bus back out to the industrial park and the international courts. The woman at the desk would not give her a pass—but yes, she said, Mr. Roscher still worked here. Kate left a message and then waited in the lobby under a large abstract oil that made her think of pick-up sticks.

When she saw him, he was deep in conversation with the carefully coiffed translator she had seen in the Italian booth. They were speaking Italian, obviously—Joaquim used his hands in the Italian way, folding the air in front of him like pasta dough. When they reached Kate they kissed cheeks and called "Ciao," and Joaquim sat next to Kate on the cushioned bench.

"So," he said, his English still slightly inflected by Italian, "You have flown back to my territory."

"Have I?" Kate looked around. The courts were letting out. Soon all the languages of the Old World would pass by her bench. "Then you must chase me away," she said.

"But you are female."

"More important," she said, "I am not an egret."

"What are you, then?"

"I think," she said, shifting her hips to turn toward him on the bench, "I am a crane."

"Then I am a crane."

"Or perhaps I'm a heron."

"My legs are long and blue."

"I think, actually," said Kate, "my mother was a swallow."

"We are good luck for newlyweds, we *hirondelles*."

"But I must know what sort of bird you are really, before I dare enter your territory."

Joaquim's face, this close up, was a landscape of pores and laugh lines, his beard a newly planted field. On his breath Kate smelled cheap mints, and under them beer and sausage.

"The funny thing about birds," Joaquim was saying, in Kate's adopted tongue, "is that the newest species are often confused with those that are almost extinct. They remain difficult to classify."

"What song do you sing?"

"Our species," he said, "utters a lyric so rare and strange that ordinary ears cannot hear it at all."

"So they mistake it for silence?"

Joaquim nodded, the scar on his neck contracting. Kate closed her eyes. Her ears opened. She strained at first, then simply waited, to hear.

On Translating and Being Translated

BY PRIMO LEVI

Genesis tells us that the first men had only one language: This made them so ambitious and skillful, they began to construct a tower that reached the sky. God was offended by their audacity and punished them subtly: not by striking them with lightning but by confusing their tongues, thus making it impossible for them to carry on with their blasphemous work. It is certainly no coincidence that the story directly preceding this one tells of man's original sin and punishment by expulsion from paradise. We might conclude that from earliest times linguistic difference had been considered a malediction.

It continues to be a malediction to this day, as anyone knows who has had to live or, worse, work in a country where he did not know the language. Or who has had to cram a foreign language into his brain as an adult, once that mysterious material upon which memories are engraved becomes more refractory. Furthermore, there are many people who believe, more or less consciously, that a person who speaks another language is an outsider by definition, a foreigner, strange and, hence, a potential enemy, or at least a barbarian; that is, etymologically, a stutterer, a person who doesn't know how to speak, almost a nonperson. In this way, linguistic friction tends to turn into racial and political friction, another of our maledictions.

It should follow that whoever practices the craft of translation or acts as an interpreter ought to be honored for striving to limit the damage caused by the curse of Babel, but this does not usually happen. Since translation is a difficult job, the outcome is often inferior. This gives birth to a vicious circle: translators are paid poorly and those who are good at it look for a better-paying profession.

Translating is difficult because the barriers between languages are greater than is commonly believed. Dictionaries, particularly the pocket-sized ones used by tourists, may be useful for basic needs, but they constitute a dangerous font of illusion. The same can be said of the computerized, multilingual translators that have been available on the market for some time now. There is almost never any true equivalence between an expression in the source language and its corresponding one in the target language. The respective meanings may overlap in part, but it is rare for them to match, even between languages that are structurally close and historically related.

Invidia (envy) in Italian has a more specialized meaning than *envie* in French, which also signifies desire, or the Latin *invidia*, which contains hatred, aversion, as can be seen in the Italian adjective *inviso* (disliked). It is probable that the origin of this family of words goes back to *veder male*, which either means to give somebody the evil eye or denotes the discomfort we feel when looking at a person we despise, which is expressed by *non possiamo vederla* (we can't stand the sight of her). But then, in each language, the meaning of the term slips off in a different direction.

There do not appear to be languages with a wider or narrower sphere: The phenomenon is capricious. *Fregare* (rub, scrub, polish, strike, deceive, swipe, etc.) in Italian covers at least seven meanings; "to get" in English is practically infinite; *Stuhl* in German and "stool" in English mean chair but, through a chain of metonymic senses, it would be easy to reconstruct how it came to mean excrement as well. Only Italian seems to be concerned with distinguishing between the words "feather" and "down": French, English and German don't care about the difference, and *Feder* in German signifies four distinct objects—down, a quill, a pen to write with, and any kind of spring.

Other traps for translators are the so-called "false friends." For remote historical reasons (which would be amusing to investigate case by case) or because of a single misunderstanding, certain terms in one language acquire a totally different meaning, neither kindred nor contiguous with that of the other language. In German *stipendium* (cf. Italian *stipendio*, "salary") means scholarship; statist (cf. Italian *statista*, "statesman") is an extra in the theater; *kantine* (cf. Italian *cantina*, "wine cellar") is a canteen; *kapelle* (cf. Italian *capella*, "chapel") is an orchestra; *konkurs* (cf. Italian *concurso* "competition") is bankrupt; *konzept* (cf. Italian *concetto*, "concept") is a rough draft; and *konfetti* (cf. Italian *confetti*, "sugar-coated almond") is confetti. *Macarons* in French are not macaroni but rather macaroon cookies. "Aperitive," "sensible," "delusion," "ejaculation," and "compass" do not mean in English what they might seem at first sight to us (Italians). To an Italian they mean: purgative, sensitive, illusion, exclamation, an instrument for describing circles. "Second mate" is the third in command. "Engineer" is not only an engineer in our sense (as we understand it in Italian) but also one who works with motors ("engines"). These "false friends" are said to have cost more than translators dearly: after the war, a young aristocrat from our south found herself married to an American train engineer on the basis of a declaration made in good faith but wrongly interpreted.

I do not have the good fortune of knowing Romanian, a language loved passionately by linguists, but it must be teeming with false friends and represents a true minefield for translators, especially if *friptura* (cf. Italian *frittura*, "fried foods") is roasted meat, *suflet* (cf. Italian *suffle*, "souffle") is soul; *dezmierda* (cf. Italian *di merda*) means to caress; and underwear is *indispensabili*. Each of the terms listed is a snare for inattentive or inexpert translators, and it is amusing to think that the trap goes in both ways: A German runs the risk of mixing up our *statista* (statesman) with an extra in the theatre (cf. *statist* in German).

Other traps for the translator are idiomatic expressions, which are present in all languages but specific to each one. Some of them are easy to decipher, or they are so bizarre that even an inexperienced translator will notice them. I don't think anybody would write lightheartedly that it really rains "cats and dogs" in Great Britain. At other times the phrase looks more innocent, and it can get confused with plain discourse. The risk of translating word for word, as in the example of a novel in which the well-known benefactor is described as having a skeleton in his closet, is possible though not common.

A writer who does not want to embarrass his translator should abstain from using idiomatic expressions, but this would be difficult, because each one of us, whether speaking or writing, uses idioms without being aware of it. There is nothing more natural than for an Italian to say *siamo a posto* (we're OK), *fare fiasco* (to fail), *farsi vivo* (to show up), *prendere un granchio* (to make a mistake), the above-cited example *non posso vederlo* and hundreds of other similar expressions, but they make no sense to a foreigner, and not all of them are explained in bilingual dictionaries. Even *Quanti anni hai?* (literally, "How many years do you have?") is an idiomatic phrase: an English or German would say the equivalent of *Quanto vecchio sei?* ("How old are you?"), which to us (Italians) sounds ridiculous, especially if the question is addressed to a child.

Other difficulties arise from the use of local terms, common in all languages. Every Italian knows that Juventus is the name of a soccer team, and every reader of Italian newspapers knows what is being alluded to with *il Quirinale* (residence of the president of the Republic), *la Farnesina* (foreign ministry), *Piazza del Gesu* (headquarters of the Christian Democrats), *via delle Botteghe Oscure* (headquarters of the Communist Party). But if the translator has not been immersed in the culture for a long time, he will be perplexed and no dictionary can help. He will be helped by a sensitivity to linguistics, which is the most potent weapon for a translator but which is not taught in schools, just as the virtue of writing verse or composing music is not taught. This ability enables him to take on the personality of the author he is translating, to identify with him. It serves him when something in the text doesn't quite add up, doesn't work, sounds out of tune, makes no sense, seems superfluous or confused. When this happens, it may be the fault of the author, but more often it is a signal that some of the pitfalls described are present, invisible, but with their jaws wide open.

Yet avoiding the snares does not automatically make one a good translator. It is more arduous than that. It has to do with transferring the expressive force of a text from one language to another, and this is a superhuman task. Indeed, certain famous translations (such as the *Odyssey* in Latin and the Bible in German) have signaled a new direction in the history of our civilization.

Nevertheless, since a literary work is born from a profound interaction between the creativity of the author and the language in which he expresses himself, there is an inevitable loss in translation, comparable to the loss when one exchanges currency. This reduction in value is variable, large or small, according to the ability of the translator and the nature of the original text. It is usually minimal with technical or scientific texts (though here, in addition to having a command of the two languages, the translator needs to understand what he is translating and must therefore have a third competence as well) and maximal with poetry (what is left of *e vegno in parte ove non e che luca,* "and I come to a place where nothing has light," if it is reduced and translated to *giungo in un luogo buio*, "I arrive in a dark place"?).

All these "cons" might be intimidating and discouraging for aspiring translators, but some weight can be added to the "pro" side. Translation is more than a work of civilization and peace; it is uniquely gratifying. The translator is the only one who truly reads a text and reads it in its profundity, in all its layers, weighing and appraising every word and every image and perhaps even discovering its empty and false passages. When he is able to find or even invent the solution to a knot, he feels *sicut deus* (like god) without having to bear the burden of responsibility that weighs on the author's back. In this sense, the joys and fatigues of translating are as related to the process of creative writing as those of grandparents are to parents.

Many ancient and modern writers (Catullus, Foscolo, Baudelaire, Pavese) have translated literary works they felt attracted to, deriving joy for themselves and their readers, and finding a certain release in them, much like a person who takes a day off from his job and devotes himself to doing something different.

One word about the condition of a writer who finds himself being translated. Being translated is a job neither for weekdays nor holidays; in fact, it is not a job at all. It is a semi-passive state similar to that of the patient under the surgeon's knife or being on the psychiatrist's couch, rich in violent and contrasting emotions. The author who sees himself on a translated page in a language that he knows feels at one time or another flattered, betrayed, ennobled, X-rayed, castrated, planed, raped, adorned, or murdered. It is rare for him to remain indifferent toward a person, whether he knows him or not, who has stuck his nose and his fingers in his entrails. He would gladly send him (one after another or all together) his own heart properly wrapped, a check, a laurel wreath, or "godfathers."

Translated by Zaia Alexander

Sima Street[*]

BY SVETLANA VELMAR-JANCOVIC

Today, Sima Nesic would be called an interpreter; in his time they called him Sima the *targuman*. But it is not such a big difference, since *targuman* means translator. Sima could translate from seven different languages and speak just as many. As a boy, he would roam for hours through the city's main trading district, called the Dubrovnik Bazaar (today a section of Seventh of July Street between Prince Mihailo Street and Jugovic Street). He walked past cramped little wooden shops listening to what Jews, Tzintzars, and Greeks shouted out loud or muttered to themselves as they traded—words and sentences that have been continually repeated by all the world's merchants from time immemorial. Sima listened to those strange and unfamiliar sounds; his ears adapted to them and gradually domesticated them. He realized that each language has its own melody, which—when you grasp its meaning—reveals not only the secrets of that particular language, but at least one of the secrets of communication in general. The laws that govern words began to interest him more than the laws that govern people, and the more he learned about the ways of words, the more he seemed to know about the ways of men. As he grew, he spent more and more time playing the game of translating sentences from one language into another, and then into

---

[*] The title refers to a Belgrade street named for Sima Nesic, a minor Serbian police official who was killed in a well-known incident at a Belgrade public fountain in 1862.

a third and fourth. He began to believe that much evil stemmed from the fact that people were unaccustomed to listening to or understanding each other—they simply did not pay enough attention to words. In the young man's opinion, people should have been taught to handle words instead of guns. The first to hear this was his father, the hide merchant Pavle Nesic, who was shocked. And when his son declared that he would like to go abroad in order to study languages, he became deathly afraid. Being a practical and well-to-do man, Pavle Nesic sent his son to the School of Commerce in Vienna.

Every morning around ten o'clock, Sima the *targuman* stands again at the corner of Sima Street and Captain Misa Street, approximately at the place where, during his lifetime, an alley separated the Turkish and the Serbian police headquarters. Here Sima Street is empty and its noises are muffled by half-darkness. Passersby are rare; when they squeeze between the parked cars, they seem to be splashed with shadows. The place is now dark because the sunlight is completely blocked out by the new building of the College of Natural Sciences and Mathematics. Underneath that large edifice, erected where both the Turkish and the Serbian police headquarters (and, later, the Glavnjaca prison) once stood, there is a covered passageway with columns that leads to Students' Square. Sima the *targuman* now considers this another example of the misunderstanding of words: why should a building in which natural sciences and mathematics are taught block the sunlight and a view of the sky? But on that day, the third of June, 1862, the place looked much different.

It was early Sunday afternoon. Sima, the interpreter for the Serbian police, was standing next to an open window. The enormous sky over Kalemegdan radiated summer light, the smell of the Danube, and a protracted subtle feeling of tranquility. He listened to the meandering drawl of Sunday voices, which reached him from the central marketplace (Students' Square is now located where the central marketplace used to be). That soft whirlpool of noises forced itself on him and goaded him into selecting individual sounds and trying to discover their origins. He had come into his own (as one would have said then)—he had children; in five days he would turn thirty-two. But he still liked to play. With words, of course. Never before—it seemed to him—had he felt so keenly how similar that urchin of yesterday was to this dignified *targuman*. Just like that boy, Sima the *targuman* believed in the power of words; just like that boy, he knew the power of inner harmony, once it was attained. He felt that life would offer him an opportunity to do something that would reveal to others how essential words are in the process of communication. As an interpreter, he accomplished a few things: he prevented misunderstandings. But that was not enough. He hoped that he might be offered a position as an envoy to a foreign land or be invited to teach at the *lycée*. Everything was possible that afternoon, and the world lay wide open before him. With the glittering June, he felt his youthful elation rise in his blood again. Glowing inwardly, Sima surveyed green gardens on the sloping banks of the Danube; he saw the upper stories of Turkish houses peeping from the greenery, and, close up, the roof of Dositej's School of Higher Learning rising above that crossroads of light. In the distance, out of reach, the mists of the Danube drifted above the slopes. Everything looked so clean in the mild June air, so free of any foreboding. But then, suddenly a cry soared up from the bottom of the green expanse. The voices grew stronger, reached him, and became distinct: they were a bad omen. The distorted sounds contained threats and expressions of fear, and Sima felt that the mildness of the day was suddenly shattered.

Soon the news reached him: over there, on the slope, at the Cukur fountain, a Turkish soldier had wounded, or maybe even killed, a Serbian boy.

So Sima the *targuman* hurried toward the fountain. If there had been a misunderstanding, who could straighten it out better than he? If some misfortune had occurred, who could find the right word as quickly as he? The *targuman* walked hurriedly; right behind him was Djordje of Nis, a jokester who spoke an impossible dialect, and two gendarmes. They leapt over the contorted shadows of rose bushes and the drooping shadows of mulberry trees (so suitable for dreaming of love). But Sima was not thinking about love: he was thinking about the well-known Viennese banker, Tzintzar Sinna, for whom he had worked as a very young man. That banker, who had the face of an intelligent rat, would inspect his employees every morning as if sizing them up for the day's work (long experience seemed to urge him to anticipate changes in their biorhythms), and he would say: "When you are in the utmost hurry, slow down. If you don't, making a mistake is unavoidable." Sima was in a hurry now, and his strides grew longer and longer, madder and madder. The banker was warning him in vain. Sima did not slow down.

He got there at the right moment. The crowd around the fountain grew more silent as it grew larger; a mute ring tightened around the Turkish soldiers. The boy was lying on the ground, wounded in the head and perhaps still alive. At his feet was a broken water jug. Water flowed from the fountain into the silence. Sima knew what he had to do. Politely making his way through the ring, he gave a sign to the gendarmes, and they quickly tied up the soldiers. Sima bent over the boy, sadness on his face. Then he raised his head. The sorrow was gone; now was the time for resolute action. He looked at no one in particular, although everyone in the ring felt as if Sima were looking straight at him (he had also learned that trick from the ratlike banker). He said that the boy should be taken away immediately; he might still be saved. As for the Turkish soldiers, they would go with him to the Serbian police headquarters; they would be tried before a Serbian court. Serbian citizens should keep their dignity. At the same time, speaking in Turkish, he told the soldiers not to resist.

This was not the first time that Sima the *targuman* saw words—his words—accomplish something: they reached people, calmed them down, and remained in their ears. And people obeyed him: the crowd, the soldiers, the gendarmes. The boy was carried away, the handcuffed soldiers walked ahead of Sima, between the gendarmes, dozens of reflections flickered like eyes from the garden greenery, the townspeople followed Sima at a distance, and the sky was translucent, spacious, and bright.

In his imagined watchtower at the corner of Captain Misa and Sima Streets, Sima the *targuman* now always shakes his head as he watches that silly *targuman*, who—many decades before—walked with the handcuffed Turkish soldiers and a group of peaceful townspeople, suddenly strengthened by his confidence in the power of words. Sima knows what that young fool will tell him in passing; it is easy for Sima to shake his head now. Since the day he died, he has had an entire century plus a few decades more to think over everything that happened. But as a young *targuman*, he didn't have it so easy then and there, he didn't have a single moment for reflection. He had to be prepared for anything.

All eyes and ears, he walked behind the Turkish soldiers and thought about nothing. He felt numb inside. But he nevertheless saw light in the spacious sky, dimmer in the vanishing June evening. The dust was drowsy, and fragrances of linden trees, mulberry trees, wild mint, and sage blended together. Only the mildness was gone, extinguished. Although Sima walked through well-known alleys, he felt that he had entered a region where he had never been before. And again he was in a hurry (there was no reason for it), and, hurrying, he erroneously took a shortcut, the wrong one, the one that led by the Turkish police headquarters.

(The problem is that bankers are usually right.) At the windows of the Turkish building (which also served as a barracks), he suddenly noticed soldiers aiming their rifles at him; he realized their evil intention and shouted a warning. As he shouted, the arrested Turkish soldiers broke away and ran toward their barracks. Djordje of Nis rushed after them, the crack of rifle fire could be heard, and the townspeople started to draw back. Sima walked toward the soldiers who were shooting at him. He saw black smiles on their faces, and—in impeccable Turkish—he began calling to them, telling them to hold their fire, to stop, that what they were doing could lead to a disaster. His words collided with the swirling air, with the shattered light, with the shots. The soldiers fended off his words furiously, as if they were some kind of accursed disease. Sima the *targuman* shouted louder and louder; rifle fire answered him more and more rapidly. Then he could no longer feel his legs and body—he became bodiless. Only his head, which had suddenly become wobbly, sank to the bottom of the shallow darkness.

Sima the *targuman* now stands again at the corner of the street named after him, uncertain which turn to take: the one to the left, the shorter one, toward Visnjic Street, or the one to the right, the longer one, toward Francuska Street. That house that Milan Bogdanovic frequented is on the left; the house in which Slobodan Jovanovic lived is on the right. The two men thought differently in politics, but they were both perfect stylists and shared a sense of historical paradox; they might help him express what has been bothering him for more than a century: how is it that his genuine desire for harmony caused so many deaths? (For the first time in his life, Sima the *targuman* is having difficulties with words.)

Immediately after Sima was killed, Djordje of Nis was seriously wounded; he died a few hours later. On the slopes above the Save and the Danube, old hatreds flared up. The Serbs quickly seized their arms and attacked the city gates, which were manned by the by Svetlana Velmar-Jancovic

Turks. The Turks began to retreat into the Kalemegdan Fortress, and the battle (in the words of the British envoy Gregory, who supported the Serbian cause at the famous session of the House of Commons, on May 17, 1863, in London), lasted the entire night. The next day, just before noon, in the opaque June glow, foreign consuls met with Ashir, the pasha of Belgrade, and Ilija Garasanin, president of the Ministerial Council, and they reached a mutual agreement and put together the Armistice Convention, effective immediately. So one could again walk the hushed streets of Belgrade with a feeling of relative security.

This historical comedy was thus postponed until the following day. The following day was Tuesday, the fifth of June, a dazzling, magic day, full of deep light. From the direction of the Stamboul Gate (located between the present Monument of Prince Mihailo and the National Theater), a procession moved toward Palilula Cemetery, in Tasmajdan. The entire Serbian population of Belgrade, anyone who could move and was not bedridden, was in that procession. They were attending the funeral of Sima Nesic, the *targuman* with excellent prospects, braver than a hero of legend, his parents' only son, the handsome interpreter who spoke seven languages. They were attending the funeral of Sima Nesic, who was riddled with bullets, and of Djordje of Nis, who was also riddled with bullets. Sobs and liturgical chants blended with the thick heat of the morning, the water from the moat at the Stamboul Gate stank, no one lamented aloud, and sweat trickled from beneath the top hats of the officials. Flocks of large storks and wild ducks circled swiftly over Terazije and the Venice pond. There was not the slightest breath of wind under the sky. They walked toward the outskirts of the city, toward Terazije, on the hard, hot dirt road (it is Kolarac Street today). They reached a small tailor's shop and stopped at the place where today, in Kolarac Street, is a branch of the Belgrade Bank and the entrance to the underground walkway in front of the "Albania" building. With his head bowed, the tailor waited to join them. Forbidden portents hid in the dust. And then, with a whistling sound, a bomb fell right from the sunny sky. The cannonball was perfectly round, not very big, and it exploded right under Sima's coffin. The Turkish guns started to thunder from the direction of Kalemegdan. The bombardment of Belgrade had begun. It lasted for four hours and turned into a hotly disputed international issue.

Foreign correspondents later tried to maintain that the bombardment was not particularly heavy, because the poorly armed Turks were poor marksmen. Bombs exploded one after another (admittedly, in intervals, not as they did in 1915, or 1941, or 1944; however, this was also a sort of beginning). The coffin containing Sima the dead *targuman* was dropped on the hard ground, and the lid slipped a bit, although no one noticed it. The whole crowd scattered, storks and wild ducks included. Through the crack in his coffin, only the peaceful *targuman* Sima Nesic, whom they would not allow to rest, stared with his right eye at the sun, which had reached its zenith.

At his corner, Sima now shakes his head again. But he is not inclined to reproach himself anymore; he reproaches Mr. Longworth, the British consul in Belgrade. This gentleman's reports to his government almost obliterated Sima's role in history. Being a Turkophile, he was convinced that the Turks were "good-natured people" who were "rightly annoyed by the rebellious attitude of the Christian population." Accordingly, he notified his government that the riots of the third of June were incited by the Serbs, not the Turks. Fortunately, both at that time and later, some British gentlemen and others thought differently, so that the truth about his death, slightly distorted, has become historical fact. But even that is unimportant now. His name has been preserved, admittedly not as a proper noun but rather as a modifier by Svetlana Velmar-Jancovic

of another noun, written in white letters on a dark blue street sign: Sima Street. The *targuman* reads this inscription on the sign several times; he listens attentively to its sound, already somewhat unfamiliar; its meaning evades him and fades away, sharing the inevitable fate of repetition. Suddenly, he is confused: does Sima Street have anything to do with Sima the *targuman*?

Translated by Bogdan Rakic

French Lesson I: *Le Meurtre*

BY LYDIA DAVIS

See the *vaches* ambling up the hill, head to rump, head to rump. Learn what a *vache* is. A *vache* is milked in the morning, and milked again in the evening, twitching her dung-soaked tail, her head in a stanchion. Always start learning your foreign language with the names of farm animals. Remember that one animal is an *animal*, but more than one are *animaux*, ending in *a u x*. Do not pronounce the *x*. These *animaux* live on a *ferme*. There is not much difference between that word, *ferme*, and our own word for the place where wisps of straw cover everything, the barnyard is deep in mud, and a hot dunghill steams by the barn door on a winter morning, so it should be easy to learn. *Ferme*.

We can now introduce the definite articles *le*, *la*, and *les*, which we know already from certain phrases we see in our own country, such as *le car*, *le sandwich*, *le café*, *les girls*. Besides *la vache*, there are other *animaux* on *la ferme*, whose buildings are weather-beaten, pocked with rusty nails, and leaning at odd angles, but which has a new tractor. *Les chiens* cringe in the presence of their master, *le fermier*, and bark at *les chats* as *les chats* slink mewing to the back door, and *les poulets* cluck and scratch and are special pets of *le fermier*'s children until they are beheaded by *le fermier* and plucked by *la femme* of *le fermier* with her red-knuckled hands and then cooked and eaten by the entire *famille*. Until further notice do not pronounce the final consonants of any of the words in your new vocabulary unless they are followed by the letter *e*, and sometimes not even then. The rules and their numerous exceptions will be covered in later lessons.

We will now introduce a piece of language history and then, following it, a language concept.

Agriculture is a pursuit in France, as it is in our own country, but the word is pronounced differently, *agriculture*. The spelling is the same because the word is derived from the Latin. In your lessons you will notice that some French words, such as *la ferme*, are spelled the same way or nearly the same way as the equivalent words in our own language, and in these cases the words in both languages are derived from the same Latin word. Other French words are not at all like our words for the same things. In these cases, the French words are usually derived from the Latin but our words for the same things are not, and have come to us from the Anglo-Saxon, the Danish, and so on. This is a piece of information about language history. There will be more language history in later lessons, because language history is really quite fascinating, as we hope you will agree by the end of the course.

We have just said that we have our own words in English for the same things. This is not strictly true. We can't really say there are several words for the same thing. It is in fact just the opposite—there is only one word for many things, and usually even that word, when it is a noun, is too general. Keep this language concept in mind as you listen to the following example:

A French *arbre* is not the elm or maple shading the main street of our New England towns in the infinitely long, hot and listless, vacant summer of our childhoods, which are themselves different from the childhoods of French children, and if you see a Frenchman standing on a street in a small town in America pointing to an elm or a maple and calling it an *arbre*, you will know this is wrong. An *arbre* is a plane tree in an ancient town square with lopped, stubby branches and patchy, leprous bark standing in a row of similar plane trees across from the town hall, in front of which a bicycle ridden by a man with thick, reddish skin and an old cap wavers past and turns into a narrow lane. Or an *arbre* is one of the dense, scrubby live oaks in the blazing dry hills of Provence, through which a similar figure in a blue cloth jacket carrying some sort of a net or trap pushes his way. An *arbre* can also cast a pleasant shade and keep *la maison* cool in the summer, but remember that *la maison* is not wood-framed with a widow's walk and a wide front porch, but is laid out on a north-south axis, is built of irregular, sand-colored blocks of stone, and has a red tile roof, small square windows with green shutters, and no windows on the north side, which is also protected from the wind by a closely planted line of cypresses, while a pretty mulberry or olive may shade the south. Not that there are not many different sorts of *maisons* in France, their architecture depending on their climate or on the fact that there may be a foreign country nearby, like Germany, but we cannot really have more than one image behind a word we say, like *maison*. What do you see when you say *house*? Do you see more than one kind of house?

When are we going to return to our *ferme*? As we pointed out earlier, a language student should master *la ferme* before he or she moves on to *la ville*, just as we should all come to the city only in our adolescent years, when nature, or animal life, is no longer as important or interesting to us as it once was.

If you stand in a tilled field at the edge of *la ferme*, you will hear *les vaches* lowing because it is five in the winter evening and their udders are full. A light is on in the barn, but outside it is dark and *la femme* of *le fermier* looks out a little anxiously across the barnyard from the window of her *cuisine*, where she is peeling vegetables. Now the hired man is silhouetted in the doorway of the barn. *La femme* wonders why he is standing still holding a short object in his right hand. The plural article *les*, spelled *les*, as in *les vaches*, is invariable, but do not pronounce the *s*. The singular article is either masculine, *le*, or feminine, *la*, depending on the noun it accompanies, and it must always be learned along with any new noun in your vocabulary, because there is very little else to go by, to tell what in the world of French nouns is masculine and what is feminine. You may try to remember that all countries ending in silent *e* are feminine except for *le Mexique*, or that all the states in the United States of America ending in silent *e* are feminine except for Maine—just as in German the four seasons are masculine and all minerals are masculine—but you will soon forget these rules. One day, however, *la maison* will seem inevitably feminine to you, with its welcoming open doors, its shady rooms, its warm kitchen. *La bicyclette*, a word we are introducing now, will also seem feminine, and can be thought of as a young girl, ribbons fluttering in her spokes as she wobbles down the rutted lane away from the farm. *La bicyclette*. But that was earlier in the afternoon. Now *les vaches* stand at the barnyard gate, lowing and chewing their cuds. The word *cud*, and probably also the word *lowing*, are words you will not have to know in French, since you would almost never have occasion to use them.

Now the hired man swings open *la barrière* and *les vaches* amble across the barnyard, udders swaying, up to their hocks in *la boue*, nodding their heads and switching their tails. Now their hooves clatter across the concrete floor of *la grange* and the hired man swings *la barrière* shut. But where is *le fermier*? And why, in fact, is the chopping block covered with *sang* that is still sticky, even though *le fermier* has not killed *un poulet* in days? You will need to use indefinite articles as well as definite articles with your nouns, and we must repeat that you will make no mistakes with the gender of your nouns if you learn the articles at the same time. *Un* is masculine, *une* is feminine. This being so, what gender is *un poulet?* If you say masculine you are right, though the bird herself may be a young female. After the age of ten months, however, when she should also be stewed rather than broiled, fried, or roasted, she is known as *la poule* and makes a great racket after laying a clutch of eggs in a corner of the poultry yard *la femme* will have trouble finding in the morning, when she will also discover something that does not belong there and that makes her stand still, her apron full of eggs, and gaze off across the fields.

Notice that the words *poule, poulet,* and *poultry,* especially when seen on the page, have some resemblance. This is because all three are derived from the same Latin word. This may help you remember the word *poulet. Poule, poulet,* and *poultry* have no resemblance to the word *chicken,* because *chicken* is derived from the Anglo-Saxon.

In this first lesson we have concentrated on nouns. We can safely, however, introduce a preposition at this point, and before we are through we will also be using one verb, so that by the end of the lesson you will be able to form some simple sentences. Try to learn what this preposition means by the context in which it is used. You will notice that you have been doing this all along with most of the vocabulary introduced. It is a good way to learn a language because it is how children learn their native languages, by associating the sounds they hear with the context in which the sounds are uttered. If the context changed continually, the children would never learn to speak. Also, the so-called meaning of a word is completely determined by the context in which it is spoken, so that in fact we cannot say a meaning is inescapably attached to a word, but that it shifts over time and from context to context. Certainly the so-called meaning of a French word, as I tried to suggest earlier, is not its English equivalent but whatever it refers to in French life. These are modern or contemporary ideas about language, but they are generally accepted. Now the new word we are adding to our vocabulary is the word *dans*, spelled *d a n s*. Remember not to pronounce the last letter, *s*, or, in this case, the next to the last letter, *n*, and speak the word through your nose. *Dans*.

Do you remember *la femme*? Do you remember what she was doing? It is still dark, *les vaches* are gone from her sight and quieter than they were earlier, except for the one bellowing *vache* who is ill and was not let out that morning by *le fermier* for fear that she would infect the others, and *la femme* is still there, peeling vegetables. She is—now listen carefully—*dans la cuisine*. Do you remember what *la cuisine* is? It is the only place, except perhaps for the sunny front courtyard on a cool late summer afternoon, where *une femme* would reasonably peel *les legumes*.

La femme is holding a small knife *dans* her red-knuckled hand and there are bits of potato skin stuck to her wrist, just as there are feathers stuck in *le sang* on the chopping block outside the back door, smaller feathers, however, than would be expected from *un poulet*. The glistening white peeled *pommes de terre* are *dans une bassine* and *la bassine* is *dans* the sink, and *les vaches* are *dans la grange*, where they should have been an hour ago. Above them the bales of hay are stacked neatly *dans* the loft, and near them is a calf *dans* the calves' pen. The rows of bare light bulbs in the ceiling shine on the clanking stanchions. *Stanchion* is another word you will probably not have to know in French, though it is a nice one to know in English.

Now that you know the words *la femme*, *dans*, and *la cuisine*, you will have no trouble understanding your first complete sentence in French: *La femme est dans la cuisine*. Say it over until you feel comfortable with it. *La femme est*—spelled *e s t* but don't pronounce the *s* or the *t*—*dans la cuisine*. Here are a few more simple sentences to practice on: *La vache est dans la grange. La pomme de terre est dans la bassine. La bassine est dans* the sink.

The whereabouts of *le fermier* is more of a problem, but in the next lesson we may be able to follow him into *la ville*. Before going on to *la ville*, however, do study the list of additional vocabulary:

> *le sac*: bag
> *la grive*: thrush
> *l'alouette*: lark
> *l'aile*: wing
> *la plume*: feather
> *la hachette*: hatchet
> *le manche*: handle
> *l'anxiété*: anxiety
> *le meurtre*: murder

The Servile Path

BY MICHAEL SCAMMELL

Translators are the ghosts of the literary profession, invisible men who don a mask and pretend to be someone else. Translating is a peculiar occupation, especially when the mask you wear belongs to a writer who is still alive, as Vladimir Nabokov very much was when I worked for him. To impersonate such a protean stylist would have been hard for anyone and certainly exceeded the powers of a near beginner like myself, but I was young and brash and willing to try. Nabokov valued me, I now think, precisely because I was green and malleable enough to bend to his whims and listen to what he said. And when in one respect I ceased to listen, our collaboration ended.

I met him forty years ago, by sheer coincidence. I was a graduate student in Russian literature at Columbia University, and in the fall of 1959 I rented a room from an elderly Russian émigré named Anna Feigin. Anna found me unbearably supercilious at first and so insufferably "English" that she longed to throw me out. Luckily she couldn't afford to: I was the only one who had answered her advertisement.

My aloofness issued more from self-doubt than from national stereotypes, and my periodic arrogance disguised an inferiority complex rather than the reverse, which Anna quickly realized. "I am extremely pleased with my new tenant," she wrote to a first cousin some time after I arrived. "He is decent, kind and modest, and works all the time." It is immodest of me to quote this, of course, but it is relevant to another part of this story. Anna was especially impressed by the fact that I had studied Russian, had spent several months living with a family of Russian émigrés in Paris, and was reasonably fluent in French as well as Russian. "In short, I've never seen the like around here. And he brought a whole library of books with him."

Anna's letter now resides in the Berg Collection of the New York Public Library, where I read it not very long ago, but at the time I knew little about the nature of her feelings toward me. I did, however, begin to get to know her better. Short to begin with, Anna was bent even shorter by arthritis; the creases in her friendly face would often deepen as she grimaced with the pain of a sudden movement. Despite having a cousin and a few friends in New York, she did not like to go out much. One of her reasons for having a tenant, she told me, was that she feared attack if she lived alone. I told her not to be afraid. I had grown up in tougher circumstances in a working-class family in England and was sure I could take care of her (those were the days before the drug boom and the appearance of guns on every street corner).

Anna was fascinated by my stories. The daughter of rich Jewish parents, and a concert pianist by training, she would have had a glittering career if the Bolsheviks had not forced her to move to Berlin. Like many Russian émigrés, she had moved to France to flee the Nazis and from there had escaped by the skin of her teeth to America on the eve of World War II. She knew about privation and poverty but had little concept of the English class system that I criticized so bitterly.

We discussed Russian literature in the kitchen she let me share with her. I expressed, among many other opinions, admiration for Nabokov's provocative study of Gogol and praised the novel *Pnin*, his affectionate portrait of an absented-minded Russian scholar at sea on an American campus. I told her that I was also interested in translation and had translated parts of Chekhov and Lermontov into English. In late fall I told her about my first publishing commission, to translate *Cities and Years*, a modernist novel by the Soviet author Konstantin Fedin. Anna made a face at the word "Soviet," but was pleased by my success. As I now know, she also reported these conversations to her cousin.

In February, 1960, Anna unexpectedly invited me to dinner. It was a unique occasion. Despite our many friendly chats, I had never been through the door that led to her parlor and private living quarters. On the night in question I knocked on her door, entered, and was solemnly introduced to a tall avuncular gentleman with an Edwardian air, a plummy English lisp, and a firm handshake, and to a perfectly coiffed, petite, white-haired lady, who looked perfectly elegant in the perfect French manner—Mr. and Mrs. Vladimir Nabokov. An immensely tall young man, about my age, uncoiled himself from a low armchair and introduced himself as their son, Dmitri.

Anna was Vera Nabokov's first cousin, and not just any cousin but virtually Vera's elder sister. They had lived in the same apartment in Berlin before Vera's marriage to Vladimir. Anna had typed Nabokov's first novel, *Mary*. The three of them had gone on holidays together, had planned to build a joint summer house, and were close neighbors throughout most of their years in Europe. It was the Nabokovs who had brought Anna to the United States from occupied France. And Vera was the cousin to whom Anna had been writing about me, which is why her letters are now in the Berg Collection.

It would be nice to say that I have a vivid memory of that first meeting, but I don't. I do remember deep armchairs, an oriental rug, vases of flowers, and a table set with fine china. But the rest is a blur. Nabokov was basking in the afterglow of his huge success with *Lolita*. The novel had turned him into a world-class celebrity and had made him rich. Stanley Kubrick had paid an enormous sum for the movie rights, and Nabokov had just returned to New York from five luxurious months in Europe—his first visit there since his hasty escape from the Nazis in 1940. He was now on his way to Hollywood to write a script for Kubrick. More importantly for my immediate future, Nabokov had just come to an arrangement with Putnam to publish translations of several of his early Russian novels in English.

A short time after that dinner, Anna casually asked if I could give her one of my translations to send to Nabokov. I handed her a short story, "Gusev," by Anton Chekhov. I received a letter back from Vera, now in Hollywood, to say that she and her husband had no copy of Chekhov in Russian to compare my work with, but would I care to translate three pages from Chapter 4 of Nabokov's last Russian novel, *The Gift*?

"If my husband suggests a sample to be translated out of this book it is because you will have no difficulty in borrowing a copy from my cousin, while we shall be able to check your version using a copy we have here . . . My husband asks me to add that the passage in question is difficult"—"much more difficult," she herself added, "than Chehov." Vera wrote that publishers would pay six dollars a page, a handsome price at the time, and that her husband was frequently asked by publishers to suggest to them the names of suitable translators.

The three pages began with a poem, which I was asked not to bother with, and a passage whose opening sentences I translated as follows:

A sonnet, apparently barring the way, but perhaps, on the contrary, providing a secret link which would explain everything—if only man's mind could withstand that

explanation. The soul sinks into a momentary dream—
and now with the peculiar theatrical vividness of those
risen from the dead, they come out to meet us: father
Gavriil, in a silk pomegranate chasuble, with a long staff,
an embroidered sash across his wide stomach, and with
him, already illumined by the sun, an extremely attractive
little boy—pink, awkward, and delicate.

Yes, this was certainly different from Chekhov.

It was a month before I sent back the three pages, not because
they were so difficult (though they were certainly that) but because
I had my graduate studies to attend to. Vera wrote to thank me
for the translation. "My husband thinks it is perfectly wonderful."
"Pomegranate," a literal translation, was amended by Nabokov
to "cerise" and later to "garnet-red"; the wide stomach became a
"big" one, and there were more changes further on, but the passage survives recognizably in the published version. Vera asked if I
would be prepared to translate the rest of Chapter 4. Son Dmitri
was planning to translate most of the novel, but he had just won
a scholarship to sing with La Scala in Milan and doubted if he
could manage the whole book. "If this offer is acceptable, I would
like to add one more thing: my husband always reserves the right
to make any changes in the finished translations. He wants from
the translator as close an adherence to the original as possible."

The offer surprised me more than it should have. Vera had covered herself by saying that Nabokov might suggest my name to
publishers if he liked my translations. Barely a word had been
said about translating Nabokov himself. I had been covertly tested
without knowing it. But I was happy to have passed the test and
had no problem with Nabokov's last stipulation. Although I
hadn't then heard of his injunction to translators to follow "the
servile path," I firmly believed that the translator's job was to

come between author and reader as little as possible. As a translator, I was servile by instinct and therefore closer to his ideal than I realized.

BY NOW it was the early summer of 1960. I had traveled out to the small fishing village of Sausalito, just north of San Francisco, where friends told me I would find the Beat poets and their allies. Oddly enough, at the very moment I was drifting into the orbit of the great mandarin of modern American prose, I was searching for his polar opposite: the literary avant-garde. As a young would-be writer of twenty-five, I preferred the "hot" prose of D.H. Lawrence and the young Saul Bellow as well as the breathless Kerouac to the chilly baroque splendors of Nabokov. True, *Lolita* had been pretty hot in its way, but it struck me as more like a baked Alaska: hot, sweet meringue on the outside, ice-cold at the core. In truth, I was less enamored of Humbert Humbert's masturbatory monologues than I dared own up to at the time.

I was too late for the Beat poets (and too early for Haight-Ashbury). I settled down to a lonely bachelor life in my room in Sausalito (rented to me by yet another Russian émigré) and started on *Cities and Years*. Vera was soon in touch with a "better plan" than before. Would I translate another Nabokov novel, *The Luzhin Defense*, in its entirety? The book, about an errant chess genius, was shorter and easier than *The Gift*, but the translation was needed "as soon as possible." I demurred. I had to finish *Cities and Years* first and would be returning to New York to prepare for my graduate orals. Vera came back with a new suggestion: Dmitri was overwhelmed by his music studies, so would I do Chapters 2 through 5 of *The Gift* and revise Dmitri's Chapter 1 to suit?

Vera already took it for granted that I would translate at least one novel, if not two, but I was still a reluctant debutant. Nabokov, it must be remembered, although an instant celebrity, was not yet a literary colossus. *Lolita* had been a *succès de scandale* as much as it had been a literary event. The nine novels, several dozen short stories, innumerable poems, and handful of plays Nabokov had written in Russian were completely unknown to the English speaking world (and also to me), while *Pale Fire*, *Ada*, and all of the later works were still to come. I admired what prose I had seen, but I was far from falling in love with it.

Nevertheless, I was highly honored and flattered by Nabokov's attention, and the six dollars a page spoke loudly to an impoverished graduate student. Vera sent the outlines of a contract. It was a wonderfully simple document, typed on one and a half pages by Vera herself. I would undertake to deliver a complete translation of *The Gift* within one calendar year and would revise the first hundred pages or so completed by Dmitri. But I balked at Vera's stipulation that the translation was to be "faithful, exact, and complete." How, I wanted to know, would the courts define "faithful" and "exact"? I didn't anticipate any difficulties between us, I wrote back, but "I would prefer to have these words either omitted or faithfully and exactly defined."

This cocksure phrase seemed rather witty to me at the time and was a hint of the tone I was to adopt in subsequent correspondence. Like many insecure individuals, I was always fiercer on paper than in the flesh. Fortunately, Vera was tolerant and quietly dropped the words I objected to without comment. Nabokov reserved the right to make "any changes and/or corrections in the finished text" he found "necessary or desirable," and also the right to dispose of it as he wished. It was enough. We signed the contract in August 1960.

AT THE end of the summer I acquired my first automobile and drove erratically to Los Angeles on the beginning leg of a transcontinental trip home. The Nabokovs were staying in Mandeville Canyon Road and invited me to lunch. We ate on a pretty terrace fringed with hibiscus, palm trees, and subtropical bushes that I did not recognize. Nabokov, little suspecting the difficulties that lay ahead, was in an expansive mood and professed himself extremely satisfied with his *Lolita* script. He warmly approved of my plan to write a dissertation on the structure of *Anna Karenina* and expressed his deep admiration for Tolstoy.

It was six more months before I could get to the translation of *The Gift*, which, contrary to my hopes, turned out to be a long-distance collaboration with the author. I started it in New York, did most of the work in Southampton, England, completed the book in Paris and Milan, and mailed the final chapter from Ljubljana in the former Yugoslavia (Vera wrote that the book had been opened by customs but had made it across the border with no losses.) The Nabokovs during this time moved from Los Angeles to Nice (spending the winter on the Promenade des Anglais), then to Stresa, Italy, to Champex in the Swiss Alps, where Nabokov hunted butterflies, to Geneva, and finally to Montreux. We did at one point discuss a meeting to go over the text together, but in the end it proved impossible, and the whole thing was done by correspondence.

Correspondence, in this case, meant correspondence with Vera. It is a commonplace that Nabokov never wrote letters. There were exceptions to the rule: the famous correspondence with Edmund Wilson, for instance. But it was generally true. As Stacy Schiff has shown in her biography of Vera, it was a convenient way for Nabokov not only to guard his time but to erect yet one more barrier between himself and the outside world. In my case, as I later saw in the Berg Collection, he annotated the letters and lists of questions I sent to him, and Vera wrote the final replies, often reproducing the exact phraseology he had used in his notes. In the three years of our collaboration, I received only three letters signed by him.

Much of the correspondence was taken up with technical matters. The transliteration of Russian names and letters into English, to which Nabokov would devote many pages in his introduction to his translation of *Eugene Onegin*, was a particularly hot topic. Reading over Dmitri's chapter after it had been corrected by Nabokov, I had the nerve to observe that "complete chaos reigns in the transliteration of Russian characters . . . particularly over the Russian vowels." I objected to Nabokov's spelling of "Chehov," which sounded funny to the English ear in place of the customary Chekhov, said I preferred "tsar" to the Germanic (and unfortunately American) "czar," and contested a number of other spellings that looked awkward or comical or Gallic to me.

Nabokov, via Vera, responded mildly to these strictures, accepting "tsar" and a number of other suggestions, and also sending me a copy of his *Onegin* system of transliteration. On the subject of "Chehov," however, he and Vera were adamant.

My husband . . . absolutely insists on Chehov (not Tchechov—a semi-Germanism—or Tscekhov, etc). He assures you that it does not matter that Chehov sounds funny to an Englishman: being much more nearly correct than the other varieties, it will gradually become more accepted . . . He also assures you that Tschekhov, Tchechov, etc. sound even funnier to a Russian than Chehov does to an Englishman.

I was riled by both the tone and the content of this little lecture, and after an elaborately polite discussion of the pros and cons of various transliteration systems and their inevitable imperfections, I couldn't resist a retaliation.

In replying to [my suggestions], you quote about five ludicrous spellings for Chekhov and refuse them all successfully—but without ever saying that I never suggested them, or that I find them as ridiculous as you do. Nor do you anywhere quote the suggestion that I did make— namely the spelling I use above . . . I trust you will not condemn me on the basis of some monstrous, mythical Tschekhov in the future.

And that was not all.

You say in your letter that "it does not matter that Chehov sounds funny to an Englishman" since other varieties sound even funnier to a Russian. Forgive me, but I was under the impression that the Russian ear had been catered to in the Russian, and that this edition was intended for the English-speaking world.

There was more in the same vein, and Vera nicely apologized in her next letter. But she did not give way on the spelling of "Chehov."

Later we got into another altercation over Tolstoy—not the name but the name of one of his works. I had written to say that my dissertation was to be a structural analysis of *Anna Karenina*. "*Anna Karenin* (not *Karenina*, please!)," replied Vera. I knew what she meant. The "a" is merely the feminine form of "Karenin" that logically shouldn't exist in English. But again I dug in my heels. "Of course you are right, strictly speaking, but . . . Anna came into English literature and into my life as Karenina, and Karenina she will remain." I then (mimicking Nabokov) scanned the two names and innocently added that to use "Karenin" would be "like translating a Pushkin line accurately and completely destroying the rhythm." Little did I realize the aptness of that lighthearted comment.

Another intricate subject was the question of what kind of English to use for the translation—English English or American English? It mattered less to Nabokov's elaborately formal prose than it would have to that of a more colloquial writer, but the question came up more often than I had expected. I boasted (unjustifiably, I now think) that I was comfortable with "either dialect" but found it confusing to come across "tram" and "streetcar" on the same page, and later complained: "You have changed my anglicisms to Americanisms and my Americanisms to anglicisms—which way do you want me to go?" It turned out that I was more worried about this question than Nabokov was; it didn't matter to him nearly as much as transliteration.

> American English, please, whenever there is an essential divergence between the two. On the whole, however, my husband thinks that the idiom should be more or less neutral. He does not mind if "tram" and "streetcar" appear on the same page.

By the end of July 1961 I had finished Chapter 4 and by mid-August was close to the end of Chapter 5. Vera wrote to say that her husband was "amazed at the speed with which you work." I, too, am amazed when I look back. To say I was inspired would be misleading. On the contrary: I wasn't moved by Nabokov's prose at all. I was too young and too ignorant. I found its rhythms florid, mannered, and artificial, and its metaphorical tropes reductive. Instead of art being ennobled by its likeness to nature, nature was likened to a collection of artistic effects. This reversal of the usual order was part of Nabokov's originality. In his ludic universe, life imitated art, not the other way round. All was artifice and device, an approach that I was able to savor only with maturity. But at that early age I did not respond; Nabokov's prose was the opposite of the spontaneity and romanticism of my favorite writers.

What was left—and it still was plenty—was the novel as a glorious puzzle, a box of tricks that the enchanted reader makes his way through as he opens more and more compartments. In some ways it was a metaphor for the very act of translation I was engaged in, since every text presents itself to the translator as a succession of obstacles to be overcome. In the case of *The Gift*, whose narrative was deliberately strewn with elaborate traps and decoys, the challenge was doubled, and there were moments when I seriously doubted my ability to cope: "Your husband's text is so crammed with nuances, so rich in diminutives, augmentatives, archaisms, slang, rare words, etc.," I wrote early on in my work, "that I despair of ever rendering even a tenth part of it into English. A pale copy seems to be about the best I can produce." But the battle of wits between me and the text strongly appealed to my competitive instincts, and I did improve with practice.

On a syntactical level, Nabokov turned out to be surprisingly easy to translate. His Russian was saturated with echoes of French and English, and his sentence structure was very Latinate: like Tolstoy's. Compared with Chekhov (despite Vera's boast), and especially compared with Gogol or Dostoyevsky, whom I was later to translate, Nabokov composed sentences that were not all that difficult to dismantle and reconstruct, and this sped up the work immensely. It was on the lexical level that he became so fiendishly difficult, and here I truly floundered. One problem was that I didn't have a sufficient number and variety of dictionaries at my elbow in England to resolve the knottier problems, whereas Nabokov's responses to my questions were littered with "see *Webster's*," "see *O.E.D.*," etc., which offered an interesting insight into his own procedures. As Homer or the Bible are to some writers, dictionaries were to Nabokov. But even with a mountain of reference works at my disposal I could never have been equal to Nabokov's immensely rich and idiosyncratic vocabulary.

I was also obliged to rush through the translation much faster than I would have wished in order to meet our agreed-upon deadline of August. If there was an excess of errors, I explained to Vera, it was due to speed more than incompetence. I needn't have hurried. Nabokov was delayed by the exacting and exhausting work required of him to finish *Pale Fire*, which was now scheduled to appear before *The Gift*, and he said he wouldn't be able to get to the translation for several months. In view of the increased time available I offered to take the last couple of chapters back and rework them, but Vera said it would not be necessary. I was still hoping that I would be able to get together with Nabokov and go over the translation in person, and there was talk of a rendezvous in England or New York, but nothing could be decided until *Pale Fire* was finished.

Meanwhile Nabokov continued to answer the various questions and problems I had raised concerning the early chapters. There was one passage in which I tried to emulate the protagonist's rhyming schemes in English. "'Crying' immediately suggested lying and dying under sighing pines on a silent night. 'Waterfall' prompted my muse to recall some long forgotten ball. 'Flowers' called for hours about bowers which were ours," and so on for the better part of a page.

Nabokov carefully read through my suggestions and sent back the following: "*Letuchiy* (flying) immediately grouped *tuchi* (clouds) over the *kruchi* (steeps) of the *zhguchey* (burning) desert and of *neminuchey* (inevitable) fate," etc. I was not to diverge from the servile path even for a moment. Those familiar with Nabokov's eccentric translation of *Eugene Onegin* (especially his commentary) will recognize the principle. Nabokov's version was more faithful to the original's literal sense, but I couldn't suppress a pang over the loss of English rhythm and wordplay.

In Chapter 3 I encountered a characteristic blizzard of butterfly names and was completely flummoxed until Nabokov sent a list of equivalents. Malayan hawkmoth, swallowtail, painted lay, Amandus blue, Freya fritillary, and so on (a list that was just as beautiful in English as in the original Russian). Determined to do better with a long description of mushroom hunting, I labored for several days and through several dictionaries to do the passage justice, but when the emended text came back Nabokov had cut the entire passage. Mushroom hunting is a continental passion that means little to Anglo-Saxons, so Nabokov took an uncharacteristically pragmatic view and simply erased the scene.

It was, of course, an education in itself to work with him even by correspondence. I remember one page coming back with a long list of Russian synonyms for verbs depicting light in the margins, with their English equivalents attached: glimmer, glow, gleam, shine, twinkle, sparkle, dazzle, coruscate, and so on. There were little lessons on verbs of motion (a complicated business in Russian), and extensive instruction on botany, zoology, entomology, and every possible aspect of natural history.

I am often asked why it was that Nabokov even needed a translator into English. After all, the author of *Bend Sinister*, *The Real Life of Sebastian Knight*, *Pnin*, and *Lolita* was hardly lacking in English prose style. I myself asked him that question when I visited him in Los Angeles, and was given two reasons. The first was that he needed the precious time to go on writing original works in English. After all, he was already in his early sixties when he made his literary and popular breakthrough, and he wanted to do much more. The second reason, he said, was that he wanted to spare himself the temptation of rewriting his early Russian books in English instead of simply translating them.

Both reasons held largely true for *The Gift*. His corrections did border on revision at times, but Jane Grayson, an English professor who has studied these matters, states that on the whole he did not try to rewrite this important novel but carried out a creative reworking of my literal translation. This can be seen, says Grayson, if the translation is compared with the translations of earlier novels such as *King, Queen, Knave* and *Laughter in the Dark*, and *Despair* (all initially translated by Dmitri), which Nabokov rewrote extensively.

My own mission was to turn Nabokov's Russian prose into more or less fluent English without either falling into the pit of literalism or sliding into the swamp of interpretation. I was adjured to reproduce the original as faithfully as I could but was expressly forbidden to be "creative." That was Nabokov's prerogative, as he confirmed in one of his rare signed letters:

Besides correcting direct mistakes I have dealt with a number of inaccuracies. In a few cases the changes are meant to simplify or clarify matters, or else they reflect my own predilections of style. I realize quite well that the odd turn of some of your sentences is owing to your desire to be faithful to every detail of the original, as I had asked you to be; but here and there you have been handicapped by not quite knowing the exact meaning of a Russian term, especially in the case of homonyms or words deceptively resembling one another. I have put an exclamation mark in the margin . . . merely in order to draw your attention to these shortcomings. The book is very hard to translate and in many cases you have found clever and elegant solutions. On the whole you have done a very good job.

In my general euphoria over the relative success of my translation of *The Gift*, and because we had not been able to meet, I tried to engage Nabokov in more personal correspondence. At one point I asked him about writers I thought might have influenced him, including Andrey Bely and the Russian Formalists. I also mentioned my admiration for the French painter Jean Dubuffet and asked Nabokov what he thought of Dubuffet's collages of butterfly wings. Nabokov's reply was succinct.

> *James Joyce*. I greatly admire *Ulysses*. *Bely*. *Petersburg* is one of the three or four greatest novels of our time. I have never read *The Good Soldier*. *Robbe-Grillet*. Best French writer—but have never read his manifestoes. *Shlovski*. I seem to remember an essay of his on *Onegin*. Never met him. What is termed "formalism" contains certain trends absolutely repulsive to me. Collage of *butterfly wings*. A ridiculous mutilation.

By this time it had been agreed that I would translate a second novel of Nabokov's, *The Luzhin Defense* (simplified to *The Defense* in English). In the interim I had married, and I successfully applied to Vera—for the first time—for an advance to help me rent a small apartment in New York. Vera sent the money instantly. She was a stickler in monetary matters but always treated me generously. I was so pleased to be paid regularly for such enjoyable work that I was the least demanding of employees when it came to money, but Vera insisted on paying for extras, such as checking Dmitri's Chapter 1 of *The Gift*, and always paid my postal expenses. Later, when a long chapter (in addition to Dmitri's Chapter 1) ran in *The New Yorker*, Vera sent me a handsome check as my share of the publication fee, which came as a complete surprise. A realist might say that such payment was only just, but I was a total novice in those days and was delighted by this unexpected bonus. I am sure that my eagerness to please contributed to our cloudless partnership that first year, and the Nabokovs responded with great courtesy and cordiality.

I started translating *The Defense* in the spring of 1962, shortly after getting married, but the work went slowly. I now had a job teaching Russian language and literature at Hunter College and was working on my dissertation in addition to translating. Since my wife and I were far too busy to take a honeymoon, we delayed it until the summer. We rented a former farmhouse in Brooklin on the coast of Maine, and I spent most of the two months we stayed there finishing the translation. Solzhenitsyn once told me that he read Karl Marx on his honeymoon. I translated Nabokov. I'm not sure which of us had the harder job, but I undoubtedly got the better deal.

The Defense was indeed shorter and easier than *The Gift*, as Vera had suggested, and by August 1962 it was completed. The Nabokovs had gone on vacation. I didn't know where they were, and we ourselves had decided to drive across Canada and visit the World's Fair in Seattle, so I took the typescript of the translation with me to await word of where to send it. In Seattle I heard from Vera that they had been butterfly hunting in Zermatt but were now in France, and could I send the translation?

At this point my relations with the Nabokovs were extremely cordial. We still had not managed to meet to discuss the translation of *The Gift* in person. Vera wrote to say that they had hoped to see me during a visit to New York in June, but I had already left for Maine. Perhaps they would manage it another time. We had also discussed the prospect of my translating more of Nabokov's Russian novels. I had recently hesitated before signing a contract to do the first American translation of Dostoyevsky's *Crime and Punishment* because of that prospect, but Nabokov had said to go ahead. There would be quite a wait before the first two translations of his Russian work were out, and we could think about the future later.

I had every reason to feel pleased with myself, and when I mailed *The Defense* from a small town in Washington State called Walla Walla, I added chattily that we were there to watch our first rodeo. Vera replied:

> It was nice to hear you have had so much fun from your trip to the West. I hope, though, that you hated the rodeo as much as I did: all those blockheads on poor deliberately tortured horses ... those miserable calves half-crazed with fright. Almost as disgusting as the corrida.

Without knowing it, I had touched a sensitive nerve: Vera's hatred of all forms of cruelty to animals. There was something in Vera's governessy tone, however, that provoked me too, and I sent off an impassioned defense of bullfights and rodeos that ended intemperately:

> Perhaps it has something to do with the masculine temperament and sensibilities. There is supposed to be an element of sadism in most of us (men) and I can certainly sense it in myself from time to time. I would be interested to know whether your husband agrees with you in this, but then he has at least one distinguished predecessor in D.H. Lawrence (*The Plumed Serpent*). For myself (and this is said utterly without rancor), I find it incomprehensible why butterflies should be stuck on pins.

The butterfly crack, with or without rancor, was indefensible, and there cannot be many instances of Nabokov being compared to

D.H. Lawrence, nor of him being asked about sadism. My jejune
letter brought forth an even more wrathful retort.

Cruelty is probably the worst evil that exists, and ever
existed in the world, and—in my opinion—should be
combatted vigorously, both within and without one's personality. And sadism is the worst form of cruelty. Yes, my
husband is with me in this appraisal, all the way. Inci-
dentally, you do not believe, do you, that anyone in his
right mind would be sticking pins into live butterflies? I
am sorry if I sound didactic but I do think that logic is
a healthy discipline for thought. But the way you reason
one would be justifying Nazi extermination camps and
Soviet Che-Ka next.

Very had clearly lost her temper, but I was too bumptious and
blind to see it. I replied:

If logic can't distinguish between prison camps and rodeos
it doesn't really recommend itself to me as a tool. I'm sure
I feel the same way as you do about most forms of cruelty
around us. It's just that I draw the line at butterflies—I
would rather see a live butterfly than a dead one (butterflies *do* die, don't they?)—and you draw the line at calves
being roped and flung to the ground (although they don't
die).

I cannot now defend my provocative comments on the sacred
butterflies, nor the shrillness of my tone, but at the time, unbe-
knownst to myself, I did find one defender. Vera was in the habit
of writing to Anna to check up on me or inform her about my
progress. After our first meeting in New York, for example, Vlad-

imir had come to the conclusion that I was gay and had continued in this delusion for about a year, until Anna informed him of my engagement. Now Vera wrote to Anna to complain about my intemperate letters. Anna replied that Vera and Vladimir were overreacting. "You completely fail to take into account that he is only twenty-five or twenty-six, and you are much older. You forget, or maybe you don't know, that he comes from a poor, and more importantly, a deprived background." Here Anna enumerated the various details of my English working-class childhood that she had picked up from our chats in her kitchen, and added: "I don't think he was ever in good society."

There may also have been a complaint about my translations, for Anna wrote: "How on earth could he ever have known Russian well enough to satisfy Volodya's demands? And why on earth did you decide to give him such an important book? I often wondered but never asked." And Anna defended me once again on the cruelty charge: "As for his remarks about sadism, I don't see any stupidity in this, I just think of his twenty-five years."

I was completely unaware of this exchange and continued to correspond with Vera as if nothing had happened. I had a long-standing ambition to do a full translation of Bely's *Petersburg* (only an abridged translation existed at the time). I wrote to Nabokov to ask if he would consider writing an introduction: his name would make all the difference in selling it to publishers. Vera replied that he "very much approves a project to translate *Petersburg*. Bely is a perfectly marvelous writer." Unfortunately, Nabokov was too swamped with his own projects to consider it. It never occurred to me to ask him simply to recommend me to a publisher, though perhaps he would have declined by then.

In October 1962 my wife gave birth to a daughter. Vera sent gifts, including a tiny loden cloak that has since become a family heirloom. The next summer we moved to England. I had been intending to read the proofs of both *The Gift* and *The Defense*, as we had agreed, but Nabokov wrote to say it would not be necessary, and with that our correspondence lapsed.

There was, however, an epilogue. Soon after my arrival in England I wrote a letter to the editor of *Encounter* suggesting that Mary McCarthy's marvelously detailed and sympathetic decoding of *Pale Fire* (a novel I did not care for) must have been inspired, if not half written, by Nabokov. It was a silly and tactless thing to write—and completely wrong. Nabokov himself was amazed by McCarthy's perspicacity and complimented her on it. Years later I apologized to Mary for my insolence, and she was highly amused, though I doubt if Nabokov was.

Later still, I was caught in the same trap I had set for Mary. In 1968 a friend sent me a copy of the *Saturday Evening Post* containing an essay by the novelist Herbert Gold. Gold had taken over Nabokov's teaching post at Cornell and later interviewed him for *The Paris Review*. In his essay Gold wrote about Nabokov's well-known penchant for hoaxes and said that the name "Michael Scammell" on the title page of *The Gift* had instantly struck him as an invention. "Scammell" was an unlikely name and an anagram for "le masque." Nabokov had translated the novels himself and hidden behind this transparent pseudonym.

Gold was eventually assured by Nabokov that I existed, but his speculation was a fine illustration of the anonymity of translators and of my own anonymity in particular. I had just translated an extremely bad novel (*A Thousand Illusions*, by the not untalented Soviet dissident Valery Tarsis) for filthy lucre, and I was looking around for a way of distancing myself when Gold's article arrived. Seizing on his notion of my fictionality, I signed the translation "Michel Le Masque," a name that is still listed in all the catalogues.

The masked translator thus acquired a mask of his own. It was pleasant to know that the supreme master of disguises was indirectly, and unknowingly, responsible for the invention of this wholly mythical translator. And it is nice to think that our ultimately prickly relationship ended with a joke.

The Task of This Translator

BY TODD HASAK-LOWY

The underlying cause was Ted's odd but well-funded entrepreneurial ambition. Here was a guy whose not-so-insignificant inheritance, intermittently delivered by bank wire at the command of his healthy-as-a-bull father, who was uninterested in the morbid suspense of wills and impatient sons, might have long ago been squandered had his visions been a bit more grand. Every eight months or so since his eighteenth birthday, Ted would be overtaken by some ultimately small, but at the time monumental, vision, a vision he cultivated and situated in his head alongside his father's own capitalist ascent (having to do with luggage). They never, none of them, not a one, ever amounted to a thing, though a few, bizarrely, developed little lives of their own, this due to lingering ads in the yellow pages and the like. All the same, they kept coming. The fourth of which interests us here. Ted would get an idea, for an invention, a service, a middleman operation of some sort, whatever, and he would first do two things: (1) name it—the invention, service, or middleman operation; and upon the completion of step 1, (2) pay a good friend with graphic-design experience plenty of money to design a logo, letterhead, business cards, ads, and anything else along these lines, seeing how money was not an object, not really.

The fourth such vision, the one of relevance here, came to the destined-to-be-wealthy-despite-himself aspiring man of means during his third year at a ferociously overpriced, nearly prestigious private college. One of his classes that year, which he took by mistake, he wasn't even in the right building, was named "Transnationalism and Borders" or something like that. Ted read only four pages, right around one-half percent, of the overall assigned readings, but diligently attended the class, where he sat silently, attuned to the goings-on with the same steady but vaguely sterile interest with which one follows a sporting event broadcast through a TV halfway across a loud bar. He gleaned nothing tangible from·the class, but the word "transnationalism" did grow on him. The instructor, naturally, used the term a bunch, and though this particular student never completely grasped its most limited meaning, let alone larger implications, Ted did develop a real fondness for the prefix "trans." It cropped up in his doodles, and over time its semantic cousins—transportation, translation, transcendence, Transylvania, transplant, transsexual, transmission—whenever they appeared, pricked him somehow. And so a vision was on its way, this one, as mentioned earlier, being the fourth in a longer, still-proliferating series. Ted concluded that all this "trans" stuff had big implications for the future—he did gather from his instructor, who seemed quite passionate about the whole thing, that the future was about transnationalism, or something to that effect—and that a business, a one day giant corporation, was waiting to sprout from this trans moment in world history. Ted looked at his trans lists—which would he bring to fruition? Transportation was mostly spoken for, transplant too technical, transsexual hardly a moneymaker, and so on until he got to translation. His would be a translation institute or company or service that would translate for people when that was needed, and, according to his instructor, this was going to be a lot.

So the first thing to do, obviously, after dishing out over $7,000 for the top-of-the-line graphics stuff, was to hire some translators.

The French and German folks were easy enough to track down, but our young CEO was stuck on the idea that the longer the list of languages his company could work with, could translate, the better. Ted wasn't a graphic-design man himself, but he did have an image in his head of the main ad listing all the serviceable languages, descending downward in some authoritative-looking font, properly spaced and all, and that the longer the list, well . . .

And this is the part that just kills Ben. He, too, attended this center of higher learning, which, again, cost so much that were his parents to have taken and smartly hidden the money required for tuition, room, board, books, phone, recreational medication, trips home—the four-year total coming in just a few bucks over $140,000—in a CD, money market, mutual fund, IRA, 401(k), tax-elusive investment setting, and just kept their child alive and fed, getting him to deliver papers or pizza or processing data or anything until the age of thirty-five just to avoid debt, he could have retired, more or less, thanks to a bull market, which, essentially, would have made him a millionaire. But his parents didn't, so he shared the same floor of a large student-housing complex with Ted the entrepreneur during their first year.

Ben, our hero, took, in order to fulfill the foreign language requirement, an obscure language. This language is a European language, but seriously Eastern European, entirely marginal in pretty much anyone's genealogy of languages, just barely getting invited to the Indo-European family table. Just barely. Balto maybe, Slavic probably. The language that balances out French and Italian on the unofficial spectrum of languages for a romantic evening. This language hardly gets much mention outside of its local habitat, though it is the language spoken by those unfortunates that every fifteen years or so, whether under the auspices of fascist, Communist, or unspecified geopolitical misguidance, rise to international attention as they and their linguistic neighbors do horrible things to each other in the name of nationality, religion, ethnicity, etc. Being a language so underappreciated, it rarely surfaces even at gigantic state universities, places where enough people learn and teach, say, Flemish, to push a few tables together at some popular bistro right off campus at the end of the semester in order to celebrate this Flemish thing they've built. But thanks to a starry-eyed partially Slavic professor, who wrote perhaps one of the three best grants this decade, enough funds were raised to create a program in this language's instruction. This instructor, who really just didn't get it, was of the mind that once this language program got off the ground and the initial inertia working against it was overcome, the students would sign up regularly, appreciating the sheer beauty of the language, wanting to learn it in order to better understand the unrest that speaks this language, unrest this instructor figured wasn't about to end. Ben, not even remotely Slavic, let alone Balto, in the very early days of that first semester, was helplessly following around a striking romantic interest, who was flattered, but no thanks, who herself was Slavic and who signed up. Ben did, too. It was more of an "I'll just hang out with her in class and see what happens" thing, expecting to likely drop the class and her, or her dropping them both, or just him, but this instructor, boy oh boy, this was no normal language class. It's not that he made Ben passionate about the language, it's just he forced Ben to see how it was his global responsibility to know this language, that to walk away from it, once being exposed on even the most superficial level, was somehow an act of inexcusable sociohistorical negligence. This kept Ben from bailing early on, and later in the semester, just as Ben's transplanted sense of history was wilting, the language was resold to him from a different angle. The instructor couldn't afford to lose students. Future funding depended on enrollment. Not only did he need them to remain enrolled, he needed them to enroll for the second semester and then the second year and on and on. Soon Ben learned that he could do nothing to earn less than an A-minus; it just wasn't possible. So he stayed on for three semesters, even after the Slavic woman transferred to Indiana. How much did he learn? Not too much. Some basic greetings and conversation, a few hundred words, a handful of strange idioms. A poem by some survivor-victim-witness-type. Enough for Ted to put this language, with Ben as the company's translator, near the very bottom of that impressive list in the ad, nineteen languages long.

"No. No. No fucking way, Ted," Ben at first protested. Ted countered, over a so-called business dinner at a pricey restaurant, that no one would ever ask for translation services in this language. The meal ended with a drunk but still-intransigent Ben. His reluctance was finally overcome in the moment he agreed to listen to Ted make this same point over a bottle and a half of the same dry but full-bodied wine at the same bistro on the same night a week later, again on the company's nickel. Because, really, what's the worst that could happen?

The letter arrived four years after the establishment of the translation institute, two and three-quarter years after its last translation services (these in Italian) were provided. It read:

Dear Misses and Misters that concern:
I am making this letter to you for to request your assistances. I am will to travel soon to your country that is yours for meeting with my extensive family in three monthes. Much years ago a difficult event happened and took place due to me that now I do not and did not am communicating with this extensive family. From this I suffer much. My luckiness today permits traveling by me to your country that is yours so to meet and encounter this extensive family that to request a forgiveness. English

but however I speak not. Please, then, please I will paying for translation. 19th October this year. I am too wanting meeting with this translating man one week earlier than the extensive family meeting.

I am thanking you.

Goran Vansalivich

Ted the entrepreneur, who long ago was already on to other not much bigger, let alone better, things, quickly drove his new Japanese sports car to Ben's apartment, letter (already stapled to some nonsensical official memo from Strictly Speaking Translators) in hand, to demand his services. An hour later Ben returned from a pickup basketball game, clad, ironically it now seems, in sweatpants from his alma mater, to find Ted negotiating over his cell phone the purchase of a small cash-machine company, which would finally, not that it mattered, make him richer still.

"Are you out of your mind?" Ben responded rhetorically in his kitchen moments later. Ted, not quite as foolish as we first thought, announced, "Here's your advance, I'll call you in a couple days with more details," casually placed a check upon Ben's filthy counter, and exited. Ben, despite the $140,000-plus forked over by his parents, truly and really needed this money, having manically abused his line of credit in everything from the methodical acquisition of each and every rare Hendrix import to his strict observation and celebration of International Sushi Night (which falls on any and all odd-dated Tuesdays). The sweatpants were, in fact, about all he had to show for his eight semesters of liberal arts education. They're great pants, but still.

This left Ben a bit over two months to (re-?)learn the obscure language in question. He miraculously unearthed some old materials—one textbook and a stack of flash cards—and with his nearly four-digit advance from his friend took to reaching the fluency he never even got a whiff of back on that high-priced tree-lined campus. Two days later, Ben had mastered the material from the second semester and was totally at home with the present tense and words like "dog," "sink," and "prime minister." In the search for more materials, Ben frantically and unsuccessfully searched the Web for his old instructor, who by now was making a killing over at the State Department, then contacted numerous schools, institutions, and bookstores for these same materials, but eventually had to settle on poring through an old copy of this language's dictionary at the downtown library. He did this for three entire days, learning words like "orchestra," "legend," and "diamond."

Halfway through day three, trying, as a sort of spontaneous exercise, to describe his burrito to himself in this language ("big," "tasty," "brown," "powerful," "sincere"), he gives up and drives home relieved, practicing resignation speeches (in English) to deliver to Ted, only to find the first half of his exorbitant appearance fee in the mail later that day.

At their preliminary meeting, for which Ben meticulously memorized a host of introductory dialogues concerning instructions to train stations and questions of geographic origins, the man did most of the talking. He was short and slight, with excellent shoes and a striking chin. His eyes were dark green. Ben listened intently and heard:

My name is Goran Vansalivich and I blah you blah. Blah years ago my brothers (passive marker?) blah by blah. I tried blah to blah (assert myself?) but I could not. Their young children (passive marker?) blah from my country and blah to your country, blah blah blah blah. I tried to explain why I blah not blah blah, but they blah blah blah anyway blah blah blah blah.

Sweating, Ben nodded his head vigorously, sipping his coffee—which Goran would soon pay for—like an aperitif, and mumbled, slurring the difference between present and past-tense markers, which had suddenly eluded him, as he said either "I understand" or "I understood." The man continued:

> Now thirty-five years blah I blah to blah with my family, with my nephews and blah. I try to blah but they blah until I blah and now I can finally blah blah blah, but blah. One week from today at the blah blah next to the blah orchestra, we will blah to blah blah with my family and I will, I hope, blah, blah (kitchen?) blah.

And he gently rested his hand on the table, next to an emptied mug, and looked at Ben, whose toes were flexed against the floor. Ben flawlessly—accent, intonation, and stress aside—delivered the line, "I look forward to assisting you next week," which he had memorized for the occasion, and raised his hand toward Goran, hoping to utter his farewell and be on his way.

But Goran continued, quicker and more upset:

> But they blah blah do not understand why blah blah blah (threat?) blah blah blah my brother blah blah blah gun from the other man blah blah blah blah blah blah. If I blah choose blah blah I blah blah then maybe blah blah door blah blah blah grave. But if I blah choose blah blah, I blah blah move blah blah (future tense?) not blah together, not blah or blah blah blah, but only, yes, only blah blah blah blah blah blah blah blah. You must blah, you must not blah, yes, I, no, blah blah blah (Goran's hand up around an imaginary throat, his voice inappropriately loud, as the Americans in the place not so subtly

turned their heads to see) blah blah, and then boom, my brothers, my brothers blah and I blah, but not, blah, no not blah, they think that I blah, but I did not, no, no, never, no, no, no, blah, oh, blah blah blah blah (idiom meaning "nothing ever ends").

And before Ben and his incomprehension could be exposed, Goran wiped his narrow brow, rose, apologized, and walked out of the cafe, leaving a brand-new $50 bill on the table for two coffees and the blueberry scone Ben had disfigured beyond recognition.

AFTER THE meeting Ben spent the better part of the next two days drunk and/or in bed, the "and" period being a particularly unpleasant gray stretch in between Saturday night and Sunday, when Ben negotiated unsuccessfully with his unfriendly, intransigent sheets. The first activity Ben managed to undertake was a visit to the video store. It meant standing up, moving around his apartment, dressing, leaving home in at least a marginally presentable fashion—teeth brushed, hair attended to, shoes—driving for five minutes, parking, being with other people, milling about, deciding, paying, driving for another five minutes. No small task, but the safest bet in his less than enthusiastic, but unavoidable quest for reinstatement in society.

The store was much too big: forty thousand titles. Some days this is what it took: forty thousand movies. Hours upon hours of transferred-to-video cinematic adventures. Some days he needed the knowledge that he could choose from over forty thousand titles, every last John Candy vehicle, six different Hell's Angels documentaries, in order to be convinced to initiate the rental of exactly one movie. But today he longed for the late 1980s resort town family-owned convenience-store inventory: fifty to a hundred choices, a few new movies (the term "new release" was as yet unborn), some strange old musicals or a Cary Grant picture, a movie or two with naked ladies, an early Steve Martin piece, and *Star Wars*. Simple enough. But this new store, this "better" store, well, now . . .

So he milled about for a long while until he felt he was in a very bad museum. He made a mental note twenty entries long of "maybes," though none called out. He milled some more, thinking about his socks. Yawned.

The last station was foreign. It wasn't always; there were days when intellectual aspirations, a dull sense of culture lured him toward this aggressively self-mannered bourgeois aisle, "Foreign." Where French pronouns and high-contrast images of the Indian subcontinent adorn small boxes with promises of a different sort. Where art supposedly resides. Crap. Today seeing a movie did not mean reading a movie. But the milling had become easy and predictable and not so painful.

The first clue was not the language itself but the chin of the actor in the picture. It wasn't that it was larger than normal, it was somehow sharper and closer to the surface. An angular, nearly threatening chin that looked like his teacher, that woman, Goran, and pictures in xeroxed newspaper articles. A strangely dominant gene. Subtitled, not dubbed. The original language undisturbed. Better yet, accompanied by English equivalents. Resuscitated and uneasy, Ben seized the tape, gently and cautiously storming the rental counter, longed-for textbook in hand.

BEN RACED home, running a lonely red light, not even turning on the radio. Inside his apartment he was aghast at how long it took the signal from the remote control to reach his TV and VCR. His combined mania and fear found him carefully stuffing the cassette into the machine. He pulled over an upholstered milk crate to sit on. Ben watched the movie in its entirety hunched over said milk crate, motionless, keys still in hand.

Over the next five days, Ben viewed the video twenty-six times. The movie was 118 minutes long. Add to this the time Ben spent rewinding, pausing, relistening, transcribing, and imitating, and we're talking ten-plus hours a day of video instruction. The second viewing, separated from the first by a hurried, silver-dollar drip of urine in your underwear piss and the seizure of pen and paper, initiated Ben's transcribing project. The smaller man—clever, but weak and apologetic—spoke softly and quickly, enraging Ben. His cellmate was animated and proud, his words, thankfully, delivered in slow, important portions, everything a speech or sermon:

"I can't help what I've done, but, I, I, I, am, am, am, sorry, sorry, sorry. Heh, heh."

"Apologies and nonsense. Nonsense and apologies. A scoundrel's best friends once he's caught."

Ben hated the little man, and was grateful that he, too, had eventually been captured and imprisoned alongside the leader he betrayed. Like a play unimaginatively adapted for the screen, scene after scene of conversations in the cell. The sadistic guard appearing occasionally.

Ben watched the first third of the movie four times in a row, determined to memorize it in its entirety and move on. On the third day, forced to run out to the convenience store to buy AA batteries for the weary remote control, Ben recited, nearly chanting:

"I made a mistake, an error. I am a man. This is what we do best."

"Wrong! This is what we do most. Our best is fighting for perfection, for justice, for truth. You will not be here forever Petre . . . how will you live when you are released? In the prison of their false freedom, or as a warrior for true liberty?"

Halfway through round four of his memorization of third number two, while the tape rewound as instructed by the gallant remote, Ben was struck with the urge to find out how it all ended.

His first viewing had somehow evaporated from memory. So he actually sat down, let the pen rest, even granted the remote some time off.

A woman, letters read aloud, a beating and then another. A second guard who is actually an insider. A payoff, or promise of a payoff. Both men swelling into lengthy monologues, sobbing wildly and uncontrollably, no cut for fifteen minutes of more despair and breakdown, unrefined, unchoreographed, and unedited.

Ben's apartment had been dark or mostly dark for a number of days now. There were unfriendly smells generating from his dwelling and himself. Things, in all senses, had gotten a bit messy—again, in all senses.

The ending seemed a bit unresolved, or at least open-ended. The smaller man is persuaded, but by whom? Who is, really, the leader? The leader is revealed, maybe, to have been broken, and is now, with his promised money, a trap? Has the small man been duped into informing once more, this time to his mentor and hero—who is nothing of the sort, really—this time unknowingly? Dammit. The ending, what is it?

Ben didn't like this. He did, sort of, but not really. More captivated than pleased. He had forgotten the whole foreign-language business in the meantime, and watched the film three times beginning to end, determined to get to the truth, going so far as to prop a body mirror in a precise position against the wall so that bathroom visits could be made without stopping the tape. He wasn't eating much at this point. Whatever was available. A banana, a can of baked beans at room temperature, a loaf of bread, one slice at a time, the rectangled plastic bag cuddled up against his side like a languid house pet.

Might the whole thing be a documentary? Is that possible? Are there hidden cameras? There are so few edits, so few changes in camera angles, almost no close-ups. Is this real?

Ben searches for the video case, for quoted blurbs from high-brow critics, for a bit of info from the studio or video company or whatever. Some clue to this thing, this devastating thing. The case is not the case, it's the generic, clear-plastic thing. He may as well have rented *Con Air*.

Ben sleeps for a while. He may or may not have decided to sleep. It's either early morning or late evening. The lighting in his apartment is poor to begin with and all the curtains are closed, and somehow got crudely taped to the wall, apparently by Ben. Ben instinctively turns on the TV and VCR from his hygienically unenviable position on the couch. The videotape doesn't respond. Ben panics and curses. The tape, it turns out, has been ejected by the machine. Ben recalls that the machine is designed to rewind the video to its beginning if a tape plays to its end, and then eject the cassette. Ben stares at the edge of the tape protruding from the machine. Its original title and an English translation, *Captives*, troubles Ben as possibly inaccurate.

Ben lies motionless for a time and takes stock of his situation. Intrigued by the film, but without much else to feel good about. In his exhaustion and hunger, in the dim light of his physiological weakness, he must relax; that is he can only, can't help but relax enough to see the unpleasant trajectory of his entire life in sad, simple focus. At his present position along the path of his days, he is in a mild descent, a yearlong undramatic descent, which followed a shorter undeniably much more dramatic descent of that earlier period, which even here on the nasty couch can only be thought of as "the breakup." The rest, the duly past part of his life, hidden on the far side of the horizon of his misery, is so much a memory as to be doubted. Something to do with potential and promise. Rising overall, unfazed by slight dips. Like the world's population or a retirement account. His present smell can only be described as wrong.

He watches the video again, crawling to the machine, perhaps in a gesture of self-irony. He collapses, again self-irony is a possibility, and watches the film on his back, directly under his television, looking out over his brow, backwards. The only thing certain is that everyone can be bought, it's just unclear who's buying who and why and in exchange for what, and who's getting the better end of the deal. In the final account, the middleman is the only obvious winner, and even he seems clueless.

After enduring twenty minutes of angry, chaotic fuzz and hiss from the unsupervised TV, Ben retreats to the bathroom. He sees himself in the mirror and is both disgusted and disappointed; somehow he had expected even worse. He runs a bath, tired and restless. As he disrobes, he is shocked by the sweet, full, rounded scent of his skin. He feels proud of this smell, as if producing such stench was the true project of the last few days, as if this is his greatest asset. He raises a bent right arm, lowers his nose toward and then into a hairy armpit, closes his eyes and breathes intently through his nostrils, savoring the last moments of his repugnance. The odor is so powerful and foreign, he must look at his image once more in the mirror to verify that this is indeed him and not some rank imposter. It is him, though his hair is up to tricks it has never and will never perform again.

The bathwater emits a liquidy version of his smell after little more than a minute. He drains the water but runs the shower at the same time to avoid the cold. The slow, staggered draining of the first tub makes Ben think of calculus, though he's not sure it should. Sitting on his rubbery ass in the now nearly empty tub, Ben soaps himself, paying extra attention to his crotch, which, despite all the water, still garners his suspicion. The second bath allows him to submerge his head and torso, the soles of his feet planted flat on the linoleum wall. He relaxes, feeling his buoyant hair forget its recent behavior. The water is silent in a droning, hummy kind of way. Ben begins a fantasy about a divinely temperature-regulated tub, picturing scantily dressed attendants with steaming water jugs, but he's too tired to develop this any further. He drains the tub, rises with the shower back on, soaps and shampoos himself twice more. He shaves twice, too. Throughout he thinks about the upcoming event, trying not to.

THANKS TO his brother's wedding nine months earlier, Ben has nothing but good thoughts about his suit, though there is little else to comfort him here on his drive to the event. He cuts an uncommon path across town, almost due east, from one aging tier of Cold War suburbia to another. Ben has been to London, Rome, Costa Rica, and even Cairo, but he has never ever been on this part of this road, which elsewhere runs right past his boyhood home. The sights say nothing to him; all he can think of, as townships regularly announce themselves every few miles, stating their population and year of incorporation, are high school football teams, stores selling guitar amps, and used-car lots.

THE HALL is cold and boxy, with a preposterously high ceiling. Goran greets him immediately. Besides the two of them, only the caterers have arrived. Goran's suit and shoes are immaculate and he holds a glass filled with a clear liquid and a great deal of ice.

"Good evening."

"Good evening."

"Did you find the blah with no difficulty? I am very blah about tonight's blah."

Ben steels himself, trying not to flinch. Fantasies of having miraculously acquired fluency through the video are mostly dashed, though Ben feels a tad more confident. He recites a line from the film. He can't recall, somehow, who said it.

"Please, it is important, please speak slowly, I'm feeling a bit strange this evening."

Goran responds to this with a measured smile, looking down at Ben's legs and feet as if to check the veracity of Ben's claim.

"Perhaps something to eat or drink." Goran responds, speaking, thank God, slower. "Here," and he reaches up to take Ben gingerly under his armpit toward the caterers. In the poor lighting of the hall, the patch of scarring on Goran's temple, the dermatological ruins of something between bad acne and a burn, shines hideously.

Ben is served a drink by a heavy black woman, who against her black vest and black bow tie is revealed to be merely brown. Getting drunk surfaces as a possibility, but is quickly stifled. Ben is already nauseous.

"Where is the . . ." He points to where he thinks it ought to be, unable to remember the word, feeling doomed.

"The bathroom?" Ben recognizes the term and repeats it, hoping to prove something to his host. "Over there," Goran points a ringed finger in the opposite direction. Ben hurries, an urgent rumbling in his intestines causing his forehead to perspire. Goran calls something out to him, cheerily, that is absolutely unintelligible to Ben. The intonation suggests the English tongue-in-cheek "don't get lost" or "I'll be here, waiting," but the only word Ben thinks he understands is "tooth."

The unfortunate spectacle of bread-diet constipation mercilessly and suddenly overthrown by a bad case of the willies is best glossed over, so let's just say that even with pants pushed down around ankles, jacket hastily hung on stall-door hook, tie needlessly swung over left shoulder, and ass firmly and squarely planted on toilet seat, Ben is convinced something somehow is bound to get soiled. The seat, even for the slightly tall Ben, is too high, forcing him into an uncomfortable anti-squat position. One bit of graffiti adorns the stall, a symbol or logo of some sort, mostly covered over in a layer of paint close to, but not exactly, the color of the rest of the stall.

FIFTEEN MINUTES later Ben exits the bathroom, walks down a short hallway he doesn't remember from the first half of the trip, and enters the main hall. Everyone has arrived. It must have been a convoy or a caravan, for everyone is now here. They stand far away from Ben and from Goran and from the bar and appetizers Goran has bought for them. Ben is stunned once more by the chin. A dominant gene of Machiavellian proportions. Through it the blood relatives are obvious, even from sixty feet. Thanks to this chin and the blond hair of one man married into the family, Ben can construct the entire family tree, which now twists awkwardly in the unforgiving breeze of the reluctant gathering. The men stand suspiciously close together, uncomfortable in suits, hands in pockets, drinkless. Moms wrestle and haggle with their young children, too young to understand the collective boycott of the snacks. Two moms negotiate fruitlessly with small whining pouters. The other women trap their own little squirming bastards between their thighs. Every minute or so, one squirts free and darts toward the goodies. The mother, furious, turns to her husband and buys some assistance with her exasperation. The dad walks quick and angry, his long gait nothing but paternal authority. Upon arrival, the child is instructed to "Come here!" The father reaches his right arm across to grab his child's right forearm. The child is turned, and his ass is slapped, less to hurt him than to propel him back to the group to which he belongs. Each of the four fathers does this or something close to it at least once.

Goran stands away from the group, speaking quickly to an older woman. She and Goran have all the gray hair in the room. The young, boycotting parents have, it appears, no parents of their own. Excitedly Goran speaks to the older woman, clutching her arm like he did Ben's, holding the woman up next to his chest. Her fat face nearly hides the chin, nearly. Her head bobs endlessly. Beginning from the upright position, the bobs pull her head toward her left shoulder. At about sixty degrees, it bounces back upright, in the spirit of a typewriter. Goran appears to love her dearly. She herself is expressionless, though her head certainly moves a lot.

Ben, who is working, returns to Goran in order to help him communicate with this woman. Goran smiles at Ben while closing his eyes. "This is my sister. I have not seen her in thirty-four years. She cannot speak. So sad. She blah a blah last year."

There is twenty minutes of this. Ben stands next to Goran and his shaking, wobbly-headed sister, listening to Goran's monologue, thanking God that he is not being asked to translate. The rest of the family continues to fester. The moms have surrendered, and the children gorge themselves on crackers, cubes of white and orange cheese, and carrot sticks. They drink soda dispensed from a special tube, a tube with access to six different sodas. The children force the black woman to prove this by testing each one. The mothers sit on folding chairs, too exhausted to maintain the postures and positions their stiff dress requires. The men are a huddle. Ben has no business here and escapes to the bathroom.

Returning to the unreunion through the hallway, Ben encounters one of the parentless parents. She is a biological member of the chin clan. The hallway is so narrow—it could not possibly be up to code—that Ben and this woman must synchronize their passage, each turning their hips parallel to the wall. She begins twisting before Ben, who pauses and stares, hoping to seize an opportunity. Her bright eyes are blue by blue-gray. Large, the skin around them is taut, crow's-feet radiating down and outward. She cries regularly. Beyond these magnificent, expressive eyes her face is part plain, part ugly. Ben is taller, but she is bigger. Her cheap polyester knee-length skirt reminds Ben of his junior high librarian. She returns his stare, impatient, while Ben registers that he is, if only by default, the best-looking of those assembled here this evening.

"Excuse me." Between polite and annoyed she says it.

Ben starts. "No, uh, mmm, what . . ." He hasn't spoken English to another person for six days. Confused, her eyes grow. Not to mention she probably needs to use the bathroom. "What, um, what the fu—" He touches his face trying to concentrate, sorting out different abbreviated phrasing for what ought to be a very, very long question. "What the hell is this?" That's his best shot.

She shakes her head. "This?"

"This," he stammers, "this fucking thing," his perplexed arms up to gesture out toward the larger space to his left and her right on the other side of the hallway only to collide with the narrow wall. The embarrassment and pain in his hands return to him his verbal facilities. "What the hell is going on here? Who are you people?"

She pauses, looking right over his eyes, like he's been asking her for the time every two minutes for the last hour. "Uncle Goran," she hisses with acidic mockery, "is a murderer." Ben refocuses and does nothing. They stare at one another without understanding. "He killed our parents," she blurts, with all the expression of the lady from 4-1-1. "Excuse me," and she lowers her massive right shoulder into Ben's right shoulder and forces him against the wall so she can go and piss.

A few minutes later, Goran approaches Ben, who has been trying to understand what is afoot in his GI tract while attempting to fill in the vast gaps of the woman's sparse narrative, returning to the phrases "prison sentence," "refugee status," and "adoption agency" with most every scenario. "We will start now," Goran says, still smiling.

"Need, can, should, um." Ben fumbles for the right modal verb to construct his sentence with. "Might you say to me what is the thing you are going to say now to all the people here?" Ben inhales, nearly felled by his own syntax.

"I don't know," Goran replies slowly. "I will apologize. You should not blah. I will talk slowly." And he raises his arms toward the two dozen chairs assembled before a podium and microphone. Loudly Goran says to the other family members, "Please sit down."

Ben, quickly rehearsing scenarios of humiliation and failure, realizes the time has come. A couplet of dialogue from the movie keeps running through his mind: "'I'm not who you think I am.' 'Exactly, you are who I thought you were.'"

"Sit down, please, everybody," he speaks loudly, almost enjoying the authority of speaking someone else's words.

The family migrates to the chairs, reluctant and lethargic. The men are expressionless. Two of them, both of whom have married into the clan, place themselves at opposite ends of the first row. The mothers round up their little ones. The one from the hallway disciplines her son with the word "dammit."

Goran moves behind the podium, too short for it, but indifferent. A pair of unneeded speakers has been set up, and so Goran's words boom: "I want to thank you for blah here tonight." Goran, still smiling, looks at Ben.

"He, uh, I want to thank you for coming here tonight." Ben returns a forced smile of his own.

"Many years blah, our family blah a very bad blah." Goran pauses.

Ben pauses. "Many years, many years ago, our family had a very bad thing happen to it. Uh, very bad thing. Real bad." Ben scans the family, waiting to see who will unmask the charlatan first, but they all just stare at Goran.

"The blah blah came into our village and made everyone choose between blah and death." Goran pauses.

Ben pauses. He pauses. He raises his glass, his thoroughly empty glass, to his mouth to stall, feeling his spot in the room sink below the rest of the outlying world, which immediately begins tumbling down on top of him.

Just then the two men seated at opposite ends rise. One is tall, the other is wide. The tall one has a horrible hairdo. Long in back, short on top. He wears cowboy boots with his suit. The other definitely lifts weights. His tie is visibly bottom-of-the-line, and he wears no jacket over his short-sleeved button-down. They walk briskly toward the podium. The room is silent, save for the static breath of the speakers. One girl, happy at the sight of her father, suddenly exclaims, "Daddy!" The bobbing head bobs much faster, like a metronome set for the allegro part of the evening's program.

In the instance before they reach him, Goran turns to Ben and says, each word terrifically enunciated, "I will need your help now."

"Motherfucker," the jacketless one says, also enunciating impressively, in the moment he arrives at the podium. He reaches out for Goran, but bumps the podium. Infuriated, he crashes the podium to the ground. The other one stutters his last step, leans back, and adeptly slugs Goran in the face. Goran goes down and the guy with the bad tie sits on him in order to beat him without having to take his stance into consideration. The translator hurries toward his client, tackles the cowboy, who topples over and onto the other two. The next three or four seconds cannot be fully known without the aid of stop-motion photography.

The main problem is the boot. First slicing up his thigh, it is now, at this very instant cleaving the translator's bottom in two and is firmly wedged into an obvious site of insertion. There are many other things happening at this very instant. The weight lifter is, more or less, lying on top of the translator. Someone's blood, it appears, is on the sleeve of the arm he is grasping. The cries of children and shrieks of women are surprisingly audible, their high frequencies undisturbed by the low, dull thuds and groans of the more proximate melee. But the hard leather cowboy boot, adorned with silver tips, up, yes, up his ass, this is the main problem. Ben's immediate objective is to pull himself up and off of the boot by using the aforementioned bloody arm as a lever. His client's voice, distinctly accented isolated vowels and consonants, can be heard nearby. Ben pulls at the arm to lift himself, but the boot follows, applying equal or greater force. The guy wearing the boots, it seems, is really working over the client, enjoying the stability Ben's ass offers him to hurt the client as quickly and efficiently as he knows how. The body on top of Ben—whose head repeatedly says things like "you motherfucker," "fucking fucker," and "cocksucker motherfucker cunt" in a distinct but difficult to place East Coast accent—shifts a bit. The client pulls the man's hair—Maine?—using his fingers to truly hurt the other man's face.

It occurs to Ben that Goran isn't just making sounds of suffering and pain. There is also something akin to laughter. The big man has rolled off Ben; the boot is nearly disengaged. Two women—he knows by their shoes—are angling into the pile, scolding the combatants, using their handbags for some unclear purpose. It occurs to Ben that Goran just may be the kind of man who views the relationship between a $3,000 suit and a brawl as anything but mutually exclusive. Much to Ben's dismay, there is a counter-roll, though the boot has been successfully dislodged.

At that moment, the pile is dismantled by the two stockiest female family members and one of the caterers, who drag the attackers away by their feet. The one who had been on Ben thrashes and flops, fishlike.

Goran rises, decidedly dignified for a man bleeding from both nostrils. The wives of the two men scream at their surly, seething husbands in unintelligible unison. The children have been hurried to the exit by the other mothers. The two men who did not participate in the brawl stand silent and stone-faced next to the woman with the bobbing head. It shows no sign of slowing, though the return point is now closer to seventy-five degrees.

Goran sits in a chair, tilts his head back, and begins a series of facial contortions. Throughout, he systematically checks the flow of blood from each nostril, dabbing the area around his philtrum with a different digit at each new expression. He settles on none of them, instead grabbing a thick pile of small, square napkins.

From among those invited, only the two other men and Ben remain. The wives, the bloody husbands, and the head have all disappeared. The caterers stand far away, safe behind a table, drinking soda and picking at the remaining cheese. The two men sit down. Both dark featured with shiny black hair. Their faces clearly come from the same source, though one of them seems to have taken his a bit further. His nose, ears, lips, and even chin are bigger, wider, thicker, and sharper than his brother's. Ben, his ass throbbing, looks at Goran, who no longer smiles as he tries to repair his face with cocktail napkins.

Goran holds a bright, newly reddened one at a distance from his face considering it like a hand mirror. He speaks in slow monotone: "They will not tell their children I killed their parents. I did not."

"You won't tell your children he killed your parents. He did not." Ben looks at Goran as he says this, his chest swelling as the words come and go effortlessly.

"He did!" one of the brothers protests. "Bastard!"

"I did not," Goran says calmly. He pauses. After a few of his more discreet efforts fail, he gives up, twists the tip of a napkin and casually inserts it in his right nostril. Half-nasal, he continues: "I did not blah them, but I could not blah them. I wanted to blah them, believe me, but I could not." This "blah" is the same word repeated.

"What does"—and he says the sound of the unknown word to Goran—"mean?" Ben asks.

Goran removes the napkin tip, studying its saturation. "To do something so they don't die."

"He wanted to prevent it from happening, he wanted to save them," Ben's voice pleads with the brothers, "but he couldn't. But he wanted to."

"They made me watch," Goran says to the napkin. Reinsertion.

"Nonsense," one of them says.

"He's lying," says the other.

Ben turns to Goran. "They think that you are . . . that this . . . that this is nonsense and lies . . . what you said."

Goran takes his eyes off the napkin, studying Ben with similar interest. "I loved my brothers and sisters. I wanted to die instead. Now I want my nephews and blah to be my family." Ben continues looking at Goran and vice versa after the latter finishes speaking. Ben looks over at the taciturn brothers, back at Goran, and then at his own shoes. His bottom smarts, but less. He starts to translate, but one of the brothers beats him to it:

"We shouldn't have even showed up today. We only did because Aunt Sonja asked us to."

As Ben begins to search for their words in Goran's language, the other brother continues: "She can't talk, and she can barely write. It took her ten hours to write a one-line note. She wrote, 'Listen to him. Nothing more. Listen. Please. To him.' Well, we're listening, but that's it."

"Yeah. Fuck him," the other adds by way of conclusion. Their anger reveals itself through the bottom of their chairs now squeaking around the floor as they use their legs to spit out their contempt.

Ben thinks he might have a very crude paraphrase for that last part, and could do the rest with no problem, but Goran interjects, "The blah is the blahest. The one who does not die is the one that wishes most to die."

Ben raises his hand to both parties, asking them in two languages to hold on and wait and shut up, please, now.

Suddenly warmed up, Mr. Big Face continues, addressing mostly his brother, who nearly smiles, apparently enjoying the intimacy of their antagonism. "I mean, how does a guy like him even get into this country or out of his own? He's a known criminal. It isn't just his own that he kills. He's notorious."

Ben feels a jolt of promise as he recalls the image of the very page upon which "notorious" and its equivalent were printed in the library dictionary. Though it may have actually been "nocturnal."

"I wait my whole life since that blah day to blah to everyone, to my family that I am blah, that I hurt no one." Goran looks down, moving the bloody napkins around the tabletop in a variation on solitaire.

"Please, stop, please, hold on," Ben continues, nearly laughing in his powerlessness.

"If I could, if I were that kind of man, if I knew I wouldn't get caught, I would kill him right now," the littler-faced one declares proudly. "I was cheering for Earl and Tommy. Quietly, because, after all, the kids. But he deserved it."

Outside of the brothers, who take turns, everyone is speaking at once. Ben is nearly speaking sign language, having vigorously added all known gestures to his bilingual gibberish in order to silence the room, but no one pays any attention. Goran regularly slams a fist upon the table each time he proclaims his innocence. The brothers counter by pointing their fingers, at Goran, at Ben, at each other.

Gritting his teeth, stomping his foot, and half spinning around in his exasperation, Ben invokes the translator's authority with a spirited "Shut the fuck up!" He repeats it in English, justly confident that Goran will understand. The startling, heartfelt integration of urgent tone and intense mini-dance was the kind of thing that might have earned him an ice cream cone or another pony ride from his mom a decade and change ago.

The hall is silent. Ben sits down, unable to decide where and how to start, uncertain as to the source and nature of his interest here in the first place. Goran has built a large asterisk, the bloody napkin ends gathered into a single point, their still-white tails radiating outward. The brothers help each other put on the suit jackets they had removed moments earlier. Ben bites his lips and shuffles around a half-dozen mixed-up phrases in his head.

Finally Goran removes a checkbook and pen from inside his suit jacket. He writes a check, tears it out, and hands it to Ben. It is written in the amount of $25,000. A local bank has issued this check, printing on it Goran's full name and a local address. "For each family," Goran says.

"He wants to give this to every family," Ben says, handing the check to the one with the exaggerated face.

"For what?"

Ben translates.

"They will believe me."

Ben translates.

The brothers whisper to each other, alternately shaking and nodding their related heads.

"Not enough," one rejoins.

Ben translates.

Goran writes another check, tears it out, and hands it to Ben. "Thirty," Ben announces.

A brother snatches the check from Ben and studies it. He reaches into his own inner-breast pocket, removes a pen, and writes on the check. He stands up to hand it directly to Goran, but Ben intercepts the check and reviews the alteration. "They want fifty each," he informs the client.

Goran motions for the check from Ben, then writes on it. As he finishes, a brother walks toward Goran to take the check. Ben raises his arm to chest level, stopping the brother, and instead takes the check himself. "Forty-two-five."

"Fuck him," one says, fed up, turning the first word into a diphthong.

For a few moments no one speaks. The caterers are carrying trays and boxes of liquor out through a back door.

Then Ben speaks his best idea in years, the kind of thing that comes to him thanks only to the chaotic distribution of dumb luck. "What if," he rubs his unique chin, "what if he pays you thirty now and another twenty in five years, but only after he checks with your children that you're telling them the truth?"

"What was that?" Goran asks, as if he has missed a potentially crucial line in a movie.

"What truth?" one of the brothers challenges.

Ben holds his index finger up to Goran and speaks to the brothers. "That he didn't kill anyone."

The brothers consult each other by looking at each other.

One says, "And if we don't?"

Ben clumsily explains the deal to Goran, who seems intrigued. The translator turns back to the brothers.

"That's the deal. Yes or no."

GORAN SLOWLY walks Ben to his car through the crisp air of the parking lot. "When I return in five years, I want you to be my blah again."

"Your what?"

"My translator."

"Oh. Of course."

Goran reaches into his breast pocket and hands Ben a check. "Thank you." The short wealthy man walks away toward an idling car.

In the poor light of the parking lot Ben needs a few moments to make out the many digits on the check. His entire torso surges as a number of internal organs—lungs, heart, colon—respond instantly to the good news. Meanwhile, the cold night makes Ben's jaw and mouth jump involuntarily, causing his teeth to click and crack together spasmodically, resulting in an irregular shoulder bounce, all of which are summarized in a dull hum Ben does not notice. Failing to wrestle control of the top quarter of his body, Ben simply nods his convulsing head and mutely smiles his open and closed mouth, unable to remember how one responds to "thank you" in Goran's language.

Asylum

BY SUSAN DAITCH

S he rode up the elevator with Krelnikov. They had both gotten to work early. Krelnikov made Eve nervous, but in her desire not to appear to be the kind of person who recoiled at any suggestion of confidentiality, she tried to hide her aversion to him and to act as if his insinuations were nothing serious.

"Hot day, again," he said.

The elevator was empty, but he stood close to her as if it were crowded, and he had intimate things to say.

"Nobody understands translation isn't an act of convenience. Every company wants their job toot sweet." He looked at her pleadingly. She wasn't in the mood for Krelnikov, didn't want to talk to him or figure out what he was trying to say.

"What do you want from me? What can I do about deadlines?"

"I'm sorry, Eve." He looked hurt.

She wondered what she had done and thought she would never stop apologizing to him.

Leaning against the polished steel paneling, he looked as if he'd spent days sitting on the edge of a chair in a dark room and could no longer stand up straight. Face wet from the heat, he punched a hole in the lid of his coffee cup and took a sip. Although he'd lived in New York for many years, he retained a strong accent.

"They forgot the sugar. You want this?"

"No thanks. I have my own. What are you working on?"

"I'm watching Spanish Conquistadors travel up the Amazon. Their boats are beginning to take on water, and they swim with alligators. They haven't figured out how to make wallets."

"Are they lost in time?" Eve watched the lit numbers as the elevator slowly ascended, feeling Krelnikov's breath less than a foot away. She made up a story. "As the ship navigates a bend in the river they suddenly find a modern city with skyscrapers and an underground train system; they see men in suits, women in short skirts."

"No, it isn't that picture."

"How much time do you have left?"

"About ninety more minutes of the sixteenth century remains. Let me tell you I wouldn't mind a little civilization at this point: a village, a trading post, signs of a market economy. A group of Jesuits, I wouldn't mind," Krelnikov explained.

"It's in German?"

"Yes, of course, it's a German movie."

They reached the eleventh floor and the offices of Talk Around the Clock, Incorporated, a business that provided translation services for foreign-language films needing to be subtitled in English and American films requiring translation into other languages. The reception area was covered by movie posters unchanged for years: Jean Seberg, Judy Holliday, Orson Welles. Krelnikov stopped in front of Piper Laurie in *The Hustler* and imitated a pool shot, bending over so Eve had to walk around his butt. She guessed the coffee cup was supposed to be the ball at the point of his imaginary cue. Krelnikov and Eve went their separate ways. His office was to her left. The only kinds of movies he got excited about had to do with angels returning to earth as temporary humans or epics about great individuals. If he wanted to live his life over, if he wanted a second chance, Eve wondered what he was so desperate to erase, to tape over.

"Who wouldn't," he said, "grab at the opportunity to do something else in a younger body? You like romances and screwball comedies, which always seem opaque to me. I never laugh at mistaken identity, misplaced trust, or puns that I waste time trying to translate. You can keep your bedroom scenes and banana peels. Give me a second chance any day, and I'll grab it."

EVE SWORE in French as dialogue was spoken, then checked what she wrote against the film, and last of all, translated the dialogue or voice-over narration into English. She kept two sets of papers for each movie, the original and her translation. The mechanics of attaching subtitles to film was done at a lab. She threaded the film through the gates, one reel for sound, one reel for image. Usually she worked from an optical print, one reel alone. The room contained a Steenbeck editing table, a telephone, an extra chair, and a shelf of English and foreign dictionaries. The blinds were drawn in order for Eve to see her work. A messenger brought cans of films from producers, and Dell, the receptionist, distributed the reels to Eve and the others.

Une femme inconnue . . .

An unknown woman, Eve wrote quickly, *checked into a hotel.* The hotel looked like the kind of place where John Barrymore had contemplated suicide in *Dinner at Eight*. It was late afternoon, but the woman, whose short brown hair and black glasses were deceptive in their severity, fell asleep. When she awoke, it was the middle of the night. Her room was not shabby but not very well kept either. Its wallpaper appeared soft and worn. The bed, night table, and chairs looked as if they had been used and cleaned too many times. The camera pulled back to reveal a view across an airshaft, glowing dark blue and gray except for two squares of yellow light: windows. The hotel was designed so that it wrapped around a central courtyard. From an exterior shot Eve quickly identified the unnamed city as New York. The telephone rang, and in a sleepy voice the actress answered it.

Yes, this is Corinne.

That established her name. Corinne hung up and returned to the window without switching on her lamp. Beside a long striped curtain she stood very still. There was music on the sound track, uninterrupted by dialogue or voice-over. Eve fast-forwarded. Suddenly Corinne saw a man and woman struggling. Their fight seemed partly a drunken brawl, but then the woman, a blonde whose hair was twisted up in the back of her head, gave a final push. The man went over the edge and down the airshaft. The blonde woman didn't scream or appear distraught. She wiped her hands on her skirt as if she'd just dirtied them and fingered the stray wisps that had escaped her twist in the effort. Less than a minute passed, but in movie time, it wasn't clear how long she sat in the room where the man had been murdered. Eve noticed the sky on the little screen of the Steenbeck editing table growing lighter. The police came. The woman was, or pretended to be, grief-stricken, as if the fall had been an accident. She handed them a letter, which they read, nodding, handling it with gloves and tweezers, then putting the paper in a plastic bag. The police went away. The woman ran a comb over her tightly twisted hair without undoing it, picked up her keys, and prepared to go out. Corinne cleaned her glasses on a shirttail, put on her jacket, intending to trail her. The camera followed the two women as one and then the other passed an appliance store whose signs were in Arabic. Washing machines, hair dryers, cameras, and radios all glowed in the shadows behind the grating. Corinne dogged the other woman's steps as she went into a drugstore, and pretended to look at magazines and birthday cards while the blonde woman waited for a prescription to be filled, struggling but failing to overhear what was said.

Dell knocked on her door. Before answering, Eve froze the two women who, once back at the hotel, had walked the corridors circling the airshaft only to bump into one another at the elevator. They came face to face but still behaved like the strangers they were.

"I'm going home, Eve. You'll be the last one in the studio tonight."

"When did Krelnikov leave?"

"A half hour ago, but he might be coming back. Sometimes he leaves early on Friday, sometimes not."

"Have a good weekend."

"I wouldn't hang around here alone, you know. People get ideas and what not. You should go home."

So far there hadn't been much dialogue; the job was mainly voice-over. She rubbed her eyes and told Dell to wait for her, writing: *The woman who just gave you her key, what was her name?*, before turning off the machine. Eve marked her place, rewound the film and left the office.

Complaining of the heat, Dell stopped to buy a Mister Softee from a truck parked at a corner. The tinkling music blaring from a speaker in the front seat of the Mister Softee van gave Eve a headache, but at the same time she found it oddly soothing and out of place on an urban street where the song had as much impact as a car horn that played the theme from *The Godfather* over and over again. As they walked to the subway Eve imagined Krelnikov wandering aimlessly around the city before returning to a long night of work, staring at shop displays, looking over the shoulder of someone busy with Space Wizard or Donkey Kong.

"PEOPLE WILL do anything to get an apartment," Mr. O'Neill said. He often sat out on the steps in front of their building reading newspapers or thrillers he found in the trash or on the street. He claimed to be the lost son of Eugene O'Neill.

"What do you mean?"

"Two men, both from Iron Curtain countries," he explained,

"shared a place over on East Seventh Street, but the name of only one of them appeared on the lease. The other, you see, had just arrived, and had been here no more than a few weeks. He murdered the first guy, cut up his body, took the dead man's credit card, went to the hardware store and bought trash bags to dispose of the parts. He might have gotten away with it, too, if it hadn't been a long weekend, but it was the Fourth of July and hot, you know, so naturally the corpse in the dumpster began to smell. When the man was caught, he claimed that his only motive had been to get his name on the lease. He just wanted his own apartment. I haven't seen your friend Lenny around lately. Does he have another job that took him to California again?"

"He just wanted an apartment of his own," Eve said.

When she got upstairs she looked up the name of Corinne's hotel in the telephone book. She thought she might walk by it sometime, just because she enjoyed seeing places she knew in the movies and seeing places where films had been shot. Hotel des Fauves, Hotel Curry, Hotel Development Assocs, Hotel Dexter, Hotel Dixie, Hotel Fane Dumas, Hotel Franconia. It wasn't listed.

THE MURDERESS didn't guess she was being followed. Corinne managed to break into her hotel room and read some letters. While she was going through the papers, the camera cut to the other woman entering the hotel, stopping for her messages at the front desk. Eve didn't like suspense. It made her feel helpless. She resisted speeding ahead to get the tension over with. There was a lot of cutting back and forth between the two women, each getting closer to the point where they would meet. Eve had to translate the contents of one letter as it was held up to the camera. She wasn't sure how much of it was important, but since only a small part of the text would fit in the margin left for subtitles she had to make a decision. Eve underlined *Dear Martine, Meet me at*

2:00 at the train station under the clock. That seemed the essential message but she wasn't certain. The blonde woman now had a name, Martine, and Martine was on her way back to her room. While she stopped down the hall to speak to one of the maids, Corinne slipped out of her room, running quickly around the corner, and so her surveillance continued undetected.

At two o'clock the following afternoon Corinne saw Martine meet a man under a clock at a train station. There was a long embrace and a long kiss but no dialogue and no voiceover. Eve fast-forwarded. She didn't want to watch. Then the man was taken up to her hotel room.

As Corinne became increasingly obsessed with watching Martine, she began to neglect the reasons for her own trip to the unnamed city. She was a buyer for a French department store and had come to the city to place orders for American T-shirts and sunglasses. Angry telephone messages and notes revealed that while caught up in her fixation with Martine she failed to return calls or attend meetings. Samples of merchandise were sent to her room in vain. Boxes and bags piled near the door. She became convinced that Martine would murder again, and in order to stop her, if that's what Corinne really wanted to do, she had to determine Martine's motives.

What linked the two men, one dead, one not yet so, together? Eve wrote, translating Corinne's voice-over thoughts as she looked out the window, watching, waiting to see if they, too, would fight. "*One-notyetso,*" Eve said out loud. The phrase sounded like a kind of martial arts gesture, but she left it.

"Give up, Corinne," Eve shouted into the air. "Martine and her friend are getting along like a house on fire." Krelnikov banged on the wall.

Corinne finally opened the boxes, scattering lids across the floor. She tried on all the sunglasses and T-shirts, then took them off. Outside all was black until Martine suddenly turned on a light, appearing naked as she walked around the hotel suite. The man she had met in the train station got out of bed, too. They began to dress, but soon abandoned the task, and the two of them could be seen lying on the floor. Corinne stood behind the curtain again, hand over her mouth laughing. "*Ah mon dieu.*"

EVE RAN into Dell in the bathroom, a series of lefts down a half-green, half-gray hall. She leaned into the mirror holding her eyes open, putting on mascara.

"That Mr. K, he takes too many breaks and comes out of his room to disturb me when I have my own work to do. I'm sick of listening to his crabbing. He makes me feel like I work on the complaint hot line at the Department of Transportation. All I can do is listen and say 'Please hold,' then he yells at me as if he thinks I should be taking notes. I tell you this, if I worked for the city I'd probably get paid more than I ever got out of Talk Around the Clock." Dell jabbed the air with her mascara wand.

"Are you staying late tonight?"

"No. No chance."

"I'll probably work all night."

"No job's worth it, if you ask me."

"I'm behind deadline."

Eve had tried to get the company to pay for cabs when she had to work late nights but the accountant, a retired chiseler named Dumphreys who worked part-time, would look at her over the top of his bifocals and tell her they were low on petty cash.

"All right, I'm leaving, you talked me into it again. If anyone asks why this job isn't finished tell them I had to leave early because I was sick. Back me up."

"Krelnikov will rat."

They walked back to the reception area. Dell dumped ashes

from the New York Sheraton ashtray she kept on her desk into an overflowing trash can.

"I've been working enough overtime to make up for it."

They were still talking when the elevator doors opened. Krelnikov jumped when he saw them. He was eating a doughnut, and his mouth was ringed with powdered sugar. He wiped his hands on his pants, saying, "Eleventh floor already. Going out for some air?"

"Yes," she lied to him.

"It's hot in my office, too."

"The air conditioner is on, Mr. K," Dell said.

"There isn't enough separation between church and state in this business, Dell." He said this as if he knew something, had seen things they couldn't begin to imagine. He often spoke this way, talking down to them in deeply inflected syllables.

Dell shrugged. Eve interpreted his statement to mean that he was still working on the jungle film and felt everywhere he went was suffocating, humid, and each transaction he faced, from ordering lunch to buying a lottery ticket, was as hopeless as conquistadors swimming with alligators.

PROSTITUTE SLAYING LINKED TO SECRETARY OF STATE
DRUG CZAR SNAGS DOMESTIC KINGPIN
MY DAUGHTER WILL KNOW THE TRUTH

Mr. O'Neill was throwing out old papers. As her eye traveled across the stacks the headlines became increasingly alarmist. He had combed his hair back from his head and was wearing an ancient but elegant suit. By taking out the garbage in a jacket with satin lapels Eve felt O'Neill was unveiling his pretensions to celebrity for all to see, but the exposure revealed only how vulnerable his aspirations were, how open he was to ridicule and curbside dirt. She hung around to talk to him, afraid he would be shoved aside by a crowd of children or an indiscriminate garbage man.

"Car got broken into down the street," he said.

"Happens all the time, Mr. O'Neill."

"This one was full of heads."

"Heads? Not real heads?"

"No, they weren't real. They were models for Downstate Medical Center's ocular unit, but the guys who broke into the car didn't know that. They sure didn't."

"What did they do?"

"They screamed. What would you do?"

"I wouldn't break into a car."

"No, you wouldn't."

Eve wasn't sure this was meant as encouragement. O'Neill sat on a stack of papers and crossed his legs.

"Ever translate *Anna Christie*?"

"No, I don't do old movies. If it was ever translated the job was done years ago."

"I met Garbo when she was working on the movie. My father took me to meet her. She held my face in her hands. 'Such a beautiful boy,' she said, 'I will never forget you.' I thought that since she lived in New York, she might want to visit me these last years. She never answered my letters."

"I think she was a recluse."

"Who in their right mind wouldn't be?"

"Well, nuts to her."

"That's what I say. Eve, will you do me a favor?"

Eve knew this meant a trip to Liquor Plus down the street.

"I used to look at people in the city as a series of open books, or open to different degrees. Now people are video games." He made binging and bonging noises as he adjusted the papers. Then he straightened up and pretended he was ramming and turning knobs, speeding around a computerized road, ramming other cars, zapping running figures whose knees lifted at ninety-degree angles. If you didn't know what he thought he was doing, he looked obscene. When Eve turned to make her way toward Liquor Plus someone turned on a fire hydrant, but no children or dogs ran through the water, and it poured into the gutter, rushing toward the stacks of papers O'Neill had so carefully assembled.

"Your friend," someone said, "is going to get wet, and so are you." Eve turned around quickly. A group of men standing in front of a laundromat didn't seem aware that she existed. One of them was sucking a Sugar Daddy, and he threw the yellow and red wrapper into the stream of water. A few of them laughed, but she couldn't tell if they were laughing at her. She couldn't tell which one, if any, had threatened.

SHE FELL asleep in the editing room. The others had long gone. Eve lay on the floor telling herself she would rest for only a few minutes, but when she awoke, it was hours later. The room was nearly pitch-black; the only light came from the square image on the editing table. Tiny Corinne had stood watching tiny Martine for hours. The square had a ghostly green light. The room smelled of sticky celluloid. Eve wanted to go home, but home seemed too far and too complicated a trip, even though it was only one fairly short subway ride. She lay down on the floor again, staring at the ceiling this time without sleeping. She thought she heard sounds from Krelnikov's room next door, a sound like a drawer opening, but she couldn't be sure. Perhaps the translator who liked angels and epics did live in his office.

Corinne asked for her messages at the hotel desk, but seeing Martine enter the hotel, she dawdled at the counter, pretending to read American Express brochures, while Martine asked for her messages. She was told that a Charles Vague called. *Vag, pas Vaig,*

Martine corrected the clerk's pronunciation. Eve didn't know what to do with this line. In voice-over, because the whole incident was being remembered, Corinne wondered if he might be some kind of partner of Martine's, rather than a potential victim.

"Finally, you figure something out," Eve said.

Corinne looked up Vague in the telephone book. The camera followed her short red nail down a column of print. There was only one Vague listed. After a telephone call, Corinne determined that he was a taxidermist and his company was located downtown, so far west the city was no longer recognizable as itself. There were empty windy avenues with wide garages and loading docks for trucks. Corinne, on the pretense of wanting a parrot stuffed, went to pay a visit to Monsieur Vague, but as she got out of the cab, she saw Martine enter the Vague door, staggering under the weight of an enormous package. Corinne stood in a doorway, watching her from the street. She waited by an empty loading dock, watching as minutes passed. (An hour, Eve figured, in real time.) Finally Martine emerged again, empty-handed, and got into a waiting car.

Watching Corinne climb the dark stairs to Charles Vague's studio, Eve felt the walls moving in. As she rang the taxidermist's bell, Eve imagined a disaster in which Talk Around the Clock would be blown up, film frames flying in all directions. Little bits of burnt celluloid like black plastic snow would fall on the sidewalk, on a fire truck, into a stack of newspapers at the corner stand.

Corinne knocked on the pebbled glass door at the top of the landing, then opened it. The room was filled, not only with stuffed animals but old glass cabinets, dusty overstuffed chairs, and stacks of unshelved books. Monsieur Vague introduced himself and asked what he could do for her. Looking concerned, Corinne told him she possessed a dying parrot that meant the world to her and when it passed away, she would like to have it stuffed. Vague was younger and more fashionable than Eve imagined a taxidermist would look.

How long have you had this parrot?
Five years.
What is it dying of?
The cause of illness has the veterinarian puzzled.
"She's an excellent liar," Eve said.

"I don't want to hear about it, please!" Krelnikov banged on the wall. He was in.

Eve turned down the sound. Vague asked for Corinne's number, saying he would send someone round to collect the parrot. She gave it to him, but insisted the bird wasn't dead yet, and there was a chance, however slight, that it might recover. *So please don't call me. I'll call you.* Eve thought, you dope, you should never have given him the number at the hotel. You'll die now.

Unable to wait herself, she fast-forwarded. Corinne, showing equal parts stupidity and courage, broke into the taxidermist's to search the place at night. The plot was simple. Martine and Vague were smuggling all kinds of things out in the animals. Drugs, computer viruses, diamonds, all sealed in Florida alligators, bald eagles, and mountain lions. In close-ups, paws were carefully slit or feathers spilled in the search. It was a diverse business, specializing in endangered species. The men Martine murdered in various ways had each been investigating her connection to Vague. She let them trace her to her hotel room, and she let them think they were acting as seducers. She was very good at what she did, and Corinne admired her, as her own life as a buyer for Printemps had been without adventure or romance. This was indicated by the irate callers and other signs of her dull, quotidian responsibilities. The sunglasses and T-shirts lying in piles were indistinguishable from one another. The film didn't go into it, but Eve imagined Corinne must have lost her job after spending weeks evading salesmen and obsessively following the woman across the airshaft. Apart from the accident at the elevator, the two never met.

Just before the very end, Eve went backwards. She was shocked by what she saw. Vague was in Corinne's hotel room. He drew the striped curtains. The room grew very dark. He threatened Corinne, but it wasn't clear to Eve, who had been skipping around, how much either one of them knew about the other. Corinne took off her clothes slowly, and then Vague too, undressed.

"He looks like a shirt ad," Eve whispered. "He's too perfect and too sinister. I don't believe she would let herself be seduced. The man probably smells of preserving chemicals. Some people will do anything to get what?"

"Pleasure in danger," Krelnikov said. "Don't you understand?" He had opened her door, just as Vague approached Corinne.

"Hi. My name's Vague. Charles Vague." He imitated James Bond with an exaggerated accent. Either he had been standing there for a while or could hear more through the walls than Eve had imagined possible.

"You had me fooled, Mr. K. Look, I have to finish this translation by tomorrow." She didn't say leave me alone.

"Just let me distract you for a moment. I'm done with the film about the Amazon." He turned off Eve's editing table, and the room instantly became dark. "I'm working on something else I want to show you."

Eve didn't want to be rude to him, she was always rude to him, but she was afraid of Krelnikov's tiny editing room where his size and neediness filled the office. The last time he had called her in, he had been translating a scene from a science fiction film in which digital waiters served dinners to humans, pouring wine and slicing rare meat with the grace of pre-Industrial Revolution etiquette in spite of their microchip hearts. It had been a story of revenge, predictable but disturbing. Sandblasted by Krelnikov's moroseness and misanthropy, she marked her place, then turned her notes over. He noticed her gesture.

"I don't want to read your translation. I don't care who the murderer is. I mean, I already know."

"I can only look for a minute, then I have to get back."

A MAN picked up half a brick from the rubble on the street and broke the glass window of a building that appeared abandoned. Its doors were boarded up; some of the windows had bars over them, but the bars were twisted in different directions as if a strong wind blowing close to the ground had swept through. Layers of dirt accumulated so densely over the decoration of the lower storeys that what had once been ornate were now like a series of blackened chunks. No longer specific; cornices, keystones, or gargoyles melted into clusters of lumps.

"It was called the Canary Island Rest Stop Hotel," said Krelnikov. "This is a part of the city in which many buildings have been abandoned. Nobody has figured how they can make any money through reclamation, so the empty offices and lofts stay empty, you see. Subways stop at the edge of the district bringing in Vietnamese and Turks who work in airless sweatshops."

"This is a German movie?"

"Yes, of course. Why do you always ask me that? It's supposed to be Berlin. You can see trucks filled with bolts of cloth, and racks of dresses and suits clog the alleys by day. At night everything, even the diners, is closed."

"Diners? You've been here too long."

"Cafés. I wanted you to understand."

"The loading bays look as if they were shot a few blocks away."

"No, I don't think so." Krelnikov was breathing hard.

The Canary Island Rest Stop still had erratically supplied electricity. Squatters lived somewhere in its recesses. There were points of light which gleamed from upper balconies looking out onto the lobby. A bank of lit elevators in a glass shaft, lambent and mesmerizing, seemed to travel without stopping.

"What goes on in the upper floors?"

"I don't know. The stairwells are completely black."

The man began to climb one spiraling flight, a series of matches illuminating his face as he ascended. His head was shaved, covered by tattoos. Gradually the sound of other voices appeared on the sound track. The man followed the murmur of the voices until he came to a room on what Eve figured must have been the fourth floor. Down a dark hall, a few light bulbs sputtered overhead, but finally he pushed open a door to find a Vietnamese family squatting on the floor, eating a communal meal. Light hit their white bowls; they looked up at the intruder, alarmed.

"You're going to have to find someone to translate the Vietnamese," Eve said.

"No, they only want the German translated." The man pulled out a knife, and Krelnikov abruptly turned off the machine.

"He's going to kill them."

"How do you know? Where's the angel?"

"Whoever said there would be one? There aren't any. So what I want you to do is listen to this scene while I'm in the hall, then tell me if any German is spoken in it."

"I don't do German. Only French." She immediately regretted her answer.

"But you know what it sounds like. I can't watch this scene, and I may not have to if there's no speech in it."

"It's late, Krelnikov. I have to go home."

INSANE   LIQUIDATORS   INSANE   LIQUIDATORS
INSANE LIQUIDATORS

Eve ran past cut-rate stores that sold piles of merchandise: blenders, toasters, computers. Past window displays of gold chains arranged like starfish and past men who asked what her name was.

by Susan Daitch

That night the city was a kind of schizophrenic whose personalities had aged differently. Some parts of the landscape had been rejuvenated from an injection of redevelopment, new if ugly. Others fell to pieces. Window grates peeled away, pried off their hinges like a lattice made of dough. The fire escapes were crowded. A city full of people who may believe they're being gypped out of their true identity and recognition; a city full of people like Krelnikov who wanted to live their lives all over again. What secrets would she bury in stuffed trophies, hunted and endangered, then mail out of the country? She couldn't think of any. She envied Dell, who did her eyes three times a day and couldn't care less.

On her way home Eve looked through the flyblown labels in Liquor Plus and the chicken dinners for two (fries and cornbread included), all for $7.95, which were sold next door. She couldn't imagine the city where fashionable women gave up on T-shirts and sunglasses, and followed a murderer because perhaps they wanted to kill someone too, but hadn't ever the nerve, and so tailed a woman who did. Even as she had waited for the elevator she could hear the sound of the translator in the room next to her, sobbing and rewinding film. You couldn't, she learned, tell him it was just a story, because he had been in that city; and he knew it was all true.

Translation and the Oulipo

BY HARRY MATHEWS

A PROBLEM IN TRANSLATION

Some of you may know the name of Ernest Botherby (born in Perth, Australia, 1869, died in Adelaide, 1944), the scholar who founded the Australian school of ethno-linguistics, and also the explorer who identified the variety of Apegetes known as botherbyi, popular in England during the years before the Great War when private greenhouses were still common. Botherby attained professional notoriety in the late twenties, after publishing several papers on a north New Guinean language called Pagulak. The peoples of New Guinea were a favorite subject with Botherby. He had begun studying them years before when, at the age of twenty-four, he undertook a solitary voyage into the interior of the island, vast areas of which remained uncharted at the time. A collation of reports by Nicholas von Mikhucho Maclay, the Reverend Macfarlane, and Otto Finsch had convinced young Botherby that tribes still existed in the New Guinean highlands that had shunned contact with their neighbors, not to mention the modern world, and preserved a truly primitive culture.

Starting from Tagota at the mouth of the Fly, Botherby traversed the river by steam launch to a point over five hundred miles inland, whence he proceeded in more modest craft almost to its headwaters. After establishing a base camp, he traveled across the plains into the mountain forests, finally arriving at the unexplored region he was looking for, a complex of valleys lying—to use the toponymy of the time—between the Kaiserin Augusta, the Victor Emmanuel Mountains, and the continuation of the Musgrave Range.

In one of these valleys Botherby discovered, as he had hoped, his first archaic tribe. He designates it as that of the Ohos. This community, numbering no more than a few hundred, lived a peaceable existence in conditions of extreme simplicity. They were hunter-gatherers equipped with rudimentary tools. They procured fire from conflagrations occurring in forests nearby but were incapable of making it otherwise. They also used speech, but a speech reduced to its minimum. The Oho language consisted of only three words and one expression, the invariable statement, "Red makes wrong." Having patiently won over the tribal chiefs, Botherby was able to verify this fact during the many weeks he spent with them. Other needs and wishes were communicated by sounds and signs; actual words were never used except for this unique assertion that "Red makes wrong."

In time Botherby signified to his hosts a curiosity as to whether other communities existed in the region. The Ohos pointed north and east. When Botherby pointed west, he was met with fierce disapproval. So it was naturally west that he next went, prudently distancing himself from the Oho settlement before taking that direction. His hunch was rewarded two days later when, in another valley, he came upon his second tribe, which he called the Uhas. The Uhas lived in a manner much like the Ohos, although they knew how to cultivate several edible roots and had domesticated the native pig; like the Ohos, they had a rudimentary language used invariably to make a single statement. The Uhas' statement was "Here not there." The used it as exclusively as the Ohos used "Red makes wrong."

Botherby eventually made his way back to the valley of the Ohos. There he was overcome by an understandable (if professionally incorrect) eagerness to share his second discovery, to wit, that near them lived a people of the same stock, leading a similar life, and possessed of the same basic gift of speech. As he was expounding this information with gestures that his audience readily understood, Botherby reached the point where he plainly needed to transmit the gist of the Uhas' one statement. He hesitated. How do you render "Here not there" in a tongue that can only express "Red makes wrong"?

Botherby did not hesitate long. He saw, as you of course see, that he had no choice. There was only one solution. He grasped at once what all translators eventually learn: a language says what it can say, and that's that.

YES, BUT WE'RE DIFFERENT

The range of the Oho and Uha languages is tiny; the range of modern languages, for instance, French and English, is vast. There is virtually nothing that can be said in English that cannot be said in French, and vice versa. Information, like phone numbers and race results, can easily be swapped between the two languages. Then again, some statements that seem informative do not really pass.

A Frenchman says, "*Je suis français*"; an American says, "I'm American." "I'm French" and "*Je suis americain*" strike us as accurate translations. But are they? A Frenchman who asserts that he is French invokes willy-nilly a communal past of social, cultural, even conceptual evolution, one that transcends the mere legality of citizenship. But the fact of citizenship is what is paramount to most Americans, who probably feel, rightly or wrongly, that history is theirs to invent. The two national identities are radically different, and claims to them cannot be usefully translated in a way that will bridge this gap.

I suggest that this gap extends into the remotest corners of the two languages. *Elle c'est levée de bonne heure* means "She arose early," but in expectation of different breakfasts and waking from dreams in another guise. This does not mean that it's wrong to translate plain statements in a plain way, only that it is worth remembering that such translations tell us what writers say and not who they are. In this respect, French and English—or Germans and Portuguese—would seem to be as separate as Ohos and Uhas.

There are also times when plain statements of fact do translate each other rather well—even the statements "*Je suis français*" and "I'm American." To make what I mean clear, let me add to them one or two supplementary words. The Frenchman says, "*Je suis français, Monsieur!*" The American says, "I'm American, and you better believe it!" You see at once that the meaning of both statements is the same: an assertion not of nationality but of committed membership in a community—"my community." So even essentials can sometimes break through the linguistic separation.

What makes this interesting is that the substantial identity of these statements does not lie in what they say—the information they contain is obviously not identical (French/American). So in this instance, at any rate, what has been successfully translated lies not in the nominal sense of the words but in other factors of language, whatever they may be. And whatever they may be, these factors are precisely the material of Oulipian experiment.

The word "Oulipo" is the acronym of the *Ouvroir de littérature potentielle*, or "Workshop for Potential Literature," a group founded in 1960 by Raymond Queneau and François Le Lionnais. The group was created to explore what becomes possible when writing is subjected to arbitrary and restrictive procedures, preferably definable in mathematical terms. Since many have found this undertaking preposterous, it seemed useful to turn to translation and its attendant problems in making the interest of Oulipian methods clearer to skeptical writers and readers.

So can the Oulipo help translators in their delicate task?

TRANSLATION AND THE OULIPO (I)

The Oulipo certainly can't help in an obvious way. Unless he wanted to sabotage his employer, an editor would be mad to employ an Oulipian as a translator.

A few samples will show why. As our source text, let's take a famous line from Racine's *Phèdre*:

> *C'est Venus tout entière a sa proie attachée.*

The literal sense—please be charitable—is "Here is Venus unreservedly fastened to her prey."

First translation: "I saw Alice jump highest—I, on silly crutches."

Explanation: a rule of measure has been applied to the original. Each of its words is replaced by another word having the same number of letters.

Second translation: "Don't tell anyone what we've learned until you're out in the street. Then shout it out, and when that one-horse carriage passes by, create a general pandemonium." Explanation: the sound of the original has been imitated as closely as possible: *C'est Venus tout entière a sa proie attachée.*/"Save our news, toot, and share as uproar at a shay"—and the results expanded into a narrative fragment. (Let me give you an example of a sound translation from English to French, Marcel Benabou's transformation of "A thing of beauty is a joy forever": *Ah, singe debotte, / Hisse un jouet fort et vert.* "O unshod monkey, raise a stout green toy!")

In these two examples the sense of the original has been quite forsaken. Even when they preserve the sense, however, Oulipian renderings hardly resemble normal ones.

Third translation: "At this place and time exists the goddess of love identified with the Greek Aphrodite, without reservation taking firm hold of her creature hunted and caught." Explanation: each word has been replaced by its dictionary definition.

Last translation: "Look at Cupid's mom just throttling that god's chump." Explanation: all words containing the letter *e* have been excluded.

The preserved sense hardly makes these two translations faithful ones. And yet all four examples can be considered translations. What has been translated, however, is not the text's nominal sense but other of its components; and we may call these components "forms," taking "form" simply to mean a material element of written language that can be isolated and manipulated. So the first pair of examples are direct translations of forms—not only the words but a form of the original has been replaced, in one instance a lexical context, in the other the choice of vowels.

These strange dislocations of the original may seem cavalier, but they are useful in drawing attention precisely to elements of language that normally pass us by, concerned as we naturally are with making sense of what we read. Nominal sense becomes implicitly no more than a part of overall meaning . . .

This view of translation is a first clue to why the Oulipo has something to teach anyone interested in how writing and reading work.

TRANSLATION AND THE OULIPO (2)

Imaginative writers officially disclaim reasonableness and honesty. That's what imaginative (or creative) signifies: they're lying. Poets and novelists are outright liars. They promise to provide no useful information unless they feel like it. Three advantages accrue immediately. First, you are released from all responsibility to the dead world of facts. Second, your readers are ready to believe you, since by admitting you lie, you've told the truth at least once. Third and best, you can discover the unforeseen truth by making it up. You are condemned to possibility: you can say anything you like.

So much freedom can be unnerving. If you can say anything, where do you start? You have already started. No one sits down to write in the abstract, but to write something. Some writerly object of desire has appeared, and you are setting off in pursuit of it. The object may be an anecdote, an idea, a vision, an effect, a climate, an emotion, a clever plot, a formal pattern—it doesn't matter; it is what you're after. What happens next? The process of translation as it is commonly practiced provides a helpful analogy. I am speaking from my own experience, but I do not think it exceptional.

Simplistically described, translation means converting a text in a source language into its replica in a target language. Both translators and readers know what happens when this process is incomplete: the translator becomes so transfixed by the source text that when he shifts to his native tongue he drags along not only what should be kept of the original but much more—foreign phrasing, word order, even words. The results hang uncomfortably somewhere between the two languages, and a brutal effort is needed to move them the rest of the way.

I learned how to avoid this pitfall. When I translate, I begin by studying the original text until I understand it thoroughly. Then, knowing that I can say anything I understand, no matter how awkwardly, I say what I have now understood and write down my words. I imagine myself talking to a friend across the table to make sure the words I use are ones I naturally speak.

It makes no difference if what I write is shambling or coarse or much too long. What I need is not elegance, but natural, late twentieth-century American vernacular. Translating the opening sentence of Proust—*Longtemps je me suis couché de bonne heure*—I might write down: When I was a kid, it took me years to get my parents to let me even stay up till nine. (This is actually mid-twentieth-century vernacular; but that's where I'm from, and that's what I might say.)

There is still work to do. But I have gained an enormous advantage. Instead of being stuck in the source language, I am standing firmly on home ground. My material is as familiar as anything in language can be, and instead of having to move away from the foreign text, I can now move towards it as I improve my clumsy rendering, sure that at every step, with the source text as my goal, I shall be working in native English. All I have to do is edit my own writing until I eventually reach a finished version.

Think of the writer's object of desire—vision, situation, whatever—as his source text. Like the translator, he learns everything he can about it. He then abandons it while he chooses a home ground. Home ground for him will be a mode of writing. He probably knows already if he should write a poem, a novel, or a play. But if it is a novel, what kind of novel should it be—detective, picaresque, romantic, science fiction, or perhaps a war novel? And if a war novel, which war, seen from which side, on what scale (epic, intimate, both)? At some moment, never forgetting his object of desire, which may be the scene of a thundershower breaking on a six-year-old girl and boy, he will have assembled the congenial conventions and materials that will give him a multitude of things to do as he works towards realizing that initial glimpse of a summer day, a storm, and two children.

BACK HOME AT THE OULIPO

A parenthetical point: the Oulipo is not a literary school. It is not even concerned with the production of literary works. It is first and last a laboratory where, through experiment and erudition, possibilities of writing under arbitrary and severe restrictions are investigated. The use of these possibilities is the business of individual writers, Oulipian or not.

All the same, several members of the Oulipo have exploited Oulipian procedures in their work. I suggest that these procedures have provided them with home grounds. How is this possible? How can methods based in deprivation become the comforting terrain on which a writer sets out in pursuit of an object of desire? Why would anybody not a masochist want to determine a sequence of episodes according to the tortuous path of a knight across the entire chessboard? Or use the graphic formulations of a structural semiologist to plot a novel? Or limit one's vocabulary in a story to the threadbare words contained in a small group of proverbs? Or, if a poet, why write using only the letters of the name of the person the poem addresses? Or conversely exclude those letters successively in the sequence of verses? Or create a poetic corpus using the ape language of the Tarzan books? Nevertheless, these are some of the things Perec, Calvino, Jacques Jouet, and I chose to do, with acceptable results.

Why did we do them? I used to wonder myself. When I first learned that Perec had written a novel without using the letter *e* I was horrified. It sounded less like coming home than committing oneself to a concentration camp.

When we were children, what we loved most was playing. After a fidgety family meal or excruciating hours in class, going out to play made life worth living. Sometimes we went out and played any old way; but the most fun I had was playing real games. I have no idea what games you enjoyed, but my own favorites were Capture the Flag and Prisoner's Base—hard games with tough rules. When I played them, I was aware of nothing else in the world, except that the sun was getting low on the horizon and my happiness would soon be over. In Manhattan last autumn, I stopped to watch a school soccer game in which an eight-year-old girl was playing fullback. She was alertness personified, never taking her eye off the ball, skipping from side to side in anticipation of the shot that might come her way. She had definitely not engaged in a trivial activity.

The Oulipo supplies writers with hard games to play. They are adult games insofar as children cannot play most of them; otherwise they bring us back to a familiar home ground of our childhood. Like Capture the Flag, the games have demanding rules that we must never forget (well, hardly ever), and these rules are moreover active ones: satisfying them keeps us too busy to worry about being reasonable. Of course our object of desire, like the flag to be captured, remains present to us. Thanks to the impossible rules, we find ourselves doing and saying things we would never have imagined otherwise, things that often turn out to be exactly what we need to reach our goal. Two examples: Georges Perec's novel without the letter *e*, intermittently dramatic, mysterious, and funny, describes a world filled at every turn with multiple disappearances. Some undefined and crucial element in it is both missing from it and threatening it—something as central as the letter *e* to the French language, as primordial as one's mother tongue. The tone is anything but solemn, and yet by accepting his curious rule and exploring its semantic consequences, Perec succeeded in creating a vivid replica of his own plight—the orphaned state that had previously left him paralyzed as a writer. I had a similar experience with my novel *Cigarettes*. My "object of desire" was telling the story of a passionate friendship between two middle-aged women. That was all I knew. I had concocted an elaborate formal scheme in which abstract situations were permutated according to a set pattern. This outline suggested nothing in particular, and for a time it remained utterly empty and bewildering. It then began filling up with situations and characters that seemed to come from nowhere; most of them belonged to the world I had grown up in. I had never been able to face writing about it before, even though I'd wanted to make it my subject from the moment I turned to fiction. It now reinvented itself in an unexpected and fitting guise that I could never have discovered otherwise.

For Perec and me, writing under constraint proved to be not a limitation but a liberation. Our unreasonable home grounds were what had at last enabled us to come home.

The Translator

BY NORMAN LAVERS

Noshi Bei Wattapornpet drags the beat-up cheap piano bench one step away from the tacky old piano, its deal finish peeling, and places it up against the 900-year-old rosewood table and sits down. The lovely smooth wood of the table has two deep rounded valleys where generations of scholars have rested their elbows. Even Noshi's tiny feather-light elbows have contributed. She is 89 years old, and was trained by her father to be a scholar from the time she was nine.

The two-room flat has only a narrow pathway in from the front door, circling the room, exiting into the next room, and circling it. Only one as tiny and narrow-shouldered as Noshi can walk the pathway facing straight ahead. The remainder is piled to the ceiling with boxes and parcels wrapped in cloth or paper, and tied about with string. The rosewood table itself is stacked high with books and dictionaries and papers, leaving only a small square workplace where she sits, with her brush and the little tray in which she mixes soot and oil to make ink.

She is translating *Hamlet*, re-forming its gorgeous blank verse into the sweeping and elaborate script of her own language, so that her nation, her people, can have this masterpiece. She is working on the great final scene, culminating in the treacherous duel between Hamlet and Laertes.

"We defy augury," Hamlet is saying.

She needs to think about that line. How can she convey it into her culture without the reader thinking Hamlet is a fool? How can an educated man, especially one who has studied philosophy, defy augury? It is like snapping your fingers in the faces of the gods, challenging them to do their worst. It is a senseless and unnecessary thing to do. (She has had a candy bar for breakfast, and now she taps a king-size cigarette out of its package, breaks off the filter, and lights it, inhaling deeply.) When she had her four beautiful husky young sons, she told everyone how ugly they were. Who would not do the same? Even with her saying that, the gods looked and saw how handsome they were, and killed every last one of them, one by smallpox, one by tuberculosis, one fighting the Japanese, one fighting the communists. Just as she had spoken poorly always about the two strong husbands she had had in her life, telling everyone they were so weak they could not even beat her properly, and did not even have mistresses, but the gods had found them out anyway, and killed them both fighting the colonialists. And her four brothers—always in twos and fours, lucky enough numbers— and always males (except her), which showed how much good luck there was in the family (that's why she is so unlucky, it suddenly occurs to her, because she is so cursedly lucky)—her four brothers, impressed into various armies of various warlords and killed fighting on one side or other. The gods, of course, had never noticed, had never needed to be jealous of her, so little and insignificant with her frail bones like dry sticks, and no muscles anywhere in her body. Her nickname is Sparrow. And that's what she is like, too, so easy to crush that nobody bothers, able to live on grit, and missing nothing with her sharp eyes.

She will skip that line about auguries for the moment and get on to the duel itself, because a duel is something understandable in any language. She drags the bench the step back towards the piano. Playing Western music gets her blood into the proper rhythm for translating a Western language.

She bangs at the piano vigorously, and sings in her piping bird voice:

> *Mia-tsee dotes an do-tsee dotes*
> *An ridder ramzee divy*
> *Uh kiddery divy too*
> *Wooden yu*

Then she sings:

> *Yu ah mah des-tiny*
> *Yu ah what yu ah to me*

Now she feels ready to begin, and drags the bench back to the table. She has given up trying to translate word by word, since that seems to make no sense in her language, and of course there is no way blank verse can be duplicated—she had learned that when she made her translation of *Paradise Lost*—since most of the words in her language rhyme with each other. Nor could she write it as a play, for in her country plays are only music and dance and beautiful costumes and go on for hours, while the audience eats and visits with friends, no one listening to the words of the songs. So she is writing it as an epic novel, trying to capture the spirit and render it into something intelligible.

THE DEMON king Claudius (she writes) went to visit Ophelia where he was holding her captive in the Kingdom Under the Water. He was smitten sorely with love of her, but she was Prince Hamlet's number one concubine. He ordered her to put her raiment aside, and took his pleasure from her young body—how could she resist a mighty king?—but she despised the odor of his aging body and the simpering expression on his wrinkled face, and in her heart she stayed loyal to her youthful lover. Claudius sensed her coldness, and ground his teeth with frustration. He had offered her half his kingdom and joint rule and everything her heart could want if she would agree to be his voluntarily, but she quietly resisted. He had tried to stay away from her, and Gertrude, his number one wife, and all his concubines and pleasure girls did what they could to make him forget her, but he kept coming back.

If this coldness is out of loyalty to Prince Hamlet, he said, then you are a fool. Prince Hamlet is not going to save you. In fact by tonight he will be dead. Then you will have no one but me.

She bowed before him in bodily submission, but in her heart she was steel.

King Claudius was depressed returning to his castle, but he felt better the moment he looked at the forces he was marshalling against Hamlet. The ghosts of Rosencrantz and Guildenstern had been converted into mighty demons, each with four heads and eight arms, each arm carrying a weapon. Laertes, mounted on a giant war elephant, was carrying a bow the size of the mast of a ship, and in it was nocked the magic arrow that could not miss. The ghost of the sledded Polack, wearing a magic armor that could not be pierced, and sending out a blast of icy cold that froze and shattered anything he touched, had gladly come to fight the son of his hated old enemy. And there was the ghost of Polonius, master of curses and deceits. Finally, King Claudius had purchased with gold the services of Fortinbras and his entire Army of the East.

Noshi pauses. In a traditional novel she would now outline Prince Hamlet's forces, and they would be equally grand and magical. But in fact, there is no one to be in Hamlet's army. There is only himself, not very brave or very strong, and with no special weapons. Horatio, his friend, who is not a warrior but a Buddhist priest. And Ophelia, but Ophelia is tiny and slight like Noshi herself, and a prisoner.

(Noshi stops chewing the end of her brush—a bad habit!—and lights a new cigarette.) She is thinking of the many times when she was herself a prisoner. Her status changed every time the government changed its policies. One time she would be a professor at the university, and have her precious rosewood table and her books and manuscripts and dictionaries, and a commission to translate a great work. Then she would write something wrong, and all her things would be taken from her, and she would be put in prison or on a work farm in the bitter north of the country. That had happened when her prizewinning translation of *Paradise Lost* had been published. First the colonials had arrested her, when she seemed to be saying the great powerful God from the West had sought to keep the native people in their tropical paradise naked and ignorant, preserving for himself the best fruits of their forest, and now the tireless Satan, with his forces in the hills, had got the people on his side, and dressed them and tried to bring them into the modern world. When the communists had thrown out the colonialists, they had released her and made her a hero. But then when they looked again at her treatment of Satan, they decided that what she was really saying was that Satan and God were fighting each other for their own selfish motives, and using the people as their pawns, and the people's land as their battleground, and that the people were just as bad off either way. At that point she was put back in prison. Then the new more liberal and open government said that the past governments were wrong, and all praise should be given to the truth tellers, who were only loyally trying to make the country stronger with their intelligent and constructive criticism. The new government actually asked for, desired criticism, the harsher the better. So she was released, given her books and her rosewood table back, and commissioned to work on *Hamlet*. All of her generation were dead, either killed by the emperor, or by the colonialists, or by the communists. They were all stronger than she was, but not as patient. Now she is out again, and has quietly picked up her work where she left off.

ALL THE people are saying these are the good times, it won't go back to the old bad days again, it can't, the government would no longer dare. The government will listen to the people's demands now, and the people have plenty of demands to make. (Some of the young people came to Noshi's apartment last night and advised her that they would be gathering in the streets today to voice their protests, and she has been hearing the rising murmur of their voices outside her second-floor window all morning.) Noshi says nothing to discourage the people, but they are all so young they have not seen the pendulum swing as many times as she has. For herself, she is writing as fast as she can, eating her candy bars and smoking her cigarettes while they are available to her. As the Westerners phrase it, she is saying "Hey!" while the sun shines.

She has been reading *Hamlet* all her life, but had always been afraid to try to translate it. Because the more she read it, the more it seemed to consist only of its beautiful words, and since she could not translate it word for word, she would have to render it into equally beautiful words in her own language. In short, she would have to be Shakespeare at the top of his power.

But while she was in prison this last time, she had got an insight into one of the themes, and thought she could weave her translation around that. She was watching the young people around her dying of starvation and tuberculosis and despair, and watching, without listening, as the aging cadre came to give them their reeducation lectures every day, and she was looking at the posters everywhere of their leaders, more ancient and doddering than she was. In a flash she understood the play *Hamlet* and the character Prince Hamlet.

The big question had always been why he was such a coward, why he hesitated for five long acts to kill Claudius when in the first he promised to sweep at once to his revenge. When Noshi was first trying to puzzle out that question, she used to think, Why didn't Shakespeare just put Othello in the part of Hamlet? And then she realized: because the play would have been over in the first act, Othello either killing Claudius or being himself killed in a reckless head-on charge against the palace guard. But that couldn't be the only reason a great writer would make Hamlet hesitate, just to fill out the length of the play. Nor, for that matter, was Othello necessarily right and Hamlet wrong. For, look, if Hamlet had been put into the play *Othello*—he never would have been duped into killing his wife. That's the answer, Othello was a rash fool, and rash fools are manipulated by the clever evil people. Laertes, after all, was hasty and rash, and Fortinbras was hasty and rash, and Claudius played them like instruments. He would have done the same to Othello.

The question was answered the moment you realized the play was a battle between youth and age, the old and doddering but rich and powerful and clever playing the young for fools, using wealth and cunning to get the young to fight each other, in order to preserve power for the old. Only Hamlet, by using patience, by holding back, by thinking and testing, could not be played for a fool. After all, he had first to be certain the ghost of his father was not a sort of supernatural Iago. And he had to be sure he killed Claudius in a way that would truly punish him. And finally, because Hamlet was young and full of imaginings and loved a beautiful young girl, it was only fair that he did not rush off at once to save his country, but had a moment to enjoy the attractiveness of life.

THE GODS had taken pity on Ophelia (she writes), and freed her so she could fight alongside her lover. On the plain beyond the river on the edge of the mountains, the two armies met.

Claudius was furious that Hamlet and Horatio and Ophelia could dare to challenge his authority, but he gloated when he saw how weak and unprotected they were. (Noshi can hear the crowds down on the street two floors below beginning to shout and chant. She has not looked outside, but she can tell by the sound they are in tremendous numbers.) First he sent Rosencrantz and Guildenstern, converted into eight-armed monsters, against them. Hamlet and his party threw stones and sticks at them, but could do nothing against the dazzling curved blades of their swords. Guildenstern chopped off Hamlet's head with a single swing. Hamlet made a groan, quickly silenced, as his head went rolling, and his body, shooting up a geyser of blood, dropped lifeless. Rosencrantz swung with one sword against Horatio, and another against Ophelia, and they both similarly dropped, spouting blood. For fun, the two monsters stripped Ophelia's clothing off, so they could ogle the private parts of her headless corpse. But suddenly the heads swelled up, and new arms and legs dangled out of them, like a crab coming out of a shell, and Hamlet and Horatio and Ophelia jumped to their feet with their new bodies. At the same time a nub appeared on the severed neck of their original bodies, and new heads quickly grew up. Now six friends were facing the monsters. Again the monsters swung, and now there were twelve, and then twenty-four. The monsters looked back at Claudius, worried, their arms growing tired. (There is louder chanting on the streets below, and a loudspeaker is ordering everyone to go home. Noshi hears the rumble of heavy vehicles slowly approaching in first gear.) Claudius called them back and now sent Laertes in with his giant bow, and his magic arrow that could not miss. He pulled the bow back and let the arrow fly. It whistled on its way, then curved, and weaving back and forth, went through the chests of all eight Hamlets, then curved and went through all eight Horatios, and all eight Ophelias. They cried out with the pain of the cruel jagged barb ripping their flesh aside, skewering their organs.

But soon they had risen, and flocks of sparrows began to fly out of the holes in their bodies, then the holes themselves closed. The sledded Polack sent out his cold . . . and the friends were fractured into pieces, but more sparrows flew out, and the body parts grew back again. There were thousands facing Claudius's embattled army. Claudius saw the hatred in their eyes and could not believe it. I was always told that everyone loved me, he lamented. He staggered back to the castle on his cane. Kill them all, he ordered his army, then went into his room where he would not have to see any more. (She eats quickly the candy bar she has been saving for lunch, and takes the cigarettes out of her package and secretes them in the hem of her shapeless old house dress.) His army was weary, and beginning to feel sick at what they were doing. (Suddenly there is shooting, and she hears the people screaming, and the pounding of their feet as they run. She stops then for a moment, and closes her eyes, and thinks to herself how beautiful all the young people are. Then she begins writing again even faster.) Fortinbras's army had sailed in chopping and cutting, and at first the easy victory, the smell of blood, the thought of how much money they were being paid, thrilled them. (She hears heavy booted footsteps running up the stairs.) But after the first surge of excitement, the blood began to smell repulsive to them, and besides, the people were coming on in bigger and bigger crowds, and even sticks and stones, when there were so many, began to hurt. And everywhere that there was blood, sparrows flew out, thousands and thousands, and fighting them was like fighting the drops of water in the sea.

THE SOLDIERS only have to hit her thin door once to knock it to splinters. She sits quietly looking straight ahead while one of them turns sideways and squeezes through the crowded room towards her. He jerks her hands up and puts manacles on them, which of course immediately fall right off her skinny hands and wrists. The soldier glares at her, then orders her to get up and accompany them down the stairs. She does not even glance behind her, so no one will notice how hard it is for her to give up her table and her manuscripts.

"This time you won't be coming back, old woman," the soldier says. It is at this precise moment that a new insight, a new understanding comes to her, which is why she raises her hand and snaps her fingers at her astonished captor, and answers him in English.

"We defy augury," she says.

The Perfect Word

BY ROBIN HEMLEY

Despite Dr. Fischer's anise-scented breath, he had, overall, a flat unlaundered smell—surprising for a man who wore a crisp suit with a silk tie, and whose thin hair was slick and parted in the middle. The trim fingernails, the closely shaven face, the speckled eyeglasses didn't fit a man whose last bath might have been in the forties or fifties. Maybe he pressed his clothes without washing them. Or somehow ironed without removing them. I had once read that Archduke Ferdinand died at Sarajevo because he had his clothes stitched to his body and the doctors couldn't cut the layers of regal wear off fast enough to attend to his wounds. Perhaps that isn't true, but it wouldn't be the first time self-mutilation and fashion overlapped.

I saw Dr. Fischer all the time where I worked, a patisserie and coffee shop called The Runcible Spoon. At the time, I was studying video at the Art Institute and working twenty-five hours a week, hoping to save up my money to move, either to New York or LA, I hadn't made up my mind. Fischer came in regularly and sat alone in a corner bent over papers. None of us had an inkling what they were, and I didn't ask. He gave no indication that he remembered who I was, and why should he? I'd taken one class from him when I was full-time at Northwestern. Chinese calligraphy. I hadn't shown much talent. I had handled the brush like a first-grader using a fat pencil. My strokes came out thick when

I wanted them thin, and anemic when I wanted them bold. I'd volunteered to run the slide projector that semester, and for this Fischer had given me an A. I couldn't think of any other reason. Even though most students considered Fischer too cerebral, they still liked him for being easygoing. The truth was, if he remembered your name, you got an A. If he didn't, he'd give you a B.

The staff at The Runcible Spoon called him Mr. Raisin or, alternatively, Mr. Crispy, because he always ordered "Raisin toast, extra crispy." No matter how many times I waited on him, he always gave me the same instructions, as though I were waiting on him for the first time. So it surprised me one day when he called me by name over to his table and started talking to me about his work as though we were old buddies.

"What do you think, Rick?" he said, pointing with a nubby pencil to an onionskin manuscript. "Do you think *liaison* is a better word than *rendezvous*? These are two country boys going fishing." He looked up at me with his frank eyes and touched the eraser of his pencil to a front tooth.

I didn't really know what he was talking about and I couldn't imagine two country boys having a fishing liaison. "Do they speak French?" I asked.

"No, no, they speak Chinese, of course," he said, rapping the pencil twice on the tabletop. "But that hardly matters. These are translations. Now which is it? Rendezvous or liaison?"

Fischer sat back in his chair and stared at me. I had other customers waiting and it really didn't matter to me which word he used. I just wanted to choose the one that would make him leave me the bigger tip.

"Rendezvous," I said firmly, and saw something fall in his eyes. "Maybe liaison," I said.

"Are you sure?" he asked. He took a sip of espresso, then set the cup down and began furiously erasing a word on the onionskin paper.

In the next half-hour, things started to get pretty frantic around the restaurant, and I was run from one corner to the next trying to meet the demands of all my customers at once. Why couldn't my boss schedule enough people for our rushes? That's all I wanted to know. He knew when the rushes were, and at that moment the place was full, and only two of us were working out front: myself and Gina, who had the counter and the register. And of course, almost every customer thought that every other customer didn't exist. When it comes to refills, customers, as a lot, can be pretty solipsistic. I almost poured my whole coffeepot on one woman who was getting antsy about her strudel and Kona refill.

"Rick, we're eighty-sixing the strudel," Gina confided as she swooshed by me. "I'm making some more Kona and we're out of cups."

"Is this your first day as a waiter?" the woman asked me.

I managed to control myself, and dashed to the kitchen and gathered a rack of empty cups. The machine looked like a huge breadbox. It had sliding doors on two sides, one for putting dishes in, the other for removing them. I slid the tray in, pushed a button, and stood back. At first, the machine made a grinding noise, then I heard the sound of rushing water, and steam rose from the cracks of the sliding doors. The steam settled and the grinding halted. This was what we called "the deception cycle." You had to pay attention with this machine or you could scald yourself pretty bad. Suddenly, steam rose again from the cracks and surrounded me. The water rushed and the rattling was twice as loud.

Gina and I did a kind of ballet out front. I traded her the tray of cups for a pot of freshly brewed Kona. An arm shot out and grabbed me by the elbow.

I dropped the coffeepot and it shattered by my feet. Everyone swiveled around. I regarded the person who had caused me to drop the coffeepot. It was Dr. Fischer, and he sat frozen in his chair, his pencil poised by his ear.

"I hope I didn't cause you to do that," he said.

"Abandon hope," I told him, and turned to get a mop.

When I returned, I gave him a clean dishtowel, for which he thanked me abundantly. "*Liaison* was the perfect word," he added. "You're not familiar with Chinese idiom, are you?"

He spoke with a thick German accent, actually Austrian, but I understood the nuances of European speech about as well as I knew Chinese. Fischer seemed like an odd combination. "I am not Chinese," he'd announced the first day of class, enunciating each word in his severe accent, like a German prison guard. This drew a laugh from the students. "I was born in Shanghai in 1930, where my father was the Austrian consul general. I was raised there until the Japanese invaded in 1937. I thought I'd explain this to you early on. Otherwise, you might think I was Chinese, and I certainly do not want to confuse anyone." And this brought another laugh.

"What are you working on?" I asked, leaning on my mop. It wasn't that I was interested in what he was doing, though I had been curious in the past. But I was also keenly aware that the woman who'd asked me if this was my first day was staring at me. Let the coffee-addled barbarian go into withdrawal, I thought. I didn't know why I was still working at the restaurant. I'd been thinking about the Peace Corps lately.

"Poems from the Tang dynasty," he said. He smiled up at me with a set of teeth that didn't look brushed. A black seed was wedged between his two top front teeth.

"Let me tell you a secret," he said. "All these years, Westerners have been reading fakes. Not the real poems by the real men. No one knows the way these men really were but me."

"Sounds great," I said.

I was about to ask him if he wanted some more raisin toast, my cue to him that I was no longer his student but his waiter. Some customers, not just ex-profs, forget that you're not there to listen to them, and have to be politely reminded.

I felt someone tap me on the shoulder. I turned. It was the woman who'd asked me if this was my first day. She carried her coffee cup in front of her like a beggar. "Am I expected to wait all day?" she asked.

Instead of answering her, I sat down at the table with Dr. Fischer. He shuffled some papers out of my way.

"Hey," the woman said, rapping her cup on my shoulder blade. I pointed to the sign above the register, which read, "If you're in a hurry, you're in the wrong place."

She turned around and walked over to Gina at the register, who gave me a drowning look. I felt sorry for Gina, but I couldn't help it. Sometimes, you have to make a stand against customers.

THE NEXT day, I received a call from Dr. Fischer inviting me over to his apartment for lunch. He was acting mysteriously, saying he had something important to discuss with me, something about yesterday, and he didn't want to talk about it over the phone. He whispered like the phone was tapped. I didn't have anything better to do, so I said sure I'd come to lunch, and took the El from my apartment in Wicker Park to the Loop, changed trains to the Howard, and changed again in Evanston. From my stop in Evanston, I walked about ten blocks to the lakefront apartment where Fischer lived.

We ate in Dr. Fischer's dining room. The lunch consisted mainly of Korean pickles the colors of Christmas ornaments. This was a pickle sampler—reds, greens, and oranges cut in every shape from julienne to spears.

After lunch, Fischer produced a folder and spread out the contents on the table: a stack of papers, some written in English, some in Chinese. He told me to look them over.

I didn't know Chinese. I had no idea which translations matched the originals, but I pretended to know, glancing back and forth between them. Even though I couldn't read the characters, I knew a little bit about them. I recognized the simplest characters, the ones for mountain, river, sun, man, and woman.

One of Dr. Fischer's manx cats, Vanessa, jumped on the dining table and flopped down on the papers. "Oh well, we can work later," Dr. Fischer said. It didn't seem to occur to him to move the cat. The other cat, Sophie, rubbed up against a table leg. Dr. Fischer had introduced them to me the moment I'd walked in.

We went into the living room, where the walls were covered with scrolls and paintings and framed calligraphy. I sat down on a brocaded couch and Dr. Fischer took out his checkbook and started to write a check.

I recognized one of the calligraphic styles on the wall from Dr. Fischer's slide lectures. The strokes were thin and long and delicate. The lines were straight and unwavering. Black lines frozen or plucked perfectly from thin air. They seemed created by someone who understood absolutes, who knew the distance and length of infinity. They had been done by the Chinese emperor Hui-tsung, who devoted all of his time and money to the arts in his kingdom. As Dr. Fischer had explained in class, the arts had flourished under the emperor, but he neglected everything else, including his military. Eventually, barbarians overran the country, capturing Hui-tsung and bringing about the end of the Northern Sung dynasty. The barbarians imprisoned him in a dungeon, where he spent the rest of his life perfecting his writing style.

Fischer looked up at me and said, "So I gather you're willing to take on the task at hand?"

I leaned forward, resting my arms on my legs. Then I straight-ened up and sat back in the couch. "What exactly is it?"

"Translator," he said, blinking. "I thought you understood."

I put my hand to my chest. "But I don't know Chinese."

"Let me tell you a little bit more about my project," he said, and he put aside the checkbook, face up on the coffee table, which was an oval of glass supported by twisted limbs of polished black wood. I glanced at the amount, seventy-five dollars, written in a hand that was equal in beauty to the way Fischer made his Chi-nese characters. "The poems you've been reading are from the Tang dynasty," Dr. Fischer said. "They're among some of the most famous poems in Chinese. Poems by Li Po, Tu Fu, Po Chu-i." The *Po* of Li Po and Po Chu-i, he pronounced *Bye*. "Surprisingly, they've never been properly translated. Do you know why that is? This might shock you."

I had no idea what he was talking about. But Dr. Fischer leaned forward and locked me with his eyes as though I understood com-pletely, and was just playing dumb.

Dr. Fischer settled back in his chair. "Many of the Tang poets would take excursions to the country together, something like Chautauquas." Dr. Fischer must have seen the blank look on me because he rolled his hand in front of his face and added, "A con-ference, a get-together. You understand?

"Would you like some anise seeds?" Fischer asked me. "They make a wonderful breath freshener." Fischer smiled, and dipped his hand into the bowl of anise seeds on the table. He tilted his head, opened his mouth, and trickled the seeds in. "What's both-ering you?" he said after a moment.

"Nothing," I said. "I thought you might be bothered by the fact that I don't read or speak Chinese."

"Bothered?" Fischer said. "I'm delighted. If you knew a word of Chinese I'd ask you to leave and bill you for lunch. Still, it's important for you to look at the originals. We must learn to respect the text even if we don't understand it."

Fischer grabbed the blue bowl of anise seeds and set it in front of me.

"Waley, Anderson, and the others," Dr. Fischer said. "They're little schoolgirls. Even contemporary Chinese scholars ignore the truth." He looked at me blankly, then opened his mouth wide, and a single sharp laugh burst out as if an animal had been trapped inside him. The laugh startled me and I dropped anise seeds on the coffee table. Fischer looked at them and waved his hand. He laughed again and I laughed too.

"As in Greek society of the same time, love, spiritual and intellectual, was reserved for men, and the Tang poets, when they went away together, wrote love poems to each other. These are the poems that survive, but they have been bowdlerized." He squeezed one of his hands like he was getting milk from a cow's udder. "In some cases, the mistakes are innocent. We have to understand that the poets disguised the sex act in metaphor. It's obvious enough, but most translators choose not to see. A fish leaping, a musical instrument, the braiding of hair. And of course, there aren't any personal pronouns in Chinese, so who is to say the speaker is addressing a she instead of a he?"

I didn't have an answer for that, but then I'd only taken one semester of Chinese calligraphy.

"I have one more question," he said, craning his neck and regarding me solemnly. "You're not gay, are you?"

"Sorry," I said.

"Sorry?" he said. "Why apologize? You're much better off. And I prefer it this way." Still, he looked slightly disappointed.

He preferred that I didn't know Chinese. He preferred that I wasn't gay. He preferred that I didn't know anything about poetry. So what were my qualifications?

Fumbling with the folder of calligraphy, I closed it as though it were a criminal file on me.

"There's a mistake," I said.

"Where?" Dr. Fischer asked, leaning forward.

"I mean, between us," I said.

Fischer took a breath. "Undoubtedly. There always is."

"Maybe I'm not the person you want."

Fischer waved his hand like he was clearing smoke.

"Will seventy-five dollars do? Keep track of the time you spend on these and count up your hours. I'll pay you seventy-five dollars per hour, if you find that reasonable." His cat had left the dining-room table, and so he gathered up his translations in a manila folder and handed them to me.

An hour. Seventy-five dollars an hour. I reeled. "What do you want me to do?" I asked weakly.

"Make changes. Make lots of changes. I'll see you in a week," and he let me outside.

That night, I lined up a dozen translations on the kitchen table and read them through several times. They were attributed to twelve different poets from the Tang dynasty, but they all sounded alike. A typical one was by the poet Wang Chih-huan:

Waiting in Vain for My Friend Wu

Woodcutters go back and forth
with their saws
felling one another's stout timber
The barbarian moonlight
Excites upward-leaping fish
along the banks of the Ch'u River.
Twin hills swell wide—
Moans fill an orchid-wood boat.

And still, because you promised,
I wait,
plucking the one-stringed guitar.

The rest of the poems were even worse. There wasn't anything poetic about these translations. They were crude and laughable, and even if Fischer was correct, he should have left them the way they were. If people didn't want to see something, there was no way to force them to see it. One was titled, "Wang Wei Remembers the Daisy Chain." Another one was called "Golden Showers at the Temple of Heaped Fragrance." The worst, though, was "In Farewell to Field Clerk Han Going Home: A Song of Bodily Fluids."

I studied the first poem but didn't have the faintest idea what I was supposed to do with it. Tentatively, I scratched out the word *excites*, and tried to think of a substitute. I wasn't sure why I didn't like the word. In fact, the more I looked at the word, the more it seemed just fine. Who was I to change around Dr. Fischer's words, even if I did think it was a stupid poem? I didn't respect the translation, much less the original.

I looked at the poem again. I wrote the word *gooses* in place of *excites*, then crossed that out and settled on *strokes*.

But whoever heard of ancient gay Chinese poetry? If what Fischer said was true, people would have known about it long before now. Maybe the whole project was a ruse. Maybe the old boy had a thing for me. A year earlier, a professor had shown up naked on the doorstep of one of his students in the middle of the night. He'd banged on her door and demanded a nightcap. The professor had been forced into early retirement. Things like this happened all the time.

Doesn't it bother you at all that he's stringing you along like this? I thought.

But he's paying me.

That was enough for one night. I put the poems away, and the next day I cashed Dr. Fischer's check.

FISCHER LED me to the dining room like he was a general and I was a scientist working on a top-secret project. Everything looked the same as before. The papers seemed untouched. The plates of food were still there as well, though browner and with a large cloud of flies surrounding them.

"What are your suggestions?" he said.

"I don't have any," I said.

"Nothing?" he said.

I shook my head.

"Nothing is a suggestion, too, I suppose," he said. "Just as inaction is a form of action. Let me see the folder," and he reached for it, but I pulled it away.

"No," I said. I had second thoughts. Maybe I'd acted brashly, bringing over the poems without having worked on them at all.

"No?" He arched his eyebrows and regarded me suspiciously. "Let me see the folder."

I handed it to him. What else could I do? They were his poems. He regarded the top poem silently for a minute, his hand cupped over his chin.

"Dr. Fischer," I said. I knew what I wanted to say, but I couldn't say it. Looking at him, I just felt pity. "I'm terrible," I said finally. "Can't you see that? I don't understand why you want me. Yesterday I went to the library and spent half the day poring over Waley's translations and Anderson's. They seem fine to me."

His face darkened and he looked at me with astonishment. He flipped from one page to another.

"'A misty rain comes blowing with a wind from the east,'" Fischer announced suddenly. "Isn't it obvious what this refers to? Here, you've missed it," and he pointed to one of the translations.

Fischer leaned uncomfortably close and read over my shoulder. Even if I had been able to understand what he was talking about, I still couldn't have concentrated.

I didn't see it, whatever he was talking about, but nodded.

Fischer pointed to a poem called "Taking Leave of Wang Wei." I recognized the name Wang Wei. He was one of the Tang poets, too.

"This was written by Wang Wei's lover," Fischer told me.

"'I will turn back home. I will say no more,'" Fischer recited. "'I will close the gate of my old garden.'"

Dr. Fischer explained the image to me. This time, I couldn't hide my shock and I laughed. "You can't say that," I said.

"Of course not," Fischer said, and smiled. "What do you suggest?"

"It sounds fine the way it is. Garden. Why can't it just be a garden?" I bent over the manuscript and pointed at the word as though I had to prove it actually existed. "I just don't see it," I said.

"You can't ignore it," Dr. Fischer said.

"Why does it have to be that way?" I asked. It was a garden. It said it was a garden. It didn't say anything about body parts.

The poem seemed fine to me without making something sexual out of it. It seemed like a simple poem about two friends saying good-bye, nothing more. And if it wasn't, I didn't have to know.

He started clearing the food-encrusted dishes from the table as though he'd just noticed them, as though I weren't there. He stacked them up and the cloud of flies broke up and then converged around his arms.

"Dr. Fischer," I said.

He didn't turn around to look at me, but kept stacking plates. "This is my work," he said. "These are my translations."

I didn't know exactly what to say. It occurred to me that it mattered. Until now, the poems hadn't seemed important. I thought that it was me. Actually, I hadn't gone to the library. I hadn't looked at anyone else's translations. I'd told him that so he'd think I was hardworking, but he seemed appalled.

Fischer disappeared into the kitchen and I heard him turn on the kitchen tap. I felt very thirsty.

Fischer walked into the dining room again. He pulled out a checkbook and a silver pen from his smelly jacket. "I want to pay you for today."

"For what?" I said. I shook my head. Dr. Fischer looked at me blankly. I pointed toward the kitchen. "May I have a glass of water?"

"There's bottled water in the refrigerator," he said.

The kitchen was covered with paintings and framed examples of calligraphy. I recognized another style from Dr. Fischer's slide lectures. If it was an original, it was hundreds and hundreds of years old. And priceless.

"Is this an original?" I asked.

"Do you like it?" he said, seeming to know which painting I referred to.

"It must be worth a fortune," I said.

I opened the refrigerator door. The light didn't turn on. The smell almost knocked me over. Most of the food was unidentifiable. There were several things wrapped in foil and a large bowl covered with green fuzz.

I shut the door, but the smell didn't subside. It engulfed me as I walked through the kitchen in search of a glass. I opened a cupboard and saw a box of saltines and three boxes of Mystic Mint cookies. That was all. There was no other food around. Plenty of glasses and plates, but nothing to fill them with. I checked every cupboard, every drawer.

I put my glass under the tap and let it run, testing the temperature with my finger. I filled the glass with cold water and drank so fast I had to stand there for a second and catch my breath. Then I filled it again and took my time.

I went into the dining room.

"Dr. Fischer," I said. "Why did you choose me?"

He paused and said, "Choose you for what?"

"For this. Translating these poems."

"Because you have a good ear, because you are honest, and because you are . . . American."

"How could you know I'm honest?" I said.

"At the restaurant. You speak bluntly. I admire that."

"But how could you tell I have a good ear? I just ran the slide projector for you."

"That doesn't matter," Fischer said. "It is your sensibility I wanted."

"You don't know my sensibility."

"You were in my course. You were the boy who ran the slide projector. If my memory is correct, you earned an A."

"You gave just about everyone an A, Dr. Fischer."

"Here," he said, handing me the check he'd made out. "Please don't cash it until Tuesday." I didn't take the check. With a kitchen like that, I was amazed that the previous check had cleared. He didn't have enough money for clothes. He couldn't afford food.

Fischer's cat Sophie jumped in his lap and he began to stroke her.

"I'm afraid you will be insulted," he said slowly, as though addressing his cat. "You see, you were the clumsiest calligrapher I've ever taught. You held the brush as though it were a meat hook. People see what they want to see. I am not so concerned about making these poems beautiful, but I want the true voices of the poets to be heard, even if I must peel them of all metaphor. In other words, my intent is to strip these poems of the subterfuge. If they are not obvious to you, then who will they be obvious to?"

What was he saying? That I was an oaf? I had appreciated the class, respected the work. So what if I didn't understand how to hold a brush, if all I was good for was advancing slides in a carousel?

"You said I was perfect."

"You were perfect," he said simply. "You couldn't handle the brush, but I thought you were sensitive. You gave a strong oral presentation. Do you remember?"

It was a video actually. I remembered. I did it back when I was sure what I was going to do with my life. The video was based on a famous Chinese poem. It showed a chair, a simple chair with a broken leg. The chair was in an empty white room and had toppled over. The camera panned around it as a woman's voice recited the English translation of the poem. As the poem was recited, the chair was slowly repaired, invisibly. First the leg was fixed and then a rich purple paint started to climb the legs to the back of the seat.

The poem was about an emperor whose enemies killed his favorite bride while he was away from the palace. His constant brooding for her turned the state into ruin, and so the people went to a Taoist priest, who was able to "summon spirits by his concentrated mind." The priest, searching for the woman among the pavilions and towers of the air, finally found her. He brought her back to earth in the form of a golden throne. Sitting on his throne, the emperor was strong and content, but when he was away from it, he could do nothing. And so he sat on the throne until his death, possessed by the spirit of his bride.

"I remembered this," Dr. Fischer said. "That's what I remembered when I asked for your help. Now I see you're a poseur, a dilettante. This is far worse than someone without ideas. You have good ideas, but you're afraid of them. I doubt you'll ever do anything with your life. I thought you would. I was sure of it."

He was right. Now I would have laughed at that emperor. I would have joked lewdly about him sitting on his wife. Or I would have told him he was sitting on a chair, nothing more, nothing less. How had this happened to me?

Fischer handed me the check, but I put my hand up.

"Take it," he said.

In Love With Russian

BY LAURA ESTHER WOLFSON

When I left my first marriage, my future ex-husband sent me this e-mail: "Don't talk about me to anyone. If someone asks why we have different phone numbers now, tell them it's for business reasons."

I teased out the implications of his request. If I stopped mentioning him to people who knew us, they would continue thinking we were married until the evidence to the contrary was overwhelming. If I didn't mention him to people I met later, on my own, this important chapter of my life would be pointlessly cloaked in mystery. Unable to please him in so many ways, I knew that this wish, his last, would also be impossible for me to honor.

Tactless people asked if our marriage had run aground on the shoals of cultural difference—had my American habits and culture and his Soviet ones clashed and ultimately proved incompatible? How I wanted to believe that the answer was no. After all, we were two individuals, weren't we?

Just as I was reluctant to admit the role of cultural difference in our marriage and its demise, I was loath to recognize that marriage to Aleksandr (not his real name) might have helped me speak Russian better. That would diminish my credentials as a translator and simultaneous interpreter, reducing them to an offshoot of wifehood.

But of course Aleksandr was central to my grasp of Russian. There are certain foreign words you are just not likely to learn except as part of a domestic arrangement: pilot light, pantry, cilantro, duvet cover, curtain rod. Building on my college major in Russian language and literature, with its emphasis on the instrumental case, *War and Peace* and verbs of motion (don't ask; I've got them all memorized, but I can't explain), I learned from him entire terminologies related to electronics, car parts and fly-fishing.

When we met in the USSR in 1987, I assumed, based on the occasional English word slipped jauntily into his speech, that he knew my language well and was just holding back so I could practice speaking Russian. And then one evening in his hometown of Tbilisi, Georgia, with separation looming as I prepared to return to my job on a cultural exchange project in Siberia, I spoke to him in English for the first time. As we started down the five flights of urine-scented stairs that led from his family's apartment to the street, I poured out my anguish.

"What happens now?" I asked. "Tomorrow I'll be thousands of miles away. When will we see each other again?"

I paused, certain that he had grasped every word.

He shot me a blank but feeling look that said, *I can tell you're very upset, and I can certainly guess what it's about, but I'm terribly sorry, I cannot respond to the particulars.* As we continued down the next four flights, I haltingly reiterated in Russian what had taken me just one flight to say in English. Now I knew that this business of expressing myself in another tongue was for real.

Aleksandr became my teacher, his Russian my model for how to speak the language. He was a skilled storyteller with wonderfully clear diction. I understood him easily when I still had difficulty with other Russian speakers. He spoke a vivid Russian, rich in comic images, retro Soviet hipster slang, and borrowings from Georgian, his second language. *Chalichnoy* was a Georgian-Russian hybrid word frequently on his lips: it described the local knack for wheeling and dealing, acquiring the unobtainable, knowing which palms to grease, and doing so with wit and grace. Another word of choice, more a sound, really, was *eef, eef,* an interjection employed mainly by men from the neighboring republic of Azerbaijan to express pleasure (or anticipation) at the sight of a well-endowed woman or the aroma of a good meal.

He didn't go out of his way to correct me when I made a mistake, but simply incorporated the proper form into his response, so that I absorbed it without effort. If I thought I might have coined a word without meaning to, and then asked if it actually existed, he would grin and say, "Now it does!"

After we moved to the United States, we found that marriage conducted in a foreign language afforded certain advantages: we could stand at a shop counter discussing a prospective purchase without the vendor listening in, and generally engage publicly in secret exchanges. But at times we went too far. Looking daggers at each other in a public place, voices raised, did we really imagine that passersby would think we were conversing tranquilly about some matter of minor concern?

Once, as a tense exchange unfolded between us in the subway, a man who looked anything but Slavic—he was black—sat next to us for several stops without giving any indication that he understood. Then he turned to us. "Oh, you speak Russian!" he said delightedly, and this he said in near-flawless Russian. "I studied the language when I was growing up in the Dominican Republic. Please let me practice with you." Startled, we complied. I now wonder if he inserted himself deliberately in order to play peacemaker.

And so the public bickering ceased, until the end, when it became impossible to contain. And still, I sometimes turn to a shopping companion to discuss the merchandise in our secret language, only to realize that we have none. Russian became the language I spoke spontaneously when awakened from a sound sleep. After I left Aleksandr, I surprised myself and a few other people by suddenly speaking Russian in bed.

About three years into our marriage, we became engrossed in Eduard Limonov's *Eto ya—Edichka* (*It's Me, Eddie*), a profanity-laced roman à clef set among down-and-out Russian immigrants in 1970s New York City. We took to emulating the main character: laughingly, playfully, we cursed each other out in the foulest terms imaginable— the book contained much that was altogether new to me, and for Aleksandr, seeing these words written down was a novelty, not to say a shock.

After a day or two of this, we'd both had our fill. "Let's get it out of our systems!" Aleksandr suggested, and like golden retrievers shaking off the water after a swim, we swore with gusto for a few moments, and then returned to the loftier registers to which we were more accustomed.

He learned English quickly, speaking it "frighteningly well," according to the Englishman who was his boss at his second job in America. But for our nine-plus years together, most of it in the United States, we carried on our relationship in Russian, switching into English only for quintessentially American topics such as credit cards, MTV and presidential primaries. Sticking with Russian for all those years suited us both. It eased his adjustment to life in the United States, giving him a piece of home to hold onto. It kept him articulate and at ease, as I had first known him on his home turf.

In later years, he would sometimes—but not often—shift into English when speaking with me. At certain moments, he would pronounce my name in a way slightly different from his usual, tipping me off that a stream of English would follow. I felt at these times that he was possessed by some alien being, and that an exorcism was called for.

When my family gathered, he often stuck with my little niece and nephew, especially early on, when his English was still shaky. They furrowed their brows and struggled to make sense of his unusual syntax. When he read to them, they corrected his pronunciation with excruciating politeness.

Once, we faced off for a playful skirmish, my nephew on Aleksandr's back and my niece on mine.

"Charge!" bellowed the little boy, aged four, bouncing up and down on Aleksandr's back.

"Charge!" he cried again, seizing Aleksandr's shoulders and shaking vigorously. "Charge!"

Aleksandr looked puzzled. "What is 'charge'?" he asked mildly, adjusting the weight on his back.

DURING OUR last months together, I was translating a book about Russian obscenities and slang for the Sexy Slang Series, put out by an imprint of Penguin. *Dermo! the Real Russian Tolstoy Never Used* was the title, which was similar to those of the companion volumes. (See also: *Merde! The Real French You Were Never Taught at School*.) The author of *Dermo!* (a word that lies equidistant between 'turd' and 'shit' on the crudeness continuum), was a plainspoken émigré living in Brooklyn who had boasted in New York's Russian-language press that he and Solzhenitsyn were the only Russian authors in America to earn their living by their pens. This my client did by churning out skillfully plotted post-Soviet potboilers punctuated with hired killings and rough sex.

"It's a smutty book," he said to me when he called to propose the project. "I would rather have a man translate it, but the translator I wanted is busy with another book. You're the best I could do."

I took the job, but decided that I would contact him frequently with queries about the filthiest terms in his manuscript. I would make him squirm.

The book, mostly in prose, also contained eight or ten obscene ditties by Pushkin and other towering nineteenth-century figures, as well as some anonymous snippets of off-color and scatological folklore. Each time I crafted a rhymed, metered English version of one of these, I would call Aleksandr at work to share my accomplishment, launching without preamble into the Russian, followed by my English rendition. He would pick up the receiver to hear me gleefully reciting something like this:

> *"Kuda nam Vasha Pol'sha!*
> *Pizda nashay Yekateriny gorazdo bol'she!"*

> "Catherine the Great had such a large twat,
> By comparison, Poland's the size of a gnat!"

Meanwhile, I kept my vow to call the author regularly. One day, some months into the project, when Aleksandr's and my marital breakdown was too clear to ignore, I phoned my client with a question. After a halting explanation of some coarse term, he sputtered, "Your husband's from over there, isn't he? Can't you ask him?"

"No," I said sadly, "I can't."

Uncharacteristically tactful, he said nothing. I daresay he was a veteran of several marriages himself.

SOMETIMES, LONG after a marriage is over, clarity comes about specific issues that sparked resentment. For years, you don't have a clue what it was you did, or you think that one thing was going on, and then discover—far too late—that the issue was something else entirely.

One of our problems had to do with garbage—but not in the way I initially imagined.

Aleksandr loved to fix small appliances. After he arrived in the United States, friends and family took to giving us broken gadgets too cheap to have commercially repaired. Soon we were the owners of some eleven tape recorders, four television sets and three or four VCRs, all of which he swiftly got into working order. Some of these devices we put to use; some we gave away; some were stacked in closets, along with the remnants of others he'd cannibalized for parts.

The sidewalks of our Manhattan neighborhood were also a rich source of electronics. Neighbors set malfunctioning appliances out with the garbage, often in the original box, including fitted Styrofoam chunks and instruction manual, the cord coiled neatly alongside. Aleksandr was astonished at the things Americans jettisoned.

I was proud of his abilities, and amused by his strange hobby. And here too, my undergraduate studies served me well, for in those years I frequently recalled that while trawling through the works of Aleksandr Solzhenitsyn as a college senior, I had somewhere come across a comparison, now suddenly germane, of the Russian soul (deep, long-suffering) and the American national character. (Among Russians, it is a truth almost universally acknowledged that to pair the word 'soul' with 'American' would be a gross misapplication of the former, even if English 'soul' has nothing approaching the fathomless depths that characterize Russian *dusha*, a word redolent of spirit, inspiration, breath and a host of other things mystical and profound.) The great man observed in Americans a tendency to discard possessions promiscuously, whereas Russians, he said, fix and reuse every sort of item imaginable, extending the useful life of things practically out to infinity. I cannot cite the source, but if I'm not imagining things (always a possibility, especially after thirty years), Solzhenitsyn specifically faulted Americans for tossing out their shoes rather than taking them to the cobbler to be reheeled.

I was quite sure that *my* Aleksandr had never read a page of

Solzhenitsyn—first, because when he lived in the USSR, he didn't move in the daring and rarefied circles where Solzhenitsyn's writings were passed illicitly hand to hand in barely legible carbon copies (typed nine at a time, because, through trial and error, some expert producer of these printed works had figured out that the tenth layer was utterly unreadable, and this became general knowledge in the samizdat crowd), and later on, in the US, because he just wasn't interested. This gap in his reading notwithstanding, my husband's way with electronics was for me emblematic of the spiritual richness, the avoidance of endless, destructive cycles of acquisition and waste and the ingenuity that can arise amidst deprivation, all of which Solzhenitsyn so admired in his compatriots, and probably also in himself.

"Would you like a Walkman?" my husband would hear me say on the phone. "Aleksandr found it in the garbage and made it work." I would say this in English or in Russian, depending on whom I was talking to—we knew almost as many Russian speakers in New York as English speakers.

I felt him seething. Why? I thought what he was doing was so admirable, required such skill. I'd never known anyone with his talent for bringing machines back from the dead.

I polled my Russian-speaking informants. *Musor*, Russian for 'garbage,' was a most unsavory word, one of them told me. Since so many people in the USSR were poor, it was the custom there to throw out only those items that were utterly revolting or unusable. In addition, *musor* was related to the Russian word *srat'* meaning 'to shit,' and its numerous colorful derivatives, such as *sral'nya*, or 'shithouse.' To the Russian ear, this person said, *musor* was far fouler than 'garbage.' And so, for a long time, I thought that Aleksandr was deeply offended to hear me say that he was rooting around in the *musor*, when in fact he was doing something much, much cleaner.

Over the years, though, I've asked many other Russian speakers about *musor* versus garbage, and I've encountered no one who agrees with this explanation, no one who finds *musor* more revolting than garbage or thinks that the word wanders dangerously close to the semantic defecation field. Just that one person, whose identity is now lost to time.

Yet I remain irrationally attached to the garbage/*musor* duality. I believed it for so long, and I want language to be at the root of everything, because language is what I do. And so I've come full circle: where once I was loath to believe that language and cultural difference had any bearing on our problems, now I see that I sometimes overestimated their role.

Garbage is *musor* is garbage, all of it vile and evil smelling. What happened was simply this: I shamed him—blindly, foolishly, inadvertently—in a way that transcended language.

The Translator

BY COURTNEY ANGELA BRKIC

When my son was an infant I memorized every detail of his body. I unfolded his softly curled hands and examined the fine lines of his palms. The creases were something a potter might leave in clay. His legs fit neatly into the hollows of his chest and his back curved like the spine of an aquatic animal, as if nostalgic for his pose before birth. At first, I did not know how his toenails would survive the air, how objects so small had the capacity to grow. His hair was soft, like the fuzz of a graying dandelion. It bore no resemblance to his father's coarse blackness or my dark brown color, and it occurred to me that even a newborn's hair is the product of residency in his mother's belly.

As my son has grown, so has his hair toughened into this world, but I could not bear to throw those first downy cuttings away. Instead, I sealed them in an envelope and identified its contents with a black pen. I keep it in a desk drawer, where his milk-teeth are soon to join it. Light of my eyes. You are shedding your toddler's skin.

He still enjoys sitting on my lap when I am working. He watches the marks my pen makes with wide, solemn eyes. He is learning the alphabet and sometimes holds a pencil inexpertly in his hand to write out the characters of his name. He can also write the names of his parents. *Mommy* is a caterpillar that wanders across the piece of paper. *Daddy*, the unsteady footprints of a baby bird.

Last week he stopped and pointed to the English letters that bled from my pen. "What are you writing?" he wanted to know.

I was translating verses from a long-dead poet, and had just finished a line about warm bread in our children's hands. "I am putting our language into their language," I told him. "So that they can understand it."

He considered this. "Why don't they just learn our language?" he asked.

The suggestion was so undeniably logical that I laughed. "Our language is very difficult for them," I said and could see him considering my words. His father has the same expression on his face when he thinks very seriously about something. And his father does not understand why I spend the hours at my desk, either.

"They don't pay you for that," he tells me. "They don't care about our poetry."

"It's important to me, *habibi*," I tell him. "It makes me happy."

But he only grins, a little bitterly, and shakes his head. "You think that if they read our poetry, it will change things."

I do not tell him, but that is precisely my hope. How could anyone read the words of those poets—the ones who lived on mountaintops but loved the world, those who spoke gently about love—and remain unmoved? It is my own response to those words, across a gap of centuries, which encourages me. So I sit at my desk until my neck aches and my eyes begin to blur, stalking words in English. Their movements have a ferocious beauty I can recognize and I occasionally stumble upon patterns so correct and beautiful, that tiny bumps appear on my arms.

Sometimes at night there is the sound of gunfire and I stuff cotton in my ears. I frequently write by candlelight—as the old masters must have done, I remind myself—because electricity is a force that seems to die on a daily basis. When I blow the candles out, I sit for a moment until my eyes become accustomed to the dark. But the strange gnawing follows me even there. *Will some young girl take a flashlight to bed,* I wonder, *and weep over these words, the way that I did with Sylvia Plath when I was fourteen?*

When I crawl into bed beside my husband, he draws the blankets over my shoulders. He presses his lips to my forehead, and tells me, tiredly, "You are dreaming, *habibti.*"

I AM an interpreter for Battalion One of the Liberation Forces.

In the beginning I traveled with them around the city, patrolling the Zones of Confrontation and helping communicate with civilians we met. On the first day, they gave me a Kevlar vest and showed me how to fasten the straps. It took me a long time to get used to wearing it. It was summer, and I sweated so profusely beneath the armor that I felt as though my body were shriveling like a raisin. I needed a hand up into their vehicles, mechanized monsters that looked like the bastard children of jeeps and tanks. My husband, who is a doctor, would massage my neck in the evenings so that I could even hold my head upright the next day.

We patrolled the city, the place where I was born and which I have known since childhood, but whose streets were suddenly alien. I was dismayed to realize that I was forgetting the way those streets looked before, as if my remembered city had been as steadily eroded as the real one had been bombed. Instinctively, my imagination added whitewash and repaired gardens but I was unsure whether the resulting picture was recollection or pure invention. It was like the face of a family member who has died, whose features you have sworn to commit to memory but which begin to fade almost immediately.

During that first week, we passed an old woman standing by the side of the road. Black smoke poured from a shop behind her. I caught a quick glimpse of her face, through a tiny window in the vehicle's door. It was like a snapshot, a single moment of clarity in an otherwise blurred landscape. Tears had cut paths through the soot on her face and she was holding something in her hands. Before I could see the object more clearly, we had passed her. Since then, I have wondered what it was. A singed pillow? I ask myself, as I lie in bed at night. A half-burned ledger for her family's business? Sometimes I believe that I saw a tiny, charred hand with delicate white branches on its palm. It seemed to wave at us grotesquely, but had clearly been clenched in the moment of death.

"What was that?" I cried out to the sergeant, twisting around in my seat and forgetting that there were no windows in the rear of the vehicle. Somewhere behind me, down the slow unfurling of days, a woman stands on the street holding an unidentifiable bundle in her arms, weeping.

Sergeant Brandt has twin daughters at home, in Minnesota. He carries a picture of them wherever he goes, and showed it to me one day when our vehicle was crawling through the city. They are five years old and sprawl on an oddly shaped sled in the photograph.

"It's a Flying Saucer," he explained. "Plastic, so they don't hit their heads on anything sharp."

He was the first to ask about my family and, thereafter, always asked after Ali. Once, he even gave me chocolate to take home to him. Ali put it experimentally on his tongue, but then grimaced and spat it out into my hand. I ate the bar myself, though I didn't tell Brandt this, and remembered Boston, where I lived for several years as a little girl.

He had also seen the woman beside the road, I am certain of it. He didn't answer me but his voice was strange when he radioed our coordinates.

MY MOTHER takes care of Ali during the day. She has been living with us since the first days of the war, or, as she calls it, the "benevolent occupation." She doesn't like that I am working for the Americans. "Is it for this that you studied literature," she asked me once, while I learned a vocabulary list in which words like "APC," "AWOL," and "Air-to-Ground" swam in front of my eyes.

It isn't that she dislikes the Americans. Quite the contrary, she has always remembered Boston fondly. She likes to reminisce about Filene's Basement and Newbury Street. Even the monstrous snow has become a thing of beauty to her.

"Do you remember, Sara?" she asks me. "How the banks would be piled so high on either side of us that we had to walk single file, and couldn't see anything but the sky above us?"

It isn't dislike but fear that makes her wary of my work. Threats have been made against "collaborators," and we do not tell our neighbors where I go every day. But we have all accepted the situation, even my husband, whose hospital wages are no longer enough to feed us. After the first few weeks, when medicines became more widely available, he became slightly less desolate. He has brought some supplies home—bandages, antibiotics, and several bags of plasma.

My mother dreads my work, but silently. She is afraid that I will be in the wrong place at the wrong time. I think she has fantasies of our moving to the countryside, where she was born, living off of fruit trees and goat milk. But we have heard that things are bad in the country, as well.

She loves her grandson, and so the two of them chatter to each other all day long. Sometimes around noon I look at my watch and know that she is cooking something on the stove, and that Ali's toys are spread on the dining room table.

"Clear that away!" she will tell him in mock severity, the way she did with me when I was his age. "There isn't enough food to share with your friends."

And he will shout to her, happily, "But, grandmother, they're hungry too!"

And she will bring an empty pot to the table, and pretend to feed his toys with a wooden spoon. "Time for us to eat," she'll tell him when she has finished.

MY HUSBAND and my mother are much happier since I have stopped accompanying the patrols. Now, I go to work each day in the "safe zone," a lengthy process and the most frightening part of my day. Although I have an identity card with my name and picture on it, I have to wait in line to cross into that enclave, which is cordoned off from the rest of the city. I keep my identity card firmly tucked in my blouse until I reach the soldiers at the gate. They have begun to recognize me but, still, we must go through the formalities. They swipe my card in a machine, look from my picture to my face and back again and I am allowed to walk past the checkpoint. I once had a nightmare that the rest of the city fell away while I was in there. That I returned to the gate in the evening and the city was simply gone. The "safe zone" was an island surrounded on all sides by water and my family floated out there, somewhere beyond the guard shack.

Two weeks ago, a car bomb exploded near that checkpoint and several people were killed. One of them was an interpreter, just like me. We had spoken a handful of times. Her husband was also happy that her work was confined to the "safe zone." The minute I heard the news, I knew there would be reports on the radio and asked to telephone my mother to tell her I was unharmed. She had already heard the news and was beside herself. "Sara," she whispered hoarsely into the receiver but did not say anything more. We are lucky that the telephone wires were working that day. I never told my husband about the other interpreter.

MY WRITING desk is my decontamination chamber. It is sufficient for me to pick up my translations where I last left off, and I am clean again. I dream of preparing a compilation of poems from my country, and write lists of whose work to include. It is a tricky business, as I have learned. Some of my favorite poems do not lend themselves to translation. Others about which I am ambivalent suddenly reveal themselves in unexpected ways in English. Each poem dies in its conversion from Arabic, and is reborn in slightly different form. In this way, I both murder and resuscitate.

My family has no idea about the nature of my other work. It is partly shame that prevents me from telling them that I work in a prison and interpret during interrogations, and partly concern for their own well-being.

Several nights ago I turned from my desk at home to find my husband watching me from the doorway. "When I am in the hospital," he told me, "I like to think of you sitting here."

But, of course, when he is at the hospital, I am sitting light years away.

I was told that some of the detained would be former members of government, others would be insurgents. A few might be civilians. My identity would be protected, I was assured. I am allowed to view the prisoners, first, through a one-way window, to make sure that I do not know them, to prevent any form of recognition. As of yet, I have recognized no one. And so, in the seemingly airtight room, I spend days repeating the interrogators' questions in Arabic, then the answers in English.

I no longer work with Brandt and his men, but with intelligence collectors. They are tougher men than Brandt's soldiers. They don't grumble to me about cancelled leaves or the heat. It is as if they do not notice these things.

At first, I thought naively that they, too, felt shame. That this was at the root of their hardness, but I have changed my mind. These men are consumed by the mission of their work. I cannot put my finger on it, but their eyes make me uneasy. Every day when we finish, I am absurdly relieved when they tell me, "You can go now." In the moments before they say these words, as they lean back in their chairs or straighten the papers in front of them, I expect them to pass judgment. I have the irrational fear that they will tell me I can't go home.

My husband thinks that I am translating documents and something in my stomach contracts painfully every time he comments on my sallow skin. "Don't they have windows in those American buildings?" he asks me. "You look like you need a day in the sunshine."

Last week we had a day off together for the first time in months. We spent it in our tiny garden, drinking coffee, reading newspapers, and chasing Ali between potted plants.

At one point he caught my hand and held it against his cheek, the way he used to do when we were first married. There is a lot of silver in his hair, now. It appeared almost overnight, and I smoothed his hair with my hand. For the first time since this all began, I felt like crying.

THE NARROW windows in the interrogation rooms are too high for me to look through. They block out the light and the air in the rooms is stale. Once, a prisoner asked what the weather was like outside. "Is the sun shining, sister?" he asked. "Are the pomegranates growing on the trees?"

The man was a civilian, and quite young. He had violated a curfew he said, by taking food to his mother. His eyes reminded me of my son's. I translated his words. It is a requirement that I translate everything, but he looked at me reprovingly. "I'm not asking them," he told me. "I'm asking you."

A MONTH after I left Brandt's unit, a pregnant woman in distress flagged them down. From the vehicle, they couldn't see that she had wrapped explosives around her belly, underneath her clothes. Two of the soldiers walked quickly towards her. The men who stayed with the vehicle said they knew the minute the two realized their mistake. In the split-second before the detonation, they stiffened as if a current of electricity had shot through their bodies, from their feet to their heads. Chunks of shrapnel, pavement and bone flew like horizontal rain at the others. One large piece partially severed Brandt's right arm, below the elbow. The doctors at the base had to amputate it, and Brandt went back to Minnesota and his twin daughters. Although I did not get to tell him good-bye, I often think of him. I picture how his left hand pulls the sleigh with the two shrieking girls through the snow behind him. The stump of his right arm carves the air in front of him.

STARS ARE flames in the bowl of night.
    No, I think, and scratch it out violently.
    At night, stars light up the sky like flame.
    I draw horizontal black lines through this one. The ink makes the paper so moist that the tip of my pen tears it like damp tissue.
    Stars, like flame, in the firmament.
    I stare at the sheet of paper, then shred it with my shaking fingers. I blow out the candle.

THE WOMAN in the interrogation room is as old as my mother. She was a minor figure in the old government and I can vaguely remember seeing her on television. As she sits at the table, her face is a controlled mask. She refuses to answer any of their questions.
    "What is your name?" she finally asks me.
    I look at her dumbly, then translate her question.
    "None of your fucking business what her name is!" the interrogator shouts in the woman's face.

"None of your fucking business what her name is," I tell her.

She is silent for a moment, considering me. A cold feeling starts in my chest.

"You are their robot," she spits out finally. "You are their tool."

"I am your robot," I tell the chief interrogator. "I am your tool."

Yet another prisoner begs me to get word to his wife. "She must be beside herself," he says, then tells me her name. "At night they beat us," he adds, quietly. "But don't tell my wife this."

I have to be very careful. Sometimes other translators stand behind the observation windows to make sure that we are interpreting exactly. I choose my words for the interrogators very carefully. One of them slams his fist on the table. "Your wife thinks you are dead!" He does not seem to register the part about the beating.

"I will try," I tell the man quickly. Then, "Your wife thinks you are dead."

I open my eyes wide, and hold my breath. If he smiles, it is over. But his face betrays nothing.

But I cannot find her family name in any of the city's old phonebooks and no one I ask has heard of her. I do not see her husband again.

THERE HAVE been more suicide attacks and my husband comes home from work with tired eyes. "Almost all of them civilians," he tells me, but will not speak more about it, only tells me, "Dead civilians. Missing civilians. Civilians in their jails."

I lower my eyes.

Only our son seems unaffected. When there is water, he splashes happily while I bathe him before bedtime. But in the middle of the night he has started crawling into our bed again, and the three of us lie side by side, looking at the ceiling. There are sporadic mortar attacks at night. Shells fall randomly on houses and in gardens, without rhyme or reason. The first night that Ali fell asleep between us, I rose to carry him back to his own bed, but my husband's whisper stopped me.

"It's better this way," he told me. "This way, none of us would be left behind."

MY MEMORY is playing strange tricks on me. It is as if the words I knew are being supplanted by the new words I must learn. As if there is only so much room in my head for vocabulary, which is strange because I was a girl who loved words the way other children love dolls. I twirled them around my tongue in rhymes and wrote their names with pebbles in the dirt.

Brandt's men taught me American slang and I taught them basic Arabic phrases. The interrogators know an odd word in Arabic, but to a specific end. They are not unfriendly, but I can see a certain suspicion in their eyes when they regard me. There are rumors of "terrorist moles" who have infiltrated the "safe zone," and there have been any number of "troubling incidents."

"How come you don't cover your hair?" one of them asked me once while we took a break.

"I've never covered my hair," I told him with a small smile. "I spent part of my childhood in Boston." I regretted the words as soon as they were out, as if they could explain it.

But he broke into a sudden smile. "Hey, I'm from Boston."

I looked at him, smothering a smile. "Why don't you wear a Red Sox hat?" I asked.

He looked at me with a blank expression, then nodded slowly.

I think I have pinpointed what differentiates these men from Brandt's men. On the city streets, those soldiers had depended on me as much as I depended on them. Without me, they were lost in a morass of language that made no sense to them. In these small rooms, however, I am incidental, and as much at their mercy as the prisoners.

Their commanding officer has the same quiet confidence that Brandt had, and the men listen to him without question. He even tells about his young wife in Georgia and that she is pregnant with their first child. I tell him about my Ali, and he looks at the photograph I carry with me.

"A good-looking kid," he tells me.

But I often remember that prisoner's words. *At night they beat us.* I think about this when I sit in the interrogation rooms, when I eat my lunch in the mess hall. I look around at the very young faces, the faces of men not so much older than my son when you consider it, and the same age as many of the people they are questioning. *At night they beat us.*

The commanding officer is a good man. His young wife smiles out from the photograph he shows me, and her arms are wrapped around her enormous belly. But there is one face that turns over and over in my mind, and I can barely concentrate in the interrogation room because of the noise it makes. *At night they beat us.* He had not even flinched at those words.

IN THE end, I have been reduced to my lowest common denominator and it is only my voice that they care about. I am a verbal alchemist. I turn our language into their language, and back again. Usually, they do not even look at me. They certainly would not care that I am withering in the interrogation rooms, that the sheaves of paper on my desk have gone untouched for days.

"Go work," my husband will tell me after dinner, giving me a gentle push.

But I shake my head each time. You were right, I want to tell him.

Conversely, I am often the prisoners' only focal point. There are days when I think I can't stand their eyes anymore. On my way home, I decide a hundred times not to return. But we need the money. And I need to see my son's face as he sneaks a hand into my purse to find the piece of fruit I have taken for him from the mess hall every day.

I have several times dreamed that my husband is under interrogation. That he looks at me in horror.

"How could you, *habibti*?" he asks me, near tears.

But their rules are such that I am unable to respond.

Sometimes I am the one they interrogate. I am seated at the table opposite them, and my hands are folded so tightly in my lap that my fingernails draw blood from my palms. Sometimes I am holding poems, translated into English. *I will give you these pages,* I think, suddenly optimistic again. *And you will understand. You will understand.*

But when I look down I realize that my blood has disfigured the writing. It has added dots and dashes that make the script unintelligible even to me. Sometimes I realize that it is not poetry that I am holding, but my son's first attempts at penmanship, in a language they cannot understand. Mommy is a wandering caterpillar, I want to tell them. Daddy, the delicate trail left by a baby bird.

The Interrogation of the Prisoner Bung by Mister Hawkins and Sergeant Tree

BY DAVID HUDDLE

The land in these provinces to the south of the capital city is so flat it would be possible to ride a bicycle from one end of this district to the other and to pedal only occasionally. The narrow highway passes over kilometers and kilometers of rice fields, laid out square and separated by slender green lines of grassy paddy-dikes and by irrigation ditches filled with bad water. The villages are far apart and small. Around them are clustered the little pockets of huts, the hamlets where the rice farmers live. The village that serves as the capital of this district is just large enough to have a proper marketplace. Close to the police compound, a detachment of Americans has set up its tents. These are lumps of new green canvas, and they sit on a concrete, French-built tennis court, long abandoned, not far from a large lily pond where women come in the morning to wash clothes and where policemen of the compound and their children come to swim and bathe in the late afternoon.

The door of a room to the rear of the District Police Headquarters is cracked for light and air. Outside noises—chickens quarreling, children playing, the mellow grunting of the pigs owned by the Police Chief—these reach the ears of the three men inside the quiet room. The room is not a cell; it is more like a small bedroom.

The American is nervous and fully awake, but he forces himself to yawn and sips at his coffee. In front of him are his papers, the report forms, yellow notepaper, two pencils and a ball-point pen. Across the table from the American is Sergeant Tree, a young man who was noticed by the government of his country and taken from his studies to be sent to interpreter's school. Sergeant Tree has a pleasant and healthy face. He is accustomed to smiling, especially in the presence of Americans, who are, it happens, quite fond of him. Sergeant Tree knows that he has an admirable position working with Mister Hawkins; several of his unlucky classmates from interpreter's school serve nearer the shooting.

The prisoner, Bung, squats in the far corner of the room, his back at the intersection of the cool concrete walls. Bung is a large man for an Asian, but he is squatted down close to the floor. He was given a cigarette by the American when he was first brought into the room, but has finished smoking and holds the white filter inside his fist. Bung is not tied, nor restrained, but he squats perfectly still, his bare feet laid out flat and large on the floor. His hair, cut by his wife, is cropped short and uneven; his skin is dark, leathery, and there is a bruise below one of his shoulder blades. He looks only at the floor, and he wonders what he will do with the tip of the cigarette when the interrogation begins. He suspects that he ought to eat it now so that it will not be discovered later.

From the large barracks room on the other side of the building comes laughter and loud talking, the policemen changing shifts. Sergeant Tree smiles at these sounds. Some of the younger policemen are his friends. Hawkins, the American, does not seem to have heard. He is trying to think about sex, and he cannot concentrate.

"Ask the prisoner what his name is."

"What is your name?"

The prisoner reports that his name is Bung. The language startles Hawkins. He does not understand this language, except the first ten numbers of counting, and the words for yes and no. With Sergeant Tree helping him with the spelling, Hawkins enters the name into the proper blank.

"Ask the prisoner where he lives."

"Where do you live?"

The prisoner wails a string of language. He begins to weep as he speaks, and he goes on like this, swelling up the small room with the sound of his voice until he sees a warning twitch of the interpreter's hand. He stops immediately, as though corked. One of the Police Chief's pigs is snuffling over the ground just outside the door, rooting for scraps of food.

"What did he say?"

"He says that he is classed as a poor farmer, that he lives in the hamlet near where the soldiers found him, and that he has not seen his wife and his children for four days now and they do not know where he is.

"He says that he is not one of the enemy, although he has seen the enemy many times this year in his hamlet and in the village near his hamlet. He says that he was forced to give rice to the enemy on two different occasions, once at night, and another time during the day, and that he gave rice to the enemy only because they would have shot him if he had not.

"He says that he does not know the names of any of these men. He says that one of the men asked him to join them and to go with them, but that he told this man that he could not join them and go with them because he was poor and because his wife and his children would not be able to live without him to work for them, to feed them. He says that the enemy men laughed at him when he said this but that they did not make him go with them when they left his house.

"He says that two days after the night the enemy came and

took rice from him, the soldiers came to him in the field where he was working and made him walk with them for many kilometers, and made him climb into the back of a large truck, and put a cloth over his eyes, so that he did not see where the truck carried him and did not know where he was until he was put with some other people in a pen. He says these other people also had been brought in trucks to this place. He says that one of the soldiers hit him in the back with a weapon, because he was afraid at first to climb into the truck.

"He says that he does not have any money, but that he has ten kilos of rice hidden beneath the floor of the kitchen of his house. He says that he would make us the gift of this rice if we would let him go back to his wife and his children."

When he has finished his translation of the prisoner's speech, Sergeant Tree smiles at Mister Hawkins. Hawkins feels that he ought to write something down. He moves the pencil to a corner of the paper and writes down his service number, his Social Security number, the telephone number of his girlfriend in Silver Spring, Maryland, and the amount of money he has saved in his allotment account.

"Ask the prisoner in what year he was born."

Hawkins has decided to end the interrogation of this prisoner as quickly as he can. If there is enough time left, he will find an excuse for Sergeant Tree and himself to drive the jeep into the village.

"In what year were you born?"

The prisoner tells the year of his birth.

"Ask the prisoner in what place he was born."

"In what place were you born?"

The prisoner tells the place of his birth.

"Ask the prisoner the name of his wife."

"What is the name of your wife?"

Bung gives the name of his wife.

"Ask the prisoner the names of his parents."

"What are the names of your parents?"

Bung tells the names.

"Ask the prisoner the names of his children."

"What are the names of your children?"

The American takes down these things on the form, painstakingly, with help in the spelling from the interpreter, who has become bored with this. Hawkins fills all the blank spaces on the front of the form. Later, he will add his summary of the interrogation in the space provided on the back.

"Ask the prisoner the name of his hamlet chief."

"What is the name of your hamlet chief?"

The prisoner tells this name, and Hawkins takes it down on the notepaper. Hawkins has been trained to ask these questions. If a prisoner gives one incorrect name, then all names given may be incorrect, all information secured unreliable.

Bung tells the name of his village chief, and the American takes it down. Hawkins tears off this sheet of notepaper and gives it to Sergeant Tree. He asks the interpreter to take this paper to the Police Chief to check if these are the correct names. Sergeant Tree does not like to deal with the Police Chief because the Police Chief treats him as if he were a farmer. But he leaves the room in the manner of someone engaged in important business. Bung continues to stare at the floor, afraid the American will kill him now that they are in this room together, alone.

Hawkins is again trying to think about sex. Again, he is finding it difficult to concentrate. He cannot choose between thinking about sex with his girlfriend Suzanne or with a plump girl who works in a souvenir shop in the village. The soft grunting of the pig outside catches his ear, and he finds that he is thinking of having sex with the pig. He takes another sheet of notepaper and begins calculating the number of days he has left to remain in Asia. The number turns out to be one hundred and thirty-three. This distresses him because the last time he calculated the number it was one hundred and thirty-five. He decides to think about food. He thinks of an omelet. He would like to have an omelet. His eyelids begin to close as he considers all the things that he likes to eat: an omelet, chocolate pie, macaroni, cookies, cheeseburgers, black-cherry Jell-O. He has a sudden vivid image of Suzanne's stomach, the path of downy hair to her navel. He stretches the muscles in his legs, and settles into concentration.

The clamor of chickens distracts him. Sergeant Tree has caused this noise by throwing a rock on his way back. The Police Chief refused to speak with him and required him to conduct his business with the secretary, whereas this secretary gloated over the indignity to Sergeant Tree, and made many unnecessary delays and complications before letting the interpreter have a copy of the list of hamlet chiefs and village chiefs in the district.

Sergeant Tree enters the room, goes directly to the prisoner, with the toe of his boot kicks the prisoner on the shinbone. The boot hitting bone makes a wooden sound. Hawkins jerks up in his chair, but before he quite understands the situation, Sergeant Tree has shut the door to the small room and has kicked the prisoner's other shinbone. Bung responds with a grunt and holds his shins with his hands, drawing himself tighter into the corner.

"Wait!" The American stands up to restrain Sergeant Tree, but this is not necessary. Sergeant Tree has passed by the prisoner now and has gone to stand at his own side of the table. From underneath his uniform shirt he takes a rubber club, which he has borrowed from one of his policeman friends. He slaps the club on the table.

"He lies!" Sergeant Tree says this with as much evil as he can force into his voice.

"Hold on now. Let's check this out." Hawkins's sense of justice has been touched. He regards the prisoner as a clumsy, hulking sort, obviously not bright, but clearly honest.

"The Police Chief says that he lies!" Sergeant Tree announces. He shows Hawkins the paper listing the names of the hamlet chiefs and the village chiefs. With the door shut, the light in the small room is very dim, and it is difficult to locate the names on the list. Hawkins is disturbed by the darkness, is uncomfortable being so intimately together with two men. The breath of the interpreter has something sweetish to it. It occurs to Hawkins that now, since the prisoner has lied to them, there will probably not be enough time after the interrogation to take the jeep and drive into the village. This vexes him. He decides there must be something unhealthy in the diet of these people, something that causes this sweet-smelling breath.

Hawkins finds it almost impossible to read the columns of handwriting. He is confused. Sergeant Tree must show him the places on the list where the names of the prisoner's hamlet chief and village chief are written. They agree that the prisoner has given them incorrect names, though Hawkins is not certain of it. He wishes these things were less complicated, and he dreads what he knows must follow. He thinks regretfully of what could have happened if the prisoner had given the correct names: the interrogation would have ended quickly, the prisoner released; he and Sergeant Tree could have driven into the village in the jeep, wearing their sunglasses, with the cool wind whipping past them, dust billowing around the Jeep, shoeshine boys shrieking, the girl in the souvenir shop going with him into the back room for a time.

Sergeant Tree goes to the prisoner, kneels on the floor beside him, and takes Bung's face between his hands. Tenderly, he draws the prisoner's head close to his own, and asks, almost absent-mindedly, "Are you one of the enemy?"

"No."

All this strikes Hawkins as vaguely comic, someone saying, "I love you," in a high-school play.

Sergeant Tree spits in the face of the prisoner and then jams the prisoner's head back against the wall. Sergeant Tree stands up quickly, jerks the police club from the table, and starts beating the prisoner with random blows. Bung stays squatted down and covers his head with both arms. He makes a shrill noise.

Hawkins has seen this before in other interrogations. He listens closely, trying to hear everything: little shrieks coming from Sergeant Tree's throat, the chunking sound the rubber club makes. The American recognizes a kind of rightness in this, like the final slapping together of the bellies of a man and a woman.

Sergeant Tree stops. He stands, legs apart, facing the prisoner, his back to Hawkins. Bung keeps his squatting position, his arms crossed over his head.

The door scratches and opens just wide enough to let in a policeman friend of Sergeant Tree's, a skinny, rotten-toothed man, and a small boy. Hawkins has seen this boy and the policeman before. The two of them smile at the American and at Sergeant Tree, whom they admire for his education and for having achieved such an excellent position. Hawkins starts to send them back out, but decides to let them stay. He does not like to be discourteous to Asians.

Sergeant Tree acknowledges the presence of his friend and the boy. He sets the club on the table and removes his uniform shirt and the white T-shirt beneath it. His chest is powerful, but hairless. He catches Bung by the ears and jerks upward until the prisoner stands. Sergeant Tree is much shorter than the prisoner, and this he finds an advantage.

Hawkins notices that the muscles in Sergeant Tree's buttocks are clenched tight, and he admires this, finds it attractive. He has in his mind Suzanne. They are sitting in the back seat of the Old-smobile. She has removed her stockings and garter belt, and now she slides the panties down from her hips, down her legs, off one foot, keeping them dangling on one ankle, ready to be pulled up quickly in case someone comes to the car and catches them. Hawkins has perfect concentration. He sees her panties glow.

Sergeant Tree tears away the prisoner's shirt, first from one side of his chest and then the other. Bung's mouth sags open now, as though he were about to drool.

The boy clutches at the sleeve of the policeman to whisper in his ear. The policeman giggles. They hush when the American glances at them. Hawkins is furious because they have distracted him. He decides that there is no privacy to be had in the entire country.

"Sergeant Tree, send these people out of here, please."

Sergeant Tree gives no sign that he has heard what Hawkins has said. He is poising himself to begin. Letting out a heaving grunt, Sergeant Tree chops with the police club, catching the prisoner directly in the center of the forehead. A flame begins in Bung's brain; he is conscious of a fire, blazing, blinding him. He feels the club touch him twice more, once at his ribs and once at his forearm.

"Are you the enemy?" Sergeant Tree screams.

The policeman and the boy squat beside each other near the door. They whisper to each other as they watch Sergeant Tree settle into the steady, methodical beating. Occasionally he pauses to ask the question again, but he gets no answer.

From a certain height, Hawkins can see that what is happening is profoundly sensible. He sees how deeply he loves these men in this room and how he respects them for the things they are doing. The knowledge rises in him, pushes to reveal itself. He stands up from his chair, virtually at attention.

A loud, hard smack swings the door wide open, and the room is filled with light. The Police Chief stands in the doorway, dressed in a crisp, white shirt, his rimless glasses sparkling. He is a fat man in the way that a good merchant might be fat—solid, confident, commanding. He stands with his hands on his hips, an authority in all matters. The policeman and the boy nod respectfully. The Police Chief walks to the table and picks up the list of hamlet chiefs and village chiefs. He examines this, and then he takes from his shirt pocket another paper, which is also a list of hamlet chiefs and village chiefs. He carries both lists to Sergeant Tree, who is kneeling in front of the prisoner. He shows Sergeant Tree the mistake he has made in getting a list that is out of date. He places the new list in Sergeant Tree's free hand, and then he takes the rubber club from Sergeant Tree's other hand and slaps it down across the top of Sergeant Tree's head. The Police Chief leaves the room, passing before the American, the policeman, the boy, not speaking nor looking other than to the direction of the door.

IT IS late afternoon and the rain has come. Hawkins stands inside his tent, looking through the open flap. He likes to look out across the old tennis court at the big lily pond. He has been fond of water since he learned to water-ski. If the rain stops before dark, he will go out to join the policemen and the children who swim and bathe in the lily pond.

Walking out on the highway, with one kilometer still to go before he comes to the village, is Sergeant Tree. He is alone, the highway behind him and in front of him as far as he can see and nothing else around him but rain and the fields of wet, green rice. His head hurts and his arms are weary from the load of rice he carries. When he returned the prisoner to his hamlet, the man's wife made such a fuss Sergeant Tree had to shout at her to make her shut up, and then, while he was inside the prisoner's hut conducting the final arrangements for the prisoner's release, the rain came, and his policemen friends in the jeep left him to manage alone.

The ten kilos of rice he carries are heavy for him, and he would put this load down and leave it, except that he plans to sell the rice and add the money to what he has been saving to buy a .45-caliber pistol like the one Mister Hawkins carries at his hip. Sergeant Tree tries to think about how well received he will be in California because he speaks the American language so well, and how it is likely that he will marry a rich American girl with very large breasts.

The prisoner Bung is delighted by the rain. It brought his children inside the hut, and the sounds of their fighting with each other make him happy. His wife came to him and touched him. The rice is cooking, and in a half hour his cousin will come, bringing with him the leader and two other members of Bung's squad. They will not be happy that half of their rice was taken by the interpreter to pay the American, but it will not be a disaster for them. The squad leader will be proud of Bung for gathering the information that he has—for he has memorized the guard routines at the police headquarters and at the old French area where the Americans are staying. He has watched all the comings and goings at these places, and he has marked out in his mind the best avenues of approach, the best escape routes, and the best places to set up ambush. Also, he has discovered a way that they can lie in wait and kill the Police Chief. It will occur at the place where the Police Chief goes to urinate every morning at a certain time. Bung has much information inside his head, and he believes he will be praised by the members of his squad. It is even possible that he will receive a commendation from someone very high.

His wife brings the rifle that was hidden, and Bung sets to cleaning it, savoring the smell of the rice his wife places before

him and of the American oil he uses on the weapon. He particularly enjoys taking the weapon apart and putting it together again.
He is very fast at this.

Her Native Tongue

BY LYNNE SHARON SCHWARTZ

Acertain woman never felt entirely comfortable speaking her native tongue. She spoke ably enough; her vocabulary and grammar were adequate to say all she needed to say, but she didn't feel at home either in her mind or in her mouth. Since she had never spoken any other language and couldn't know what degree of comfort others felt, her discomfort was vague and amorphous; she knew only that she had to search uneasily for words and phrases as if they came from a second language and not a first, that the contours her mouth formed and the paths her tongue traveled did not take shape as readily as she imagined they should. She even suspected she might speak differently were her tongue more at ease. She would express herself with richer and more subtle nuances, and in the process her opinions and attitudes themselves might change and grow more subtle. In other words she might be a different person or, more precisely, a self, waiting inside her, speechless, would find speech.

One day while riding on a bus she overheard a conversation in an unknown tongue between a man and woman sitting behind her. Though she couldn't understand what they were saying, the sounds of the language seemed familiar, like the features of a distant relative. The broad, lingering vowels, like amber deserts or rose-tinged skies, called up dormant affinities in her vocal cords and in the pathways of her brain; the harsh, craggy consonants suggested jagged cliffs or surf hitting rocks, unlike her native language whose vowels sounded like cream and custard, the consonants like pastry crusts.

From the strangers' tones she could distinguish questions and answers, interjections and phrases of surprise or dismay. After a while she could make out the shapes of sentences, syntactical groupings that fell into patterns. She felt she was starting to grasp the curves and the trajectory of their conversation—she lacked only the subject matter. The more she listened, the more she had the uncanny sense that at any moment she would understand what was being said, as if what barred her from understanding was not her total ignorance of the language but rather a thin veil she could almost, but not quite, see through. She had the excited feeling that at any moment the veil would be lifted or else she would penetrate it. Before the couple got off she turned around to ask—in her native tongue, the only one she knew—what language they were speaking. It was the language of her ancestors; she had never heard it spoken because her grandparents had died before she was born and her parents either could not speak it or didn't wish to.

Some time later, in a taxi, she heard the dispatcher on the intercom instructing his drivers in what she recognized as the same foreign yet familiar tongue. Now and again she distinguished the name of a local street, and perhaps because of these intermittent known words and because the subject was obvious—where to pick up and discharge passengers—she felt even more strongly that at any moment the veil would lift and she would understand everything. When she reached her destination she told the driver she'd changed her mind and wished to be taken elsewhere, just so she might keep listening. She tried to fix certain syllables in her ear—rough and pebbly, yet musical—repeating them under her breath to see how they felt on her tongue, wondering what as yet unknown nuances of herself they might be made to articulate and who she would be as a result. This pleased her, yet the pleasure was frustrating: the veil did not lift or become transparent. Still, if she listened long enough, maybe it would happen. Or if the veil did not lift, she would burst through it.

She yearned for the feel of words coming instinctively to her tongue and for the new self that would emerge along with them. Meanwhile, her native language was feeling more and more cumbersome. Rather than study the alluring language in books, she decided to go to the country where it was spoken. Once there, she acquired the most essential words and phrases and picked up others from signs and shop windows as strangers do. But she resisted studying the language in any methodical way. She felt it was already wholly inside her, and once the veil had lifted, the words would spring instantaneously to her tongue.

She wandered through streets and shops and parks, her ear taking pleasure everywhere in the sounds it had longed for. Always she felt that the veil was about to lift. And she did begin to grasp fragments here and there, but simply as strangers do, not in the instantaneous way she expected and thought she merited.

She stayed a long time, learning to shape the craggy consonants and the broad amber vowels. The language required that her mouth take new positions, more open and flexible ones, and that her tongue, moving in new patterns and at different speeds, strike against her teeth and palate at new angles and with different degrees of force and subtlety. All this she did well; her accent was good, and over time her vocabulary increased and her grammar improved. She was able to say most of what she needed to say, although she was not aware of saying anything she might not have said in her native tongue.

After some years she was fluent, and her mouth and the pathways of her mind felt comfortable as they had not with her native tongue, which she remembered but rarely used: that felt like a foreign language now. She even began to think and dream in the new language. And the nuances of her manner of expression did change somewhat—but she could never be sure whether this came about through the new language on her tongue or simply through the passage of time and the effects of leading a new life in a new place.

In the end she came to speak the language of her ancestors as ably as she had wished, but she never had the satisfaction of seeing the veil lift and understanding everything instantaneously. Now, when she overheard conversations on the bus, she understood perfectly, but without the sense of wonder she had anticipated. Nor did the self she now was strike her as wondrous either, since she had been present at its gradual evolution—as she would have been in any language. So while she was contented speaking her adopted language, her contentment was marred by uncertainty: had she learned to express herself so well because of an ancestral affinity in the pathways of her brain, or had she simply mastered a new language by proximity and long residence as any stranger might? Perhaps it was a mistake to have come. If she had remained at home, listening to occasional random snatches of the ancestral tongue, waiting and trusting, perhaps the veil might one day have lifted to reveal its entire lexicon and structure. And if so, then she had spent years earning what would have been hers effortlessly, and laboring to become the person she would naturally have become in time.

Author Biographies

ZAIA ALEXANDER is a writer and literary translator. Her publications include *Wende Kids: A New Generation of German Authors*; "Primo Levi and Translation" in the *Cambridge Companion to Primo Levi*; "The Translator's Diary" in *Suitcase: A Journal for Transcultural Traffic*; and "The Danube Exodus: the Rippling Currents of the River" (coauthored with Marsha Kinder) in *Future Cinema: The Cinematic Imaginary after Film* (MIT). She holds a PhD in Germanic Languages and Literature from UCLA and served as chair of the PEN Center USA Translation Jury in 2007.

CHANA BLOCH (1940–2017) was a poet, translator, scholar, and teacher. Bloch's last book of poems, *The Moon Is Almost Full*, appeared in 2017. *Swimming in the Rain: New and Selected Poems, 1980–2015* includes work from *The Secrets of the Tribe*, *The Past Keeps Changing*, *Mrs. Dumpty*, and *Blood Honey*, as well as new poems. Bloch co-translated *The Song of Songs* (a Modern Library Classic), *The Selected Poetry of Yehuda Amichai* and his *Open Closed Open*, and Dahlia Rakovitch's *Hovering at a Low Altitude: The Collected Poetry*. Her work has also appeared in *Best American Poetry 2015* and *Pushcart Prize XL*, *The New York Times Sunday Magazine*, and *The New Yorker*. For poems, translations, reviews, interviews, audio, and videos, see www.chanabloch.com.

COURTNEY ANGELA BRKIC is the author of *The First Rule of Swimming* (Little, Brown and Company, 2013), *Stillness: and Other Stories* (Farrar, Straus and Giroux, 2003) and *The Stone Fields* (Farrar, Straus and Giroux, 2004). Her work has also appeared in *Zoetrope*, *The New York Times*, *The Washington Post Magazine*, *Harpers & Queen*, the *Utne Reader*, *TriQuarterly Review*, *The Alaska*

Review, and *National Geographic,* among others. Her translations of Expressionist poet A. B. Simic have appeared in *Modern Poetry in Translation.* She teaches in the MFA program at George Mason University.

SUSAN DAITCH is the author of four novels and a collection of short stories, most recently *The Lost Civilization of Suolucidir,* published by City Lights Books. Her work has been the recipient of an NEA Heritage award, two Vogelstein awards, and a New York Foundation for the Arts fellowship in fiction. Her short fiction and essays have appeared in *Guernica, Tablet, Conjunctions, Slice, Tin House,* and elsewhere. www.susandaitch.net.

LYDIA DAVIS is the author of, among others, *The Collected Stories* (Farrar, Straus and Giroux, 2009) and a chapbook entitled *The Cows* (Sarabande Press, 2011). She is also the translator of numerous works from the French, including Marcel Proust's *Swann's Way* (2003) and Gustave Flaubert's *Madame Bovary* (2010), both of which were awarded Annual Translation Prizes by the French-American Foundation. In 2013, she received the Man Booker International Prize for her short fiction, and in 2014 another collection appeared from FSG—*Can't and Won't.* She is currently assembling a collection of translations of very short stories from the Dutch by A. L. Snijders.

LUCY FERRISS is the author of ten books, mostly fiction. Her novel *A Sister to Honor,* set partly in northern Pakistan, was a WNBA 2015 Great Group Read; her novel *The Lost Daughter* was a Book of the Month pick. Her work has won several national awards and been translated into five languages. Recent short fiction and essays appear in *The New York Times, Missouri Review, The American Scholar, Michigan Quarterly Review, Arts & Letters,* and weekly at the *Chronicle of Higher Education*'s "Lingua Franca." She lives in the Berkshires and Connecticut, where she is Writer-in-Residence at Trinity College.

TODD HASAK-LOWY is a writer, teacher, and translator living in Evanston, Illinois. He is the author of four works of fiction, one scholarly monograph, and a co-written narrative memoir for young adults. His writing has been translated into ten languages. He began translating Hebrew literature into English about a decade after writing the story included here, and he won the 2013 Risa Domb/Porjes Prize for his translation of Asaf Schurr's novel *Motti*.

ROBIN HEMLEY has published twelve books of fiction and nonfiction and won numerous awards for his writing, including a Guggenheim Fellowship, the Independent Press Book Award, an Editor's Choice Award from the American Library Association, and three Pushcart prizes in both fiction and nonfiction. A graduate of the Iowa Writers Workshop, he directed the nonfiction writing program at the University of Iowa for nine years. He is currently director of the writing program, writer-in-residence, and professor of humanities at Yale-NUS College in Singapore, professor emeritus at the University of Iowa, and adjunct professor at RMIT University in Melbourne, Australia.

MICHELLE HERMAN's most recent books are the novel *Devotion* and the collection of essays *Like A Song*. Born and raised in Brooklyn, she has lived for many years in Columbus, Ohio, where she teaches at Ohio State University. She also writes a weekly advice column for *Slate*.

DAVID HUDDLE is from Ivanhoe, Virginia, and he taught at the University of Vermont for thirty-eight years. His fiction, poetry, and essays have appeared in *The American Scholar, Esquire, The New Yorker, Harper's*, and *Green Mountains Review*. In 2012 his novel *Nothing Can Make Me Do This* won the Library of Virginia Award for Fiction, and his collection *Black Snake at the Family Reunion* won the 2013 PEN New England Award for Poetry. His most recent book is a collection of poems, *Dream Sender*, published in September 2015 by LSU Press.

NORMAN LAVERS grew up in Berkeley, California. He got an MA in English at San Francisco State, and was awarded a writing fellowship to the Iowa Writers Workshop, where he received a PhD. He taught literature and creative writing for thirty years before his retirement in 2000. He has lived in various parts of Europe and Asia. Nature and settings in remote parts of the world figure often in his writing. His short stories have won numerous awards, including the O. Henry and Pushcart prizes. His books are available on Amazon and Kindle.

Author Biographies

PRIMO LEVI was born in Turin, Italy, in 1919 and earned a degree in chemistry from the University of Turin in 1941, but had trouble finding work because of Italy's racial laws. In 1943, as part of a fledgling partisan group, Levi was arrested by the Fascists and spent a year in the concentration camp at Auschwitz. His skills as a chemist enabled him to work indoors and survive the harsh conditions. After the war he wrote over a dozen books of memoir, fiction, essays, and poetry. The work that brought him to international attention was *Survival in Auschwitz*, 1947 (not available in English until 1959), an account of his time in the camp. *The Truce*, 1963, recounts his ten-month journey through Eastern Europe to reach home after the liberation. His other widely known works are *The Periodic Table*, *The Monkey's Wrench*, *The Drowned and the Saved*, and *Other People's Trades*. Levi is revered worldwide for the moral rigor, wisdom, and eloquence of his testimony. He died in Turin in 1987 from a fall down a stairwell, which some judged to be suicide.

HARRY MATHEWS (1930–2017) published novels, poetry, and short fiction and translated from French. A master of inventiveness, he worked in experimental modes, with bizarre settings and plots. His best-known novels are *The Conversions*, *Tlooth*, and *Cigarettes*. Mathews was a member of the French literary group Oulipo (*Ouvroir de littérature potentielle*), which used verbal and mathematical constraints that produced highly original prose.

SHARON MAY's stories have appeared in *Best New American Voices*, *The Chicago Tribune*, *Tin House*, *Mānoa*, *StoryQuarterly*, *Crab Orchard Review*, *Other Voices*, and elsewhere. She co-edited *In the Shadow of Angkor: Contemporary Writing from Cambodia* (*Mānoa: An International Journal*/University of Hawai'i Press) and a special issue of Cambodian literature in translation for Words Without Borders. She conducted research for Columbia University's Center for the Study of Human Rights and was a Wallace Stegner Fellow in Fiction at Stanford University.

JOYCE CAROL OATES is the internationally known author of dozens of novels and story collections, as well as poetry and criticism. Her novel *them*, dealing with racial conflict in Detroit, won the National Book Award in 1969 and several other of her novels have been nominated for the Pulitzer Prize. Among her best-known works are *Because It Is Bitter, and Because It Is My*

Heart, We Were the Mulvaneys, and *Black Water*. Her many awards include the National Medal for the Humanities and the PEN/Malamud Award for the Short Story. Her most recent book is the autobiographical collection *The Lost Landscape*. Oates is currently the Roger S. Berlind Professor in the Humanities at Princeton University.

BOGDAN RAKIC is a translator from the Serbo-Croatian. His translations include *How to Quiet a Vampire* by Borislav Pekic (Northwestern University Press, 2005), *Death and the Dervish* by Mesa Selimovic (Northwestern University Press, 1996), and, with John Jeffries, *Tesla: A Portrait with Masks* by Vladimir Pistalo (Graywolf Press, 2008).

MICHAEL SCAMMELL is the author of two prize-winning biographies, *Koestler: The Literary and Political Odyssey of a Twentieth-Century Skeptic*, and *Solzhenitsyn, a Biography*, and has translated many works by Russian authors, including Tolstoy, Dostoevsky, and Nabokov. He has also translated from Serbo Croatian and Slovenian, including (with Veno Taufer) *Nothing Is Lost, the Selected Poems of Edvard Kocbek*. He is currently working on a memoir.

SVETLANA VELMAR-JANKOVIC (1933–2014) was a Serbian novelist, essayist, and chronicler of Belgrade, her birthplace and lifelong home. She became a journalist while still at the university there, and in the 1950s became an editor at the local Prosveta Publishing House. She wrote five novels and several collections of essays, short stories, and plays, and won every major national literary prize. Her work has been translated into English and major European languages, as well as Korean. Her father, Vladimir Velmar-Jankovic, was also a well-known writer, but was discredited because he served in the collaborationist Ministry of Culture during the war, and later went into exile in Spain.

LAURA ESTHER WOLFSON's distinctive blend of essay, first-person narrative, and musings on language and books has appeared in *Bellingham Review*, *Gettysburg Review*, rumpus.net, *The Sun*, *Zyzzyva*, and elsewhere, been repeatedly listed as "notable" in *Best American Essays*, and appeared in Swedish and Russian translation. She has worked as a diplomatic, conference, and court interpreter and literary translator. Her translations include works on Russian obscenities and gulag slang and on Stalin's persecution of Yiddish authors. She works at a large international organization headquartered in New York City, where she translates from Russian, French, and Spanish into English.

LYNNE SHARON SCHWARTZ is the author of twenty-four books, including novels, short stories, non-fiction, poetry, and translations from Italian. Her latest publications are a collection of poems, *No Way Out But Through*, the essay collection *This Is Where We Came In*, and the novels *Two-Part Inventions* and *The Writing on the Wall*. Her novel *Leaving Brooklyn* was nominated for a PEN/Faulkner Award, and *Rough Strife* was nominated for a National Book Award and the PEN/Hemingway First Novel Award. She edited *The Emergence of Memory*, a collection of interviews with and essays on W. G. Sebald. Her work has appeared in *The Best American Short Stories*, *The O. Henry Prize Stories*, *The Best American Essays*, *The Best American Poetry*, and many other anthologies. She has received grants from the Guggenheim Foundation, the National Endowment for the Arts, and the New York State Foundation for the Arts. She teaches at the Bennington College Writing Seminars.

Acknowledgments

Chana Bloch, "Crossing the Border," adapted from "Learning from Translation," the Judith Lee Stronach Memorial Lectures on the Teaching of Poetry, 2012. Reprinted by permission of the author. © The Regents of the University of California.

Courtney Angela Brkic, "The Translator," from *Stumbling and Raging: More Politically Inspired Fiction*, ed. Stephen Elliott, 2005. © Courtney Brkic 2005. Reprinted by permission of the author.

Susan Daitch, "Asylum," from *Storytown*, by Susan Daitch, Dalkey Archive Press 1996. © Susan Daitch 1996. Reprinted by permission of the author.

Lydia Davis, "French Lesson I: *Le Meurtre*," from *The Collected Stories of Lydia Davis*, © 2009 by Lydia Davis. Reprinted by permission of Farrar, Straus and Giroux. UK edition, © Lydia Davis 2010, reprinted by permission of Penguin Books Ltd.

Lucy Ferriss, "The Difficulty of Translation," from *The Michigan Quarterly Review*, 2001. © Lucy Ferriss, 2001. Reprinted by permission of the author.

Todd Hasak-Lowy, "The Task of This Translator," from the collection *The Task of This Translator*, by Todd Hasak-Lowy. © 2015 Todd Hasak-Lowy. Reprinted by permission of Houghton Mifflin Harcourt Publishing Company. All rights reserved.

Acknowledgments

Robin Hemley, "The Perfect Word," from *The Big Ear*, John F. Blair, Publishers. © 1995 Robin Hemley. Reprinted by permission of the author.

Michelle Herman, "Auslander," from *Twenty Under Thirty*, ed. Debra Spark, Scribner's, 1986, reissued 1996. © Michelle Herman, 1986. Reprinted by permission of the author.

David Huddle, "The Interrogation of the Prisoner Bung by Mister Hawkins and Sergeant Tree," from *The Secret Life of Our Times: New Fiction from Esquire*, ed. Gordon Lish, 1973. © *Esquire Magazine* 1971. Reprinted by permission of the author.

Norman Lavers, "The Translator," from *North American Review*, V. 277: 3205, 1992. © Norman Lavers. Reprinted by permission of the author.

Primo Levi, "On Translating and Being Translated," from *Complete Works of Primo Levi*, © 2015 by Liveright Publishing Corporation. Translated by Zaia Alexander. Reprinted by permission of Liveright Publishing Corporation and Zaia Alexander.

Sharon May, "The Wizard of Khao-I-Dang," from *Best American New Voices*, ed. Richard Bausch, 2008. © Sharon May 2005. Reprinted by permission of the author.

Joyce Carol Oates, "The Translation," originally published in *Tri-Quarterly*, Fall, 1977, collected in *Nightside*, by Joyce Carol Oates, Vanguard Press, 1977. © 1977 by Joyce Carol Oates. Reprinted by permission of John Hawkins & Associates, Inc.

Michael Scammell, "The Servile Path," from *Harper's*, May, 2001. © Michael Scammell 2001. Reprinted by permission of the author.

Lynne Sharon Schwartz, "Her Native Tongue," from "Twisted Tales," in *Referred Pain: Stories* by Lynne Sharon Schwartz. Counterpoint

Acknowledgments

Press 2004. © Lynne Sharon Schwartz, 2004. Reprinted by permission of the author.

Svetlana Velmar-Jankovic, "Sima Street," from *The Prince of Fire: An Anthology of Contemporary Serbian Short Stories*, ed. Radmilla J. Gorup and Nadezda Obradovic, © 1998. Translated by Bogdan Rakic. Reprinted by permission of the University of Pittsburgh Press.

Laura Esther Wolfson, "In Love With Russian," from *Columbia, A Journal*, 2008. © Laura Esther Wolfson 2008. Reprinted by permission of the author.

ABOUT SEVEN STORIES PRESS

Seven Stories Press is an independent book publisher based in New York City. We publish works of the imagination by such writers as Nelson Algren, Russell Banks, Octavia E. Butler, Ani DiFranco, Assia Djebar, Ariel Dorfman, Coco Fusco, Barry Gifford, Martha Long, Luis Negrón, Hwang Sok-yong, Lee Stringer, and Kurt Vonnegut, to name a few, together with political titles by voices of conscience, including Subhankar Banerjee, the Boston Women's Health Collective, Noam Chomsky, Angela Y. Davis, Human Rights Watch, Derrick Jensen, Ralph Nader, Loretta Napoleoni, Gary Null, Greg Palast, Project Censored, Barbara Seaman, Alice Walker, Gary Webb, and Howard Zinn, among many others. Seven Stories Press believes publishers have a special responsibility to defend free speech and human rights, and to celebrate the gifts of the human imagination, wherever we can. In 2012 we launched Triangle Square books for young readers with strong social justice and narrative components, telling personal stories of courage and commitment. For additional information, visit www.sevenstories.com.